# OPERATION BLUE HALO

*Also by Richard Joyce*

*Operation Last Assault* — featuring Johnny Vince

# OPERATION BLUE HALO

Richard Joyce

OLIVER & LEWIS

Copyright © Richard Joyce 2015
First published in 2015 by Acorn Independent Ltd
Revised edition published 2020 by Oliver & Lewis
www.richardjoycebooks.co.uk
oliverandlewispub@gmail.com

Distributed by Lightning Source worldwide

British Library Cataloguing in Publication Data
A catalogue record for this book is available from the British Library

ISBN 978-0-9935750-1-3

Typeset by Amolibros, Milverton, Somerset
www.amolibros.com
This book production has been managed by Amolibros
Printed and bound by Lightning Source worldwide

# ACKNOWLEDGEMENTS

All the characters, and any military operations, mentioned in this book are fictitious. However, I have tried to make the book as factually accurate as possible and, at the same time, show the courage and sacrifice of the Armed Forces.

First and foremost, I would like to thank the brilliant writer, Damien Lewis, who inspired me to take on the monumental challenge of writing a novel.

Thanks to Steve Snape and Becki Eddowes for your military input, even though I have sometimes pressed for quicker answers, forgetting you have busy lives on the battlefield. Many thanks also to Gary H and Paul (Pablo) Volante for your RAF insights and detail. I hope you all enjoy the book.

To Hilary Johnson and her authors' advisory service, a bucket-load of appreciation.

I'd also like to serve a big plate of gratitude to my family, who haven't seen much of me lately, and who, when I have come out of the 'writers' trench', have had to put up with my tired moods.

More seriously, I would like to thank the British Military who are safeguarding our country in these difficult times, especially the seldom-mentioned heroes of the UK Special Forces.

Lastly, and not by any means less, Jane Tatam, from Amolibros, thank you for enabling me to get this book published.

# ABOUT THE AUTHOR

Following the success of this first novel, *Operation Blue Halo*, Richard Joyce has also published this second in the series *Operation Last Assault*, featuring that novel's hero, Johnny Vince, now retired from UK Special Forces. However, retirement is the last thing Johnny wants, and he accepts a contract as a mercenary. Filled with trouble from the outset, it turns into a race against time to rescue a wealthy American, Larry Schultz, from captivity by Somali pirates. It soon becomes apparent that other groups are also interested in Schultz, making it hard for Johnny to know who to trust, especially when he learns that his brother, Oliver, is being held in ransom for Schultz.

The third in the series is *Operation Poppy Pride*, publishing in 2020.

# PROLOGUE

In 2011, mainly through British Intelligence, it transpired that a new band of terrorists was emerging. To start with, the reports trickled in. Small villages were being seized; women, children, and men were beaten, raped, or killed. No one knew the name of this terrorist group; villagers were too frightened to talk.

It wasn't until early 2012 that whoever was masterminding these new militants, began enforcing Taliban loyalists to switch sides. The Taliban set up a meeting with the Afghanistan government, who in turn brought in the British government. It seemed that the new group was gaining ground over the Taliban. Anyone from a local village man up to a Taliban leader who did not conform, was tortured, and killed. Further sickening atrocities were unveiled. The terrorist group had conflicting names, the latest being known as L-khaba-a, pronounced Elkhaba, which experts believed translated to 'The Hidden'. They were seen as modern day Vikings.

By the end of 2012, recruits in the Afghanistan National Police and army, including certain government officials, were being bought by the Elkhaba. 2013 saw the prospect of British troop withdrawal from Afghanistan. The British government knew the Elkhaba would upset their withdrawal plans, jeopardising the fragile stability, and the hard work the British military had done so far. An opportunity was seized to strike a deal with the Taliban. This did not go down well with the Americans. This deal, classified 'Top Secret', did not enter the public domain. Still though, there was no known official name for the main leader. A quick agreement was thrashed out to eradicate the growing Elkhaba and find the leader. The emphasis on the deal was on British terms rather than those of the Taliban. Obviously, sacrifices had to be made, and, as ever, money was involved.

Personally, I didn't trust either the Taliban or the Afghan government, and I had my reservations about our government. However, I viewed this as an opportunity to do my job; the job I loved. I was summoned by my commanding officer, Dick Brown, to oversee the drawn-up mission details. He was annoyed that his own son, Lee, also in the Special Boat Service, had not been chosen. The CO's boss overruled his decision and chose me, saying I had a complex character, right for the task. I didn't know what he meant by this, but I grabbed the chance. The mission was called Operation Blue Halo; my suggestion. This was the breaking point for my CO; it seemed to him his bosses weren't taking his pleas seriously, and he stormed out of the office. I put forward the squad I wanted with me, and this was agreed. I was also informed that I would lead the operation; a massive privilege.

Further intelligence located the terrorists' stronghold and the main areas in which they operated. Because of other missions, we [SBS] would be sharing the task with the SAS. A concern was the amount of time we would spend on the ground. Air cover and further support was assured if required, but I took this with a pinch of salt. We were excited, and we were tooled up for the job, almost too much so. There wasn't one of us who didn't want to take the fight. Many of those who weren't chosen were deeply jealous. I wasn't too happy with the time left in which we had to train when we were informed of the insertion date of 25th March 2013, but life isn't perfect. There would be no stand down: this was it.

# CHAPTER ONE

The first extraction of eight SAS guys, an interpreter, two Supacat HMT400 vehicles, and a further two quad-bikes, seemed ages ago. What should have been a simultaneous two HC2 Chinook extraction had now turned into a return flight for the first Chinook. I was only informed prior to the landing zone being set up, that one Chinook had had a serious malfunction and all others were on operations elsewhere. I was relieved the malfunction had been detected before take-off and not on our withdrawal, but I still felt a little anxious. I was sure the more our squad waited, the more we would encounter an enemy force bent on revenge.

As I lay there listening for the distant sound of the Chinook's thump, thump, thump, my thoughts returned to the overall mission. Our SBS squad, X squadron, and the other SAS squadron had completed a successful mission; if honest, beyond even our audacious expectations. After nearly six weeks, Operation Blue Halo had achieved the covering of hundreds of kilometres, capturing more than one Elkhaba stronghold, and after many vicious firefights we had captured two suspected leaders. With only superficial injuries, and one immobilised Supacat, which we destroyed to prevent it getting into the hands of any fanatical religious extremists, we were all on a high, keeping us motivated. Underneath though, we were all exhausted and malnourished. All the same, I couldn't have of dreamt of a better bunch of courageous men. Most importantly, we all watched each other's backs throughout the operation. Yeah, it was tough going, but that's the nature of the beast.

Again, I cupped my hand, holding a very small Maglite torch around my watch. With a pinhole cover over the lens I studied the time, making sure no light escaped. Time check: 05.17 hrs. Where the hell was the Chinook? Dawn would be breaking soon. I looked up to scan the surrounding area. We were positioned in a dip in the featureless desert.

I caught the eyes of Fish looking back at me, probing for any signs of worry. I guessed he had the same questions going through his mind. As squad leader, I gave the youngest member of the troop a thumbs-up and a smile. I mimicked the beer can to mouth action.

Tony 'Fish' Fisher was from Dorset, a single twenty-four-year-old lad who relished the idea of beer and women. He boasted on many a drunken night in town how he could pull any bird, and of how many birds he had notched up in his previous conquests. His chiselled jaw and model-like face set him aside from some of the uglier brutes. Not only was he a good-looking lad, he was very intelligent, almost a human encyclopaedia. He used knowledge rather than brawn when in an argument or any piss-taking. He was six foot tall, with no great build, more athletically lanky. He always had bags of energy, especially when it came to the ladies, and he hardly slept. His love for sport drove him on to try different activities.

His baby-face appearance now seemed different though, not just with the hair growth and grime, but maybe Operation Blue Halo had matured him. On this, his first mission, he had seen some violent and brutal sights, making more than one kill. I would congratulate him personally, and inform the Head Sheds that he had stepped up to the mark. I knew he would party hard and boast for days after, and bore us all to death.

I glanced over at the others. Gary 'Shrek' Harding was guarding one of the suspected Elkhaba leaders. He stared back at me, appearing as calm as ever. Shrek was thirty years old and from Hampshire, an ugly-looking brute you would really have to think twice about arguing with. His large forehead almost overhung his eyes, his nose was flat, and his eyes were sharp and intimidating. He was about my height: five foot ten inches. He had the aura of an ogre about him, hence the nickname Shrek. The only difference was he wasn't green. He'd had a shady upbringing, one he rarely mentioned. He had the temperament of a rattlesnake, leave him alone and he was fine; poke him and he would bite. As I got to know him better, I realised his looks were deceptive. Shrek was kind and generous to his mates and family. He was married with two kids. He would always be the first at the bar buying rounds. He'd chip in to help anyone who asked, or who didn't ask. But as an Elite soldier, he was ferocious in a firefight, brutal in unarmed combat, and always the first to get stuck in. His fearless approach sometimes had to be questioned as lunacy; however, he never put anyone else in danger. I could always count on his support.

The last man of our team was Robert 'Planet' Archibald, my best mate. The biggest bloke I've ever seen. At six foot ten and with an enormous stature, his reputation in the troop was formidable. He was a hard, aggressive Scotsman with tough, Action Man rugged looks. I'd rather whack a rhino with a stick and take my chances than pick a fight with him. Planet lived and breathed the SBS; nothing else really mattered. His hands were massive, his fingers like bunches of bananas. The first time we met was in the Paras. I was in the gym catching up on some reading, ignoring the piss-taking from the other beef-heads pumping weights. He swaggered over and stood over me. Nonchalantly, I raised my eyes without lowering my book. He stood there staring me out, looking displeased. I lowered my book and turned to the others, who had stopped working out.

"Is an eclipse due this month?" I asked.

A few laughed, or should I say sniggered quietly. This encouraged me, so I turned to him, catching his glare.

With a kind of *I don't care* attitude and putting on a posh accent, I said, "Are you lost, young man? You really shouldn't be; a chap your size should have his own postcode."

He didn't make any attempt to reply, but his stare became more threatening. Being a black belt in Go-Kan-Ryu Karate, I stood up, looking into his steely-fixed gaze. It was then I really got a sense of how huge he was. As we locked stares the atmosphere in the gym thickened with anticipation; silence fell upon us. Honestly, at the time I wasn't comfortable with the situation; maybe I had bitten off more than I could chew.

Mimicking a posh major, I said, "You're blocking the light of my favourite book, old boy."

He smiled, breathed through his teeth, then turned around and strode off like a giant. He slammed the door behind him, vibrating around the gym. It was only then I felt relieved. After this little incident, the other lads changed his nickname to Planet.

Fortunately, I didn't come up against him in the Paras milling bout. As no one matched Planet's size, the instructors volunteered the next smallest bloke, and he subsequently was pulverised. We both passed our training and achieved our wings. I didn't have much to do with him after as I found a different circle of friends.

Over the years, after passing selection, we became best mates. As our friendship grew, I found out I'd not upset him in the gym, but complimented him. He thought I'd had either balls, or no brain. If Planet hadn't liked me, he would have smashed me up there and then, he'd said. Thank fuck.

★

The cold started to seep into my bones as I lay there. A gentle breeze whipped around my body, making me shiver. Tiny granules of sand and dirt rolled over my wrists. The night was spectacularly clear. The moon and stars shone on us, almost pinpointing our position to any enemy. I pulled my Diemaco C8 retractable stock in closer to my shoulder, reminding me I was in charge and alert to any possible threat. My weapon could lay down eight hundred rounds per minute over an effective range of five hundred metres. I also had the 40mm under-slung grenade launcher fitted; a formidable weapon.

For ages I hadn't decently eaten. My stomach started to growl, thinking the whole of Afghanistan could hear it. Reaching down, I pulled out some chocolate, cramming the lot into my mouth.

'Hey, Vinnie, ye gonna share that? I'm fucking starvin'. If not, can I eat the prisoner?' Planet said in my earpiece.

Shrek chipped in, 'Well, it would be better than eating that haggis shit you normally eat. But, I suppose the crusty arse of the prisoner is the same as the crusty arse of a sheep.'

'Maybe a few Highland thistles thrown in could help our wee little Scotsman,' remarked Fish.

'Fuck ye all,' came the expected reply from Planet.

'I'm not sure he only *eats* the sheep, Fish,' Shrek said. 'I've heard he's not getting too much lately. Maybe you could take him out to find a *real* woman.'

'I'll twist ye fuckin' balls off when we get back,' retorted Planet.

As big and aggressive as Planet was, he was prime material for a wind-up. After all the years together, he still took offence at his Scottish heritage being slated, much to the enjoyment of the others. It was still good to hear after the fierce firefights and hard routine; the camaraderie was still in them. I let this run for a short while, until almost simultaneously the banter stopped as the first sounds of the Chinook could be heard. I knew it would be hugging the contours, utilising its on-board screen technology's night enhancement package, turning night, to day. This could pinpoint enemy positions, even a goat turd.

I knew my squad would be scanning their arcs, looking for the first indications of the approaching Chinook in the green world of their night vision goggles. We were very alert, listening through the eerie darkness for the slightest sign of an enemy counterstrike. After making my way over to the Supacat to set up the Satcom, I made the necessary call to the Chinook pilot. I confirmed we had no further enemy contact, all infrared markers were in position, and the LZ was secure. All was good to go.

The pilot returned, 'Bravo Zero Bravo, this is Bravo November One, received clear. Five klicks to LZ, Supacat first, you know the drill. Don't hang around guys.' A slight pause, then the pilot continued, 'And Vinnie, we don't want any trouble. I'm due my fry-up in an hour.'

Roy 'Rabbit' Franklin was the pilot for Special Forces operations. I had met with him on a few operations and training exercises. Ever since I'd had to teach him the basics of escape and evade, we had never got on. Even socialising, I found his wit and banter went too far. I reckoned he thought he had a right to fit in with us. However, he had not earned my trust. He would wind me up at the drop of a hat. The others got along fine with him, so rather than cause a scene, I just found a group of others to chat to. Roy had been in the RAF since leaving school. He was pushed in by his parents, his dad being an ex-serving member. At first, Roy hated it and wanted to quit, but his dad and some of the officers talked him out of leaving. Many years later, he admitted he had been wrong, acting like an arse when he tried to quit; I didn't disagree.

He was the finest SF operations pilot available, no doubt about it. He was a brilliant forward thinker, planning everything in detail. His downside, apart from his sarcastic humour, was his fiery temper. When provoked, he would not shy away from a fight. In his spare time he made babies, or that's how the lads would piss-take him. Six children to his name, and at the age of thirty-six he was destined for more.

'You have time for a fry-up?' I said. 'I thought you would be off making more babies, you know, get more child benefit, and tax us hard workers. How's the wife, by the way?'

'The other SAS blokes on the first extraction have cleared out the canteen of all hot breakfasts, so only muesli left for you guys, but I suppose that will make a nice change from all the posh dining you SAS nancy boys have been used to,' retorted Rabbit.

'Don't think I didn't hear that, dickhead, it's SBS,' Planet chipped in. 'I think a wee little rabbit will be on me main course when I get back.'

Rabbit ignored him. 'On landing, don't hang around, boys, out.'

'Yeah, out, wanker,' I said.

Dusk was emerging from the black night; time was crucial for this second extraction. I didn't want to spend another day in this shit-hole, especially so close to the Pakistan border, where the continuing influx of fighters joining the crazed world of the insurgents was ever-growing. It wasn't just the religious fundamentalists joining the Elkhaba and Taliban; in fact, very few were joining. Now a mixture of fighters joined their cause: the unemployed, uneducated, poverty-stricken, and generally misguided young men. Some of these men were the sons and brothers of simple village families who had been accidently killed by British and American forces; this sparking more to join in for revenge. Those who were prompted to join and didn't, sealed their own fate. I was only there to carry out the mission orders set in front of me, not to decipher the difference between a crazed religious fundamentalist and a young man low on luck. Any person who pointed a weapon at me could expect a deadly retaliation.

My tense shoulder muscles relaxed, as coming towards our position fast and low was the Chinook, giving off its eerie blue halo glow. The static electricity formed a dust-flickering radiance, whipped up by the Chinook's twin rotors; a magnificent out-of-this-world sight. The Chinook circled, and as always, the last seconds of descent looked as if the hulking beast was going to belly-flop, but instead, the aircraft floated to the ground. Truly amazing, taking balls to fly into a hot zone to extract your men. I held a big respect for all Chinook crew, and even Rabbit, when he wasn't getting on my tits.

We all wrapped our *shemaghs* around our faces. With the tail ramp down, the crewman could just be seen. We waited a few seconds for the brownout to disperse, caused by the downwash of the rotor blades engulfing the Chinook with sand and dust. First up was Fish. He steadily drove the Supacat towards the illuminated sticks being waved, and parked it nicely inside. Shrek grabbed one of the prisoners and dragged him across the short run to the tail ramp, throwing him into the cabin. The leader tumbled and landed flat on his face as his wrists were restrained with cable ties. I found myself chuckling at Shrek, and I bet the other lads enjoyed it, too. With both crewmen and us scanning our arcs, next was Planet, dragging the remaining prisoner. He wasn't any less vigorous when showing the leader to our finest military flying asset. Following up the rear, I ran up the tail ramp, meeting the loadie.

'I'm the last,' I shouted. 'Let's get the fuck out of here.'

On all previous operations and training exercises I'd always stipulated where my seat was: next to the tail ramp. I felt at ease with the outside view, and the crewman with his high-powered fire-rate M60 machinegun. As I entered the Chinook's fuselage, I was shocked to see Planet in my seat. No use trying to drag him out, so I vented my displeasure, bellowing at him to move his fat arse. He cupped his hand to his ear above the Chinook's engine and rotors, with a look seeming full of revenge.

'Pardon?' he bellowed. 'Can't hear ye, mate.'

'I'm not joking, fucking move. This is my seat,' I shouted.

'Sorry, ye'll need a satnav to find ye own seat. Need a postcode?' He roared with laughter.

He began to fasten his seat straps, so this time I cupped my hands to his enormous ear.

'You Scottish wanker,' was the best I could reply.

This made him laugh even more.

Not a second after I was sat next to the now smug Planet, the loadie sent a message to the pilot that we were all present. The noise from the engine increased and the nose of the Chinook dipped forward. As the craft shook, its speed surged. The dust that filled the air soon dispersed. Removing my webbing, *shemagh*, and NVGs, I put my Diemaco downwards-facing on the floor. I was shattered, and more than likely looked like a bag of shite, like the rest of my squad. Through the fuselage's red-light gloom there was a relief from the others, even though we weren't out of trouble yet. Any of the Chinook's components could malfunction, and there were the threats from small arms fire, and, even worse, a surface to air missile or a lucky RPG. Even though it was sketchy, intelligence revealed that SAMs were being shipped in through Pakistan. Another fear was the Taliban-favoured DHSK mounted on a vehicle, known as the Dushka, or sweetie. It fired at six hundred rounds per minute at an effective range of two thousand metres. It was a serious threat, and could easily make mincemeat of the Chinook and anyone inside. I put these concerns to the back of my mind.

Still annoyed at not having my seat, I gave Planet my best evil stare; however, even though gaunt, six weeks of facial growth, dust, and matted hair, I probably wouldn't have scared a nun. Amazingly, Planet turned away and swiped his fingers in the cut-throat death gesture at the two leaders, with a crazed smile. Maybe the capture of my seat had gone to his head. We had lost two great SBS blokes in a recent Afghan operation; perhaps this was Planet's way of mourning. I looked across at both prisoners: one looked terrified, but the other appeared untroubled.

The second made direct eye contact with me and grinned. His teeth were like old toppled gravestones. His stare looked as if he was hiding something; something evil. An unnerving chill ran down my spine and the hairs on my neck stood up. At this point he read my fears, and then nodded, muttering something. I could speak a little Pashto and even less Arabic, but I couldn't work out what he was saying, let alone hear him. He mouthed it slower, his evil eyes piercing mine, but I still couldn't understand.

With my neck hairs raised like a wolf's hackles, I turned to Shrek.

'Gary, did you search both prisoners?'

'Sure did, boss.'

'Are you sure?' I made a point of looking concerned.

Shrek frowned. 'Yes, boss. Not all folk from Hampshire are stupid pig farmers and eat raw potatoes.'

This was a regular piss-take for Shrek from many of the lads. I nodded my appreciation and turned back to the Elkhaba leader for more answers, but his face had gone blank, continually staring at the floor. It had only been three minutes into the flight. I felt uneasy, but didn't have a clue why. My sixth sense had proved right on other occasions. Maybe being tired and hungry was playing on me. I wasn't superstitious, but I wondered if it was because of not having my favourite seat.

Pulling out my earpiece, I reached for the headset, linking me to the pilot. Listening in for a while, chatter relayed between Rabbit, the co-pilot, and HQ. We were flying at one-hundred and twenty knots and hugging the contours. I waited for a pause in the conversation.

'Anything to report, Rabbit?' I asked.

'Negative, Vinnie. All's good. We're just coming up to your initial drop off zone, just beyond the small forest. I'll get your milk chilled for the muesli.'

'Just keep your senses alert.'

'Shut your eyes, chill, and enjoy the flight,' Rabbit said. 'I'll send the busty hostess in with a few refreshments.'

Closing my eyes I thought of sitting on my newly-laid patio, drinking beer with friends and my beautiful wife, Ella. Life was damn good at the moment. Married last year, a new house, and great friends; also, loving my job. To top it all, Ella and I had spoken about starting a family, but the downside was she wanted me to give up the army. That wouldn't happen; it was the first time I had heard Ella talk about leaving. Maybe one day I'd catch up with Rabbit's kid total. Some of us were due some

R&R, and I had vowed to take us all on a big trip to Italy. It took Ella some time to get around to the idea of sharing a villa with Planet, Shrek, and Fish. The compromise was Fish having a separate apartment far away in the main town.

# CHAPTER TWO

I wasn't too sure how long I had shut my eyes for, when I was startled by the sound of voices in my headset. They weren't frantic, but the tempo between Rabbit and the co-pilot was serious and heightened. I didn't want to interject with questions; this wouldn't help them concentrate. I understood many enemies were spread out far ahead on the Chinook's FUR Screen. A few moments later, my listening was sharply interrupted by the rear crewman letting rip with bursts of fire from the M60. Almost simultaneously, nearer the front of the Chinook, a crewman fired his M134 Minigun into life, spewing out three thousand rounds per minute on whatever target had been acquired.

The flames lit up the crewman's faces and those all around, casting sporadic shadows over the inside of the fuselage. Hot shells poured out around their feet; some falling into the abyss below, or rolling back at our feet. Hyper-alert, we grabbed our weapons simultaneously; not that they would help. The noise of the Minigun and M60 drowned out the noise of the Chinook. From the rear, tracer rounds came in from all directions, like a firework party, but without the fun. I was sure rounds were hitting the fuselage and rotors.

'Shit. It's coming from everywhere. You onto this Roy?' I shouted down the mic.

'Of course I fucking am. Now let me deal with this. You've done your bit. I'm in command.'

This annoyed me, but I decided to back down. However, I was sure I would bring it up again. Above the smell of cordite, I got the distinct smell of diesel. Had our main tank been hit? In the red gloom I studied the Supacat. From the rear, diesel was trickling out from the underneath. Both crewmen rocked left and right spewing out more rounds, hopefully chewing up the enemy below. I caught glimpses of the lads' wide eyes reflecting the flames from their heavy-weaponry. They all looked concerned, but not frightened. The leader, who had looked terrified at the beginning of the flight, was now screwing up his face, his eyes shut tight. He couldn't block out the noise as he still had his hands cable-tied. The co-pilot informed Rabbit of the list of warning lights and malfunctions. Rabbit was calm and stayed in control, operating various switches to activate backup systems. More rounds hit the Chinook, and Rabbit informed his co-pilot of every serious hit. The problem was I was hearing this as well. I tried to rise above the fear, blocking it out and remaining calm and positive.

An ear-piercing alarm rang through my earpiece as the Chinook manoeuvred to avoid being hit; it was the missile approach warning system. Automatic counter measures dispersed from around the Chinook, adding to the firework party. Both pilots' voices intensified in my ear. Then I heard it: SAM, SAM. I gripped my Diemaco.

'Oh fuck, fuck.'

I wasn't sure if I'd just thought this, or yelled it down the mic.

'Johnny, brace, brace,' Rabbit shouted.

Further chaff and flares deployed, and I braced myself for what was coming. I went to shout to the others, but they were already bracing themselves. I stared out the rear: a bright white light flashed from where we had just flown, followed by a wave of turbulence that rocked the Chinook and all of us in it. It was as if the bulking frame was groaning. More tracers and rounds came in, hitting the Chinook. I wondered how long before one of us took a round, blowing parts of body off, adding to the display of terror.

Undeterred, the crewmen endlessly poured death into the terrain below. The Chinook weaved left and right. I found myself grunting and taking large breaths as we hit the maximum G-force. The missile alarm went off again, screeching in my ear.

'Lock on, lock on... close,' Rabbit bellowed.

A bright flash lit up the fuselage with a deafening boom. Everything seemed to slow down after this, all sound muffled and sluggish. Through blurred vision, weird lights patterned around the black silhouetted figures. An enormous pain hit the right side of my forehead; I lifted my hand to it. My face felt warm, glowing, like sunburn. I started to shout, but had a strange taste in my mouth, a sickly-sweet taste. In slow motion as everything was, I couldn't register what was going on quickly enough. Amid the surreal mayhem, the Elkhaba leader sat there unnervingly in his white *dishdasha* and black turban, still smiling at me. I studied his features, looking at gaps in his blackened-toothed smile, scars on his face, and his piercing eyes. Searching those evil eyes, I realised why he was grinning: he had known of the attack.

I tried to shake my head, but it wouldn't move. I must be dreaming all this, I thought. Everything around was blurry and chaotic, but he just sat there like on a bench in the park on a sunny day. In an instant, my vision turned black with the sound of wind rushing around me. I tried to flap my arms and grab something, but they weren't responding. Was I falling? Was this a dream? Surely I would wake up with Rabbit telling me breakfast was due. The rushing wind stopped. I knew I had my eyes open, so I searched for a light, a sound, a smell, my mates, but all were gone. A blackness enveloped, a pure blackness, as if an evil cloak had been put over me. There was a sudden crashing, like a tree falling, branches cracking and ripping, but this was all I could sense. I had no feeling or sight. Then, silence fell again. I couldn't see, hear, or feel anything. I'm dead, I thought. This is death, now leaving only memories of my wife, family, and great life.

★

My parents had moved to Newquay when I was a young boy. I loved Newquay and the rest of Cornwall. At fifteen years old, I'd joined a rock-climbing club. Later, a girl called Ella joined. The chemistry between us just oozed. Ella was short and petite, with silky blonde hair, making her sharp crystal-blue eyes shine. We spent all our free time together. My parents welcomed her into the Vince clan. Ella's parents weren't keen on me, making it awkward, never inviting me around their house. I never bothered to ask Ella or them why. I persuaded Ella to join my GKR lessons. At sixteen, through my fantastic sensei, Trevor Angrave, I graded to black-belt. My parents had been taking me and my brother, Oliver, to karate since the aged of six. At times I wanted to quit, but my dad kept pushing me to continue. We had many arguments about this. We were a shouty family. We all seemed to air our opinions, sometimes all at once, but there was heaps of love and respect between us. My parents strived for me and Oliver to have a good education, telling us to try our hardest at everything and never give up. I never really thanked my parents for being truly inspirational and for the effort and sacrifice they both put in. As much as my dad was proud of all our achievements in the armed forces, he really tried to persuade me not to join, but I had made up my mind. At seventeen, I joined the army, knowing what path I wanted to take.

After a while, my isolated senses began to return. First, immense pain flooded my whole body; mainly my left leg and head. I tried to scrutinise in my mind parts of my body, as movement didn't seem an option. I had horrific thoughts of limbs missing, becoming aware of a ringing in one of my ears, a high-pitched noise that seemed to follow the rhythm of my heartbeat. Through the maddening ringing I picked up other sounds, which I tried to decipher. A crackling, like logs on a fire, and wind through leaves on trees filtered in. I'm not a religious man, but I wondered if maybe I'd been given a chance to live again.

I decided to shout for help, but my voice was different, mumbled, gargled, like I had food in my mouth. I spat whatever it was out. What was I doing?

'Fucking training, Johnny,' I chided myself. 'Why don't you just alert the enemies with a party banner and invites.'

I felt annoyed with myself, but at least I had started to think about the situation. I tried to open my eyes, but they were glued shut. My left arm wouldn't move; it was numb and pinned to my side. Through gritted teeth and sheer determination, I managed to move my right hand and touch my puffy face; it was covered in a sticky stuff. My face was pressed up against something. This must be the floor, I thought. My face and right hand were stinging, like a hundred paper cuts. I managed to wipe the eye that wasn't pressed into the floor, just being able to see lights in the distance. They were blurred, but unquestionably lights. What the hell were these lights? My head was thumping and spinning.

With a sense of relief, I had concluded they were vehicle headlights, hopefully a rescue party, but I still couldn't comprehend what had happened and where I was. I started to feel woozy and faint like I'd had too many drinks with Planet on one of our mad evenings out on the town. My thoughts immediately turned to my best mate. Where the fuck was he? Images and sounds came flooding back in a rush of jumbled matter: the operation, the Chinook, loud noises, bright lights, mates, shouting. I had great difficulty organising. Fucking work it out, Johnny, I mentally screamed.

I must have drifted off as the pain disappeared. I was back in Poole having fun with my wife and friends again. This was a nice pain-free feeling; I liked this better. My eye opened suddenly, and the nice, secure feeling was replaced with pain and nausea, like I'd been hit by a herd of buffalo. For the first time I could smell something awful. It was familiar, but I couldn't grasp where I had smelt it before. Staring back at the lights, they weren't as bright, as if they'd moved further away. Why the fuck haven't they found me? With sickening body sensations returning, I raised my right arm again and felt around. Soft, sharp, and cold objects teased my mind as I touched blindly. Cleaning more of the sticky stuff from my face, I spat the remaining mess out and blew my nose, sending pain spasms through my head. I looked at the gunge I'd blown in my palm, resembling blood and dirt mixed together. Searching objects that were closer, I realised there was a lot of green and brown foliage; also, I was some height off the ground. Shards of sun were starting to break through the dim leafage; swirls of haze lit up in these beams.

The sitting position slightly hampered my breathing that I was in. I still had an awful taste in my mouth. Arching my neck forward, I raised my pounding head, but my neck was stiff and restricted. My right leg felt OK, but my left was very painful. Looking at it, I noticed something sticking out. Oh shit. Was that bone? A wave of nausea came over me, so I rested my face back on the soft surface. I still hadn't worked out the situation. What the fuck was going on? I needed to get a grip. Closing my eyes, I shut out the ringing and pain, remembering waiting for a second extraction. The Chinook had taken off and cruised along. I was watching the Elkhaba leader's facial expression. Suddenly, all hell broke loose, but why? Oh hell, the SAM. Yes, we had come under attack, tracer rounds came in and then Rabbit shouted "SAM". Where the fuck was Rabbit now? In fact, where were all my mates and the Chinook? I started to breathe heavily, panic set in.

'Johnny, calm down,' I said.

I had made sure I spoke quieter this time, trying not to alert any enemy that might be out there, realising the vehicle lights could have been an enemy search party. The lights had almost disappeared. Listening hard through the numbing ringing in my head, I craved to go back to the nice, painless sleep with thoughts of home and Ella.

★

Ella was the only one to back me at first when I announced that I was joining the army. Her parents told her to finish with me as army life would bring nothing but trouble. Eventually, my parents realised it was a waste of time trying to stop me. I sat a few tests at the recruiting office, which I passed with ease, and told the officer I wanted to join the Paras. After a bit of arguing, he relented. My farewell to my family and

Ella was emotionally draining, but it was all part of achieving my goals. I had set my sights; nothing would get in the way. I trained and lived at the Para base, but on leave, I would travel down to Newquay for a quick family visit. Most of the time was spent on the beach, walking and talking with Ella. She had remained true to me, even with the pressure from her parents to finish it.

When I received my wings and a better wage, I invited Ella up. We ended up looking for a flat to share. After a few months topping up our savings, we put a deposit down and, at last, we moved in. Her parents nearly disowned her for moving in with me. My family were thrilled with my progress, and they regularly visited. After four years of going up the ranks, I started making noises about joining the 22 SAS Regiment, and asked to be put in for selection. For some reason, my platoon officers were totally against this and they made life awkward. It was almost as if I was shaming them, but I was persistent. Perhaps this was a test to see if I was focused on achieving. I spent months and months training in my spare time, which didn't go down too well with Ella at first, but again, she stood by me. I went for selection and passed. After a while we moved down to Poole in Dorset, where our lives became amazingly good. We purchased our first house, which although small, it was our kingdom.

★

*Johnny, wake up.*

I hadn't shouted this. Startled, I opened my eyes, lifted my head, and scanned the area—nothing.

'What else happened, Johnny?' I mumbled.

Then the words "Lock on, lock on... close." echoed round my mind. That was the key piece to the mystery jigsaw: we had been hit by a SAM. The Chinook must have crash-landed. I needed to get out of this position and search for survivors. A dreadful thought rushed into my mind: oh God, were the vehicle lights those of a friendly force search party? Were they now leaving without me? In a hurry, I tried to wriggle free, but couldn't.

'I'm here, over here,' I shouted.

I listened, wanting a reply, but only silence came out of the gloom. I managed to feel what was now apparent; a tight squeeze around my waist. Still strapped into the Chinook seat, I fumbled with the buckle. As it released, I lurched forward, jerking my arms and legs. Facing the ground, the blood rushed to my head and limbs; it was excruciating. I tried to resist yelling out, but the pain was too much. After, I laid there for a few minutes, trying to deal with the pain and nausea. Opening my tightly-shut eyes, I focused on the floor below, reckoning the drop was only about ten feet or so. The area was mostly covered in leaves and branches. I wasn't sure what time of the day it was, or how long I'd been trapped in this confined position.

Lurched forward, I was able to move my stiff left arm. I looked for my watch to get the time, but it was missing; it angered me. My watch was a twenty-first birthday gift from my mum and dad. It was very expensive and indestructible. My dad will be so mad with me, I thought. Then I smiled as I saw the funny side of this. At least my arm hadn't gone missing with it. Taking a better look around at the trees and branches, just above my head, behind my seat, was part of the Chinook's inside fuselage. It became shockingly obvious that I'd crash-landed in part of the Chinook into dense woodland. I had trouble getting my head around this. Where was the rest of the Chinook? I tried to remember map details of the area we'd had to study repeatedly before the operation. This must be the forest the Chinook was heading for when the Elkhaba got lucky with their SAM. This was our first night's lie up position on our deployment. Leaning back, I looked over my left shoulder. To my horror, I saw a British Army combat shirt; I was lying on a body.

With my head spinning with pain and my heart missing beats, I realised this must be my best mate Planet who I'd sat next to. I curled my arm over and shook him.

'Planet, wake up,' I said in a low voice. 'Planet. Rob, *Rob,* are you OK?'

He was unresponsive. I yelled again, louder this time, and shook his body more vigorously. At this point I realised what the smell and the sticky stuff that had been nagging me was: Planet's death and blood. Running my hand over him, he was very cold and wet. I started to gag, my body twisting with pain and the fear of loss. I felt his body further; it had sharp points protruding through it. Finding his neck, I pushed my fingers, desperately wanting to feel a pulse—nothing. I moved my fingers around a few times, but there was no sign of life. I began to shake, tears welled, and my throat began to harden. My parents had always told me not to bottle emotions up, but to let them out, share them. My training told me otherwise. I tried to stifle my sobbing in case I was heard.

'Nooooo,' I cried, but then shouted, 'Fuck it, come and find me, and please help my best mate.'

After what seemed ages of weeping into the silence and staring into nothing, I was sure I heard a voice from below saying, *Get down and get a move on.* Was this real, or was it my mind?

'Hello? Is anyone there?' I said. 'If there is, then get me the fuck down.'

I waited for an answer, but there was nothing but the gentle breeze through the trees. I desperately needed to get down and assess my situation. With one arm gripping the seat, I leaned forward and tried to swing my legs round. As I did, the pain increased and shot up my left leg and right through my spine, feeling as if my head was going to explode.

'Arghhhhhhh,' I screamed.

Inch by inch, and in excruciating pain, I continued to move my legs until I hung by my arms. The blood rushed all around my body, like millions of ants infesting me. Facing outward, Planet's cold, wet body was on my back. I didn't want to drop. Was it ten feet, or thirty feet? I tightened my grip, screaming inside to let go; my heart was thumping out of my chest.

'Let go,' I growled.

I didn't have to wait long; my grip had weakened, and I dropped.

# CHAPTER THREE

My dad was really annoyed as he stood over me, continually shouting; I'd let him down. I was sixteen years old and he had found me reading one of his signed military books. This was a restricted area, the big no. My dad collected signed military books, keeping them in his oak glassed cabinet. The hundred or so collection of books ranged from World War Two to the war in Afghanistan. Most of the authors had written about their military role in conflicts around the world. A few books were written by war correspondents and journalists. I would remove a book and take off the dust jacket. Wrapping the same dust jacket around a dummy book, I would then put the impostor back. Little did my dad know up until this point that I'd read at least thirty of his books, probably starting from when I was ten years old.

The first book I read was *Bravo Two Zero*, by Andy McNab. Since then I have read other soldiers' accounts of this SAS operation. I've inherited my dad's passion for reading and collecting signed military books. Most of the books I'd read at an early age I found shocking, but at the same time exciting. I knew if I got caught I would be in serious trouble, but this added to the excitement. I wasn't a lover of authority and rules, especially at school, and could be a bit of a rebel at times. The only place that I really respected was my karate *dojo*. I enjoyed taking on the higher belt grades and the older kids, testing myself, pushing my boundaries. I knew I was going to join the army when I left school and my goal was to join the Special Forces. I tried my hardest at school, but only in the subjects that interested me. My friends were more important to me than schoolwork; fun was easier. I was looked up to, so maybe I took leadership easily. I would retaliate if any of my friends were picked on as I hated bullying. My parents wanted me to be a zoologist; my second love was for animals and their surroundings.

My dad was now shouting at me, "Get up and put the book back now. You're grounded for two weeks, and you can forget seeing Ella."

I sat upright, cold, clammy, and couldn't understand where my dad had gone. The agonising pain swept over me again, realising I had been dreaming from passing out after the drop. I scrutinised my body.

'Nothing broken,' I said, and sighed with relief. 'Could have been worse.' I managed a stupid half-smile.

My clothes and hands were covered in blood. The priority was to find out where I was losing blood from. It had to be my leg, which was still very painful. Looking down, I'd forgotten the sight of the bone sticking out, which wasn't any more pleasant than at the first observation. I had trained in hospitals, A&E, and even helped in surgery; all part of my further training. I had seen many types of injury, including some similar to mine, in my extra training after passing selection. However, it was a different matter when it was your own body.

Hauling my leg up for a further look, I focused on the protruding bone. Luckily, it wasn't, but a part of a shredded branch, a massive splinter about twelve inches long that had skewered my calf. It had pierced an inch under the skin, narrowly missing the main muscle. The splinter followed the curvature of my calf. A sense of relief came over me, but strangely, I became annoyed that after all the years of training I had first diagnosed it wrong. Strapped around my chest was my utility belt. I felt for my knife and unbuttoned it. This wasn't a knife for killing, as in an attack, your main weapon does that, but it was for emergencies or when cutting was required. It seemed comical that the only part of my trousers that wasn't shredded was around the splinter sticking out.

'Typical,' I said. 'Bet I get a fucking fine for all my damaged kit.'

I ripped open my trousers and inspected the entry and exit wound. It was best not to cut the object out until I could get better medical supplies. I could hear Shrek saying in his *Monty Python* voice, "'Tis but a scratch, a mere flesh wound. Come on, you pansy."

Shit. I needed to find Shrek and the others. My anxiety built as I searched the gloom of the forest. This certainly didn't feel like our first LUP, more like a scene from a horror movie. Surely my remaining squad and crew must be nearby. If the exit and entry wound wasn't losing blood, then why was I covered in it? I decided to stand up and take a better look at myself, which was relatively easy, my leg causing the most discomfort. My head was still banging and, feeling dizzy, I put my arms out as I began to sway. Gently running my hands over my thumping head, I had a lump the size of a golf ball, but oddly-shaped, more like a garlic bulb. To the side of my forehead and face I felt crusted blood; the head wound must have stopped bleeding. I searched for any signs of major cuts leaking blood through my clothes. Parts of my uniform were shredded at the front, maybe by the initial SAM blast or crashing through the trees.

Taking a good look at the ground, I was standing in a congealed pool of blood, now being consumed by the earth. I tried to work out what could have produced this. Then the enormity of it hit me like a plank of wood across the head; this wasn't my blood. Up through the shards of light in the middle of the tree, some twenty feet up, part remains of Chinook with the seats and straps hung. I sharply turned away. How could I have forgotten that my best mate was up there? I'd let him down.

I had to check for certain that he was dead. I had seen many dead human bodies before and known army colleagues who had died, but this felt more personal, making the situation more critical. I psyched myself up.

'Take a look. You owe it to him.'

Raising my eyes again, I focused first on the outside of the wreckage and then dragged my eyes across to the lifeless form of a massive body hanging. My stomach knotted, and I wanted vomit. His bulky mass was covered in blood; it was his congealed mess on the ground. Was it his blood I could taste in my mouth? I shuddered. Planet's head was horrific; something had ripped most of his face off. Maybe he had shielded me in the blast or fall. I reached forward convulsing, but nothing came out. Staggering away as far as I could, I took refuge against a tree, and cried. Guilt made me angry.

'That was *my* seat. Why the fuck did he take it? I should have dragged him out, ordered him.'

Deflated, I started to reminisce about the previous operations and the SAS selection process.

★

I had met Planet on the first days of selection. Putting our first encounter behind us, we got along well. Through the books I had read, I knew what was expected of me to pass. Battling through the punishing process, we always wanted to outsmart and outdo each other. This kept us motivated and fixated only on passing; failure was not an option. Nothing, though, prepared me for how extreme the selection programme was, not even from numerous books I had read.

As I sat slumped thinking about Planet and the rest of the lads, something sparked deep in my subconscious: wake up and smell the coffee, you've survived. Stop moping. Get off your arse and search for any survivors. Find a radio and call HQ with a sitrep. My orders to get me back on track were like a double-dose of espresso mixed with Red Bull. I felt for my earpiece as I thought of making contact; however, only the wire protruded from under my collar as it had been ripped off. I started making my way through the forest towards where I had seen the lights. It was a slow, agonising walk, dragging my left leg behind as the splinter flexed between my calf muscles, walking at a funny angle so as not to knock the splinter with the other leg.

The sun was shining through the canopy of trees. The coolness had turned to humidity. I was certain I saw figures in the dimness, but each time I froze and checked, they were just shadows, adding to the eerie atmosphere. With no main weapon or pistol, my nerves were somewhat fraught, holding my breath on many occasions. After a hundred metres or so, a burning smell hit my nostrils. The further I pushed on, the more powerful the reek became.

Approximately fifty metres ahead, small plumes of smoke smouldered from the earth. Trees had been partly flattened; twisted branches were entwined in weird shapes. To the far end of the forest, the trees were totally flattened, like a lawnmower the size of a bus had ploughed through them, cutting down all in its path. Continuing towards the edge of the forest and, through gritted teeth, I got down on my front. I then crawled another few metres into a small thicket. Very slowly, I cleared the remaining bushes away, so I could have eyes on the clearing.

I wasn't prepared for what I saw. Approximately twenty metres in front was the wreckage of the Chinook, barely recognisable. It had massed into a charred, twisted frame of different-shaped metals. It could have been any military vehicle, aircraft, or even from out of this world. Smoke still smouldered amongst the remains and the earth around was heavily scorched. It hadn't been the headlights of a search party I'd seen earlier. I further examined around the wreckage, but only small, twisted remains were half-buried in the ground. Leading to the crash site were tracks made by more than one vehicle; scores of footprints were scattered around. If any of the remaining crew or my mates were in that, then they would have been burnt to dust. I closed my eyes at the thought.

Maybe the tracks and footprints around the crash site had been the rescue effort. If not, I knew very soon HQ would have, or would be preparing to send out a rescue force. Crawling back the way I'd come, I tried to keep my calf off the ground. I stood up slowly and wanted to move in a crouched position, but this was too painful. Vulnerably standing, I ventured back into the forest to widen my search. Moving around the damaged trees, I combed for survivors, and even started checking the tree canopies. After about an hour it had become increasingly obvious I wouldn't find anyone, but I still buried these negative thoughts and continued.

At that pivotal moment, out of the corner of my eye, something didn't look right about a bush. Staring for a while, I then decided to move closer for a better look. As I got within five metres, I froze. Fear started to take over, but immediately a wave of calm squashed the fear as my training took control, a sign that I was returning to my former-self. I detected the form of a human; its hand was just evident. Had the enemy left one sentry behind, or even worse, was he one part of a larger force left to watch the area?

Standing perfectly still, I controlled my breathing. I had no pistol, only the remains of its holster straps secured to my leg. Bollocks, I'd left my knife on the ground after cutting my trousers. That was fucking sloppy. I hated making mistakes, but there was no time to dwell, I'd bollock myself later. I had to deal with the figure in the bush, who I believed hadn't noticed me. Checking the ground, looking for the quietest path towards him, at race-speed, my mind went through the options. What would I do if he turned now and looked at me? What would I do if he was asleep?

Creeping forward, hardly making a sound and barely breathing, I was now within two metres. The figure was in a slumped position, head and shoulders rolled forward. I studied the body through the bush in the dull light. My heart skipped a beat as I had realised the uniform was that of a British Army soldier, one of my mates. I felt a surge of relief. Painfully slowly, I got down on my front and made a small hissing noise in case I startled him. He could be suffering from concussion, and I didn't want him to shoot me.

'Fish? Shrek?' I said, raising my voice slightly.

I had decided to use these nicknames, so he would know it was one of his mates. Again, I hissed these names a little louder and waited. A worrying thought entered my mind: maybe the body was booby-trapped. However, I had to take the risk, so I inched forward, hyper-alert to any noise or movement. My eyes were on stalks, searching for any signs of foul play. The pains in my leg and head were not even noticeable. I investigated the ground around the body for any traps. Satisfied, I gave the body a little shake, but it was motionless. I shook harder, and again it was unresponsive. Getting onto my knees, I gradually pulled back the bush and searched for his neck. His head was bowed forward, so I rolled the body over. Booby-trapped or not, I had no choice. His musty stench was awful, adding to the diesel smell. The body was cold and stiff, his clothes ripped, and he was covered in scorch marks and blood. Clearing the debris off his face, his eyes were still open. I scrambled back, my heart coming out of my mouth.

'Fish,' I shouted, in an exhaled breath.

I knew he was dead, but I still crawled back and checked for a pulse... I was too late.

Exhausted and demoralised, the sense of another loss overwhelmed me. As the tears ran into my thick beard, rage flooded through me. Tightening my fists, I clenched my teeth.

'Bollocks,' I said.

Maybe if I'd got down from the tree quicker, I could have saved him. I wanted revenge against the person who had fired the SAM. My fury was so great, I desired revenge on the entire enemy force that had fired upon us, almost exploding with temper; never had I felt so consumed by fury. I knew I had to get a grip though, as this would cloud any decisions. Eventually I calmed down, putting the thunderous anger to the back of my mind; hopefully, using this later if things got a bit messy.

I guessed the tracks weren't from a rescue force after all as they would still be searching the area, and definitely would have found me, Planet, and Fish. I reckon the Elkhaba or the Taliban had stripped the area. Hopefully they would have taken any survivors, and at least be looking after them. I pondered on this thought, but was sharply reminded of accounts of torture atrocities of other service personnel who had survived to within an inch of their lives. I shook my head, knowing I had to stay positive; this was a big factor in a survival situation.

Deciding to search Fish, I found myself talking to him whilst I did;

it comforted me. He still had his utility belt on with his knife attached, and his pistol was still holstered.

'Good lad,' I said.

I removed his gold coin belt to be used as bribery for help if he had to evade capture. We were all issued with the gold coins. His Maglite torch worked, and he still had cable ties in his pocket. I felt for his watch and undid the clasp. Rubbing dirt from the face, the time read 05.39 hrs, but the second hand had stopped. I stuffed it in my pocket, deciding to correct it later. I also made a mental note to return the watch to Fish's parents. Apart from a packet of soggy fags, which were no good even if I did smoke, I couldn't find anything else. I quickly made a search of the surrounding area. Something hard underfoot stopped me. Clearing the dense undergrowth, I touched the head of a canister. Picking it up, it was a blue smoke canister.

What I really wanted to find was his main weapon, webbing, and water canister. His webbing would have had an E&E Kit. Although each soldier's kit would differ slightly, depending on the environment and climate, all should have the basics. Each soldier sorts his own kit and kit brands. I store my gear in a sealed waterproof Pelican micro case. On this operation I had stored purification tablets, filter paper, a straw, button compass, brass snare wire, Gigli saw, thin penknife, signal mirror, whistle, pencil, paper, flint and steel, can opener, book-matches, windproof matches, candle, repair tape, sewing kit, safety pins, key-rings, cotton wool tampon (filter/dressing/tinder), condom (water carrier), scalpel handle and spare blades, surgical suture and thread kit, wound pad, plasters, alcohol wipes, thermometer, cotton-buds, butterfly closure strips, painkillers, tiny micro torch and spare battery, tiny syringe and a small tin of aloe vera. All SF would be 'sterile' of any ID tags, uniform markings, and personal items.

# CHAPTER FOUR

I couldn't bring myself to leave Fish. Assuming this was where the rescue force would arrive, I sat there for a while, thinking of good times with the lads. I promised I would drink to them both on my return. Standard operating procedure was never to return to a previous LUP. No matter how careful you were, tell-tale signs could be found and an ambush set. Maybe the enemy search party wouldn't return if they had concluded their search after finding the damaged wreckage, and, with any luck, survivors. Staying put was the best option. Water had to be nearby as the forest was stuck between the lower parts of valleys. The forest itself would shield me from enemy eyes and the harsh sun. Both squadrons had moved out from this previous LUP through a wadi under cover of darkness, boxing around a small village spotted by some of the SAS guys on a reconnaissance.

Even though the forest didn't have a supply of animals, I would surely find vegetation that was edible, or even small insects and scorpions which could be eaten for protein. Making a good shelter from cold winds at night with the foliage around would be easy. I was also sure it was possible to find further weapons, a Bergen, and webbing holding an E&E kit. If I found more equipment, I would set up human traps as I'd been taught in my jungle training. A reflective piece of metal tied to the top of a tree, faced to the sky, could reflect the sun towards any aircraft. Most pilots would see this as a signal, especially if looking for survivors. At night I could move to the top of the valley and set up another LUP monitoring the surrounding area in the day, keeping a close eye on any enemy forces and, with luck, friendly rescuers before too long.

'Great, now you're thinking straight and becoming the trained solider you are,' I said, a bit more optimistic.

Suddenly, a small noise filtered through the trees, carried along by the gentle breeze. What was that? I strained my ears. There it was again:

a clinking sound, like a metal on metal. The noise became louder and recognisable; an engine accompanied this. Friend or foe? I quickly covered Fish's body the best I could and picked up my scavenged gear. I ran as fast as I could, even though the protruding splinter kept hitting my other leg. The pain was sickening, but I had to move quickly. As I reached the end of the clearing, the sound was very close, and certainly more than one vehicle. Strangely, I found myself thinking if it was a SF rescue party I was going to give them hell for not tying down loose objects on their vehicle; this could alert you to the enemy.

Taking a sharp detour to the right of the clearing, I hid in the undergrowth, right on the edge of the forest. I buried as deep as possible and positioned my face down into the soil. *You need to look,* my subconscious voice said. Very slowly, I lifted my face up a couple of inches and looked out into the surrounding landscape. The sun's dazzling brightness bounced off the scenery. The terrain gave off a water mirage effect. Into view, about a hundred metres away, drove a large vehicle, heading towards the position of the wreckage. Following behind this large truck were two white vehicles, probably Toyotas.

I fought to shut my eyes at the brightness after being in the darkened forest. They started to water, and I was tempted to wipe them, but I knew that any movement would be spotted. I lay still, my head and leg pumping with pain. Not for the first time, I brought my breathing and heart under control. As the vehicles drew closer, I recognised they were not friendly. I hadn't even had time to prepare an escape route, or to check how much ammo Fish's pistol held, or even if it worked. I should have done this first before reminiscing about times with him and the lads. I was pissed off with myself. If I got through this, I would start to focus and become the trained soldier I was. I would have been RTU'd by now if on SAS selection process.

Watching the enemy convoy advance, the needle on my threat senses rocketed, nearly going off the scale. Breathing slowly, remaining perfectly still, I counted the enemy fighters: four males to each Toyota and two males in front of the truck. It was difficult from my angle to see truck's rear, but I made an educated guess it wouldn't be empty. Each Toyota had a rear-mounted Dushka and gunner. It was more than likely these vehicles were the ones firing at our Chinook. I wanted revenge, but it would be suicidal to move. If Shrek had been next to me, I'm sure I would have had to restrain him. Each vehicle drove within five metres of my position, showering me with dust and exhaust fumes. As I consumed these, I needed to cough, but resisted. I lost sight of the vehicles as they drove towards the wreckage. Even though out of sight, my hearing followed all the sounds, until they stopped. The occupants disembarked.

Someone shouted Arabic orders to search the area. I was totally hidden, and I had not showered for at least six weeks, blending into my environment, smelling like the shit I was in. Nevertheless, I was sure I would eventually be found. I contemplated my options: should I lie still, hoping they wouldn't search this far? But what if they came back later in larger numbers, or even with a local mutt? What if they found me now? Could I shoot my way out? If I tried to surrender, would they kill me, or imprison me, torturing me to a slow death? I couldn't stay here anymore was the resounding answer. I had to move far away from this threat.

Lifting my head as slowly as I dared, I scanned the area around my hidden position. To my right, the landscape was made up of flat, soft ground with stones and small rocks. Beyond this was the start of the valley slopes with their jagged rocks. Parts of the slopes were covered in a green and purple plantation, with living and dead trees. There had to be a crevice to hide there. To my left, the aspect mirror-imaged the right, except the valley slopes were further away, but this direction took me past the Chinook wreckage. Straight ahead was the route the enemy vehicles had driven in. The outgoing tracks disappeared over a mound-like hill; I didn't know what was beyond that. Maybe more vehicles were parked; my neck hairs stood on end.

From my initial map briefing, I could just about remember where the wadi was. My presumption was straight ahead, but it had all looked different at night. I didn't need my hunch to tell me to head right. Should I run flat-out, or try a sneaky squat-run? I knew the run would be very painful. Should I crawl on my belly? Too damn slow. After a little more contemplation, I decided I would start in a squat-run, and if this hindered me, I would break out into a sprint. The rest of the plan: to get to the base of the right valley and find somewhere to hide. Don't, whatever you do, look back whilst you are running. My negative side, or was it the sensible side, of my mind started doubting this plan, gluing me to the ground, saying, don't be stupid, stay where you are.

Right, *do it*, I overcame my doubting mind. Very slowly, I shoved the gear away, but kept the pistol in my hand. Rolling over, I raised my head and investigated the forest behind, but my view was limited because of the bush I was in. My heart was pounding, pushing acid into my throat.

Painfully and slowly, I rose onto my knees. I could just hear their voices, but could see jack shit as the forest was too dense. I started to tremble, and told myself this was adrenalin, but really, I was kidding myself. My hands were sweating, my head was pounding. This was it, by strength and guile. I took a deep breath, like before a dive into a swimming pool. Go, go, go, rang around my mind. I started running in a squat position, the pain wasn't as bad as before. Adrenalin does funny things to your body and mind. Questions were bouncing around my head at lightning-speed. Where to hide? What was the ground like? How far to go? What was happening behind me? Could I hear any weapons or shouting?

I'm sure I was listening so hard that my ears had turned around like a cat's. Although I had reached the first small scattered rocks, I wasn't too sure how far I had run, focusing on not falling over. I'd been holding my breath, concentrating so hard that I had barely realised; I exhaled, quickly gasping another breath in. No sounds came from behind me, only my feet pounding the rough ground, the stones and small rocks scattering. I cursed myself for not being more careful and silent. My body wanted to give up, but my determination pushed me on.

Reaching the bottom of the valley, six metres up was a large boulder that had fallen and rested on another group of small rocks. I clambered quickly up. Not the best rock climbing I'd done, I thought. Hiding behind a large boulder, staying completely still, I was rasping heavily. My throat and mouth were as dry as the desert I was in. I started tuning into my environment, listening for any signs from where I had just run, the position of the shadows, the ground's surface to dig a shallow scrape. If I burrowed in, was there any breeze to carry the dust out into the open? Would any smaller rocks be disturbed?

Beads of sweat trickled down my face and back. My clothes were saturated. The pains in my head and leg had worsened. It felt like hours had gone by, but it was probably only twenty-five minutes. I reckoned now was the best time to tuck under the boulder and then try to peek at where the enemy were. Grabbing a few handfuls of dried grass and heather, making a small pile at the fringe of the boulder, I buried under the earth at the base. Lastly, I covered the pile of foliage over my head. I shuffled forward with a gradual movement like a caterpillar, just to the outer edge, peering through the makeshift camouflage towards the forest. I was shocked to see how far I had run. The distance seemed a lot further than I had first estimated in the forest, guessing two hundred metres. A positive wave surged over me. For the first time since I had crash-landed, I felt exultant. It lifted my morale and suppressed the injury pains. I told myself I had done extremely well, and if things got tough, or I became negative, I was to think back on this triumphant run.

Laying still for what seemed an eternity, with my adrenalin subsiding, I shook like a leaf. My sweat-saturated clothes had turned my skin cold. Parts of my body went numb. To relieve this, I leant over an inch and gently wriggled my toes and fingers. I was starving and thirsty and desperately wanted a piss. This played on my mind, but it also gave me something to concentrate on. I needed to suppress the urge to go. If I could find a container to urinate in, I would leave it in the sun to heat up, then transfer the moisture to a connected cooler-covered container and drink it.

Each time the breeze gently whisked over the land, I shivered slightly; it had now become colder in the shadow. All was deathly quiet. I had started to smell something different, apart from the bag of shite smell that I was getting used to. Analysing the new odour, I believed it to be my leg wound, probably now infected. I needed medical attention, water, and food, and quick. I didn't have a lot of choice but to move on and search for these.

As our squadron had boxed around a small village on our first night, I decided I would have to take a massive risk and find the essentials there. I wanted to stay close to the compromised crash site, but had to weigh up my percentage of survival without the necessities. Gold coins could buy me help with the right people. Although, as soon as they were shown, I could end up being robbed, shot, and left to rot, or worse, handed over to the Taliban, or the Elkhaba.

As the sun started to set, the remaining heat from the ground seemed to follow it. A Toyota emerging from behind the wreckage site alerted me, followed closely by the truck. There were figures crouched on the benches in the back of the truck. As it went past, the rear was filled with something. I squinted to focus better, but couldn't identify the objects. Maybe they had found the bodies of Fish and Planet? If they had found my mates, I hoped they would be treated with dignity and not paraded all over the internet as propaganda, but who was I kidding? Bringing up the rear was the last Toyota. The male fighters in the back were jubilantly shouting and waving. One of them fired his AK47 into the air. I counted the entire enemy to make sure none were left behind, but I couldn't guarantee this as I didn't know exactly how many had come in on the rear of the truck.

I waited for the small convoy to fall silent and be replaced by the gentle desert breeze. I moved unhurriedly from under the boulder and then sat against it, out of sight of the forest. The surface still retained some heat. The sun was setting to the west. From this I surmised the time to be around 18.30 hrs. On the ground I drew a map of the area from details I remembered from our mission. The forest was approximately one hundred and fifty kilometres north of Khost, and fifty kilometres from the Pakistan border. Roughly, I drew the valley, wadi, and the village we had boxed around. My next plan was to find this village. With the light fading fast, I pulled out the watch I had salvaged from Fish. Winding it, I then checked to see if the second hand moved, but it didn't. I listened, but there was no ticking. I shook it and tapped it—nothing.

'Probably got it from Poundland, knowing Fish,' I muttered.

Stuffing it in my pocket, I picked up the pistol: a very reliable Swiss-made SIG Sauer P226. I checked the extended twenty-round magazine; it was fully loaded as expected.

Just before the sunset, I examined my leg where the splinter had entered and exited. The skin looked angry and swollen around both sides. Gently pushing the warm area, the pain worsened; a small amount of yellow puss oozed. With my knife, I started to cut the end of the splinter to stop it hitting my other leg, but it sent the agony further up my leg like a fire-bolt; a wave of nausea followed. Clenching my teeth, I continued to cut. Halfway through, I became dizzy; my focus was blurred, watering in bucket-loads. Gripping harder, I continued. Once through, I took in a deep slow breath and let it out.

'Well done Johnny, well done,' I said. 'Now find your bollocks, stop being a wuss and get moving.'

Wiping the tears from my eyes, I licked the moisture off the back of my hand. Without waiting for the searing pain to subside, I rolled my trouser leg down and stood up in the remaining light.

I inspected the slope, but couldn't see much. As night descended, after forty-five minutes I knew my eyes would adjust better, but only so much. It was too dangerous to use my Maglite. If the night was clear and the moon high, my vision at maximum could see a silhouetted human standing around two hundred metres away on the plains. The earth's surface curves out of sight at around five kilometres. But our visual acuity extends far beyond the horizon. If the earth was flat, or if you were standing on top of a mountain surveying a larger-than-usual area of the planet, you could perceive bright lights hundreds of kilometres in the distance. On a dark night you could see a candle flame flickering up to forty-eight kilometres away, a car's headlights around four kilometres distant. There are exceptions though, according to how many particles of light, or photons, a distant object emits.

The sun had fully disappeared and the stars and moon were shining bright. I marvelled at how beautiful the night sky above was compared to the barren landscape below. Studying these stars, I followed an imaginary line down from the Southern Cross; a constellation of five stars which provides a signpost to the south. I placed two fingers abreast this and started to move off in this direction. I knew the moon took the same rough transit as the sun when setting, so I could also navigate off this. The route took me up the side of the valley at a shallow ascent. I tried to keep away from the small rocks as any noise at night would be amplified. I wished I had a pair of NVGs. Nearer to the top of the valley, the steepness increased and the smaller rocks became larger. Even as an experienced rock climber, it was difficult climbing with no equipment in the dark.

The terrain took a sinister turn. Larger rocks and scoops in the ground played havoc with my legs. Bushes and trees played tricks on my mind. I tried to go around as many as I could, but sometimes it was necessary to hitch up and climb over. With my injured and aching body, the ascent drained energy from me. From the outset of my hide behind the boulder, I counted seconds as best I could. After six hundred seconds, I would stop for a rest. This count also gave me a goal. From this simple task I guessed my approximate distance covered from previous climbing and hiking. A further six hundred seconds elapsed. Stopping, I crouched down the best I could for a breather, not wanting to sit down as getting up used too much energy. It wasn't just the physical I would battle with, but the mental to get up and continue.

Rested for approximately five minutes, tuning into my environment, my mouth and throat were dry and lips were chapped. I ached from head to toe, but a small price to pay for being alive, I thought. As fatigue gripped me, I really had to force myself up. I checked my direction before moving off. After another six hundred second count, and battling with the energy-sapping, punishing terrain, I was nearly at the top of the valley slope. This would be the tricky part. I couldn't just stand on top as I would be silhouetted against the moonlight backdrop like a black shadow, and I had nothing to blend into, like a treeline. Now hurting more than ever, I got down onto my stomach again.

Crawling the remaining three metres, I slowly lifted my eyes over the ridgeline. My heart was beating faster and I was holding my breath. Neck and shoulders tensed, hands digging into the ground, I eased another few inches up till I could see further. Remaining perfectly still, listening, I squinted, not wanting them to stick out like great big white dinner plates in the moonlight. With no sign of life, I opened my eyes fully to survey the surrounding area. In front were smaller rocks on a flat surface. I couldn't see the ground beyond about ten metres as it seemed to disappear into the night. This must be where the flat area hit the opposite ridgeline; I must be getting close to the village.

I needed to find an LUP so to have eyes on the village. Sliding back the way I had come, I decided to go along the ridge; another laborious count. This was murderous on my leg; I become dizzy. Pain, fatigue, and the lack of food and water forced me to stop and rest early into my count. Eventually, I achieved my goal, but I hadn't travelled as far as before, or as far as I wanted to. I went through the same procedure with looking over the ridge, but became heavy and started to enjoy the rest. I had to drag myself up to the flat area, but I desperately needed a break, so I laid my head on the cool shingle. My eyes started to close.

As soon as they had shut, an alarm went off in my head. Not like an alarm bell, but like a shock. Immediately, I opened them wide, hyper-alert. What the fuck was that? Training and instinct, I thought. I must get a move on and find the village, and most importantly an LUP. Scraping over the ridgeline, I slid a further fifteen metres on my belly, taking me over small rocks and stones. This wasn't pleasant, playing hell on my bollocks. My bladder reminded me how seriously I needed to let go and my leg reminded me how bad it had become. I gritted my teeth.

'Nearly there. Keep going, you fucking tart,' I hushed.

I'd used words Fish had recently said to me on a training exercise. After falling into icy waters, I was having trouble getting out. Fish ran past, leaving me slapping and clawing at the edges of the freezing death hole. It was then he turned and, running backwards, shouted this at me. I got mad and wanted to catch him up and give him a whack or two. Now thinking back on this, I ignore my doubts and I picked up my pace.

What little saliva I had landed on my cracked lips, stinging as I licked them. The flat surface in front disappeared; I'd reached the new ridgeline. Laying still for a short while, I listened for any sounds before I looked over. The silence was as dead as the blackness beyond. I slid down like a snake, trying to muffle my agony. I came to a mound of rocks with heather around the base, like a rockery in some sweet little garden back in England. It felt unnatural compared with the surroundings. I crawled up the mound to look over the top, then I stopped, realising this must be someone's grave.

A memory flashed into my mind: I was at my Nan's funeral as a kid. My mum was telling me off for standing on someone's grave, saying that it was disrespectful and to get off immediately. But to me it looked like plain old grass.

"It's only grass Mum," I said innocently.

My mum, fuming, cuffed me round the head. "Someone's loved one is under there."

Now lying on somebody's grave, I felt as if I was disrespecting my mum and the deceased again. This unnerved me a little. Knowing my hunger, thirst, fatigue, and pain were stripping my positive barrier, I had to stay on top of the mind games. Realising there must be civilisation around, with a rush of energy I moved to the top of the grave mound and stared into the darkness. In the distance were tiny glowing lights. This must be the village. Judging the distance to be two to three hundred metres, and feeling strengthened, I moved down towards the lights. I came across another three mounds of stones; more were positioned further away. Every fifty metres I stopped, lowered my body, and listened. When I got within approximately a hundred metres, I searched for an LUP.

I found a hollow in the ground with part of an old tree trunk on its side, so crawling in, I then pulled the dead bark and dry soil over me. Through a small crack, black silhouettes of walls and paths were outlined in the moonlight. The glowing lights had dimmed, almost extinguished. I made a mental detailed plan of the village. The distant sound of a dog barking startled me; my eyes widened with fear. I hoped it was tied up as it could easily compromise my position. I was going through shivering spasms and insects crawled over me. The barking subsided, so I shut my eyes, this time allowing myself to rest. My first thoughts were of my wife and family; however, these were bombarded with the Chinook wreck and sickening images of Planet and Fish. I tried hard to put these out of my mind, but they kept haunting me.

# CHAPTER FIVE

I had drifted into the sleep of all sleeps, almost a coma. Waking, cold, groggy, and stiff, my throat was sore and my lips dry. I wondered if I had been snoring, as Ella always used to complain at home that I did. Had she been informed I was missing in action? Was she coping? I imagined her face with tears and sadness, but quickly blinked these images away. In my confined space the smell from my leg had become more pungent. Peering through the gap in the trunk, the sun blinded me temporarily. Carefully moving the bark and dirt from myself, I let the sun through and, waiting for my eyes adjust to the daylight, let the energy and warmth warm my numb body. The sun was low; I reckoned it had to be early morning. My shorts and trousers were wet. I must have let my bladder go in my deep sleep.

Looking down on the village, it was vastly larger than I had first estimated last night. Different-sized buildings were linked together, but with no architectural design. Various types were scattered around randomly. A few to the left of the village were half-built, showing a more modern breezeblock structure. Many were in disrepair, with their roofs and walls collapsed. Around the whole perimeter of the village, a substantial wall stood with parts demolished and eroded away. It was pleasing to see further greenery as different-sized groups of trees popped up in the village, like little oases. A track snaked through the village. At one end, nearest to my position, it disappeared round the valley slopes. In the other direction it led off into the far distance, but I lost sight of it as the landscape was built up with uneven ground and features of trees and mounds.

To the other side of the village, closest to my side, were irrigated farmland, ditches, and two old brown tractors, silently baking in the sun. Crops had been stacked on old wooden trailers, and some had been piled high on the ground. Over the far side of the farmland and track was by far the largest building. It was distinctively different from the others. High walls surrounded the compound. The inside structure was made up of three sections, like terraced houses. A small dome sat on the roof of the middle section. From this angle I couldn't see the main entrance to the compound. With the windows covered by ornate bars, it reminded me of a town hall or the chief elder's house. Overall, the village looked a good prospect for water and food compared with some I had sadly witnessed on our mission through different areas. As for life, all that I could see were chickens and a group of goats, all wandering aimlessly in the centre. I lay there, waiting for further life to appear.

I was drawn to the movement of a figure coming out from a single building nearest to me. This woman was dressed head to toe in black with only her eyes evident. She was carrying two empty buckets and walked across the village behind another building, after which I lost sight of her. I looked up and marvelled at the endless clear blue sky. Against this blue background, high up, in the very far distance, was a dot-like object. The item travelled across at a very slow speed. Cupping my hands like a telescope, I concentrated hard on it. As it travelled it didn't leave any white trails like a plane. The object stayed at the same height, but changed its course, staying in direct line above the track heading towards me. My eyes again started to water, so I dipped my head, slowly wiping them. Looking up and focusing again, I positively identified it as a white plane-shape, but it was completely silent.

'It's a fucking UAV,' I whispered excitedly.

This drone is being controlled either autonomously by computers in a vehicle, or by remote control by a pilot on the ground. The UAV must be sending direct pictures or live video back to a friendly force, most probably American. Were they searching for me? I contemplated standing up and waving madly at it, but then had second thoughts. How do I grab the UAV's attention while staying low? My knife blade was made of matt-black carbon fibre, so that wouldn't reflect the sun. In a eureka moment, I pulled out Fish's watch and tried to catch the sun's reflection off its silver metal underside casing, but it was too late; the UAV had passed and was heading out of sight. I cursed myself for not thinking and acting quicker. The list of fuck-ups was building; I really needed to slap myself into focusing. Putting away the watch, I gazed back at the village.

Behind the large building, the woman in black returned with her two buckets filled with water. My thirst now became desperate as I visualised drinking from the cool water. I tried to lick my cracked lips, but it only made them sore. She disappeared back into her house. A wonderful smell grabbed my nostrils, filling my mouth with saliva. The aroma of bread baking was heaven, and my stomach growled, urging me to go and get some of this tantalising food and not wait till night. I couldn't last another day in the heat without water, food, or medical supplies. Yet again I had break SOP, but this was now a case of survival.

I crawled out of my sleeping quarters; not the best I've slept in, I thought, looking back. Embarrassingly, I had a piss patch all down my trouser groin area and leg, but then I looked like bag of shite anyway, so I shrugged it off. I set off the slowest I had moved so far, but the thought of water and food played tricks on my mind, telling me to speed up and fill my boots.

After what seemed like a dying man's crawl, I reached the wall behind her building. Removing my pistol from the rear of my trousers, ever so quietly I cocked it and took off its safety catch. Hugging the shadow of the wall, I ran forward into the building's shadow, remaining still and quiet. I could just about hear some movement inside, and the cooking odours were to die for—well, not literally. I quickly worked out my escape route if it went noisy, the outer wall behind me being my best option. Crouching, I moved cautiously around the front, checking the surrounding village as I did. My heart was thumping like the sound of a distant Chinook. Jesus, could nobody else hear it? I peered around the entrance, which only had the remnants of a door frame. Instead of a door, there was a piece of what looked like a hessian sack. Taking a slight inhale and, with my Sig out in front, I went through the hessian.

Inside, staring down my pistol, I searched; my eyes adjusted to the shade. Embers were glowing in one part of the room; rods were set above them. In the centre of the fire was a clay pot, which perfumed the room with baking bread. Around the room was basic furniture: an old table, three rickety chairs and no personal items. Pots, pans, and cooking utensils rested on a small upside-down crate, which was covered by a dirty white cloth. The buckets of water stood next to the crate. Tearing my stare away from the water, I turned my attention to a doorway with no door that led to another room. The woman had her back to me; my eyes narrowed. Thoughts sped through my mind. What was she doing? Had she heard me and was waking someone? Did she or anyone else in the room have a weapon?

I tightened the grip on my Sig. She turned around and our eyes met. Behind her hijab was her frightened eyes. She dropped her plate and cup, frozen to the spot. She then lowered herself to her knees, terrified; my pistol followed her. My eyes lifted to search the darkness of the room. Blankets covered a timber-framed bed, and at the end of that, a small table was covered in religious artefacts. Further small statues were placed on a shelf. I stared back at the woman, her body now shaking. I tried to remember my best Pashto.

'*Pregda?*'

She didn't reply.

'*Pregda?*' I said friendlier.

The woman gently nodded. So, she was alone.

I wanted to let her know I was a soldier. '*Askar,*' I said, and to inform her I was her friend, '*Dost.*'

She raised her head, her eyes less afraid, and she nodded again.

I was having a mental block on my Pashto. Maybe it was the blow to my head. I was hoping it was correct so far; at least it seemed to be working.

'I'm sick... *za naroogh*. Help? *Mrastal?*' I pointed around to the rest of the village and asked her for a doctor, '*Daak tarr?*'

The woman continued to stare.

I gestured a drinking a glass to my mouth action and said, '*Oba, tgay.*' Again, I repeated, 'Friend... *dost*. Help... *mrastal.*'

The woman lowered her stare to my Sig, which was still pointing over her.

Putting the safety catch on, I slowly moved the pistol to the back of my trousers. I smiled at her, although probably a cheesy smile. I held out my hand again, but she didn't take it. She stood up slowly. I couldn't see her facial expression, so I kept eye contact.

'What is your name? *Sta num tsa day?*'

Again, she didn't reply, but I think she understood, or maybe she was pissing herself with laughter at my attempted Pashto.

Moving back to the centre of the main room, I pointed at the pot and then signalled to my mouth. I couldn't remember what the translation for bread or food was, even though I had learnt it. She continued to stare at me. Oh for fuck's sake, Johnny, just grab the fucking food and water. You're getting nowhere with this woman, I thought. I frowned at her. She gingerly moved into the centre of the room, not taking her eyes off me. I purposely blocked her exit route, but tried not to make this obvious. We stood there looking at each other in total silence. A funny voice entered my mind, *awkward*. A smile came to my face and, as it did, her eyes relaxed. I thought of the gold coins and then placed my hand in my pocket. As I did, the woman's eyes became anxious. I put on a bigger cheesy smile, slowly pulling out Fish's belt of gold coins. Removing a few coins, I held my hand out to her. The woman's eyes lit up like fireballs, staring at the coins for ages, before her watery stare looked back at me.

'*Daak tarr*… Doctor. *Za naroogh*,' I said.

I prompted her to take the gold coins. She moved closer and held out her trembling hand. Her hands and nails were filthy, but I suppose mine were no better. She wouldn't take the coins, so I placed them in her hand. She clasped them immediately, a death grip of life, and then held her hand to her chest. She nodded, and I nodded back.

'Please help. I need a doctor,' I pleaded.

She nodded at the doorway.

What did she mean? I pondered, and then she did the same gesture again. Of course, you idiot, Johnny, you're blocking the doorway. I stepped to the side and she moved slowly to the door without removing her glare from me.

Just as she got to the hessian, I said, '*Insha Allah*.'

As she left, I trusted my last comment of "God willing" had secured my future. Creeping back to the window aperture, I slightly pulled back the hessian; the woman had disappeared. I drew my Sig as I became slightly apprehensive of the next outcome. Should I just grab some food and water and leave?

Keeping an eye through the hessian-covered window, then back towards the hessian-covered doorway, I became anxious of her return.

'Fuck it, she's gone forever. Let's get out of here,' I said.

In the corner was a jug with a small lid, so I went over to it and dipped my finger in to make sure it was water. Assured that it was, I started to sip it. I fought the urge to gulp it down, knowing I would probably bulk it up. My cracked lips soaked up the water like an African dry riverbed receiving the first trickle of heavy rain. The water was cool and eased my sore throat. The refreshing liquid entered my stomach. It was like one of those moments after a long, hot, stressful day, when you go to the pub and there on the bar is a crisp pint of lager with condensation droplets running down the outside of the glass: pure liquid gold. I couldn't drink it all at once, I had to get my stomach used to it, and I wasn't sure when would be the next time I would find water. I replaced the lid.

With my boot, I nudged off the lid of the pot sat on the embers. A beautiful waft of fresh bread took me into a state of pure ecstasy. Bending over, I grabbed a chunk of soft dough, but it was too hot, sticking and burning my fingers.

'Shit, shit,' I hissed, shaking my hand in desperation to get it off.

Once it had cooled a little, I thrust the remains of the sticky dough into my mouth, not thinking of my filthy hand's hygiene. My taste buds were having a wild party as my mouth salivated. There wasn't much to swallow, but it tasted amazing, my stomach welcoming the food with further spasms and gurgles.

I went back into the other room and pulled the sheet off the bed to wrap up the hot bread. I noticed the sheet hadn't been washed in a while, if ever, as it was heavily stained; dropping it immediately.

'Rank,' I murmured.

I searched the room for something else to use, but couldn't find anything. I didn't want to use the hessian off the window as this could alert anyone else to my presence; however, it was the only thing I could find. Nearing the window, I caught the sound of voices outside. Immediately, I pulled out my Sig and lowered myself under the frame. The voices were coming nearer; the safety catch came off. Both were speaking in Pashto. I moved quickly to the shadows of the other room and, crouching, raised my Sig at the hessian-covered doorway. I was calm and relaxed, but felt ready to kill if necessary. First through was the woman in black, and my brain within a split-second registered her as friendly. Following her was another woman; I scanned for weapons and immediately judged if she was a possible threat. Both turned and faced me, looking startled. There was an awkward pause and the second woman came to the forefront.

'Don't worry. I'm here to help you,' she said in near-perfect English with an Afghan accent.

'Are you alone?' I asked.

'Yes, for now. It not safe here. Please, put your gun away. I will help you. I am a doctor.'

I lowered my Sig and tucked it in my trousers and said, 'What's your name?'

'Let me examine you first,' the doctor said soothingly. 'You are very bad. Please, sit on the bed.'

Her long, slender hand waved out in front of her. The woman in black, who I had now named Betty, lit a candle from the embers. Betty came into the room and started to light more candles.

'What's your name, please?' I asked again.

The doctor pulled the strap from her shoulder and swung a bag in front of her. It resembled a cool bag, but it had a red cross on the front with some words in Arabic.

'Please take clothes off,' she said, ignoring my question.

She walked in the room. In the light, the doctor was even more beautiful. She had long brown hair tied in a bunch behind her. Her wide eyes were a deep brown and she had amazing teeth. Her lips and nose were thin and perfect. Her figure was slender and tall, dressed in white blouse and black trousers. I found myself staring at her, probably a bit too long.

'Please take clothes off,' she said again, then sighed.

'Oh… yeah… err… OK,' I rambled.

Standing up, I placed my Sig on the bed behind me; in my reach, but out of reach of the other two. I stripped off everything but my boots and boxer shorts, acting casual. I looked down at my body. Holy shit. I'd lost a lot of weight, and I had bruises, lacerations, and small cuts all over. My left calf had swollen further, looking very angry, almost fit to burst. I was filthy and stank to the high heavens. My boxer shorts were piss-stained, which had merged with red stains, the blood of my best mate. I noticed, in disgust, little lice. Not the best look for standing in front of a young, beautiful woman. I looked up, feeling like a naughty boy that has messed himself at infant school. The doctor never even batted an eye, though Betty's were now on stalks. I found this a bit unnerving.

'Please take boots and pants off,' came the robotic order from the doctor.

'What? We've only known each other five minutes and it's our first date, luv,' I said in my best jack-the-lad impression—my wit didn't even earn a raised eyebrow from her.

'Take boots and pants off,' she said sternly.

'What, and no screen to go behind?' It sounded as pathetic as it was.

Sitting on the bed, I took my boots and socks off. The swelling and pain from my calf rushed down to my ankle and foot. There was an imprint where the top of my boot had been. God, my feet were humming. They were white, wrinkled, blistered, and it looked like a layer of cheese was growing; a lump came to my throat.

'I'm very sorry,' I said.

Without even as much as a nose twitch, the doctor said, 'Stop stalling, soldier. Take pants off. You wasting valuable time, your time.'

I was starting to piss her off. It was like being a private again, getting a telling-off from a higher-ranking soldier.

Standing up, I took off my stained boxer shorts and threw them with my other clothes. The doctor started to get professional medical items out of her bag. I made out English writing on some of the sealed packets. Betty's eyes were firmly fixed on my tackle. My hands automatically covered my parts. The doctor seeing me do this turned to Betty and raised her voice, gesturing at the same time. Her orders were too quick for me to translate properly; however, I translated the word "water" and, I think, "clothes". Betty left the building sharply.

'On the bed, on your front,' the doctor ordered.

I thought of a witty reply, but decided best not to say it. I was glad to lie on the bed, as looking down I caught a glimpse of her silky cleavage. I persisted asking the doctor's name. Eventually she sighed.

'My name is not important,' she said.

'It is to me.'

'OK, my name is Haleema.'

'That's a nice name,' I replied—how cheesy. 'Do you want to know my name?'

'No. It's no matter to me.'

Haleema continued to examine me. Jesus, this was like drawing blood from a stone. I reckoned even Fish couldn't have scored with this woman.

'Soldier, you have bad leg wound. I need to attend this first, then attend all other minor cuts and clean you up.'

I was sure this pretty, young doctor had been turned into a robot, perhaps brainwashed. I mustered up my best robot impression.

'What about the big lump on my head?'

In an exact copy of my robot voice, she replied, 'I not notice any lump.'

I stared at her in bewilderment, but noticed a small wry smile just before she dived into her bag. I placed my face back on the bed, laughing inside. What a moment. After all the pain and suffering, and the evil surrounding me, here I was sharing an impression of a robot with a stunning doctor, a stranger. To top it all, I had a woman dressed in black who was transfixed on my tackle, and who was probably a man underneath the outfit anyway.

'I will numb the leg and cut out the object. This will hurt you,' Haleema said.

'Haleema, I trust you. I am also a trained medic. You have a caring nature and you don't seem bothered about my injuries or who I am. Thank you.'

Her eyes fill with tears, twinkling in the candlelight. This had touched a raw nerve with her, but at least we shared a common interest. The hessian in the doorway flew inwards. I grabbed and aimed my Sig in a split-second.

'No,' Haleema shouted at me. 'No more bloodshed... please.'

It was Betty, and she had frozen. Haleema ranted off something which I tried to translate, but I only managed to translate the word "slow". I must brush up on my Pashto when I get back home, I thought.

'Nobody but us will come in this home,' Haleema said. 'They my orders to the others in the village.'

I apologised to them whilst Betty brought a bowl of steaming water and some clean cloths. I was glad she didn't use her bed sheet as a cloth as I would probably have died from septicaemia within seconds.

'I know this is going to hurt,' I said, 'so please tell me how you became a doctor, to take my mind off the pain.'

This wasn't exactly true as I normally had a good pain threshold; also, I trusted Haleema to be caring. I just wanted to find more about this amazing young woman. I had also started to enjoy her voice. What was she doing in this deprived village?

'I will tell you after I finish surgery on your leg. I need to concentrate as you could die. I not even know your name to put on your cross, your Western ways.'

I was now getting used to her weird sense of humour; well, I hoped it was humour. 'Did you get a diploma in bedside manners?' I mimicked.

She harshly frowned. God, what a plonker I was, and I raised my eyes to the ceiling.

'My name is Johnny Vince, but you can call me Vinnie.'

'Vinnie, please be still. I am starting.'

I began to slightly tense, so I took my mind off to home, thinking of friends and family. I imagined myself climbing high on a cliff in Newquay, taking in the views and sounds of the sea. I was relaxed, but strangely, also alert to any threat.

# CHAPTER SIX

Haleema placed her medical equipment beside me in a neat line and then drew latex gloves over her slender hands. A tourniquet was put on the upper part of my leg, two finger spaces above the wound to prevent any blood loss. She filled her syringe with ketamine and injected 10-mg into my leg to ease my pain, and then proceeded to flush the wound with 20-ml of a saline solution. Opening the sterile gauze pads, Haleema continued to clean the wound and surrounding area. After the injury had been cleaned, she picked up a bottle of lidocaine, a one per cent adrenalin injection, and filled up a syringe. She then injected the four aspects of the wound to numb the area.

Next, she ripped open the top of a new packet and took a scalpel out. Without the slightest hesitation or tremble, she made an incision along the length of the splinter. She pealed back the outer skin with a pair of surgical clamp tongs, leaving the splinter exposed. With another pair of large surgical tweezers, she pulled it out. When all the fragments were removed, the gash was flushed through with more saline, and again cleaned with sterile gauze pads. After unclamping the wound, she opened a sterile suture set and stitched it up, finally applying an emergency care bandage.

'Your leg done now,' she said.

I sat up; a bit lightheaded. 'Please may I have some water?'

'Yes,' Haleema said, and asked Betty to fetch some. 'Are you feeling all right? Are you going to be sick?'

'Hopefully projectile.'

This time, I gave her a wry smile as she looked up. I drank the water. Haleema pouted, then turned to Betty who was collecting all the used medical waste. Betty disappeared through the doorway.

'I need you cleaned up. You not smell good. Off the bed. Stand up.'

Haleema had returned to her robotic monotone voice. So much for progress, I thought, but I kept my opinion to myself. I stood up, feeling a little awkward again, standing stark bollock naked.

'I would love to hear how you became a doctor,' I said.

Haleema changed her latex gloves and began opening another pack of sterile gauze pads and further surgical wipes. She sprayed my body with Betadine spray and cleaned the small cuts and lacerations. I tried not to wince at the stinging, knowing this would encourage her weird humour. Last off, she cleaned an area on my right upper thigh and injected 10-mg of morphine. As she stood up and cleaned my head wound, I could see the concentration in her deep brown eyes. Stupidly, I stared down her silky cleavage. I'd only ever been this close to one girl: Ella. I looked away at objects at the end of the bed. Then, as she cleaned the rest of the grime with hot water and cloths, she began to speak.

'As young girl of fourteen, my parents took me on long, slow trip to Kabul. We borrow old orange car from village chief elder. My parents pack a bag for me. I was driven to a friend of my parents, Baha Udeen. I stay for very long time. Baha Udeen got me work. I study at Kabul International Hospital. It is private hospital. At weekends I have to pay him part money I earned. This was agreement between my parents and him. Baha Udeen is owner, and respected. I spend many hours working and studying. Every three months I return to my village. I get lift with hospital porter who was friend of Baha Udeen. We make many deliveries on way. The back of car was packed full of medical supplies. Most were out of date, and some had been supplied to hospital by other countries.

'After four years, I drive a car lent to me by Baha Udeen. This was fun, but very dangerous. It take me long time to learn to drive better. I take trips to my village on my own. My village was always busy with many workers and children. My parents and whole village welcome me on my return. On my last visit my father told me not to come here for a while as we have enough supplies. Trip was too dangerous. I tell him not to worry, it was OK. But he insisted. My father had harsh and worried look. I only know now what he was saying to me.

'I return to Baha Udeen house in Karte Naw opposite hospital. My studying get harder. I work more hours, seven days a week. I pass all exams. I would also be treating and saving lives of Afghans caught in war. On one occasion, against Udeen rules, army bring in two wounded. Soldier friends brought them in. I try to save lives of two British soldiers who not have time to be rescued. I try hard to save them, but both died. I am very sorry. We hide dead bodies until they collected. It is known

Taliban walked around the hospital. I was very sad for soldiers. This is my first loss as a doctor, the death was painful. Udeen found out and he slapped me.

'I do not return home for long time. I was very busy. I had been saving hard. I was very tired. Baha Udeen help me buy first car through friend of his. It was a black Toyota, a Tacoma, very fast and shiny. I decide to take three weeks off work. This angered Baha Udeen. I load new Toyota with medical supplies from hospital. All are British and American supplies. I paid for some supplies, but also, how you say in English, 'borrow' some every day. My Toyota was very full. Baha Udeen never asked questions about medical supplies. It had been three years since I return back to my village. The porter was murdered in his car one year before. It was said he was talking to Taliban. It was dangerous, long drive, but I make it. If stopped at checkpoints I would say I deliver for Baha Udeen. It was OK after.

'When I return to my village, I see no children playing, no farmers working. My family and friends not run out and say hello as I drive in. My village was different. It felt wrong. I got out of car and walked to my parents' home. Someone walk behind me. I turn. He hit me hard in face. I fell to the floor. I feel kicks to my body. I start to scream. This angered evil man. He dragged me by hair through door of my home. This is where you stand now, Vinnie. I try to defend myself, but was very hard. My mother come screaming into the room. She attack evil man as he ripping my clothes and touch me. As he turn around, my mother grabbed me, then cradled me. She take many punches and kicks. My mother was dragged out this room. I find out later who this evil man was: L-khaba-a leader.

' "We have been expecting you," he say.

'He shout at me lots of horrid names and ask where have I been for many years. I was taken outside to my car. Other L-khaba-a men were looking through car and take medical supplies. I keep quiet. I was very frightened I would be killed. I looked around for my mother and wondered where my father was. Where was village elders to help me? I was sexually touched by many hands. I hope my parents would not see. I tried to stop evil men. When I did, they hit me. I was asked many questions. These were medical supplies for village, our people. I asked where my mother was.

' "She is safe if you do as you are told," the leader say.

' "Where is my father and village elders?" I asked.

'He swipe me around face, and say, "Too many questions, but as you ask, they are all dead."

'I feel very sick and dizzy. It hurt like nothing else. I cry. This make the L-khaba-a men very happy. They all laugh at me. Through tears I ask, "Why have you done this? We are peaceful village. Where is my father buried?"

'The leader laugh. He point to valley, and say, "He is up there with so many others."

'In valley were many piles of stones. I plead where my mother was. I was told if I left the village he would kill her and rest of village people. If I was caught they would torture me to slow death. He grab my cheeks and try to kiss me. I struggle and he laugh. They all laugh. He tells me I would now only treat his injured and dying men. If I let one of his one men die, he would kill one in the village as punishment. If I help, my mother and me will be safe. I have been trapped here for two years.

'I hear terrible stories from friends in the village. Women and children have been raped, tortured, or killed in front of their fathers. Some villagers try to run away. Some have just gone missing. If men of village do not fight alongside the L-khaba-a they are beaten and killed. When men return from fighting, villagers have to prepare them food and water, and clean their clothes. They smoke many drugs and force villagers to sex, including men and children. My mother and me are safe, but we cannot hide from screams. My mother has been raped before I come back, but they don't touch her now. I tell the leader I would not help his men if they continued to abuse village. He go berserk and beats me. He drag my screaming mother out of her home and beat her in front of me. Our clothes are taken, and we left in sun all day naked. I never say anything to him again like this.

'In lower part of village is big building. I turn into hospital. I treat and save many L-khaba-a lives. I also not saved some. Each time I hear gunshots, I know what I cause. We are left to bury village people. My father was beaten, flogged, and shot just for stealing food from store to help others. My mother forced to watch. She cried and wailed. She shout at killers. She spit at them. They cut her tongue out. The woman you first see in our home is my mother. We trapped in this evil. Our only survival is to do as they say. We get to eat and drink, but not live our lives in peace. The only pride I take is I help rape and mutilation injuries of village. I do in secret in middle of the night when L-khaba-a men take drugs and pass out. I sneak in and take children and woman from the sleeping L-khaba-a rooms. It make me sick to see villagers and children like this.

'When they return from fighting and been fed and watered, the villagers disappear into their homes. They hide in fear. The children only play and farmers only work when they have gone. We never know when they return. They say fighters watch the village. If any of us leave, they will kill us. The L-khaba-a leader take my car. I think many times about stealing it back, and my mother drive far away, but I know what would happen to my village.'

There was a short silence and then Haleema told me she had finished. I wasn't sure if she meant her story, or treating me. My eyes had tears and my head was bowed. I hadn't even noticed Haleema's mother had come in. Betty had been a piss-take name. How could I call her this now? Even though revived after the water and medical treatment, my stomach was knotted and I felt sick. I wanted to say something, but I couldn't find the words. Looking at Haleema and her mother I wanted to say sorry, but couldn't speak. I think they understood as the mother came over and touched my arm. I sat back down, staring at the floor, going over what I'd been told. I had a mixture of emotions: angry, incensed, and sad. I had known of these atrocities happening in Afghanistan and other conflicts, but I had never heard it from the victims themselves; the same people were so willing to help me.

Haleema brought me some bread and water, disturbing my thoughts. 'You must eat now,' she said.

I said nothing, eating and drinking the best I could, having lost my appetite. Haleema brought over some new clothes. These were Afghan *dishdasha*, flip-flops, and a *shemagh*.

'They my father's. Please take.'

I felt guilty, but I had to tell her I needed my own clothes back to be identified by friendly forces, not mistaken for an insurgent carrying a weapon. I plucked up the courage.

'Thank you. But I really can't take these. I need my clothes back.'

'These my father's,' she replied, cross.

'I understand, but I can't travel like this. I will keep the *shemagh*, thank you. I will wear it with pride and think of you and your mother.'

There was an awkward pause, but then Haleema's frown evaporated with her lovely smile, taking the remaining clothes from me. Putting on my old clothes wasn't as easy as it seemed. They were filthy, ripped, and stank. Maybe this wasn't such a good idea. Haleema's mother's eyes looked puzzled as she watched me put on these unfit clothes.

'What's your mother's name?' I asked.

'Anoosheh,' Haleema said proudly.

'You must be very proud of her, and she must be of you.'

'You very kind man, Vinnie. Please go home to motherland, before terrible L-khaba-a or Taliban kill you,' she said caring.

'Please, Haleema, translate to Anoosheh what I am going to say. Thank you both for helping me. Without this I would have probably died. I am very sorry for your loss and what has happened to your lives and your village. When I have reached my army friends, I promise you the Elkhaba will pay for what they have done. You and your village will not suffer anymore after this.'

I waited for Haleema to translate. My anger energised me, so I continued, 'I want to return and kill all the Elkhaba. I have also lost very close friends to these terrorists. I will hopefully lead an operation to rescue your village, so it can return to better days. Haleema, you will get your doctor's job back in Kabul. Both of you have so much courage and integrity. I will not forget what you have been through and what you have done for me. I will tell my friends, my wife, and my children one day.' Leaving a small pause for Haleema to catch up, I continued, 'One more thing. I would like you to have these.'

I pulled out the remaining gold coins and held half of them out to Haleema.

'What is this?' she asked.

Hoping I hadn't insulted, I replied, 'These are for you. I have given your mother some already. Please, when you are rid of this evil, and mark my words you will be, I want you to help your village.'

She took them from my hand and held them close to her chest. Her eyes were filled with tears and moved gracefully towards me, wrapping her slender arms around me—her heartbeat touched me.

'I believe God and fate bring you,' she said. 'You must go, but please first wait. I have something for you.'

She released her warming embrace and signalled to her mum. Anoosheh gave me a leather satchel. I looked inside to see what it held: stuffed full of medical supplies. There was also bread and a small bottle of Evian; a miracle bag came to mind. I thanked them both and hugged Haleema again.

'Please not be angry,' she said sheepishly as I released her. 'I have something to tell you.'

I smiled. 'What could I possibly be angry about?'

She rubbed her hands nervously. 'When helicopter come down, L-khaba-a bring back dead bodies, but one soldier lived.'

'What?' I yelled, in disbelief. 'Say that again.'

'I am very sorry not telling you,' her voice quivered. 'I not sure if he still alive now. I had been treating L-khaba-a leader who come in at same time for burns on feet and legs. I then see soldier alive.'

'Where? What's his name? Where is he now?'

Haleema slightly lowered her head. 'Please not be angry. He in makeshift hospital at bottom of track, past farmer field. He badly beaten, injured in bad way like you. I not know his name. I sneak in, give him water and bread. I cleaned his wounds.' She lowered her head, even more ashamed. 'To do this, I let guard touch me all over. He heavily-manned by L-khaba-a. I heard they moving him. I not sure if he been moved or is alive. I not want to tell you. You might go to him and find he gone, or dead. I not want you to get killed. I am very sorry, Vinnie.'

# CHAPTER SEVEN

My mind was a jumble of questions and images; I was stunned. Shrek was mentally and physically strong and I was sure he would have survived his injuries and beatings. I had to see if he was still there.

'I'm not angry, not at all, elated in fact,' I said. 'I'm sure your bread and water and medical help saved his life. I need to get him out with me now. I roughly know where the hospital is. Thank you for not keeping this a secret.'

After I gave Haleema another massive hug, I then went into the other room, sorted my shit, and gave Anoosheh a quick embrace.

'*Insha* Allah,' I said as we parted.

I turned to the hessian doorway and peered around it to check the coast was clear.

'Wait,' Haleema said.

She produced something wrapped in rags. As I took it and undid them, I grinned. It was an old AK47. I didn't need to ask where it came from; I just nodded at her. This strengthened my resolve to escape with Shrek. A vehicle's brakes squealed, momentarily breaking our stare and my thoughts. Our eyes engaged again; her expression was of horror. I darted over to the hessian-covered window and sneaked a look. My heart almost stopped. I gripped the rag-covered AK47.

'Oh fuck, not good,' I whispered.

I turned around to say what I'd seen, but Haleema and Anoosheh were frantically hiding any evidence. They knew.

At the bottom of the village were two Toyotas, four more in the centre, and a further two near our building. All were heavily-laden with male fighters and supporting Dushkas. A male dressed fully in black got out of one of the vehicles in the centre. The Toyota had a small symbol painted on its door. He looked around, then began to shout. I couldn't at first work out what he was saying, but as he got louder, he was yelling for Haleema. He didn't look happy. My mind raced: fight or flight? My body shook whilst I gripped the AK47 even tighter. Adrenalin was surging in bucket-loads; my heartrate must have been off the scale. Calm it, Johnny. Get a grip. Plan your move, I thought.

I couldn't go through the main doorway because of the two vehicles parked close outside; most probably I would be spotted straight away. The window and roof were no good either; not a lot of options. Haleema grabbed my arm and pulled me into the other room, now gloomy as the candles had been extinguished.

'Quick, hide, hide. I distract them,' she whispered.

Haleema let my arm go and quickly ran outside. I wondered what her fate would be. Pushing my gear under the bed, I crawled after it and tucked myself against the wall as tight as I could, like playing hide and seek as a kid with my brother. But there would be no more games if I got caught this time. Anoosheh threw the blanket over the bed. I didn't care how rank it was now; I was just glad of some camouflage. My heart was racing, trickles of sweat ran down my back. I listened in the deafening silence. In the rush to get under the bed, I'd not unwrapped the AK47. Bollocks. I did, though, have in my hand my trusty Sig, but even this couldn't take on the whole force outside. Options ran through my mind: how would I escape if compromised? Should I make a break for one of the Toyotas parked outside? How long would it take me to get my AK47 ready? I had trained with the AK47, but I wasn't even sure if it was loaded, let alone working.

The hessian was thrown back in the doorway. In came a male who I believed was the leader as he had an air of authority about him. He stood tall, dressed in a white *dishdasha*, black jerkin and a black turban. His leather boots were old and dusty, but his clothes looked clean. His hands and face were brown and wrinkled, like old leather gloves. From his chin hung a jet-black beard. He was carrying an AK47 strapped over his shoulder, looking much newer than the one I had behind me. He looked my way first. I lowered my breath rate, my eyes squinting straight at him. My grip fastened on the Sig, finger ever so slightly squeezing the trigger for a clean shot. At the same time, I watched for the any indication he had spotted me. He then looked back to the main room and started hollering abuse, gesturing angrily with his hands. I could imagine Anoosheh cowering in the corner, intimidated by his ranting. He pointed to his feet as if he were punishing a dog and then continued to shout orders. With his eyes on stalks and his breath puffing through his gritted teeth, a pause of silence echoed around the building. Annoyed, he strode out of view; the sound of slapping resonated, like a hand around a face. My anger grew, but I had to stay calm and hidden. On every slap, he yelled one-worded abuse.

Suddenly, a Dushka let out its distinctive short bursts, clachang, clachang, clachang, echoing around the village and inside our building. It must have been one of the vehicles closest to us. The leader stopped his brutality against Anoosheh and moved quickly to the doorway. Another burst of fire resounded through the village. He ran out outside, shouting more abuse. Small clouds of dust came floating under the hessian, like swirls of mist, from the after-shakes of the destructive power of the weapon. As the cloud engulfed me, my eyes became gritty; I blinked furiously to clear them. I felt the urge to cough as the dust entered my nostrils. Fortunately, the vehicle started and then moved off, followed by the rest in the same direction. More dust seeped under the hessian. I placed my forearm across my mouth and nose.

Listening to the fading vehicles, I thought I heard the distinctive sound of a distant Chinook, although very faint. I had the urge to look, but my sixth sense batted those feelings away. Staying put, I lost the sound of the Chinook, feeling abandoned. Was it really a Chinook I'd heard? Yes, I was positive I had. This must be part of the rescue force; the other part would be a ground offensive. I had to make my presence known to them somehow. I should get back to the area of the woodland, but what about Shrek? I pondered the priority. Shrek came top, not SOP, but my gut feeling over-ruled my mind on this; after all, he was my mate. If he was still at the hospital and I left him, the Elkhaba would take him away, torturing him to death.

I went to crawl out, but my sixth sense was screaming at me to stay still. Why? I had to listen to it as it had proved right on so many occasions. Footsteps came towards the building, too heavy for Haleema. I prepared myself, pulling the Sig close in front of my face. In came the leader again. He started verbally spewing, spit flying, only this time, he'd pointed his AK47 directly at Anoosheh. His finger clearly was over the trigger. My mind raced. I knew I had to kill him before he fired his weapon. His rage intensified. Some words he screamed I managed to translate: "whore", "bitch", and "die". Lowering his AK47, he moved from my aim towards her. Not only could I hear the slaps this time, but the sound of muffled fist blows to her body. Her small muted cries yelped at every strike. Anger raged through me again. Sickeningly, he started throwing her around the room, screaming further. She bounced off the table, knocking over the chairs, and then she landed in a crumpled heap.

The evil bastard then picked her up and threw her again. She landed face first on the floor by the doorway, letting out another muffled moan; the only movement were her trembling limbs. I willed her, almost shouting, to get up and run, or to fight back. He strode over and kicked her, his boot disappearing in the crumpled mass of her clothes. She let out a long whine and gasped for air. I winced, feeling her pain. Standing over her, his discoloured teeth grinning through his black beard, he ripped her clothes off until she was naked. Her body shook with fear, and she had wet herself. She was covered in black bruises from recent beatings, and now new red marks from his blows were emerging. He picked her up by her hair as she tried to hide her naked body from him, or was it me? Did she know I was watching? Was she wondering why I was not helping her?

He threw her to the other side of the room and stood there, triumphant. He then calmly took off his *dishdasha* and stood naked, his grin eviller. He was sexually aroused.

Oh no. No, you sick fuck. I took aim at his head, my finger close on the trigger, but I stopped. If I missed, he could pick up his AK47 and return a hail of death. There was no way I would miss, but I wasn't sure if any other armed Elkhaba were nearby; yet, I couldn't let this unspeakable act happen. Touching himself, he walked slowly over and out of my sight. Fuck; I'd hesitated. I should have slotted him. You know you are a brilliant marksman. I was seething, my rage building to an unbearable level, greater even than when I'd found my dead mates in the forest.

That was it: breaking point; the fuse had been lit. I crawled out from under the bed, placed my pistol in my trouser band and didn't even think about what would happen next. Infuriated, but, weirdly, calmly in control, I marched around the corner, fists clenched. The leader had his back to me. His naked wiry body stood over Anoosheh. As I walked up to him, he half-twisted his upper body. His expression was one of shock, and then I saw his fear. In that glancing look he must have read what was coming. In that glancing look a second had elapsed and I raised my right boot up, slanting it towards my left knee, firing a powerful kick to his right side leg just above his knee. His bones cracked as I pulled my boot back. Even before his realisation of the pain of his broken leg, I followed with an elbow strike to his face. Blood spurted in all directions as his nose crunched. His hands went to his face as he spun around to the floor, letting out a hideous moan. As he landed, I lowered my stance and followed up a deathly right hand fist strike, immediately with a left hand fist strike to his hands that were trying to cover his face.

I stood up and, as he tried to raise his head and shoulders to get up, I delivered a front kick to his forehead, striking it with a thud. The full force of my boot sent his head hard to the floor. Lying motionless, I placed boot on his neck, pressing down as hard as I could. I calmly looked through the gap in the hessian covering the window. After a short while, I knew he was dead. *'Threat neutralised.'*

I'd always had this computer gaming voice say this in my head whenever I had confirmed a kill. It was something I couldn't shake off. As a teenager I played many war games on the Xbox. One, the name of which I couldn't now remember, always said, 'Threat neutralised'. As a professional Elite solider, it's not the kind of thing you tell your mates and work colleagues. It was very unprofessional and annoying. I couldn't exactly go to the in-house-quack and tell him of my gaming voice.

Taking a nonchalant glance at him, I then looked at Anoosheh. She stared at him as blood poured from his face, saturating the dirt. I wasn't sure if she was relieved or sickened by my aggression, and to be honest, I couldn't care less. I had no emotions; he'd got what he deserved. I took my foot off his throat and, walking over to Anoosheh's clothes, handed them to her. With trembling hands she took them, but we never made eye contact. I tried to save some of her dignity by not staring at her battered nakedness. Grabbing all my gear, I then sorted myself out and took the dead Elkhaba leader's AK47. I found the magazine off the AK47 from under the bed, wrapping the weapon up and putting it back. I peeked through the hessian-covered window and then the doorway. The village was silent, just the odd chicken still roaming about.

Lifting the dead man's legs by his boots, I dragged him outside, leaving a trail of blood behind, but I knew Anoosheh would hide any evidence. I checked the village first, before I hauled the body behind the wall and continued for about fifty metres. Through his grime I spotted a small tattoo on his shoulder, which matched the symbol on the side of Toyota. I was breathing heavily; my strength was fading. I found some large shrubs around a group of trees and dumped his corpse. No use trying to hide him. It wouldn't be long before the buzzing of flies and his rancid smell in the heat revealed his location.

I removed the AK47 strap from my shoulder and checked the magazine. Excellent; it was full. Returning the mag, I switched the safety catch to semi-auto. I hadn't quite got my breath, but I had to find Shrek, and quick. Running along the shadow of the wall towards the farmed field, I felt in better shape after the food and water, plus the adrenalin was still surging through me. My treated injuries now allowed me to move much better, but I knew the anaesthetics and painkillers would soon wear off. As the wall ended to the rear of the village, I crouched and slowly checked the fields for any Elkhaba. My eyes followed the track down into a lower area of land, about two hundred metres away. I saw the large building. Its walls were about two metres tall and there was a pair of large wooden gates at the front which were folded inwards. Again, I watched for any signs of movement. Sprinting off in a crouched run, I followed the ditch to the side of the field. The ditch's mud clung to my boots. The further along, the harder it became; water now covered the mud. It smelt stagnant, I hated to think what was under foot. I slowed my speed so as not to fall over. The sloshing had become a concern. I stopped; this was not the best route for speed and stealth.

Taking a short rest to catch my breath, I glanced over the ditch edge. Apart from a large stack of dried grass, the only cover was a small treeline situated at the end of the field. I could use this cover to cut across to the compound, but I would have to make an eighty metre or more dash across the irrigated cropped field to reach the treeline. Contemplating my plan, I reminded myself of the crazy run I'd made from the edge of the forest to the boulder. At least this time I was armed with a decent weapon; I smiled. This optimism with the thought of finding Shrek alive, galvanised my plan to run across the open ground.

'Fuck it. Let's do it,' I urged.

I scanned all around me, but it was spookily quiet. Go, I shouted in my mind. Without hesitating, I scampered up the bank and ran towards the treeline. My satchel bounced off my body, seeming deafening in the silence of the village. The earth was soft and clung to my wet boots, sucking at them, slowing my momentum. The ploughed earth made it tricky and I stumbled a few times. As I got within three metres, I noticed movement to my right. I dived to the ground in a cloud of dust, my AK47 pointing at the possible threat. Once the haze settled, I'd zeroed in on a small group of goats munching a patch of vegetation and dried grass. The hot sun fried the sweat on my back as I lay perfectly still. The blood pumped around my body in tune with my thumping heart. Keeping my weapon on the target, I scanned my arcs. I was expecting to see at least a goat herder or a farmer. The village seemed devoid of human life. I jumped up and made the last sprint for the treeline.

Reaching it, I was panting for breath as I dived into the large gully behind. Quickly scrambling around, I took cover, pointing my weapon over the edge. I slowed my breathing and scanned my arcs again, trying not to cough on the haze of dust. When I felt it was safe, I blew the shit from my nose; it clung to my beard. I wiped the sweat from my forehead. Beads ran down my back. Shit; it was seriously hot. The ditch smelt pungent, like a sewer, but at least it was dry. I reckoned this was the cesspit for the village, baked by hours of sun. A swarm of flies descended on me, sticking to my clothes. I wasn't in the best prone position; also, the smoke grenade dug into my side. Waiting a short while, I slowly got more comfortable, trying to stop the flies entering my nostrils.

Looking back the way I had come, I congratulated myself on another great run. A few objects lay on the ground where I had hit the dirt, the sun reflecting off their silver foil. I focused on these, realising the objects were packets of medication. One of the satchel clasp straps had broken. I cursed under my breath for losing precious items and for leaving a sign which could grab the attention of a curious enemy. I undid the other strap and took out the bottle of Evian water. The seal had been broken and the water didn't look clear, but I had no choice. I took a measured sip and then retrieved the bread. The smell was still tantalising as I unwrapped it. Tearing off a small amount, I ate it quickly before it became the next meal for the flies. Never again would I take for granted simple bread and water. In truth, I wanted to eat and drink more, but I had to ration it. I was sure Shrek would be pissed off if I didn't save him some. Looking through the satchel further, I found some paracetamol and swallowed two with another sip of water. Everything back in the satchel, I fastened the remaining strap.

Taking another look over the bank, to my horror the goats were heading my way.

'What is it with fucking goats on operations?' I said.

I thought back to books I'd read about Special Forces being compromised by goats. I had to keep the momentum and adrenalin pumping, and not get compromised because of a fucking goat. I scurried along the ditch, the ground sending up wafts of putrid shit with every step. As I neared the end, into view came the main entrance to the compound with the two large wooden gates. I stopped and lowered, careless of where I lay. I observed the truck I'd seen back at the forest.

A short distance from it was a black Toyota, almost certainly Haleema's. Around the inner of the high wall was an elevated walkway; thankfully no guards were on duty. I wished I had a pair of binoculars. Checking back along the field and ditch, the goats were now poking their heads through the treeline where I had lain.

'Fucking goats,' I muttered, shaking my head.

Getting up slowly, I darted to the outside of the compound, searching the inside with my weapon raised, tucked firmly in my shoulder. I'd trained and been in similar situations many times; I was calm and in charge. My eyes narrowed with anticipation. Senses on maximum, I moved into the compound, staying in the little shadow there was at the base of the wall. Beyond the vehicles were linked buildings with wooden doors to the middle and right structure. The left side of the building had a window, its wooden shutters closed. Further left was a smaller separate store with a single door, maybe a for food, weapons, or ammunition. I made a mental note to check this out later. At the furthest point of the compound a large mound of metal and other objects were piled high. Studying these, I clearly made out the twisted wreckage of the Chinook. Buried amongst the mass were the charred remains of a Bergen. In addition to the burnt reminders were items I could not distinguish. I started to envisage human forms. I pulled away; I had no time to think about this.

Creeping to the truck door, staying out of the view of the mirror, I instantly stood up, pointing the AK47 through the window aperture. I let out a small sigh of relief. The keys were in the ignition. I opened the door very slowly; it creaked. I cringed, screwing my face up. When I had enough room, I leant forward, taking the ignition keys and went to throw them under the truck. On the other hand, I thought, I'd better check the Toyota had its keys in the ignition first. I stuffed them in my pocket. As I shut the noisy door, I caught my own reflection in the door mirror. I was shocked to see how awful I looked. My face, where I had no beard, was covered in little cuts and bruises. I had sunken eyes with black, puffy bruising around them. The whites of my eyes were discoloured, with tiny red blood vessels running through them. My beard had all kinds of shit and living things in it. The blackened lump was prominent on my forehead. I looked like a zombie from a horror movie.

Skirting around the rear of the truck, hugging its sides, I peered over the end. On the baking hot metal floor were patches of dried blood, with swarms of flies still trying to use this as a source of nourishment.

In the corner of the truck's floor were spent cartridge 7.62 shells and a green strap from a Bergen. I squatted and moved slowly to the rear corner, scrutinising the black Toyota for life inside. It was empty and the windows were closed. Scanning down my weapon, I moved up to the driver's door, gently lifting the door handle. The door clunked open slightly. Opening it further, the door open alarm signal chimed as the keys were in the ignition. The soft chime seemed very loud and alien-like in this confined compound. Heat wafted out of the gap, like opening an oven. This would be my escape vehicle. I decided to leave the keys in the ignition rather than take them. I could see me frantically trying to get the keys out of my pocket and into the ignition under a hail of bullets. Slowly, I closed the door and took off the satchel. Opening it, I searched for the surgical tape I'd spotted earlier when I was in the ditch. I opened the door again and put the satchel under the seat. Then, shutting the door quietly, I moved around to the Toyota's rear and peeked over the tailgate—empty.

Now within five metres of the two wooden doors, I studied them for bolts, latches, and padlocks. Only an old-style round door handle with no key lock was evident. I pondered which door I would take first. On a hunch I decided the right. Pulling the Maglite from my belt, I then taped it to the front underside of the AK47 and checked it worked. I set the fire mode to single shot and then psyched myself up. Taking in a sharp inhalation of breath, I then played out the "Go, go, go" I had heard so many times before.

I sprinted to the door, kicked it in and went through as the door bounced off the inner wall back onto my shoulder. Weapon tucked firmly in my shoulder and aiming down the sights, the Maglite's beam picked out the features of a bearded man, sitting dozing at the end of the corridor. He was cradling an AK47. In that split-second, as he was startled from his sleep, I'd registered the threat and squeezed the trigger. The first shot echoed and lit up the confined corridor, hitting the threat's forehead. Immediately, I followed up with another single shot to the same place. The area around him sprayed with a red mist, the wall behind him capturing the remains of his head. *'Threat neutralised.'* As the second shot had hit, I was already moving forward. I kicked the door to the left of the dead threat and searched the gloom. Moving the sighted beam around, I caught sight of another man huddled on the floor at the back of the room. I registered: no weapon, British RAF trousers and shirt, eyes glowing frightened in the Maglite's light. In that split-second, I registered, friendly.

I swept around to my left. In front of me was a young man cocking his AK47 in a panic. I squeezed the trigger and in an instant he took two rounds to the head and then a further one in the chest. In his red mist, Threat-2 fell back against the blood-splattered wall. *'Threat neutralised.'* I searched the rest of the room.

'Clear,' I said.

Making my way back to the door I had entered, I swung my weapon around the door edge, leaning into the corridor. As I did, in the rays from the outside sun, I spotted a figure pointing a weapon. I heard the deafening sound of his AK47 and watched the flame shoot off from the muzzle. I dived to my right, the timber and wall disintegrate under the hail of fire. Threat-3 had his weapon on fully automatic; I was lucky he was a shit shot. Even though I had dived out of sight, he continued to spray where I had been standing. Threat-1's body jolted and spurted blood as it soaked up rounds. When the AK47 ceased firing, I leapt into the corridor, only to see Threat-3 changing his mag. Already taking aim, I fired off two shots to his head and one to his chest. He fell back through his own red mist and scattered head bits, bouncing forwards off the door, landing in a heap. *'Threat neutralised.'* I wished this gaming voice would fuck off.

I moved towards Threat-3, keeping my sights on the doorway. I stood on the body and edged around the door frame, looking back into the compound. My eyes took a few seconds to adjust to the brightness. I crouched back in the shadows and tuned into any noise or movement outside. The haze and the smell of the cordite smoke wafted past me in the sunlight. All was quiet except the ringing in my ears. I yanked Threat-3's body back inside the corridor and shut the door. Picking up his full magazine off the floor, I stuffed it in my belt. I moved back in the main room and, closing the door behind me with the sole of my foot, shone the light at the friendly on the floor. He looked absolutely terrified. He held his left arm up in a surrender position.

'Don't shoot, don't shoot. I'm British,' he croaked.

# CHAPTER EIGHT

'Roy. How the hell did you survive? Where's Shrek?' I said.

I was shocked to see him, and not Shrek. I lowered my weapon making it easier for him to see, but he kept his hand up.

'Roy,' I said again.

'Who's that?' he croaked

'Rabbit, it's me, Vinnie... Johnny Vince. Lower your hand,' I said in a calming voice.

Rabbit dropped his trembling hand; it was then I could see the extent of his facial injuries. His face and lips had severely ballooned. He was cut and bruised and had part of an ear missing, which had scabbed over with dried blood. His right eye was so badly bruised it had swollen shut. His remaining bloodshot eye searched my face in the poorly-lit room. He started to shake and cry, trying to talk, but found it too emotional. I walked over to him, knelt, and held his shaking hand.

'It's all right, dude. We'll chat later, maybe over that big fried breakfast. For now though, we need to get out of here and quick.'

He nodded, still transfixed on my face. Jesus. What had the sick bastards done to him? I slung my weapon over my shoulder and put his shoes on his red swollen feet. Placing my arms around his shaking body, he let out a sharp groan.

'Sorry, but we got to move now,' I ordered.

He tried to hang on to my shoulder with his good hand, but he was too weak. Lifting his body into a standing position made him wince and tremble all the way. Once he was up, he embraced me for a few seconds and then pushed me away slightly, staring.

'I got it from here, mate,' he mumbled through his swollen lips.

That old British pride, I thought. 'Can you walk OK?'

'I could run all the way home to get away from this hell hole.' He tried to grin, but it was too painful.

'I'll call a taxi. Oh, and the beers are on you back at the hotel,' I said, trying to raise his spirits.

'Sorry, mate, they took my credit card. Looks like you're going have to pay,' he replied, dribbling.

'I don't earn as much as you, as you've told me before,' I retorted.

Leaning him gently against the wall, I made my way over to the dead body of Threat-2. I picked up his AK47 and wiped the blood on my sleeve.

'Right, take this, Rabbit, but don't shoot me,' I said, and then grinned.

'I've broken my arm. I won't be able to use that. I'll probably shoot you in the back, accidentally of course.'

'Let's have a look at your arm.'

His arm, which was held tightly to his chest, was a black, weird-shaped mess. I reached behind and pulled out my Sig.

'Well, this will have to do then, but don't fucking lose it, as it's…'

I paused. I'd better not let him know Fish was dead as I wasn't sure how mentally strong he was.

'What?' he asked.

'It's owned by a good friend of mine,' I finished.

I cocked the Sig and took off the safety catch before handing it to him. He took it and marvelled at it, then a last look around the room. The dimly-lit area was bare of any furniture. The only thing remotely like furniture was some small planks of wood, probably used to beat him with. The walls were covered in inscriptions carved by whoever had been held captive, maybe for their last time. Along with the inscriptions were dark splats and stains; I imagined the horror of what they were. There was no toilet area, the captive just defecated in the corner. Next to Threat-2's body was a seat, drinking vessel, and a bowl. The air was humid and musty, which had now become more apparent as the strong smell of the cordite had subsided. Rabbit nodded at the door.

'Let's go. I'm ready,' he mumbled.

'Yeah, me too. Let's get the fuck out of this hell hole.'

Unclipping the magazine from Threat-2's AK47, I stuffed it under my belt, throwing the weapon back at his body. At the door to the corridor I told Rabbit to stay close behind me. For the second time I peered around the door, but with more apprehension. Looking down my sights as the Maglite lit the way, I was glad not to be met with a hail of death this time. I stole another magazine from Threat-1's weapon and stuffed it with the others. As we reached the door leading to the compound, the spent cartridges slid under my boots.

'I need to look in the other building next-door. I need to check for Shrek and any of your crew,' then quickly I added, 'also Planet and Fish,' in case he got suspicious and asked why I had not mentioned them.

He placed his hand on my shoulder, and said, 'Planet, Fish and the remaining crew didn't make it. I don't know about Shrek. I think he burnt alive in the crash.'

Not wanting to believe, I retorted, 'Well, I have to check to be a hundred per cent certain. Follow me to the black Toyota and I'll help you in.'

He squeezed my shoulder more formally. 'Don't go in there, mate. It's just an empty building.'

I narrowed my eyes. 'How do you know?'

'I've been in there. It's just a bare room, mate.'

Again I ignored this, as I knew Haleema had said she'd set up a makeshift hospital. But why was he lying to me? I opened the main door and peered through the gap. Once my eyes had accustomed to the daylight, I moved forward.

'On me, Roy,' I said.

Reaching the rear of the Toyota, I turned to check on him. Roy had the back of his hand across his eyes in distress of getting used to daylight. I'd forgotten he had probably been held in that darkened room for some time. Through his squinting, watery eye, he made his way to me.

'If I'd known it was this sunny I would have brought my trunks.'

Again, he tried to smile through his bloated lips. I held his good arm and led him to the passenger door, opened it and started to help him in. As the hot air drifted out of the Toyota's furnace, I got a nose full of Rabbit's body odour, including the familiar smell of an infected wound.

'OK, nice and easy,' I said.

I carefully helped him, knowing he was in pain, but he tried to keep it from me.

'Right, see anyone, sound the horn and duck down,' I whispered.

'Fucking sure, mate.' He glared at me.

It dawned on me that, with his one partly-good eye and broken arm, it was a pretty dumb thing for me to say.

'Please ready yourself for what you are going to find in there, Vinnie.'

'I thought you said it was empty,' I said.

What he had said made me more determined to look. I left the car door slightly open as it was stiflingly hot. I crept over to the left wooden door. Taking a sharp breath, I yelled the familiar words in my mind: Go, go, go.

I kicked in the door and followed it in, sweeping to the right first with the sights and Maglite on. The room was bright and airy with many beds laid out in two rows. Tables were full of used medical supplies, blankets, and water jugs. Moving forward, I scanned back to my left. In one of the beds was a man with his hands up; his legs were bandaged up to his thighs. As I looked at his face, alarm bells started ringing in my head. My thoughts went back to the Chinook as it came under heavy fire. I shook my head and tried to concentrate. Johnny, what the fuck are you doing? Get on with it and slot him, I mentally said. I took aim, but I couldn't pull the trigger; instead, I eased off, lowering my weapon. I stared at the man in the bed, working out why he was familiar. Then it hit me. I took in a deep breath, face snarling.

'You,' I bellowed.

The man in the bed was the Elkhaba prisoner from the Chinook, the one who had been staring at me and mouthing something before we had hit by a SAM.

In a rage, I walked quickly over to him and cracked him on the head with the butt of the AK47. A gash appeared and, putting his hands out to protect himself, he pleaded in Arabic. I raised my weapon and took aim.

'This is your fucking fault, all of this. You knew, you fucker. Now I'm going to slot you and enjoy it. Wipe that fucking smile off your face. This is for my mates.'

A voice came from behind. I turned, my finger caressing the trigger, but it was Rabbit. I released the pressure, tears were welling.

'Johnny, not like this,' Rabbit said. 'Don't get me wrong, I would love to do it. I'm in this mess because of him. But it will haunt you. Leave him and let's go.

'I can't, Roy. He's got to pay.'

'He's unarmed in a bed, burnt. Even his bollocks are burnt, never mind his hands.'

'I can't just leave him. Best you wait outside,' I retorted.

'No. You do this and I will tell.'

'You what?' My anger and impatience grew.

'You heard. You can't just kill him in cold blood.'

'Well, maybe I should. Maybe you're not going to make it anyway.'

He was right, of course, and I now knew why he didn't want me to enter this building. Burying my killing desire and, slinging weapon across my shoulder, I turned to the injured leader and grabbed him by his arms. He started to wail and protest, so I punched him hard in the stomach. He stopped howling and gasped for air.

Bending down to within an inch of his ear, I said, 'You're lucky he was here.'

I dragged him out and, still screaming, I gestured silence by putting my finger across my lips. Pulling him to the doorway, I threw him to the floor. He let out a cry for help. I took hold of Rabbit's hand and pointed his Sig to the cowering leader's head.

'If he moves, blow his fucking head off. You think you could manage that, Roy?' I fumed—he didn't reply.

From the expression on the Elkhaba leader's face, he'd got the message. I did a quick search of the room for any survivors, but really I knew this was in vain. I desperately wanted to find Shrek. Only the small building next-door to search, I thought, as I sifted through the cupboards. I started to imagine Haleema working here, frantically trying to save the injured and dying to protect her village. I gave an evil stare at the leader. He lowered his head.

'Think we better get going,' Rabbit said.

'Sure, we'll take this piece of shit along with us.'

'Why, what's the point? He'll slow us up or starve to death.'

'Because I fucking said so,' I snapped. 'I'm in charge, got it? Anyway, he didn't give a shit about you dying in the room next door, did he?'

I snatched a half-empty bottle of water and a few large folded cloths which sat on the side. I ordered Rabbit to follow me and to watch my back. Picking the leader up by the scruff, I hauled him to the Toyota. As I reached it, lowering the tailgate, I threw him on the back. He squealed in pain and wriggled around like an injured break-dancer as the floor was burning hot. Ignoring him, I jumped up next to him and slid him to the back of the Toyota. Taking cable ties from my utility belt, I tied his burnt wrists to the railing guard behind the rear window. Pulling them extra tight made him wince. I patted him on his bandaged legs.

'Enjoy the ride,' I said.

Jumping down, I got a buzz out of hearing him wail.

Rabbit was already in the passenger seat, which showed he was either recovering or his adrenalin was pumping. I ordered him to stay put as I wanted to search the last building.

'No... no, please don't, we need to go. There's nothing in there, trust me on this, Johnny.'

'That's what you said the last time, and looky here what I found.' I pointed to the back of the Toyota.

'I want to get the hell out of here now, before they all come back,' he pleaded.

I stared at him, seeing real pain and anxiety.

'Please Johnny, let's just go,' he implored.

My sixth sense had perked up, telling me to listen to him on this one. Rabbit had always been wise and a great planner, so I agreed. I leaped into the driver's seat and, reaching under, retrieved the satchel. Undoing the strap, I pulled out the water and then unscrewed the cap, passing him the bottle, knowing how he felt as I watched his face light up. I placed the new bottle of water in the satchel.

'Sip it, don't gulp it,' I warned him.

He took the bottle in his trembling hand and put it to his swollen lips. He sipped the best he could, but most of it ran down his chin.

'Didn't they teach you manners in the RAF?' I said.

He lowered the bottle; further dribbles of water ran down his chin.

'Fuck off,' he mumbled.

'Chew on this then.'

I took out the bread and ripped a piece off for him. Passing it to him, I waited for the same sort of reply, but he continued to sip the water. I leant across and opened the glove compartment.

'Anything in there we can use?' I asked.

He lowered the bottle, putting it between his legs, and then started to sift. He pulled out a packet of Canary Kingdom cigarettes and a black lighter with a bull logo on the front

'Fucking jackpot,' he said.

'Wow,' I said. 'There is a God after all.'

Even though he knew I didn't smoke, he replied childishly, 'Well you can't have any. They're all mine, mine.'

'Dickhead,' I said, and sighed. 'Anything else?'

'Err, mirrored sunglasses... old map... chewing gum... magnifying glass... and a pistol... nope, nothing of use.'

'Stuff it all in the satchel,' I said, my impatience growing.

Even though I found him annoying, I had to admire his humour after the shit he had been through.

As the Toyota purred into life, I Immediately lowered the windows to let the heat out. Suddenly, I caught a glimpse of a man entering the compound in a crouching position, clutching an AK47. I opened the door, leapt out, swung my weapon up and fired three shots in succession through the door window aperture, hitting him in his torso. As he pivoted around, falling to the ground, he grappled with his weapon. I took aim and followed up with two further shots to his head. A sea of red pooled around his body as I kept my sights on him, but then my eyes watched the gates for any further surprises. *'Threat neutralised.'* I quickly made a mental note of the rounds fired so far, thirteen, and then I leapt back in.

'Slacking, Vinnie, tut tut,' Rabbit said, enjoying the piss-take—at least his morale was good.

'Don't worry, I've kept one in the chamber for you. I won't miss your fat, swollen head.'

'What is your problem? You've always got it in for me. Come on, out with it,' he said, spit flying.

'Not now. Kinda busy.'

I rammed the vehicle into gear and floored the accelerator. Haleema was right: this beast was quick. As we wheel-spun out of the compound gates, I swung the Toyota left. Directly in front was yet another Elkhaba fighter, who took aim down his AK47. We were only four to five metres from him, so I drove the beast towards him. He looked petrified and then pulled the trigger. I braced myself for a hail of bullets, but nothing came. By that point we had hit him and the Toyota jolted as we went over him. I took a quick glance in the rear-view mirror: amongst the settling dust was a heap of arms, legs, and clothes. Strange, I thought, I didn't have the gaming voice in my head, but no sooner had I thought this, it entered my mind. *'Threat neutralised.'*

'Should always stop, look, and listen,' said Rabbit gleefully.

The dashboard digital clock read 12.47. I didn't have a clue where I was heading, but was sure I wanted to get us away from the village. My thoughts turned to Haleema and Anoosheh. Where had Haleema gone? Was she forced onto the enemy's Toyota as they left? Jesus. I hoped they were both all right. I was dragged away from my thoughts by the sound of a fast jet approaching. Rabbit was already looking up, his fat face literally pushed against the screen.

'Stop the car and clear the screen,' he demanded.

I stamped on the Toyota's brakes and looked for the jet-wash lever.

'Why? What's it doing?'

'Hurry, clear the screen,' shouted Rabbit hoarsely.

I fumbled on the levers, the water jets sprang into life, the wipers working the dirt away; it steamed in the baking sun.

'That's an American F-16 tipping in for a bombing run. Best fucking move,' he spluttered.

'Are you sure?'

'Just get us out of here.'

I floored the Toyota, wondering how the hell he knew this from the jet's distance, and with only one good eye. Ahead in the far distance was a wadi and, keeping the accelerator down hard, I left the main track and headed towards it. The uneven ground was made up of small rocks. It shook the Toyota, the rocks bouncing underneath was deafening. On every jolt, Rabbit let out small moans, gasping for breath. He stuck his head out of his window and followed the F-16.

'Fuck. He's let one loose. Get us out of here,' he said, back inside.

Within an instant a small whistle sounded, then an almighty deafening explosion. I looked in the rear-view mirror: a massive mushroom cloud of sand and smoke filled the blue sky. A fireball rose and blossomed through the cloud. An enormous shock wave almost lifted the Toyota into the air. For a moment the air was sucked from my lungs. We were only about one hundred and fifty metres away, dangerously close.

'Holy shit, what was that?' I gasped.

'Reckon that was a lovely, big 1,000-pound JDAM.'

'Lovely? That nearly wiped us out.'

'I reckon the pilot has spotted us and he probably thinks we're the enemy. Best we ditch the car and make it on foot to the wadi, and quick,' Rabbit said, lips inflamed and a half-closed mouth.

In the rear-view mirror another fireball erupted. The leader's hands only were visible and he was frantically trying to break loose. As we got to within a few meters of the wadi, I swung the Toyota around. We both got out and Rabbit hobbled towards the edge.

'Bloody hell, it's a long way down,' he said.

'Jump,' I shouted. 'I'll follow you, but I've just got to do something.'

Rabbit searched for the F-16 and said, 'What are you doing, mate? There's no time to hang around.'

'Jump, you twat.'

Rabbit sat over the edge and launch himself off. I turned to the Toyota, picked up a decent-sized rock and jumped in. I selected first gear and moved off slowly under the engine's steam. I slipped her into second gear and, leaning forward, placed the rock on the accelerator. The Toyota shot forward. Maybe a smaller rock would have been better, I thought. I jumped out, trying to run alongside it to shut the door, but

I ended up falling head over heels. I quickly picked myself up, ignoring the pain, and to preserve a little bit of pride. The Toyota had sped up, careering to the left with the driver's door still open. The panic-stricken Elkhaba leader wrestled with his cable ties and then started to shout at me. I nonchalantly raised my hand and gave a slow wave, mouthing, 'bye-bye'. This infuriated him and, screaming, he struggled further. The distant sound of the F-16 filtered in, so I fled towards the edge. Not stopping, I careered over. Rabbit was spot on; the sides were steep and long. As I tumbled over I tried to grab with my hands, but the sides caved in. Sand and rocks followed me down. The dust overwhelmed my lungs. I hit the bottom with a thud, winded.

It was a horrible feeling lying there trying to catch my breath, but at the same time coughing and spluttering the dust from my lungs. Murky water spewed from my nose and mouth. When I eventually caught my breath, I rolled over onto my back and thought of a similar moment on a night exercise when I had fallen over a ravine. I had hit a large flat slab of rock at the bottom and winded myself, again trying to breathe and cough up the debris that followed me down. I had taken a bad knock to my head and shoulder. In excruciating pain, I wondered if I'd broken my back. My Bergen's weight kept me pinned to the rock. I couldn't slip my arms out. As I lay there helpless, all around was black and silent. The freezing weather soon got its grip on me. I lay there for ages, shouting repeatedly for help, thinking this was where I was going to die. The deadly effects of hypothermia seize me; I knew the dangers and symptoms. It was my best mate Planet who had turned back to find me, who carried me out and called in a MedEvac.

The scream of a missile, followed by another explosion, brought me back to the present. In the direction of the top of the wadi edge, I saw what wasn't vaporised of the Toyota fly high through the air. I imagined the face of the tied-up leader's last seconds in the back of the Toyota, without the smile he'd had in the back of the Chinook. The aftershock wave rumbled through the ground. A wave of dust and debris rolled over the wadi edge. I rolled over and cupped my hands round my mouth, I'd had enough of the Afghan dirt in my lungs for one day.

Once the scene had settled, I raised myself from what felt like a shallow grave. Dusting the dirt and dust from my hair down to my boots, I continued to cough and spew my lungs up. I became aware of laughing in the distance, knowing Rabbit was enjoying the spectacle. Making out I hadn't heard him I got my gear together and pretended to search for him. This made him laugh louder. I started to chuckle and then went into a roar of laughter. Facing Rabbit, who was about ten metres from me, he was sitting up laughing. His swollen face and lips reminded me of a manatee I'd seen whilst diving off the coast of West Africa. I erupted into a another fit of laughter, drowning out his mirth. As I tried to gather myself, wiping the tears away, Rabbit stopped, his face expressionless.

'What the fuck's so funny?' he asked.

'Are you related to a sea creature, by any chance?'

He didn't get it.

This sent us into another fit of laughter; a relief valve for all the suffering we had been through, the realisation we had found each other, and survived the jet's missiles.

After the laughter died down to the odd chuckle, I walked over to him and helped him up. We didn't say anything, but instead embraced each other.

'Thanks for coming back, mate,' he said.

I didn't answer, just patted him on the back.

We parted and he dusted himself down, and said, 'Well that was fun. Shame about the car. I wonder if the prisoner enjoyed it. I'm sure I saw his shit fly through the air.'

We both let out a further snigger, but we also knew how close we'd come to being vaporised for the second time.

'Right, I reckon we should follow the wadi to the end. We're bound to find a good LUP and some shade amongst those trees. If you need a rest, please say, OK?'

I didn't wait for a reply, but set off trudging towards the target.

After two hundred metres or so, Rabbit said he needed a rest and a drink. With the sun doing its best to cook us, I moved over to a shadow in the overhang of the wadi wall and then beckoned him over. I undid my satchel and pulled out the water bottle that I'd pinched from the makeshift hospital. It was cloudy, but I had nothing to sterilise it with. I passed this and the bread to him as he sat down next to me.

'Get it down you. We've got a long way to go,' I said.

He nodded in appreciation, taking bigger swigs, and forcing the chunks of bread in his mouth.

'So how the hell did you survive?' he asked with his mouth full.

'Jesus, manners. Anyway, not now Rabbit, we need to find an LUP.'

Out of the peace and quiet that enveloped us came the distant sound of a firefight. We stared at each other for a second.

'Are they chasing us?' Rabbit asked.

'Shhh, let me listen.'

'I think we better move on,' he said, interrupting my thoughts.

'Will you shut up and let me listen for God's sake.'

It was very far away. The firing was sporadic, but intensified with the sound of Dushkas. Then more cheerfully, that of Browning .50 cal machineguns that had range up to two thousand metres, with the stopping power to take on light armour and soft-skinned vehicles. I wasn't too sure if it was British, American, Special Forces, or even a mixture of all three returning fire. Between machineguns further small explosions sounded, most probably from an under slung 40mm grenade launcher, or a light anti-tank weapon. As the battle raged on, sounds of mortars entered the cacophony. As both sides used these, I was hoping it was the good suppressing the evil.

'That's some battle,' Rabbit said. 'Best we get ourselves over there and get ourselves rescued.'

Normally I had him down as a great forward thinker and planner, but this was a foolish idea. I could understand his reasons as I was as desperate as him to be rescued and as far away from Afghanistan as possible.

I tactfully said, 'That's a dumb fuck idea. As soon as we're spotted by either side, they'll think we are trying to flank them and they'll open fire. At a thousand metres we could be enemies of each side.'

Rabbit looked a little flabbergasted. 'I fucking knew that, mate. I was only testing to see if you were firing on all cylinders,' he replied, trying to excuse his dumb idea. 'What's your plan then?'

I considered our options for a minute, then said, 'Right, first you can stop drinking all the water as we have a long way to go. Secondly, you can stop whinging you're tired and stopping every two hundred metres. Thirdly, we need to find a LUP further along the wadi and get your stinking mess of a body cleaned up. Next, when the sun has gone down, we are going to traverse around in a big arc heading towards the Pakistani Border. We will have to tab about thirty klicks and stop every hour for a five-minute rest to check our position. Hopefully the stars will be out to make navigation easier. Once we've tabbed another thirty klicks, we'll look for a LUP and then take our final rest. We'll then have a ration of water and bread. We'll stay hidden under daylight until night and then continue to tab approximately twenty klicks back towards the rear of the firefight. Again, resting for five minutes after every hour. I'm hoping we'll find the camp of the friendly fighting force.' I decided to quickly add a bit of sick humour, 'I will send you over to make friends as you look more like a scruffy goat herder than me, plus it's best if you get shot first. Any questions?'

He paused, and then replied, 'I liked my plan better.'

We picked ourselves up and I started moving across the dry wadi floor. Rabbit followed, still mumbling, giving me hard time. He knew I was listening to his banter and that soon enough I would answer.

'Fucking nancy SAS boys. Give them a gun and they think they can shoot four terrorists, drive over one, dodge a JDAM and Maverick missile, and invent a plan to get us out of here. Try flying a Chinook in the dark and under fire. SAS, special Elite, my arse.'

'It's SBS, not SAS, you twat,' I replied, giving in.

'Are you sure? Could you have spelt it wrong when you joined up?'

'Piss off.'

'Anyway, I thought you called yourself the Shakeys, Shakey boat service,' he said.

'That's right, and lads in the SAS don't say they're in the SAS; they say the Regiment. Why the hell am I even having this conversation? Shut the fuck up.'

He'd stopped mumbling, but now he sniggered.

I knew it was only banter, but this time I'd let it get to me. However, I suppose it seemed to make the trudge a bit more entertaining. I was still scanning for any threats and the slightest movement, or something that looked out of place; a natural instinct. I hoped Rabbit was keenly doing so. We had travelled about three hundred metres before we reached the trees. Arriving first, at the lowest point of the bank, I lowered myself onto my stomach and then investigated the small cluster of trees and bushes. Peering over my shoulder, I was glad to see Rabbit taking my moves seriously as he had moved to the higher part of the wadi bank, watching the way we had come. I knew his banter could go a bit far, but on the other hand I knew he had a professional side to him.

Moving into the cluster of trees, its location had good concealment with great vantage points for us to view the surrounding terrain. The only thing lacking was a hidden escape route, other than the bottom of the wadi that we had just trudged through. It also gave us a little shade from the relentless scorching sun.

After clearing an area, I then took off some of my gear.

'Rabbit, on me,' I said.

'How much water, food, and ammunition have we got left?'

It was good to see the forward thinker coming out in him. For his SBS piss-take I thought I'd get my own back. 'Don't you worry about that. I'm in charge as you're only a GBD.'

He looked over at me puzzled. 'A GBD?'

'Right, we need to get your injuries seen to, so strip off to your shorts, dude,' I said.

This reminded me of the situation I had been in with Haleema; I smiled. Rabbit caught this as he stripped off.

'Not going all gay on me, are you, mate? Bit late to come out of the closet now. I mean, I've always suspected.'

'Piss off,' I snapped.

Undoing the strap on the satchel, I emptied the contents.

'Where did you get that lot?' he said, amazed. 'You mean I've been suffering for the last half a day and you've been keeping it hidden?'

'I could have treated you back at the hospital in the village. But now imagine your body blown to bits by the *lovely* JDAM. Now stop complaining and get down to your shorts,' I said, cutting off any further banter.

# CHAPTER NINE

Examining his body, he had similar injuries to mine. He was covered in different-sized lacerations, cuts, and bruises; lice crawled amid of the filth. Around the larger cuts, the blood had scabbed. His left arm, which he still clung to his chest, was black and severely swollen. The stench billowed from him.

'Nothing a bit of Right Guard won't cure,' I quipped.

'Well, don't ask me to put both my hands up then,' he replied, imitating the Right Guard TV advert.

'I won't. Your armpits are worse than chemical warfare.'

Like Haleema, I laid out all the medical supplies and instruments in front of me. I sprayed his body with a Betadine spray and cleaned his minor cuts and abrasions. He started making a fuss that it stung like hell, so I told him not to be such a girl. The back of his neck had a large burn that had started to weep. The skin had rubbed off the burn and was covered in dirt. Dabbing the wound with a clean cloth and water, rolls of skin came off around the edges, causing him distress. The rest I cleaned with a saline solution. It was fortunate that a burn roll was in the satchel, so I added thin layers over the top, trying to keep the air from it.

Opening a syringe packet, I filled it with morphine and then injected 10-ml of it into his unbroken arm. After I had helped him back on with his filthy clothes, I gently took hold of his broken arm, which had bruised quite severely around the lumpy break. My diagnosis was he had broken his radius bone and would not have a range of movement without extreme pain. Taking out the large cloth and, cutting a forty-inch square from it, I folded it into a triangle. I slipped one end under his swollen arm and over his shoulder, bringing the other end over his shoulder around the dressing on his neck. I fastened both ends near his elbow with a safety pin, but left it quite loose for movement. For

75

good measure, I handed him two 400-mg ibuprofen tablets, which he swallowed. I also took two for myself.

My calf throbbed for the first time in a while as I sat down next to him. I undid my boot, the blood rushing to my toes caused them to ache. Rolling up my trouser leg, I noticed the dressing had turned red, along where the stitches were underneath. Carefully, I undid the dressing. The last bit had stuck to the wound, so I slowly peeled it off. As the last of the dressing came free a new trickle of blood seeped. One of the stitches had torn, probably where I'd fallen over. I opened one of the last remaining saline solutions and cleaned the wound.

'Shhhhhhit,' I hissed.

I waited for banter from Rabbit, but he had fallen asleep. Seeing him lying there, his breathing slightly husky with dribble running out of his fat lips, made me realise how knackered I was. I yearned for some sleep, but one of us had to stay on stag.

I opened the last of the bandages and redressed my calf wound. Standing up, I checked the rest of myself. Haleema had done a fantastic job. The rash between my thighs was becoming irritating. I took off my remaining boot and socks and wiped my feet with the last surgical wipes. The smell wasn't any better than the last time; I turned my nose up in disgust. Fresh blisters sat on top of old blisters, so with my knife I oozed the fluid from them. It was only then I became conscious that the fierce battle had stopped. Between the gaps in the tree and bush foliage, I marvelled at how tranquil the area could be. Vast areas of sand and dunes waved out over the enormous landscape. The only outstanding features were the peaks and ridges of mountains in the far distance, set against the pure blue sky.

Once I had dressed, I laid all our gear out in front of me. It was as if the heat and humidity had been turned up. Even in the shade I was frying in my own juices. Rabbit's heavy breathing was now turning into a loud snore, like an old vintage motorbike slowly revving. I had to look around to see if anyone else could hear it. Trying to ignore the Triumph motorbike, I broke down and cleaned our weapons. I had four full AK47 magazines, but one only had three rounds in. I added these to my remaining seventeen rounds in the first magazine. The pistol Rabbit had discovered was an old, battered Soviet Makarov pistol, which had a full magazine of eight rounds. I wondered how reliable it was. I measured out the remaining water, sharing it between the two bottles, and then tore the rest of the bread in half. The packet of chewing gum was out of date. It had gone soft and gooey in the heat, but this would take our minds off the intense hunger, thirst, and tabbing ahead of us. I would give the sunglasses to Rabbit if a sandstorm blew up as I had my *shemagh*, but only in this eventuality because we could be compromised by any reflection from the sun.

Last of all I pulled out the map. It didn't take a genius to work out where the fags and lighter had gone. The map wasn't in the best condition. The paper had been torn along the folded creases and parts were missing altogether. It was obviously quite old. Fully opened, with the magnifying glass I studied it. The details were very sparing and any text was in Russian. A circle marked in pen showed Haleema's village. From this I worked out approximately our current LUP. Working from the north direction arrow, I planned a route to get to our designated place, measuring the approximate distance in kilometres from the scale. On route there seemed to be a small mountain range with a network of rivers, even though these rivers could be long gone. I stored all the gear away and left only the Sig out for Rabbit, who by now was moving frequently and mumbling crazy stuff in his sleep, guessing he was reliving his terrifying ordeal.

My eyes and head drooped a few times, to the point I'm sure I joined Rabbit in a motorbike chorus. I woke suddenly and took a quick look around. It must have been a few hours of watch and I couldn't last the pace any further. Rubbing my eyes awake, I moved over to Rabbit and shook him gently. He frantically sat up and looked around for reassurance, so I patted him on the back.

'It's OK, dude. It's your turn to keep watch. Reckon we're going to have some nasty visitors alerted by your bloody snoring. I need some rest. If you see anything, wake me immediately, but stealthy.'

I gave him my Sig, but he still looked shocked.

'And no fucking smoking,' I ordered, getting comfortable.

I found it hard to settle, even though I was dog-tired. I kept hearing the repeated words from Rabbit that Shrek and the crew had not made it. I had really thought it was Shrek when Haleema said one of my soldier friends been found alive. Not having the time to reflect before, the sadness was now crushing me. Then it dawned on me: she had told me she had been treating an injured leader with burns to his legs and feet who had come in at the same time. I'd missed the connection, probably because I was in a state of shock. I didn't know the Chinook crew members, but equally they had died trying to save us; true bloody heroes.

I felt myself being gently rocked by Rabbit.

'Vinnie. Vinnie, wake up.'

I rapidly sat up, taking stock. The sun was setting, bringing a different perspective to our surroundings.

'Jesus. How long have I been asleep?' I said.

'I reckon about three hours, and shit, do you snore loud.'

'Must be the painkillers knocking me out. How's your arm by the way?'

'Oh, yeah, great, cheers. I'll being doing cartwheels pretty soon,' he said.

'Never happy, are you? Always moaning. It's always about you isn't it.'

Rabbit glanced over at me. 'What the fuck's that supposed to mean?'

'Ah, doesn't matter.' I shrugged my shoulders, not wanting an intense argument.

'Well, obviously it does or you wouldn't have said it. If you've something to get off your chest, then let's get it off, *mate*. Don't think I haven't noticed your attitude over the last few years.'

'Noticed what? What do you mean, my attitude?' I replied quickly, not being able to resist being drawn in.

'You look down your nose at me. You think I'm a lesser man, or so I hear,' he said, raising his voice.

'Oh bollocks, do I.'

'So why is it you always socialise with others and not me? It's like you're trying to ignore me or something. Is it because I'm in the RAF and not in your Elite squad?'

'I'll be pleased to fill in the missing gaps. First, I don't think less of you, and definitely don't look down my nose at you because I'm in the SBS and you're in the RAF. That's just you being pathetic. I've kept my distance from you as I think you can be a dickhead. Your banter sometimes goes a bit too far. Well, actually all the time. You've upset quite a few people, or so *I've* heard. You push all my buttons. I'll end up thumping you. Now can we drop this. We've got to head out, but I'm sure we will pick it up later.'

'Maybe you should get to know me better before casting aspersions. You never know when you are going to need my help, *mate*. And Johnny, you thump me, I'll kick your arse.'

'Be careful what you wish for, Roy,' I said, and glared.

'I thought I'd left the enemy behind. It's like you're disappointed you found me and not the others.'

I ignored that. 'We need to move out. Make sure you don't leave any signs we've been here,' I said, finishing the conversation.

With the sun setting fast, the gentle breeze dropped in temperature. The moon was taking over the skies. After double-checking our route by the stars, I started to walk. I let Rabbit know he had to keep up and, furthermore, not lose sight of me. There was an atmosphere between us and I was sure it would thicken later. I started a good-paced march, knowing I could walk five klicks in forty minutes. I counted the seconds in my mind. Every now and then I checked back on Rabbit. To his credit, he was keeping up. He would look me directly in the eyes and say, 'Yeah, I'm still keeping up.' He was obviously contemplating what I had said earlier.

The route wasn't as straight as I had anticipated, with small crevices that had opened in the ground trying to swallow us in the dark. When I reached three thousand six hundred seconds, I stopped and got down on one knee. I turned around to find Rabbit a little way back. His march had amounted to a plod. It was as much my responsibility to check on Rabbit, but he should have told me he was falling behind. I waited until he caught up and, when he had, he was struggling for breath, and sank to his knees.

'I'm fucked, man. That's it, no more,' he said.

Shit. I had set the pace and distance too hard. No disrespect, but he wasn't up to my stamina, even though I wasn't either. I pulled out the water and bread, lifted his head and told him to drink and eat. Dehydration is a killer in any climate, be it the heat of the Arabian Desert, or the depths of the North Pole. Any physical action produces sweat, and even the breath we see when we exhale in the cold is further moisture lost. There are basic signs of dehydration: waves of nausea which can make you lose more fluid if you are sick. Your speech will slur and your movements will slow. Sometimes you are unable to walk. At this stage you could die from dehydration.

As he ate and drank I asked if he was feeling sick. He shook his head and then went to say something.

'Tell me the alphabet as quick as you can,' I butted in.

'I'm not dehydrated, mate, just fucking knackered,' he replied, annoyed.

'Well, you may not see the signs, so do as I say.'

He sounded off the alphabet and finished with the Peter Piper rhyme for good measure.

'We all hate a show-off,' I said, with a laugh.

'Obviously there's a lot you hate about me. Oh, sorry, feeling sorry for myself again. Or maybe it's the fact I've also lost fucking good friends on this mission.' He squared up to me, looking me straight in the eyes. 'So, put your ego away. We're both in this together. Or is it you can't because you're *highly trained.*' He did the annoying double-finger speech mark gesture. 'Admit it, you wish you had found your squad instead of me.'

'Squad? You mean my mates. Yes, I bloody wish it,' I yelled.

He took a step closer, putting his face right in mine. 'Well that's tough. I wish it was my crew that had rescued me rather than an egotistic, uncaring, and cantankerous thug.'

'Yeah, *rescued* being the important word, you ungrateful twat,' I replied, my face snarling.

He pushed me a step back and then put his face even closer against mine.

'You reckon Planet would be acting such a cunt as you?'

'Get out my face, Roy.'

'Or what?'

'Or I'll kick your sorry arse home. You're starting to really piss me off.'

I pushed his nose with mine and he took a step back.

'Well go on then, try it, you useless piece of shit,' he provoked.

I moved up quickly and grabbed him by the shirt, lifting him slightly. 'What's your fucking prob...'

I didn't have time to finish as a sharp pain hit my bollocks where he had brought his knee up. However, I didn't let go of him and threw him backwards onto his arse, taking a deep breath from the pain. Striding over to him, he tried again to kick me, but I grabbed his foot and swung it away to my right. Quickly, I knelt on him and raised my fist. His expression wasn't one of fright, just a look of urging me to do it.

'Well go on then. What are you waiting for? Finish me,' he shouted, his eyes welling, catching the moonlight's reflection.

'I don't want to fight you, Roy. You've been through enough.'

'I've got awful shit going on in my head. I don't know if I can take it home with me. Do you understand?'

'I get it. You just gotta lock it all away until we are home.'

Loosening my grip, I pushed him away and took myself off to find my own space to cool down.

'Anyway, you did fucking good to bring the Chinook down the way you did,' I said. 'You owe it to yourself, and I owe you.'

I sat about ten metres from him and thought about what had just happened. I had a long look around, searching for answers. My bollocks were aching as I had my ration of water and bread. My body sweat turned me colder, goose bumps raised over me.

We had rested for about twenty minutes. In a softer voice, I told Rabbit we had better make a move.

'I can't go at your speed. Can we slow it up a bit?' he said, shivering.

'Yeah, sure.'

He was now shivering uncontrollably.

'OK, up you get,' I demanded.

I tried not to make it sound like an order, but really it was. I couldn't afford to let him suffer from hypothermia. Bit ironic, as I could have killed him a little while ago. He gradually stood up and handed me back his water bottle, which was now empty. Damn, I should have paid more attention and not let him finish it, but there was no point reprimanding him now.

'You lead then. I'll put my hand on your shoulder, so I don't lose you,' I said, but really I wanted to push him at a half-decent pace.

'OK. Sorry about earlier.'

Feeling a bit shit, I said, 'Nothing to be sorry about, Roy. Just save your energy and enthusiasm. You might need it later.'

We set off and I counted as per usual, but we were moving at a slower pace. To keep his concentration, I asked him to tell me what happened after the Chinook took incoming fire and how he had survived. I wasn't sure how mentally strong he was. Had he buried it deep? Was bringing it out in the open going to send him ga-ga?

He started to tell his side of the events.

'We were alerted to signs on our sensors and then watched the first incoming tracer rounds. Then all hell broke loose. I knew the Chinook was taking serious flak. I could see many enemy vehicles set out in a fan shape, all firing with their AA guns. Ashley Kellett, my co-pilot, listed the warning lights that flashed and sounded. I tried to manoeuvre to make it harder for the enemy to hit us. The bastards below hadn't any search lights, they just poured fire in our direction. A few times the old girl shuddered and shook. I knew our rotors were taking hits, some being partly shredded, but I had to get beyond the fan of death and as far away as possible.

'As the firing intensified I had doubts we would make it all the way back. The old girl was in a bad way. I had to keep low in case of engine failure rather than we drop out of the sky. I could see the wooded tree area and decided to use this for cover, so I lowered her as much as I dared. Alarm signals sounded for an incoming SAM which we counter-measured and took up evasive movement procedures. The AA guns continued to pound us as we flew past them. As the second SAM locked on, we were too low to do any proper manoeuvres. Our countermeasures didn't deploy as quick as they should, maybe a circuit had been damaged. I knew the SAM was sneaking up behind us at a rate we couldn't out-run. I'm not sure if you heard, but I tried to warn everybody. Just before it made its impact our flares did deploy, but it only stopped us being hit directly.

'The SAM exploded at the rear, shaking the shit out of us. As I fought the controls, Ashley unbuckled and looked back. His view was partially blocked due to your Supacat. He turned back, looking stunned. He told me we had lost the ramp with Matt, the crewman. The right side of the Chinook had been partly ripped open and was hanging out into no-man's-land. The right-hand engine had malfunctioned. I told him to buckle up and take emergency procedures as we were going down. Ashley made a frantic mayday call. As he did, I tried to land the old girl before the trees. However, we were travelling too fast and she wasn't responding properly. As we flew over the forest I tried to pull up our descent.

'The old girl shook uncontrollably. All the warning captions were lit up and alarming. The engine screamed. My hands turned white trying to bring it under control. The vibrations blurred my vision. I thought that was the end and I started having flashes of my family and my beautiful children.'

Rabbit paused for a few seconds, overwhelmed with emotion. I squeezed his shoulder.

'As we skimmed the trees, I felt and heard an almighty bang. Ashley said we had lost the part of the rear that had been hanging. I couldn't hold her up any longer and the inevitable happened. We crashed through the forest. I can still remember the noise of the trees snapping and scraping the sides. It all seemed to be in slow motion, but the sound stayed the same speed. The racket was deafening. I remember seeing the front and side screens smash, sending shards of Perspex over us. I turned to my side to protect myself, putting my arms over my head. I opened my eyes as something come through the window and then straight through Ashley's chest, pushing him further back into his seat. Blood spewed from his mouth like projectile vomit; I knew he had died instantly. It was a fucking nightmare, so I screwed my eyes shut. I was tossed around like I was in a bumper car in the dark, being thrown all over the place, my head wildly tossing. It lasted for a hell of a long time, or that's the way it seemed.

'I didn't feel the old girl hit the earth, perhaps out cold, or even dead. I woke up by the sound of myself taking a sharp intake of breath. The sun was blazing through the smashed windows, which were still shrouded in branches that been had ripped off. The engine had stopped, but all the alarm noises continued. The smell of exhaust and hot engine fumes filled the air. Dazed and battered, I tried to reach down and undo my belts, but I couldn't move my right arm as a large branch pinned it. How it had not gone through me was a miracle. A burning smell entered and I heard the crackle of a fire as it engulfed the rear.

'The terror of burning alive made me panic, so I wrestled with my arm. The fire became more aggressive, things were popping and cracking. Weird odours floated in with the smoke, the heat burning the back of my neck. Fright engulfed me as I coughed and spluttered. I pulled and twisted my arm. Suddenly, a surge of pain followed a cracking sound. My arm had become free, but I'd broken it. I managed to undo my belts and grab my E&E bag and, scrambling out of the cockpit window and branches, I fell, landing awkwardly. I tried to get my breath, but was having big trouble breathing as the toxic smoke poured from where I had just been sitting. I was glad Ashley had died instantly and was not being burnt alive.

'In severe pain, I crawled as quickly as I could away from the wreckage and managed to stand and run around the side. The heat was extreme. As I reached the rear, I spotted the form of a body inside. Then an explosion erupted, losing that person forever from my view. Landing in a heap, I momentarily blacked out. When I awoke, I was looking up at the bright-blue sky with patches of cloud passing over. Then I realised it was smoke, not clouds. I sat up immediately, feeling the pain of my arm. The wreckage was burning fiercely out of control. The heat was unbearable; my boots were smouldering, the soles slowly melting. I shuffled back on my arse with my one good arm.

'I sat there totally overwhelmed, I'm not sure for how long. I questioned why I was the only survivor. I felt a lot of guilt. I then heard vehicles, so I moved back into the forest. I hid in the undergrowth and armed myself with my pistol. The vehicles assembled around the burning wreckage. Some of the men started cheering and firing their guns in the air. One of them filmed on his phone the carnage and the other jubilant men. I had read the accounts of John Peters and John Nicol, of their own struggle for survival once captured. I didn't want to go through that. I wouldn't survive mentally or physically. Not wanting to be caught by these sick bastard animals, I took off my helmet and put my pistol to my head. I shut my eyes tight and pressed my pistol harder into my temple, repeatedly telling myself to pull the trigger. Even though I knew they would torture me when they found me, I couldn't do it.

'Not wanting to fail, again my finger poised just that extra couple of millimetres to end it, but all I could see were images of my children's faces. I dropped the pistol. The group started to search the forest. I wasn't very well-hidden, but I dared not move. Then they started to holler and wail. I wasn't sure what was going on. My arm was so painful that I wanted to throw up. I rolled onto my side and watched them dragging someone off. I thought it was one of our boys, but as they came closer I was shocked to see it was one of your prisoners. His legs and hands were badly burnt, but he was alive and he screamed in pain. As they dragged him past I thought I'd got away with it, but his head turned and he pointed at my position, yelling something in his own language. I fumbled for my pistol, but then a boot came in, nearly taking my head off.

'From that point it was my last hope of freedom. They took great pleasure in hauling me out and giving me a beating. They all crowed around me like yobs rioting at a football match, continuing to lay into me. Inside, I hoped they would finish me there and then, but instead they threw me on the back of a truck. I was blindfolded and driven away. The men in the back of the truck wailed and hollered; some even let off rounds. On the journey I was repeatedly kicked, punched, and hit with something hard, which I guessed to be their weapons. It was insane. It wasn't the pain that got to me; it was the thought of what lay ahead.

'The truck came to a stop and I was manhandled to the edge and thrown off. I was winded, but the boots and fists kept on raining down on me. I got to my feet and tried take off my blindfold, but they hit my arm down. I put my hand out to protect myself, but couldn't see anything. I could taste blood in my mouth. I took one heavy blow to my bollocks. This sent me to the floor, curled up in a helpless ball. All of them laughed and jeered. That kind of did it for me. I took a few deep breaths in and ripped my blindfold off. I stood up and launched myself at the nearest bloke, calling him a rag-head cunt, kicking, and punching him with my only good arm. As he went down, one of them grabbed me from behind around the throat. I bit into his forearm as hard as I could. He pulled away screaming. I still had part of his arm in my mouth. I turned around spitting blood from my mouth and ran at the next man, who looked terrified. He raised his weapon, but I managed to rugby tackle him to the ground. I landed on top of him and started unleashing my fist into his body, neck, and face. Then I felt a sharp pain at the back of my head and all went black.'

# CHAPTER TEN

I came around with my hands tied behind my back, slumped against a cold wall. I wasn't too sure how long I'd been out, and I'd been blindfolded again. My head was throbbing and there wasn't a part of me that didn't ache. I had no sense of smell; my nose was bunged up. I ran my tongue around the cuts inside my mouth, only to feel I had missing and broken teeth. I couldn't hear any sounds, but I felt someone was close to me. I shouted, but only heard my gargled voice bouncing off the walls. A door swung open and banged off the wall. I heard feet coming my way. I curled up, expecting punishment, and it came in the way of more fists and slapping. The worst sound, a kind of crunching, was when I took a direct smack to my nose; the blood run down my throat. The stinging pain of coughing blood up made me dizzy.

'I was dragged up by my arms and I let out a scream. My blindfold was harshly pulled off, ripping at my sore eyelids. In my face, nose to nose, was a man with his eyes wide, staring into mine. I could feel his hot breath. I couldn't move from his gaze. I was shaking uncontrollably. The two guys holding me up took a firmer hold of me. I tried to cover my bollocks as I expected he was going to knee me. He took a step back and in broken English he told me of our recent operation in detail, including how many people were aboard our helicopter. He also had great pleasure telling me it was him who shot us out of the sky and he and his men were going back to search for missing soldiers. I realised your prisoner had told him all the details. I prayed that this might relieve me of the torture to make me talk.

'His robes were pristine white, with a small black waistcoat over the top. He paced around the room.

' "I am going to let you live for now as you were only the pilot. You brought your helicopter down and saved my brother's life. But you must pay for helping your friends invade my country," he said.

'He clicked his fingers and the blindfold was roughly replaced. I heard him leave the room and the door slam. Next, I felt a sickening pain across my back as something whacked me. I fell to the ground and crawled along the floor like a scared dog, hoping to find a table or bed to hide under, but there was only the wall. My hair was pulled back and I was repeatedly hit. One of the sick bastard animals laughed as he grabbed my broken arm and squeezed. I tried not to scream, but the pain was too much, and I blacked out again.

'I woke, startled by someone taking off my blindfold. I panicked, instinctively lashing out with my feet.

' "It is OK. I am here to help you, not harm you," a woman softly said.

'It was like a slow, soothing melody in the midst of anarchy. I could only see out of one eye. I focused in the dim light to see a beautiful woman. She offered a jug of water to my lips.

' "Please, drink," she said.

'I thought it was poisoned, or part of their sick mind games; good cop, bad cop. I shook my head.

' "It's fine. You must drink. I have not much time. I am doctor," she said.

'I sipped the water. She lowered the jug and gently wiped my swollen lips before holding it up again. She did this until the water had nearly gone. She broke pieces of bread and rolled the chunks in her delicate hands, and then she popped them in my mouth.

' "You must now eat," she said.

'Taking two large tablets out of her pockets, she put them in front of my mouth.

' "Now take medication,' she said. "They help your pains."

' "Are they going to kill me?" I asked.

' "No, they only painkillers, trust me. I hate L-khaba-a men more than you."

'I didn't mean the medication. I meant the sick bastard animals out there, or maybe she knew this and tried to gloss over it. I could tell she was a good person. I let her place the tablets in my mouth and she continued to give me water and bread. She brought a bag around and took out medical items.

' "I need to clean your wounds. You are in bad way," she said.

'This wonderful doctor held my hand and then started to gently clean my wounds. She put my arm in a sling made from a dirty cloth. I thought for one moment I was dreaming. Was she an angel? She got up to leave, and I hated that.

' "Please stay. Maybe they will stop beating me if you are here."

' "Stay strong. *Isha Ally*," she said, or something like that.

'My pains eased and I drifted to sleep.

'I was rudely awoken by the door being swung open. This was like an alarm clock for another beating. With my blindfold off, I saw them coming, so I put my feet out to protect myself. Instead of a beating, though, I was lifted to my feet and hurried outside. The fresh cool breeze was lovely on my face, but the daylight was too bright and I bowed my head. I was hit hard in the back and my head was yanked back by my hair.

' "Fuck off," I screamed.

'My eyelids were forcibly opened. I shook my head to stop them.

' "OK, OK, I'll look."

'In front of me again was the man in white robes. He sat on the back of the tailgate of the black car, the same one the jet had pulverised later. He sat there all proud in front of his cronies.

' "Are you going to be a good boy, or are you going to attack my soldiers?" he asked.

' "As long as you don't kick me in my bollocks," I said. "I need these for making babies."

'He looked over at one of his cronies, one translated the last part. He roared with laughter and made his way over to me. I brought my knees together and tried to curl up tight ready for a fist or kick, but instead he just patted me on the back.

' "I like you, Mr Pilot. What is your name?"

'I stayed silent for a few seconds to think of a name, but before I could answer he repeated the question in a more threatening tone.

' "I asked you your name."

'Thinking quickly, I blurted, "My name is Chris Ryan."

' "Well, Chris, tell me who looked after your arm and took your blindfold off?" he said, tugging at my sling.

'Trying not to smirk after he called me Chris, I answered, "That was one of your guards. He also gave me his bread and water. Very nice man, he was."

' "What? Who was he?"

'Looking displeased, he ranted off to one of his cronies, who then ran off.

' "Yes, Chris. It was very nice of my men to look after you very well. Now, *you* will do a favour for me in return. We will drive you tomorrow to our best hotel and feed and clean you. I would like you very much to make a nice recording for us of how you came to Afghanistan, my country, and killed many innocent people. We will help you what to say, OK?" He stupidly grinned.

' "I'm sorry, I can't do that."

' "Why not, Chris?"

' "I'm camera shy, and anyway I think that's against my human rights," I said.

' "Oh, really, *Mr Ryan*?" His voice had changed. "Well, I have something to show you that will make you change your mind."

'He ordered his cronies to follow him, with me in tow. I was manhandled over to a small building where he opened the door. A ghastly smell of decay flooded out, followed by a profusion of buzzing flies; I heaved. I was forcefully pushed into the room and the door shut behind me, then bolted. The stench was over-powering and again I started to gag. I put my hand over my mouth and nose, but I couldn't take it, and vomit spewed between my fingers. It was semi-dark as I strained to try to work what was in the room with me.'

At this point Rabbit stopped walking and turned around to face me, crying. He wiped the tears from his face with his sleeve.

'I'm sorry for crashing and killing your mates and my crew, Johnny. It's my fault they're all dead.'

I gave him a hold and then patted him on the back. 'No, Roy, it's not your fault. It's the man who fired the SAM. It's the twisted fucked-up enemy out here in this mad country, but this is war. You were only doing your job. You managed to save my life and yours. And now we are going to make it home to our families.'

I let him go from my embrace and he lifted his face.

'You don't have to tell me any more,' I said.

'It was Fish and Planet in that room with me,' he said.

Rabbit began to walk on.

Eventually I caught him up, I put my hand on his shoulder. I'd lost my count halfway through his version of events, so I guessed it was time for a rest.

'Rabbit, let's stop for five minutes. I'm absolutely knackered.'

This wasn't completely true, but I was trying to make him feel better. We stopped and sat down. I passed a larger chunk of bread than mine to him and let him sip most of my water. We took the last of the ibuprofen. He looked mentally and physically shattered. I thought about making light of the story he'd told me.

'So, Chris Ryan, did you enjoy giving those Elkhaba cronies a pasting?'

'Hmm,' he replied, looking slightly pleased.

'Wouldn't want to get on the wrong side of you. I'll be telling my CO to get you signed up.'

A grin appeared. 'If I sign up, can I miss out the fitness training?' He laughed. 'Yeah, you should have seen their faces. I can still taste that bastard's arm. Didn't have much meat on him, a bit like us.'

'What made you use the name Chris Ryan?' I asked.

'I read his book recently, *The One That Got Away*.'

'Well, let's hope you end up escaping like him, and you get home to your family. I hope your bollocks are still OK.'

Looking down at his groin, he said, 'I should have asked that beautiful doctor to check them out. Who the hell was she?'

'Tell you what, dude, let's find a LUP and I'll tell you all about her.'

His eyes lit up as I carefully lifted him to his feet. I turned him around and pushed him gently in the direction I wanted to head. The pace was slower, not only because of Rabbit, but I was spent as well. It had been around six weeks since I'd had a decent, fresh meal. I counted to three thousand six hundred seconds as best I could, but I had fumbled a few times. We had both started to shiver. Worried about the effects of hypothermia, I had to find an LUP quick to conserve the remaining body core heat.

Keeping a proper internal body temperature is crucial to survival. In extreme heat or cold environments your core temperature will rarely diverge more than two degrees either side of 36.8 C, your body, limbs, skin, etc. being a few degrees cooler. If your core rises to over 42.7, or lowers below 28.8, death is imminent. Shivering is your body telling you are getting cold, losing heat faster than it is being replaced. Your body generates heat and energy as it burns fuel.

Shivering exercises numerous muscles. This reflex increases heat burning more fuel, but if your core temperature drops by a few degrees, shivering will not sustain your core temperature, or make it rise. Your brain has a thermostat, a nerve tissue, which controls and monitors your body's maintained correct temperature level. When going into hypothermia, this thermostat responds by commanding heat to be drawn from parts of the body to the core. The feet and hands become very cold and stiff and your core will drain the heat from your head. With heat loss from the head, your brain doesn't get the sugar and oxygen it requires, and the circulation reduces. A danger sign hard to spot, is when the shivering stops and you become very irritable.

At this stage you will stop being concerned about your condition; a 'couldn't care less' attitude will take over. If this happens, you are on the way to dying as you lose the ability to warm up. It's not enough just to put a blanket over you; you need to stop your body temperature from dropping. It's very easy to go into a semi-conscious state, eventually becoming unconscious. This is fatal. The best cure is to get heat from another source, hot fluid, or hot food, or light a fire. A well-known remedy is to share body heat with someone who isn't suffering with hypothermia; best embraced in a sleeping bag.

Ahead, looming out of the earth, was the large side of a mountain. After the recent flat desert we'd tabbed across, it looked out of place and mightily threatening in the dark. Rabbit's head had dropped and he was walking on autopilot.

'Nearly there,' I said. 'Reckon we can find a nice LUP in that mountainside.'

He didn't even lift his head.

Shit; this wasn't a good sign. The temperature had dropped dramatically. I pushed him a little quicker. As we reached the bottom of the slope I searched for LUP. A thin path led about fifty metres up to a cave entrance. I didn't have time to go and recce it; I had to get us both warm. I pushed him up the track, but he kept stumbling, hampering our progress.

When we reached the cave entrance, I helped him sit down. I had to forget about SOP; it was a race against time to get us both warmed up. I turned on my Maglite and swung my weapon in, searching the forbidding darkness of the cave. The remains of an old fire sat in the middle. The roof was charred black. To the outer edges were a few old blankets, some made of animal skins. I turned the light off and picked Rabbit up. He had now become lethargic.

'Welcome to the Hotel Flintstones,' I quipped.

I stepped over a small wall made of rocks and then laid him on the skins and blankets. I got down next to him, pulling more blankets and skins over us, cuddling up to his shivering body.

To keep him conscious, I asked, 'Rabbit, want to hear about the doctor?'

Between his chattering teeth, he replied, 'Yeeaahhh sssure, in ffffact you ccccan tell me how you ssssurviveddd.'

'On one condition though: you tap my thigh with your hand, so I know you're listening.'

'Is ttthisss one of your cccoming out mmmmoments again mmmate?' he replied.

As he started to tap his hand on my leg, I began from the point when I'd found Planet in my seat before lift-off. I didn't leave out any details, even the bloody goats. When I finished my account, up until the point I'd seen him in my searchlight, I told him how brave and defiant he had been.

'You didn't fail when you didn't blow your brains out,' I said. 'Everyone, including myself, says they will keep one round in the chamber for themselves rather than getting caught. But the reality is, I don't know anybody who really would squeeze the trigger, and I know of some seriously mean blokes. On reflection, I know I wouldn't. I would rather die shooting my way out.'

'Thanks, mate, that means a lot,' he said.

We had warmed up considerably and stopped shivering. We even shared a few jokes, but we were both on our chin straps. Eventually I followed him into a deep sleep.

# CHAPTER ELEVEN

I hadn't slept so well in ages. I didn't have any nightmares or even dreams. I stretched out my curled-up body and let out a yawn.

'Come on you lazy git, stand by your bed,' a sharp voice said.

Heart fluttering, I sat up instinctively, and for a moment I thought I was back in the barracks. Sitting there, smoking, and wrapped in blankets, was Rabbit. Around him on the floor were a few fag butts. It was pointless telling him to put his fag out now. Instead, I shook my head at him in disapproval. He just smiled whilst his smoke wafted through a hole in the cave's roof. The hole was only the size of melon and it narrowed into the rock without me being able to see where it ended. Looking back, he took his last drag of his fag before stubbing it out.

'What's a GBD then, mate?' he said.

'Glorified bus driver,' I said gleefully.

'Did you make that one up yourself?'

'No, it's well-known throughout the army and navy.'

'Piss off.'

Getting up, I noticed the blue sky had been covered by grey clouds. I was glad to be out of the relentless scotching sun. Hopefully, if it rained we would have a chance to replenish our now zero water stock; on the other hand it would be impossible to navigate at night.

'About last night, I never got to finish my account,' he said.

'There's no…'

'No, I want to finish telling you,' he interrupted. 'After vomiting because of seeing the bodies of Planet and Fish, I went into a frenzy, hammering on the door to let me out. As soon as the door opened they didn't have the chance to drag me out as I'd already thrown myself out. I sat there in shock, listening to their mocking.

' "You see, *Mr Ryan*, if you do not do as I ask, you will come back and spend many nights with your friends in there. So, do you agree to help, *Mr Ryan?*" the leader said.

'I nodded my head, but was sharply kicked by one of his cronies. Reluctantly, I replied, "You're a sick bastard. Yes, I agree to help you."

' "Good choice, *Chris.*"

'Clicking his fingers, I was helped to my feet.

' "Some bloody choice," I mumbled.

'The crony who had run off earlier entered the compound clutching another frightened-looking crony, with a pistol to his head. He was pushed to his knees, still with the gun aiming at him. The pistol was cocked.

' "So, Chris, is this the guard that helped you?" the leader said, clearly getting some joy out of the moment.

'I stared at the crony, who was now rocking backwards and forwards in the praying position. He was mumbling the same prayer repeatedly. As much as I loathed every one of these evil scumbags, I couldn't bring myself to see him shot for no reason.

' "No, this isn't him," I said, the relief on the captive's face.

' "Are you sure?" the leader said, disappointed.

' "Yes, I'm sure."

' "Do you see the man around me?" he snapped.

'I pretended to look around. I had a mad thought of saying that they had all helped me, hoping they would all be shot, but instead I said, "They all look the same, but I'm positive he's not here."

' "Maybe you have some integrity, Chris. I think we are going to get along fine. I have so many questions I need answers to," he said, stroking his black beard.

' "You already know everything, so I wouldn't waste your time."

' "Remember, you can always spend a night with your *friends*," he said, and he laughed.

'The rest of the cronies joined in, cheering. I doubt if they even knew what he'd said. They were just shit-scared of him.

' "And you remember the Geneva Convention ruling," I replied.

' "Please take Mr Ryan away. Be sure to remind him we don't believe in the Western laws."

'I was hit in the back of my legs, sending me to the ground. I knew I had pushed it a little too far. Maybe this is what you meant, Vinnie, by me going too far with my gob.'

I didn't reply.

'I was dragged back to my holding room and given a bit more of their hospitality. Only this time, my boots and socks were removed and a leather belt taken to the soles of my feet. My only relief was that I yelled every obscenity I could think of at them. I was left with my hands untied and without a blindfold, with just an armed crony guarding me. I was fucked in every way. Through my half-good eye the bastard kept smiling at me. Vindictively, he ate and drank slowly. I watched, longing for a handout.

'On guard changeover, the crony who'd had the pistol to his head came over to me. I feared the worst, putting my hand over my face and curling up in a ball. But to my surprise, he handed me some food in the shape of a dumpling which tasted of cheese. I devoured three of them, thanking him as he sat in the corner of the room. I drifted in and out of sleep, my pain dissipating as I thought of my family. My dreams were constantly troubled by thinking of the fate that lay ahead. I imagined myself talking on a video with a gun pointed at my head, making sure I co-operated. I was wearing an orange jumpsuit. In front of me was a glass of water, dates, and a script. When I finished, they stopped recording and it all took a sinister turn. I was pulled from behind the desk in front of the camera, my head bowed forward. Very much alive, my neck was hacked with a machete. After, my head was paraded in the town. I woke suddenly when I heard your shots.'

'Jesus. Sounds like you had it bad,' I said.

'Thank fuck you got me out. At least my dream never came true,' he said, and sighed.

'Well, the good news: I reckon the Elkhaba leader who started to like you, *Mr Ryan*, was the same guy who got his comeuppance before he tried to rape Anoosheh. The bad news: we're out of bread and water, so we're down to chewing gum and scavenging. It's not good to steal from the locals, but if you need to survive, then you must.'

The sound of bells clanged. I knew exactly what they were and I grabbed my weapon, making it ready.

'What is it, mate?' said Rabbit, unnerved.

'Get your pistol ready.'

I took a quick look over the cave's foot-high stonewall. In the distance from the right came a group of eight goats with clanking bells around their necks. Trailing a short distance, the goat herder came into view, walking with his long stick in his hand. He was of average height, very thin, and probably in his late forties, but out here most folk looked a lot older than they were. It didn't look like he had washed and shaved for a long time. His robe was filthy.

Suddenly, he took a small run to the edge of the rocks and quickly lifted his robe. Grossly, out squirted some bad shit; he was obviously having diarrhoea issues. He then proceeded to wash his butt with his hand and a water bottle. The goat herder got up and continued walking as if it was a run-of-the-mill thing to do.

'Oh that's gross,' Rabbit whispered. 'Remind me not to shake hands with him.'.

'It's better if you bow to a new acquaintance, as that's their tradition,' I put him straight.

'Reckon those goats are following you again, mate. Must be your animalistic aftershave.'

'Well, this time I'm pleased to see them as we need food. I reckon I could buy one off him. Give me your pistol and stay here. Keep watch and don't come down.'

'Sure. See if he's got any fags please.'

I pulled out the last of my gold coins and tucked my Sig away. Leaping over the wall, I crept down to a large boulder halfway down the slope. As the herder and goats went by, I sneaked down the thin path we had come up the night before. The slope was made up of different shades of grey, jagged chunks of rocks. Trees and shrubs were trying to survive, but most had died. As I got to within five metres, the goat herder turned around.

'*Salaam aluikum*,' I greeted him.

Bowing quickly, I casually walked up to him. Jesus, did he stink, and he was a bit unsure of me.

'*Salaam aluikum*,' he said.

He held out his right hand, leaving his shitty hand on his stick. He continued to look beyond me, puzzled where I'd come from. I quickly touched his hand.

'*Khushala shum pa li do di*... pleased to meet you.' I pointed at the small goat, 'How much is this... *Da somra di?*'

The herder rambled off, shaking his head, and laughing. I didn't have a clue what he was saying, but I didn't give a shit, because one way or another I was having that goat. I pulled out the remaining four gold coins and showed them to him. He grabbed the little bleating goat, picked it up and showed me.

'*Ao, ao, ao.*'

Good, he wanted he deal. He stuck out his filthy right hand, his yellow nails were filled with dirt. I handed him a gold coin. He examined it and held it back at me.

'Don't worry; its real,' I told him.

'*Ma ta ra kraa*,' he said, and shook his hand.

I placed another in his hand as he had asked, but he continued to wave his hand for more.

'Piss off, that's your lot.' I frowned and shook my head.

He stood there for a while shaking his hand, but I didn't relent. In the end he handed me the goat.

'*Insha Allah.*'

I replied with the same courtesy and watched him and the remaining goats wander off.

Clutching my goat, which smelt a lot better than the herder, I reached the large boulder halfway up. Putting the goat on the ground, I turned it on its side by holding its four hooves. Placing my hand across its face, I turned it to the side so its throat was uppermost. After a little bleating, the goat was pacified. I drew my knife and slit its throat. There was a small struggle. I held the goat for a while until it was dead. I then laid it on the boulder, letting its blood run out. I raced back to the cave, thrilled.

'Well, that went according to plan. Got us some top nosh,' I said.

'I'm a vegetarian.'

Accustomed to his weird wit, I said, 'Fine, you're gonna starve to fucking death then.'

There was no way he was going to last another night tabbing on an empty stomach. Any glow from a fire at night would be seen from far away. I reckoned it was still early morning and the crazed insurgents would still be stoned to the eyeballs. This left no option but to cook the goat now. Together we grabbed as much dead wood and dry shrubs as we could scavenge. Rabbit only collected a small handfuls at a time, because of the injury to his arm. In the cave I made a three-foot diameter circle out of rocks and stones, stacking them about twelve inches high.

'Give me your fags and lighter,' I asked.

He shrugged. 'What fags and lighter, mate?'

I was getting a bit sick and tired of his games. 'The ones from the Toyota. The ones you were smoking earlier. I'm not daft.'

'They're all gone, mate, honest,' he said, tapping his pockets.

After a little argument, I eventually got hold of his lighter and fags. I started by making a small nest of dried grass and twigs. Ripping open the fags, I crumbled them on the nest, along with the empty packet; Rabbit looked on with pity.

'Sorry, *mate*,' I said. 'Need to improvise, adapt, and overcome. They're bad for you anyway.'

'Get stuffed, *dude*. Hope you choke on the smoke.' He broadly smiled.

'It's good to see your lips are letting you smile.'

I didn't need to use the fags, I just hated smoking. Sparking up the lighter, the flame took hold of the nest, the smoke rising.

'Quick, get a lungful of the last of your fags,' I said.

'Oh piss off,' he sulked.

As the nest burst into flames, I added smaller twigs. When these had taken alight, I placed the larger branches. I ordered Rabbit to go find some more.

'What a waste of fags. Who put him in charge? It's the only perk I had,' he mumbled on the way out.

I had to laugh at his sense of humour; he had started to grow on me.

With the fire raging, I went back to the goat, which was covered with an array of insects. Slitting the length of its belly, pulling out all its innards, I tossed them at the base of the boulder. As I entered the cave, the warmth was truly amazing and almost smokeless.

'Bet this brings you back to your time in Girl Guides, mate,' he said.

I ignored him and laid the whole goat on the fire as I didn't have time to skin it.

'Bloody hell, did you skip a few pages of *Jamie Oliver's Cook Book*?' he said, a little stunned. 'Aren't you supposed to skin it and stuff it with rosemary and garlic?'

'The guts and intestines will boil nice in its body. When they have, I'll scrape them out and throw away the carcass. We'll live on the intestines like kings... mmm, nice.'

I fixed him with a crazy grin, holding my knife up.

'You're a mad twat.'

The cave was filled with the stench of burning hair and skin. However, underneath was a beautiful odour of meat cooking, lifting my morale. I couldn't remember the last time I'd had hot meat; my mouth watered. The smoke funnelled up the hole in the cave roof. I wondered if outside it looked like a house chimney pouring out smoke. I decided to go and check, but there wasn't any smoke coming from the mountain. Back in the harmony of the cave, Rabbit was snoozing. It was probably best to let him doze whilst I kept watch.

Boredom set in, the only joy being to put a few more branches on the fire and turn the goat. After about two hours it was a mass of charcoal. I kicked Rabbit and told him scoff was ready. I cut off a chunk of goat. The outside black charcoal skin was tough, but inside the meat was succulent. I tried to cool it before I tasted it, but still managed to burn my mouth and lips. It was amazingly delicious.

'Oh, dude, that's the best meat I've tasted for years.'

'Well bloody share some, mate. I'm dying over here,' Rabbit said, frustrated.

'You can't. Remember you're a nancy vegetarian,' I said, and then stuffed the last piece in my mouth. 'Oh God, it's nice. Mmm.'

'I was also a smoker until you trashed my fags. I've now converted to a heathen meat eater. Come on, I'm starving, mate.'

I sliced a larger portion and passed it over. It was quite funny watching him blow on the meat. His lips were still slightly swollen, resembling a Botox procedure that had gone wrong.

'I see your manners haven't improved,' I said—he didn't reply. Blimey. He must be hungry, I thought.

Taking the goat off the fire, we continued to carve off the meat. It didn't take long to fill our empty stomachs. The only thing we really needed now, well, except for beer, was water.

'Right, we need to find water. I remember seeing some rivers marked on the old map. Trees are a good sign of a water source nearby. If we can find any of these, or even a natural spring, we can replenish our water bottles for tonight's tab. I want us to head out as the sun goes down. Moving at night lessens our chances of dehydration. Put the goat back on the embers to keep any flies away. We'll eat again before we go. Grab your water bottle and your pistol and let's move.'

Rabbit didn't move. 'Why don't we just head off now and on the way look for a water source? It's still cloudy, so we're out of the sun. It saves coming all the way back. We could put the meat in your bag.'

It was a better plan than mine, reckoning we only had an hour left of light anyway.

'So?' he asked.

'Well, again, it's one of your dumb arse plans. However, on this occasion I'll go with it.'

'Really?' he asked.

'Come on. Don't just stand there. Get your shit together.'

'You weren't attached to the Third Reich were you, for fuck's sake?'

I tried to hide my smile as I stuffed the meat in my satchel, and then I stepped over the wall.

'Down, down,' I hissed.

Signalling for him to get out of sight, I then dived onto my side, nearly bringing up my meal. Advancing from the left at speed, about three hundred metres away, were two vehicles, leaving a large dust cloud behind them.

'Two vehicles approaching from the left, Roy. Arm yourself with my Sig and take cover in the shadows of the cave, but keep eyes on. I'm moving down to the boulder. You must stay here. Don't let them see you,' I whispered, in some urgency.

I crawled to the boulder, right into the goat's blood and guts; a swarm of flies went flying frantically in all directions. Very slowly, I peeked around the side and prepared my AK47. Removing my other magazines, I laid them next to me, all the same way around. The vehicles were approximately a hundred metres away and had slowed down. I searched back for Rabbit, but couldn't see him. Shit. I wanted to be able to contact him.

'Psst. Psst. Roy.'

'What?'

'If they stop, don't shoot unless they come up to our position. Only open fire when you hear my command. Got it?' I ordered.

'Roger, mate.'

Both vehicles were white Toyotas. The leading one had a rear-mounted Dushka with its gunner; the second Toyota had a rear crew-cab. Even though I wasn't religious, I was praying they were going to drive past, but like most of this nightmare we were living, the Toyotas stopped at the bottom of the slope. Bollocks. With minimal movement I brought my weapon in front, aiming down its sights. My heartbeat had started pounding quicker. I hoped Rabbit was staying calm. They all got out, seven men in total, plus a gunner who had stayed with his Dushka. They were all young fighting males, appearing menacing. One of the men who had got out of the crew-cab was being jostled to the front. He was continually being hit with weapon butts. All the men were brandishing AK47s: Elkhaba. As the lone man demonstrated with his arms, I recognised him: the goat herder. Had he turned me in? Why? For more money? If so, I hoped he gets what he deserves.

One of the Elkhaba aimed his weapon at the herder's face. The herder pointed to the direction he had travelled and then up to the narrow path where I had appeared. I couldn't hear word for word, but could sense what was coming next. They all raised their weapons at him. He pleaded by gesturing in the praying position. More shouting continued and he began walking slowly backwards. Backed up about three metres away, one Elkhaba fired his weapon in the air, making the herder jump. He turned, fleeing for his life. I kind of felt sorry for him as I hated bullies. The man standing at the front took aim, but didn't fire, he just held his position. Then he fired a single shot. I panned my view back to the herder, but he was still running. Looking back at the group, the next man fired a shot. As he missed, the rest laughed and slapped each other. This had become a sick game. They took it in turn to try to bring the herder down as if he was a defenceless animal. With each shot, I glanced back at the escapee who by now had made some ground. He lost a shoe in the process and turned back to get it. I yearned for him not to get hit, but as another round blasted out, he spun to the ground.

The herder tried to crawl off, clinging to the floor in a fight for survival. Spats of dirt flew up around him as they continued to take it in turns to shoot. Then the herder stopped crawling; he stopped moving. That was it for him, and game over for the sick bastards. Perhaps the herder hadn't come willingly to turn me in, but was forced to reveal my position. But how did the Elkhaba know he had seen me? That puzzle would have to wait as right now three of them were making their way up the narrow path. This led past me to the cave. If they didn't split up, I could stop them before they reached it. I doubted Rabbit had much chance with his pistol. He would have had training, but not to the extent I had. I also questioned had he ever shot another human being. He could hesitate or freeze, which would prove fatal.

Controlling my breathing and mind, I went into relaxed mode, but, simultaneously, that of a killing machine. I wanted revenge for the goat herder. As soon as all three men entered my defence arc, approximately four metres from where I lay, I would open fire. They wouldn't even know what had happened until it was too late. I switched my fire mode to fully automatic and waited.

Four metres… three metres… two metres… my finger squeezing the trigger a little more, one metre… wait until the third man is in my zone. Fire. Without standing up, I gently squeezed the trigger, keeping it down and only moving off Threat-1 when I knew he was dead. With the trigger still down, I moved onto Threat-2 and systematically onto Threat-3. You don't exactly know when they are dead, but you can see at this range the impact of your rounds in their upper body chest area and head. It's like small explosions of cotton followed by bursts of blood. If the round goes through, you can see flesh and body parts in a spray of blood come out behind. The body twists and buckles as each round hits. This all appeared to be in slow motion, but the ambush was probably over in five to seven seconds. *'Threats neutralised.'*

Crawling forward, I changed magazine and put down a hail of fire onto the two Toyotas, hitting a little too low. The remaining Elkhaba had already taken cover behind the vehicles as soon as I'd poured death on the three on the narrow path. As I paused and adjusted my aim, the Dushka's gunner returned fire, rocking the Toyota. All I could do was take cover from the barrage as they smashed into boulder, sending splinters in my direction. The surface vibrated as every round hit. They continued to pump into the rocks and earth around me; it was deafening. I huddled tight for protection, but instinctively I wanted to face the threat full on. I had to get out from the killing zone and return fire as quickly as possible.

The relentless destructive power of the Dushka ceased. I grabbed this opportunity; hopefully the gunner had a jam, or it had overheated, or maybe he was changing ammunition. I got up and moved the opposite way around the smoking boulder and flicked my weapon to semi mode. Down on one knee, I let off a burst at the gunner, rounds smashing into the bodywork below him. Aiming higher, I fired again, making the gunner duck. I had him bracketed. Adjusting slightly as he looked up, I let out another burst. His body twisted as rounds took their designated target; finally, the threat fell forward over the Dushka. *'Threat neutralised.'*

Incoming rounds whizzed over my head in succession and I ducked back behind the boulder. They weren't very accurate as only a few hit the massive rock. Feeling energised, and with the enormous killing power of the Dushka gone, I picked up the remaining magazines and raced down the slope. Small shingle and rocks followed my sliding feet. My mind had registered a shallow scrape in the ground, feeling like I'd had time to study a map before I'd set off knowing its position. More rounds pinged around my feet; the aim was becoming more accurate. Changing mags rapidly, I aimed through the shingle dust blown up on my entry into the shallow. At first I couldn't see my intended target, but I had to suppress the incoming fire. I returned a stream of rounds, normally liking to fire and move, but I couldn't.

The target's head was just above the Toyota's front wing as he took refuge. I took aim and waited. As soon as he popped up to return fire, I fired two bursts. He was still moving upwards as my first rounds hit his face, lifting him backwards off his feet. The second burst shattered his neck and shoulders. *'Threat neutralised.'* Where were the other Elkhaba? No movement came from the Toyotas. I searched beyond into the distance in case they had fled, which was highly unlikely as they may not be the best trained, but they were fanatically crazed in not giving up. My neck hackles stood on end.

The distinctive sound of my Sig opened fire. Ten shots had been fired by the time I had made my way back to Rabbit's position in the cave. As I reached the entrance with my weapon, scanning, Rabbit still had the Sig pointed over the wall. He had frozen with shock. No more than four metres in front of him were the bodies of the three remaining Elkhaba. I don't think he had noticed that one of the men was still alive, trying to crawl to his weapon. I fired a burst into his head. To make sure, I followed short bursts on the other two. *'Threats neutralised.'*

I lowered my weapon and slowly took the pistol from Rabbit, who had now begun to shake.

Trying to make some relief for him, I said, 'Thanks, Roy, you just saved my arse. Where the hell did you learn to shoot like that? Fucking awesome.'

He shook his thoughts. 'Well, *someone* had to do something. I couldn't wait for your fire command as you'd run away.'

I was glad to hear his humour, but the reality was he was in shock and this event would haunt him, like my first killing had.

★

My first kill was serving with 3 PARA in Afghanistan, 2006. I had previously been in a firefight situation, but had never a hundred per cent positively identified my kill. Helmand Province was the Taliban stronghold and the powers above thought it a good idea to set up a FOB right in their back yard to stir up the hornets' nest, which it certainly did. On this morning we left our base on a patrol mission to draw the Taliban out. We headed into a medium-sized village. Through intelligence we knew one compound housed a Taliban leader and his fanatical followers. Whilst we were supposed to make it look like a routine patrol, we had another patrol set out at the same time, heading in a different direction. The plan was the other group would enter the village from another angle and have good eyes on the compound. We also had close air support on standby.

Even though I was with one of the best units in the world, a courageous battle-hardened group of lads, I was shitting myself. I knew deep down this was going to kick off big style. And it did. The first rounds came in, not from the compound, but the buildings and alleyways opposite. As we all took cover and returned a barrage of controlled fire, the whole village seemed to come out and have a go. Small arms fire, heavy machinegun fire, and RPGs, smashed into our cover of walls and buildings around us. Our Sergeant Major still screamed orders amid the chaos. As the support group entered the battle, it appeared we were turning the tide of aggression and winning the fight.

Out of the corner of my eye, I spotted a lone figure jump out of a window onto a balcony area and then brazenly open fire. Peter Homes took the rounds to his body and head right in front of me. I drew my SA80 and fired burst after burst of rounds, hitting the man on the balcony. Through my sights, I watched his upper body and arms dance crazily around. He was sent back against the wall and dropped to the balcony floor, disappearing. The only reminder of him was the blood-stained wall. I didn't have time to reflect as Homes was our main priority. We radioed in a MedEvac. After the battle had ceased, we pulled out under the watchful eyes of Apache pilots. Later that evening we learnt that apart from Homes' banging head and bruised torso, only one round managed to penetrate his foot. His body armour and helmet had saved his life. It wasn't until I tried to get some sleep that evening that the death of the Taliban man on the balcony came back to haunt me with slow images playing repeatedly. Over the next few months, with further battles, I'd killed more; however, we lost some fine blokes. My first kill diminished into a lame memory.

# CHAPTER TWELVE

'Best we get the fuck out of here. Grab your kit,' I said.

'Sure,' he replied vacantly.

'You OK?'

'I think so. Are they all finished?'

'You mean am I inviting them to tea? No, they're all dead.'

Unclipping three magazines off the dead men's AK47s, I then gave Rabbit the Makarov pistol after making it ready. We made our way down the slope by using the narrow path. Before reaching the Toyotas I aimed on the dead body hanging over the Dushka, telling Rabbit to check the other. It was a bloody mess: no question he was dead. Rabbit confirmed the other fighter was dead as half his head was missing. I jumped up and pulled the dead man off the Dushka, dragging him off the end.

'Find out which vehicle has the most fuel,' I said. 'I'm going to check on the herder.'

I jogged off towards his lifeless body.

Rolling the frail, smelly herder over, I couldn't see any loss of blood, so I checked for a pulse. He had a good strong pulse, so I slapped him around his face, telling him to wake up. He opened his eyes shocked at first, and then smiled ear to ear. He hadn't been hit but was playing dead; a dangerous decision to make, yet he had got away with it. The herder stood up and proceeded to give me a hug, I wasn't sure who smelt worse.

He chanted, '*Insha Allah.*'

As he continued a load of other stuff at a fast pace, I had only understood "God willing", and that he had lost something. He took my arm and led me back to the Toyotas. Once he had searched the bodies of the dead Elkhaba, he stood up and raised his hand.

'*Gould,* gould,' he said.

I believed the Elkhaba found him with the gold coins after searching him, or maybe he had been showing them off and they had got wind of it. You couldn't trust many in this country. After an intimidating interrogation he was probably forced to show where he had sold the goat to me. I pointed to the bodies on the slope and he ran off to check.

'So, what's the story on the fuel?' I asked Rabbit.

'The car with the Dushka has a quarter of a tank; the other has three-quarters of a tank.'

I didn't know the exact distance and any change in terrain we would need to cover. It made sense to take the Toyota with the fuller tank, but weighing up the odds in coming across more Elkhaba or Taliban, hell-bent on sending us to our graves, I chose to take the Toyota with the Dushka.

'Right, we'll take this one,' I said. 'Search the other Toyota for any items we can use.'

The herder came joyfully running and shouting down the path with something in his hand. When he reached me, out of breath, he showed his find. He emptied a small brown leather pouch containing his gold coins. Rabbit then appeared clutching a large two-litre bottle of water, the ignition keys, and a pipe with a pouch of tobacco.

'Jackpot again, mate. This time if you try to take them I will have to kill you,' he said. 'Oh, by the way, there's an RPG in the rear foot-well if that's any good to you.'

'Are you taking the piss, Roy?'

He jogged back to the Toyota, leant in the crew-cab, and pulled out the RPG and a further warhead.

'This any good, mate?'

'And the tobacco is more important? Sometimes, Roy, you astound me,' I said, in disbelief.

I snatched the keys off him and gave them to the herder, who by now didn't have a clue what was going on. Again, he hugged me, his odour grabbing my nostrils. He then turned and embraced Rabbit.

Not missing an opportunity of revenge, I said, 'Coming out of the closet are we, Roy? Nice.' I winked at him.

As the herder continued to hug him, Rabbit's face was priceless.

We watched the herder jump into the Toyota and faff around before he eventually started the engine. The gears crunched and then it kangarooed backwards. With the gears crunching again, it jumped forwards, before wheel-spinning off. It continued to swerve as it sped off. He may have survived the Elkhaba's sick game, but I doubted if he would make it back to his destination alive.

Before we set off, I jumped back on the rear of our Toyota to reload the Dushka. Opening the top cover, I fed a new belt of ammunition in, slammed the top cover, locked it, and cocked the centre handle. I lifted the sight up to made sure the ammunition belt was free to run. With the butt of my weapon, I smashed the rear light lenses and took out the bulbs. I zeroed the speedometer and took a note of the time: 17.55 hrs.

'Right, you drive and I'll take over when it's dark as we will be driving on black light,' I said.

This I knew would be nearly impossible without a pair of NVGs, but I was relying on the clouds lifting to give a clear moonlit night. I pointed at the small mounted dashboard compass.

'Stay as close to this heading as possible,' I ordered.

Heading slightly northwest, we set off. I was amused at how he changed gear with only his good arm whilst keeping his knees on the wheel. I kept my eyes on the terrain all around us, searching for any unexpected wadis, craters, and pointed rocks; also, scanning for expected trouble. As we drove around the side of the stunning mountain slope, a smaller set of magnificent mountains stood in the distance. It was almost as if these mountain ranges were part of a territory border, like dividing your own posh garden from your neighbour's shit-hole of a garden, as directly opposite the landscape consisted of miles of barren desert. My eyes were straining to keep open, so I undid my window fully. I leant down and picked up the water bottle. It looked clear and the seal hadn't been broken, but I still checked it was water before I gulped it down. I handed it to Rabbit and he took a long swig. I wasn't too bothered about rationing as way off in the distance the mountain had a snow peak with greenery dotted down its slopes. This meant a water supply we could tap off. As the lifeless terrain became monotonous, I drifted off into a sleep.

★

I began helping Haleema in her village, which was now thriving with farming and children playing. My dream took an ominous turn when a convoy of dead Elkhaba men driving black Toyotas rolled into the village. They got out of their vehicles and floated across without touching the ground, grabbing children, slitting their throats. The rest of the villagers ran into their homes, but I was stuck to the spot. The more I struggled, the more I sank. The ghostly figures were covered in bullet holes, some with parts of their faces missing. On the bonnet of one of the Toyotas was the main leader I'd killed saving Anoosheh from rape. He stood defiantly naked. His leg was clearly deformed. His face grinned a toothless smile and his nose poured blood. These were the victims of my killings. The leader ranted off, spitting more blood. As the blood landed, it fizzed and melted the Toyota paintwork below him.

At the other end of the village, a convoy of SAS pinkies entered. At the front of the convoy walked eight blokes. I felt warm and safe, as if the village would be saved. The eight walking the convoy in were Planet, Fish, Shrek, and the remaining Chinook crew, all looking the picture of health. Out of the building walked Anoosheh, Haleema, and Rabbit. They greeted the convoy. The Elkhaba leader waved his arms furiously and his eyes turned as red as the blood from his nose. He yelled and pointed at the convoy. Out of the sky came a missile; laughter shrieked. Sitting on the missile, dressed in his gleaming white *dishdasha*, was the other leader who had been vaporised. He smiled at me, the same as he had in the Chinook. A wave of helpless fear come over me. I tried to shout to the convoy, but they couldn't hear me. The missile headed towards them, and then a white flash consumed my dream.

I woke suddenly, banging my head on the side of the door frame. The Toyota was swerving from left to right and the air was filled with a weird smell. The vehicle was going too fast for the environment.

'Stop,' I yelled. 'Stop the fucking car.'

Rabbit slammed the anchors on and the Toyota skidded to a stop. I faced him. He was calmly smoking the pipe he'd found earlier, oblivious to what was going on around him. He was drugged to the eyeballs on whatever it was in that pipe. Now I knew why my dream was weird: I'd been inhaling his smoke. Furious, I got out and, stomping around to his side, dragged him out.

'You fucking idiot,' I ranted. 'You could have killed us both.'

He looked at me and just smiled. I snatched the pipe and threw it away, with him looking on. He held his hand out like a kid losing a toy. I manhandled him by the scruff and, still cursing, threw him in the passenger seat and put his belt on. Angrily, I slammed his door, but his expression was still contently happy.

Light had faded. I had to squint through the blackish-grey dimness. Back in the driver's seat, the time read: 19.15 hrs. The speedometer read: 45 miles. I couldn't believe I'd been asleep that long and, more to the point, not been killed at the hands of a drugged driver. At least we were still going in the right direction rather than having done a U-turn. With both windows down, I roared the engine into life and sped off, still annoyed. As dark descended, by sheer luck, the clouds started to disperse. Maybe our luck was changing. It took a while before my eyes became accustomed to the moonlit landscape. The terrain took on a new mood, like it was waiting for a lapse in my concentration to claim the Toyota in a prize of death. My eyes were fixed on the ground in front, looking for any unwanted signs.

I couldn't see the dashboard dials. I stopped the Toyota and took a bearing off the stars and then headed off again. The flat desert narrowed to a track-like feature. On one side were the slopes of a mountain with fallen rocks and trees; on the other was a wadi with its forbidding deep sides. For a while I drove at a very low speed with my heart in my mouth, my neck and eyes straining. I had to rest, so I stopped and leant into the foot-well between Rabbit's legs, grabbing up the water bottle. Tilting my head back taking a swig, a flicker of light grabbed my attention in the rear-view mirror. The light flashed through the frame of the Dushka. Putting the top back on, I threw the bottle back. Rapidly, I ripped out the interior light and got out. The door-open alarm sounded, so I shut it behind me. To the right, in the very far distance, were sets of vehicle headlights. I estimated they were about six to eight kilometres away. The headlights' beams weaved around. I counted four vehicles at best.

I took a few steps to the front of the Toyota to work out where our track went. At the maximum point of my peripheral sight, the track widened, proceeding into the wadi, giving an entry point. I thought about hiding in the wadi, but without knowing if the ground was compact, I didn't want to chance getting bogged down. And, more importantly, if we were compromised, I hadn't found an exit point. What I did know was that the vehicle lights seemed to be following the path I'd driven. With a burning desire to get away, I got back in and shook Rabbit, who was asleep. He was probably in a world of multi-coloured psychedelic shapes and magic mushrooms. He didn't respond, so I punched him in the face, which shocked him awake.

'What the fuck?' he replied groggily.

Before he had the chance to drift off, I picked up the bottle and splashed his face.

'OK, OK,' he spluttered.

'Listen, you twat. You've compromised us and now we're being hunted.

I need you to get back in the real world and focus. You hear me? Get your shit together before I slap you silly.'

It was harsh, but I was still pissed with him. He probably didn't know the tobacco was weed. He hadn't really compromised us, but I wanted him to realise the potential shit we were in.

'I'm really sorry, Johnny,' he said. 'I just started to enjoy the moment, and then the tobacco seemed to relieve my worries. Why have we been compromised?'

Feeling a little guilty, I relaxed my tone, 'I've spotted headlights behind us, about four vehicles approximately six kilometres away. Maybe even closer now.'

The full impact of this was on his face as he looked through the rear glass. 'Where? I can't see them. Are you sure?'

'I need you to update me on those headlamps. I want their approximate distance, how many, and if they're closing in.'

I set off, grappling with the track against the edges of the wadi.

I had slowed down to a crawl in second gear. We had been driving for quite a distance and Rabbit had not updated me for at least half an hour. The shadow of the mountain made it impossible to see where the tracks led. I brought us to a slow stop.

'What's the latest?' I asked.

'I lost sight of the lights about twenty minutes ago. I reckon they've given up, or have headed in another direction.'

'I doubt if they've given up. They're a tenacious bunch of fanatical loonies. It's no good, I must switch on the headlights. If not, we either stop for the night here and they find us, or continue on black light and possibly drive over the edge of the wadi.'

'Why don't you use the fog lamps rather than the headlamps?'

Brilliant thinking, I thought, but without giving him credit, I replied, 'That was my next suggestion.'

As I held the light stalk, my soldiering screamed inside not to turn the fog lamps on, but I eventually I did. Out here in the complete blackness it felt as if someone had just turned on a football stadium's lights. My grip tightened on the steering wheel and my shoulders tensed.

'Keep watching the rear. I feel we're sticking out like a spare rib at a vegetarian party,' I said.

The drive became much easier, being able to view a good five metres in front. We were making good progress; however, after three hours I was seriously feeling the strains.

'Just spotted them,' he said, reeling me back in. 'They're bloody close, about a hundred metres behind. Their lights just appeared out of the dark. I reckon they've been driving without their headlamps on, mate.'

I was annoyed with myself for not thinking of this earlier when we had lost sight of them.

'They're getting closer, Johnny,' Rabbit said panicking.

I floored the Toyota, but had to let off as I fought to stay on the track. My brain was digesting all the data of the terrain, the pace, and all I had learnt in my advanced driving course. I was now in the zone; noise and memory weren't important. I was purely focused on moving at high speed in our precarious position. Survival was paramount.

My concentration was detonated by a wave of firing from a Dushka from behind. In my rear-view mirror the headlamps beams waved. Then another small flame burst out from the Dushka, followed by its fearful sound. We took a hit on the Toyota's rear, sending us momentarily into a fish-tail slide. The sound and force were like someone taking a wrecking ball to our vehicle. I regained control. Out of the corner of my eye I saw Rabbit ducking low behind his seat.

'I need you to keep eyes on, not hide. That seat won't protect you if we get hit again,' I shouted—although, I wanted to duck as well.

As the track rounded a bend, my heart almost stopped for a second. It looked like it had ended with a sheer drop. My foot slightly lifted off the accelerator ready to hit the brake pedal, but it was too late. We'd became airborne for a split-second before the tyres gripped the slope. We snaked down towards the wadi. It was littered with stones and rocks, which at this speed made it even more treacherous. We weren't quite level with the bottom of the wadi. I slammed the anchors on.

'What the fuck are…?'

'Shut it,' I interrupted. 'Get out and man the Dushka. As soon as you see the first fucker come over the crest, let rip. It's ready to go. Just hold the grips and squeeze the trigger, letting off short bursts. Go, go.'

We both jumped out, leaving the engine running. Leaning over the Toyota's side, I picked up the RPG as Rabbit sprinted to the Dushka. I scrambled down the side of the bank, sending dust and shingle into the air. I wanted a position for a side strike. I had to be a minimum of twelve metres away for the RPG to take effect. I ran across the bed to the other side. As I reached it, the deceiving crust on top gave way and I sank in, totally covering my boot. With my other foot still on the bank, I struggled to get out.

With all my strength, I pulled free, falling back on the slope. Picking up the RPG, our Dushka fired a burst of fire. I turned sharply to see a Toyota land over the crest, swerving out of control. Almost immediately Rabbit roared into life with further bursts. The lights of the Dushka lit up his silhouette. He had taken his arm out of the sling and was holding both handles. He must have been in excruciating pain, but hopefully his adrenalin was suppressing it. The Toyota hit the mountain slope and turned broadside on. In those seconds, rounds penetrate the Toyota, smashing chunks of bodywork into the air. More deadly bursts followed, obliterating and rocking the Toyota. Smoke and steam poured out from the engine block and the tyres burst, adding to the chaos. The two men in the front were chewed up in no time. As the second Toyota sped over the top of the crest, the gunner of the first vehicle popped his head up and started to swing his Dushka round towards Rabbit, who was still firing. I put the RPG on my shoulder and took aim at the rear side of the first Toyota. I was about forty metres away. Just as I squeezed the trigger, the second Toyota careered into the broadside stationary Toyota and the gunner went flying backwards.

*Whoooosh*...

I lowered the RPG, its trail of destruction rocketed off towards its target. As the warhead travelled at one hundred and fifteen metres per second, there was nothing the rest of the occupants in the vehicles could do. The warhead penetrated the rear body and then ignited, sending out a huge fireball explosion, ripping through the first Toyota and shredded the second one, including everyone in it. The fireball rose into the air, lighting up the carnage and wadi below. I didn't take much notice of the voice '*Threats neutralised*', as I quickly ran back and scampered up the bank. Rabbit started to fire at another Toyota's headlights that had halted on the crest, but it quickly reversed out of sight. No time to slap each other on the back. I put the RPG in the back and caught sight of the spent shells around his feet and outside our Toyota. Jumping in the motor, I quickly placed my seatbelt on.

'Hold on tight,' I shouted.

Adrenalin pumping, I rammed it into gear and raced off. In the rear-view mirror, between the moving silhouette of Rabbit hanging on for dear life, another huge flame exploded from the burning mass of destruction. The track bottomed out, level with the wadi. My steering became light as we slid and swerved through the mud. I countered every slide, turning the wheel opposite and adjusting with bursts of the accelerator, but we were losing speed. Ahead lay an option to go left further into the wadi bed, or right up the track slope. I nosed the Toyota to the right, almost going broadside, but managed to get us under control as we climbed the track. A bumpy, uneven track replaced the slippery mud surface. I was being slightly lifted out of my seat. As we came over the crest, the track took a sharp left turn, so I took evasive action and swung us left. A crashing noise alerted me, like boxes falling over in a cupboard. Had Rabbit fallen over?

I glanced in the mirror, but couldn't see him. As I looked forward, the Toyota tilted to the side. My heart sank. In that glancing look I had taken my eyes off the track and we had started to roll over the edge. I turned the wheel and accelerated, trying to compensate, but it was too late. The angle became too steep; we were going over. Automatically, I stamped my foot on the brake pedal. As the Toyota went over in slow motion, I took my hands off the wheel as it could snatch round and break my bones. I put my forearms around my head to protect myself, becoming disorientated as the Toyota rolled over and over down the bank. The engine screamed, the body creaked, and objects flew around me, but I couldn't focus on any point. My body was jostled in all directions. I slammed into the door, making me gasp. As the insane roll came to a halt, I tried to regain my composure. The engine was still screaming as my foot had slid off the brake pedal and was now wedged between it and the accelerator. I yanked my foot out and the engine reduced into an idle purr. The side of my face was through the door's open window and flat on the bed of the wadi. The only light in the pitch blackness came from the dashboard illuminated lights.

Panic set in as a wet surge come up from the crusty surface, being substituted for a thick slimy rancid mud as the weight of the Toyota sank. I lifted my head and neck out of the gluey mud as it started to enter my mouth and nose. Trying to find my seatbelt release buckle, I started to take in the fluid that lay on top of the mud. I spat out as much as I could. I had to breathe through my nose as my mouth was now completely submerged. My neck strained to its maximum and I panted for air. The Toyota eventually stopped sinking, so I continued to frantically reach back for the buckle. My eyes were bursting out of their sockets with fear. Every time I moved or relaxed, my nose moved below the few survival millimetres under the stagnant water.

I tried to slow my heart and breathing as I blew the water from my nose. Lifting my hand up, trying to grab the seat opposite, I managed to hold on to the seat's arm rest and heave myself up an inch. The engine stopped. Smoke and fumes filled the air as I took in a few gasps. Abruptly, the arm rest came down and I was dumped back into the mud, but this time I was completely submerged. Holding my breath, I desperately waved my arm out to grab something. I shook my head and tried to lift it up, but the mud seemed to pull me back. A massive dread came over me. Was this it? Drowning in a wadi of shit? I'd come so far; I didn't want to give all that up. I struggled further, lashing my legs to try to get a foothold, but nothing was working. My heart was beating in my ears, like lying in a bath underwater. Images of my family and wife filtered in, calming me. I became weak, and the pressure of holding my breath became too severe. I tasted the muddy water leaking into my mouth as I fought to keep it shut. I knew in a few seconds I would give in to the overwhelming pressure and take a gasp of the mud and water.

I'd forgotten about my thrashing hand, which had now stopped and just stood still like a flagpole. I was disturbed from the last moments before death as something squeezed my hand and then pull my arm. My face came out of the mud and I took a huge breath, consuming some of the grime. I started to choke, but then something forced my mouth open. A rancid sticky mess shot out, clearing my airwaves. My shirt tightened around my neck and I was heaved up further. The gooey shit was cleared from my ears and eyes.

'Breathe, you bastard, breathe. Don't you fucking die on me now, Johnny.'

In the murky darkness, Rabbit had hold of me.

# CHAPTER THIRTEEN

A small fire had broken out under the bonnet; more hot fumes filled the car. Rabbit unclipped my belt and screamed at me to get out. His urgency spurred me on to wriggle free and, with his help, I climbed up the seats and out into freedom. The heat of the fire from the engine compartment was intense. We both jumped off and sank to our shins in the mud.

'Hang onto the car and pull yourself to the bank,' he instructed.

As he led the way, hanging on with one arm and pulling his feet out of the mud, I followed him, trying to use his steps. Grabbing the underside of the Toyota, I put my hand on something hot and it fizzed.

'Fuck,' I said.

I'd hung onto the exhaust. Trying to ignore the burn, I continued to grab and move. Rabbit held out his hand and, as our hands locked, he pulled me towards him. We both fell onto the bank with me on top of him. Breathing erratically, we locked our stare. He was traumatised, but elated at the same time by my near death; I must have looked the same. Huddled on top of him, our faces were inches apart.

'Looks like we've both come out the closet this time, mate,' he said, and laughed. 'Let's get away before we're toasted.'

The fire had by now taken a good hold of the front of the vehicle, the heat warming my wet clothes. Whizzing noises zipped over our heads, followed by the sound of a murderous Dushka: 'clachang, clachang, clachang.' We hugged into the sandy bank as the debris off the ridge exploded over us. The next rounds hit our Toyota, rocking it with every strike and sending shards over us.

'Move, move,' I shouted.

Racing to my feet, I followed the bank towards the end of the wadi. Rabbit didn't need telling, he was in hot pursuit. We were under the cover of the bank and darkness, which gave us a lifeline as more rounds thundered into our Toyota. We had covered about a hundred metres when a massive explosion erupted. We dived for cover. Turning my upper torso, a bright flash lit up our burning wreckage, which had flown and landed on its roof. The whole area lit up and then faded to a glow. Another explosion split the Toyota in half, blowing out the sides, the noise echoing for miles. That must have been the other RPG warhead. We didn't hang around to watch any more of the display.

When we reached the ridgeline in the far distance, I turned back to see the headlights of another vehicle. It had driven over the crest and had stopped short of the still-burning wreckage of the two Toyotas. I estimated they were one hundred and fifty metres away. The Dushka gunner continued to fire, hosing the area around our burning wreckage for good measure. After he had finished, a deathly silence fell, but then faint jubilant celebrations shouted. Another set of headlights drew up to the crest of the track. More jeering and small arms fire rang into the black night, echoing off the mountain slopes. As their track was blocked, this gave us time to move out. I didn't have to give any orders, both knowing this was our opportunity.

Under the cover of the wadi we moved silently and quickly. After four hundred metres or so I was out of breath and had to stop. Laying with my back against the cold sandy bank, I was surprised to see Rabbit doing the same; he had easily kept up with my pace.

'You OK, mate? You look like shit, literally,' he said.

I looked down: I was covered in black, stinking slime and the sand had started to stick to that.

'Thanks, Roy, thanks for back there, I owe you...'

'You owe me twice now, mate,' he cut me short. 'Reckon that should keep me in fags for the rest of my life.'

After all the crazy shit we had been through, we burst into laughter. I wondered how much of this was nerves. I rested my head back on the ground.

'What the fuck happened back there?' he asked.

'After the turn at the top of the crest, I checked to see why you had jumped and made a run for it. Then the edge gave way,' I replied, in jest, feeling slightly embarrassed and waiting for him to bite.

'Funny, mate. Not. After *your* erratic driving, I was *thrown* from the back. Once I stopped bouncing, I looked up to see the underside of the Toyota disappear down the bank. Ignoring my arm's excruciating pain that was out of its sling, I scaled down after you. Worse, smoke began to pour from the engine. Then I took a path through the gruelling mud. Climbing the side of the Toyota was murder. As I looked over through the door, I saw your head under the water with your arm stretched out. I feared the worse, Johnny. I leant through up to my waist and took a hold of your arm. It took sheer determination to drag you out. You're a fat bastard.'

I laughed at this, but really, I knew his courage and determination had saved me from the grip of death.

'Well, like I said, I owe...'

Before I could finish, Rabbit got up and pulled me to my feet. He then did something unexpected: he proceeded to impersonate me.

'Right, first we are going to head that way.' He pointed forward in a silly manner. 'Second, we are going to run without stopping all the way home.' He did a silly jog on the spot. 'Thirdly, no eating or drinking, but you *can* smoke the funny tobacco. Lastly, let's goooo, fuck-wit.' And he did a silly run ahead along the bank.

I followed him with tears in my eyes, not just from the laughing, but the realisation that Rabbit was turning out to be a good, solid friend. How wrong I had been.

Eventually, I had taken the lead. After a few rests we came to the end of the wadi. I looked back: all but a tiny glow sat amongst complete darkness. The moon was in the last stages of going down. I thought of Rabbit's piss-take earlier, so I decided to change the start of my next sentence and not point.

'OK, this is the plan. Let's find a decent LUP as high up in the slopes as we can. This way they won't be able to bring their vehicles up. Also, it will give us good eyes on them. I reckon we have only an hour of darkness left.'

I climbed up the bank without waiting for any further piss-taking from him.

As we tabbed on, every now and then I made sure he was close behind me. In front, apart from the mountain, was a featureless plain. I'd counted two thousand five hundred seconds and then stopped for a well-earned rest. Hunched over with my hands on my knees, I was exhausted. Rabbit followed up in a worse state.

'That's it for me mate... no more... I need to rest,' he rasped.

I couldn't have agreed more. 'Right, let's grab five, then one more climb up the mountain slope to find an LUP.'

'For fuck's sake, mate, don't you guys ever stop?'

'Nope, we're just a bunch of nancy boys, remember?' I said, rather smug.

'Point taken. Can't wait to go back to being a GBD. Tell you what, my arm is fucking hurting. Got any more of those tablets?'

'Sorry, dude, we've had the last of them.'

My teeth and gums still had the sticky mud residue around them. I needed a drink to wash it out, but then a sudden shock hit me. In the blind rush to get away from the burning Toyota and the incoming rounds, I had left the water, food, and my AK47.

'Roy, did you pick up my satchel, or even the water?' Before he could answer, I carried on fretting about it, 'What about my weapon? Do you have your pistol?'

Looking worried that he had let me down, he replied, 'I'm sorry, but I didn't have time to get any of it. You were more important. I think I lost my pistol as I fell out the car.'

'Oh fuck,' I said.

'Does this mean we've got jack shit? No food, water, or medical supplies?'

'And no fucking weapons!' I snapped. 'Why did you not think to grab them?'

'Because I thought the engine fire was going to take a serious hold and blow us to kingdom come.'

'Jeez, we are right in the shit now,' I said, almost blaming him, but it wasn't his fault; it was all down to me.

Not feeling good about the situation, I grumpily moved up the mountain slope. Rabbit kept his distance to about ten metres behind. Maybe he wanted to let me stew. The slope was covered by loose rocks and gravel with larger scattered boulders. Trees and bushes hampered the climb further. After a treacherous ascent in cold conditions, we had made it almost to the top where a sheer face of rock ascended into the stars. I jumped and grabbed the rock ledge that hung over us. Heaving myself up with the last of my energy, I swung my legs over. Sprawled out and face down, I rested and took stock of my position, completely knackered. I had to unclip the smoke canister and move it round to beside me. The rock slab ledge jutted out from a hollow in the rock face. The hollow was a small cave in which two men could easily shelter. The ledge I lay on was about three metres in length and two metres in depth. Above this lifeline cave, the wet and sheer precipice meant we couldn't go any further.

I sat up, admiring the view as the sun broke. I caught sight of Rabbit's one-handed fingers grabbing the edge and then disappearing. Again, they tried and failed. I found this highly amusing. He began cursing. I slid over the side and jumped down.

Still laughing, I said, 'Wanna hand, dude?'

'Piss off.'

He put his foot in my cupped hands and I lifted him as hard as I could, but he grappled with his one arm.

'For fuck's sake, hurry up,' I said.

'Well bloody lift me higher, for God's sake.'

I did, but this was sapping the last of my energy. He put his feet on my shoulders and pushed himself over the ledge. Again, I had to find the strength to pull myself up and over the ledge. We took refuge in the small cave. I had begun to shiver; my clothes were still wet and I really did look and smell terrible. We huddled together for warmth. Annoyingly, I had to endure Rabbit's incessant snoring. I was dog-tired, but I couldn't sleep. My body kept going into spasms of shivering just as I started to drift.

After a few hours I felt like shit; also, I was sick of his snoring. The sun's golden rays had started to creep along our ledge. I moved him off me and crawled out of the shadows into those rays. Straight away my shivering body warmed. I lay completely flat on my front, as if basking on holiday; steam rose off my shirt sleeves. A chilly breeze whisked over the top of the ledge, gently blowing the steam. As my body heated, I stopped shivering, but this was replaced by huge hunger pains. My belly rumbled and gurgled; I felt sick with hunger. I realised I needed to take a shit, and quick. All SF are supposed to bag their shit and carry it with us when on a mission. We weren't allowed to bury it, as local dogs and bloody goats could sniff it out. We normally squatted over cling film and bagged it up. There was always the joker in a team who would stuff it in someone else's Bergen.

I tried to fend off the motions, but it became quite an urgent matter. Holding on desperately, I eased myself off the ledge. Walking in an uncomfortable fashion, I shifted to the edge of a bush, where flustered, I whipped down my trousers and shorts and ungracefully let it out. I had terrible diarrhoea, black in colour, smelling absolutely rank. Not really the type you would want to wrap in cling film, but a great laugh to a prankster. Hopefully, I was not coming down with diarrhoea and vomiting, but I'd been in some dire situations without proper hygiene.

Perhaps it was the after-effects of an unbalanced diet and the rich goat meat. The rash on my inner thighs had now spread further and my bollocks were itching. Cleaning myself up the best I could, I hitched up onto the ledge. Rabbit was still curled up asleep. Back into a prone position in the sun, I searched the landscape from where we had travelled earlier. I could just see the wadi we'd exited, including the track above it. I followed the track and wadi as far back as I could, but they both veered left, following the contour of the mountain.

This LUP wasn't as good as I'd first thought. Even if we stayed in the shadow of the cave, remaining perfectly still, we could easily be spotted from the adjoining slopes. It was a risky position. Looking at the mountain slope above the track, I spotted a small path in the distance. We were easily in sight, even inside our cave. We had no water, food, and proper insulation if the weather worsened. Against SOP, we had to move in daylight and find a better LUP, and more importantly, water, food, and weapons.

I slid across to Rabbit and shook him slowly, he felt cold to the touch. As he stretched and yawned, he started coughing and clearing his throat, probably due to the lack of cigarettes. As he woke up properly, I explained my next plan and the reasons for it.

'Yeah, that was my plan too. Reckon you're learning from the old master at last,' he said cheerfully, and winked at me.

'Good. Then you jump down first and head towards the bush at the base of the ledge and take cover. I'll follow the master.'

'Really? You sure you want me to lead and navigate?' he replied, with enthusiasm.

'Sure. You've showed real initiative recently. Now get down and find that cover and let me know when it's safe to follow, before I change my mind.'

I helped him over the edge and waited like a little kid, wanting my prank to succeed.

'Oh for God's sake, what the fuck is that?' he seethed. 'I've just trodden in some fucking animal shit. That's outrageous. Oh my good God, it stinks.'

I tried to keep my fits of laughter in as I got down off the ledge, but it was made even harder watching him wipe his boots on the ground.

Trying to stay serious, I said, 'Reckon that's from a big Afghan black mountain bear. He must have come close last night.' I let out a fit of childish giggles.

'It's not fucking funny, Johnny. We haven't even any weapons to fight off this black bear.' He looked around, alarmed.

'Well, I've got my knife, but I'm sure the *master* could use his bare hands,' I said, my sides hurting from laughing.

'Piss off, Johnny, this is serious shit,' he said, frustrated.

This set me off even more.

'Keep it down. It could be close,' he said.

He stood there looking at me in disbelief, and then started looking around for this supposed bear. When I regained my composure, I pulled my knife out and handed it to him.

'Here, you lead the way.'

'Sod off, you lead the way.'

I set off with him sticking close behind, the aroma stuck with him. At least he was looking alert, even if for the wrong reasons. We tried to stay hidden using the natural landscape we traversed. Many boulders, trees and bushes were at our disposal. On occasions we had no cover, which made me feel very vulnerable. I was constantly searching all around for any movement or life, especially from behind. I wondered if the remaining Elkhaba had cleared the track blockage and had now descended on our burnt-out Toyota. It wouldn't take long to spot our trails leading away. Once they found them, the tracks would lead them to the bottom of the mountain. It wouldn't take a genius to guess where the LUP was. We hadn't had time to cover our tracks last night, so this made my decision this morning to move in daylight the right choice.

After travelling about five hundred metres, we came to the edge of the mountain slopes where they went back on themselves. This left a vast open landscape of desert. We were still up high on the slopes.

'Right, let's take a five-minute rest over there by the group of trees and rocks,' I said.

We reached what seemed to be a little oasis and sat in partial shade, away from the merciless sun. There were dried-out droppings scattered, which might indicate a water supply for goats. My stomach cramps had worsened and I was feeling dehydrated.

'How you feeling, dude? Are you hungry and thirsty?' I said, asking the plain obvious.

'Yeah, both mate, and my arm is becoming unbearable.'

'Jeez, let me look at that.'

Lifting his sling, his arm had ballooned to an alarming size and looked fit to burst. I gently put my hand on it; he flinched.

'Shhiiit,' he hissed.

'Sorry.' I undid his sling. 'Raise it above your head whilst we wait. I'll see if I can find some water.'

I lifted a few of the large rocks and found a few tiny, murky pools of water underneath. Cupping my hands, I managed to get a small amount of the cool liquid. I poured some on his warm arm and then went back for more. I achieved this several times. Then I put some on my face and head to cool me down. Lastly, I took another handful carefully over to Rabbit.

'Here, drink this.'

'What about washing your hands first?'

'Fuck off, just drink it,' I retorted.

As I scavenged for the last few drops for myself, I was alerted to the sound of a vehicle.

'Keep low and still,' I whispered.

Very slowly, I lifted my head over the large rock in front. I'd momentarily lost the sound, but then I heard it again. I turned my head and ears in its direction.

I spotted a motorbike being ridden along the track. A small cloud of dust followed the back wheel. As the motorbike got nearer it wobbled as it hit the bumps in the track. Riding the motorbike was a bearded man, dressed in khaki shirt and trousers, and also a *Pakol*. In front of him sat a small child, probably no more than four years old. Behind the adult, hanging on for dear life, were two more children, of about eight in age. They passed below and then continued to ride off up the track. At times I lost sight of them behind trees and the uneven landscape. Just on the limit of my eyesight, a small cloud of dust plumed behind the motorbike. Then it disappeared behind a group of trees.

I whispered to Rabbit, telling him what I'd just witnessed. My plan was to take the same route towards those trees as I reckoned there would be a village where we could get provisions. We were hidden here, but I knew the hunter force would be scouring the slopes for us. We had no chance if they had dogs, we had no chance without any weapons. I guessed Rabbit didn't have the energy to run for his life, and to be honest, I don't think I did. I also knew I couldn't leave him alone. The last thing we wanted was to get caught. We both knew this was our last throw of the dice. We set off cautiously down the slope to the track. I'd never felt so vulnerable.

# CHAPTER FOURTEEN

With the sun frying us on our every step, it became apparent this was beyond even my expectations. Bloody typical, this was certainly the hottest day so far, I thought, looking up at the sun. It must have been over forty degrees. We both stopped on many occasions for a rest, longing for water. The terrain gave us a decent amount of cover through wadis and trees, but the heat was unbearable. Rabbit was sunburnt and in a great deal of pain with his arm. We had only been moving for approximately thirty minutes when he called a halt. He slumped to the base of a tree, irritably pulling at his wet shirt.

'I need a rest again, mate. I've got to get out of this fucking sun and heat.'

'Don't mind if I join you,' I said, and wilted next to him. 'Lift your arm up like I said.' My speech seemed slower.

'Oh, yeah, forgot. Think the sun is cooking my brain. Don't want to sound negative, but how long before we hit that village? I can't go on much longer.'

'Well, your choices are, turn back and ask the pursuing Elkhaba hunters for a drink of water. Lie down here and die here. Or, dig deep and find the strength to carry on.'

Shrugging his shoulders, he sluggishly replied, 'Suppose I'll turn back and ask for a drink. I'd probably get more sympathy.'

'Wait here while I go forward and look.'

I left him in the shade and squatted through the remaining bushes and trees at a right angle to his position. I found the edges of a track; well, not so much of a track, but vehicle tyre marks were evident. Staying out of sight as best I could, I lifted my head to look along the trail in the direction of the motorbike. Another kilometre in the distance was an entrance to a compound with high walls around it. Just a short way in front, on the other side of the track, was a small group of buildings.

I made my way back to Rabbit. He was holding his arm up and looked to be in agonising pain.

'Listen, Roy, I know you're in a bad way. There's only another few hundred metres or so to the village.' I had to lie to him to keep him motivated.

'Great.'

'Right, grab your shit together. We need to make that village.'

'I haven't got any gear, mate,' he replied, baffled.

'I meant your shit state.'

I helped him up, his body shook.

The next five hundred metres was gruelling, punishing us both to our limits. Climbing down into a narrow ditch first, I helped Rabbit down. We sat down together, looking like we had just got out of a swimming pool, totally dressed. I took stock of our position again: we were within three hundred to four hundred metres.

'Let's take five,' I said, exhausted.

'How much further?' Rabbit asked, sounding a bit delirious.

'Couple of hundred metres, I reckon. Think we should hit the buildings on the other side of the track first, but this means crossing the track in the open.'

'Think you underestimated how far the village was,' he mumbled.

I threw him a big grin. 'But you made it, right?'

'Wanker,' he said, with his eyes now shut.

I laughed. 'Let's look at your neck burn, and then you can check yourself over. Give us time to rest.'

'No point. Not as if we have any clean water and medical supplies, is it? Some dumb arse fuck left them in the car. Needed to save his own arse, bloody selfish git.' Rabbit threw me a stupid grin.

'Point taken,' I said.

'What happened to that chewing gum, mate?'

I had forgotten about it, so I pulled it out of my pocket. The packet came out with a handful of dried mud. I brushed most of it off and handed it to him. He hardly had the energy to unwrap it. The gum pieces inside had melted together and had turned black. I was amazed to see him wipe them and put a large amount in his mouth.

'Want some?' he garbled; the juices ran down his chin.

'Err, no thanks.'

I checked over my cuts and bruises. The rash between my legs was driving me mad. The bandage around my leg was soaked red and it didn't smell too good either. My fingers had started to swell around the lacerations, making it painful to bend them. The part of my face not covered by my beard was tight from sunburn. I had sand and dirt everywhere. My eyes and mouth were bone dry, but at least I was in better shape than Rabbit; he looked in a sorrowful state.

Again, I helped him up and we moved slowly off in the direction of the small group of buildings. The open fields got greener. The small irrigated ditches around them were damp under foot. I took a lengthy look at the harvested crop in one field. A few stems were still protruding out of the sun-baked earth and the wrinkled warty leaves were dying in the sun and heat.

'Wait here a minute,' I said.

As he lay in the shade, I made my way quickly to the edge of the cropped field and pulled at a few of the stems and leaves, making a hasty retreat.

'What you got there, Titchmarsh?' he croaked.

'I think it's chukri, like a kind of rhubarb.'

Peeling back the outer dried skin in the stem revealed a softer inside, though it looked passed its best. I took a bite and munched away. Rabbit watched with bated breath.

'Any good?' he asked.

I threw him a few stalks and told him it was better than nothing. He started to peel back the skin.

I left him in the shade while I moved on the edge of the track. Laying down, I scanned the surrounding areas, and then watched the buildings for any sign of life. I would normally like to watch for a day or so, to monitor and record any movements. However, time was against us. I snuck back to Rabbit, who was still eating.

'Wait here. I need to take a quick look around the buildings. If it goes noisy, find a good hiding place on the edge of the other village. Wait till night and search the village for water and food, OK?'

'Then what?' he croaked.

'Find a way out of here.'

'You're making out as if you're not coming back.'

I didn't reply. I knew it was harsh, but the fact was I might not be returning, if I was compromised.

After checking both ways up the track, and again around the buildings, I summoned the energy to dart across and hide behind two large, empty, rusted barrels at the base of a small building. Inside the barrels were used plastic bottles, food cartons, and general rubbish. I quietly moved up to the window, listening first for any signs of life. A thought entered my head: maybe I'd been seen and a weapon was waiting for me to pop my head up over the aperture. The heat was messing my mind. I quashed this negative thought and pulled my knife out. Peering into the room and checking rapidly, there was a bed and a chair. Standing up, I took a better look, but these were the only two objects.

I moved around to the next building. Timber protruded from the top of the walls; these were the rafters holding the roof up. The structure was crudely made. Before I looked inside, I noticed in the distance, at the edge of a rutted field, small piles of earth. Next to the earth mounds were the holes, surrounded by the soil. They were too small for graves and the dirt had gone solid. I guessed they had been dug a while ago, possibly to hide weapons. I went through the same procedure of checking inside. Again, there was the same furniture, only this time there was a table with a candle and some pliers. Just before I moved onto the last building, something caught my eye on the floor under the table. The object was a red strand of cable, about two inches long. I stared at this, slightly unnerved. I asked myself why this piece of red cable was there. Then the realisation hit me: could this be a small improvised explosive device set-up?

The last building had shutters on the windows. It was unlike the rest. The sides were made up of traditional stone and mortar. I scuttled across to it and checked the only door, but it was bolted and padlocked firmly. To me, the building looked recently finished. Desperate to find food or water, or even weapons, I thought about kicking the door in. But maybe it was booby-trapped, and to be honest I didn't think I had the strength. Even climbing onto the roof didn't seem an option. Just behind this secure building was what seemed to be a well of water with a metre-high brick wall around it. Bingo. Checking the coast was clear, I quickly moved to the well. The wooden frame to haul up the bucket looked very fragile. I lifted the wood slats off and peeked over the edge. The rising stench made me pull back straight away. It smelt strongly of chemicals. Holding my breath, I tried again to see the bottom, but it looked endless. I picked up a small stone to throw over it, when unexpectedly, I heard an approaching motorbike.

I had nowhere to go. I lay down and curved my body around the brick wall, my heart started to beat faster. With any luck, it would be another family driving to the village. The motorbike pulled in just behind the first building and its engine switched off. Bollocks. Could this be the end of my nine lives? I had one very close eye on the building. Two men walked into sight and my heart sank as one of them was carrying an AK47. They were both in their twenties and didn't look dishevelled. I lifted slightly up onto my hands, ready to explode out of my silly hiding place if necessary. I listened to them talking; they were coming closer. The fear of getting caught on my own gripped me, almost forcing me to freeze. I didn't have to tell myself the trouble I was in if caught, and the dilemma Rabbit would be in out there on his own. The decision was made for me: I would do whatever it took not to be captured and not let Rabbit down.

The padlock was being unlocked and then the large wooden door creaked open. I relaxed slightly, knowing this could be my break. I got up onto my hands and knees. My calf muscle burned again as they began talking inside the building. I contemplated running up to the door, slamming it, and putting the padlock through the latch. But what if the padlock was inside the building? Would they shoot through the door? Maybe I should just make a run for it? Could I take on both men, unarmed? OK, decide, Johnny.

One of the men, still talking, started making his way over to my position. His voice seemed relaxed, so I knew he hadn't seen me. Plan B. What was plan B? As his footsteps stopped at the base of the well, he shouted something back in the direction of the way he had come. Shit; I hadn't put the cover back on the well. Then the other bloke started yelling. I was even more shocked to hear the most unexpected thing: Rabbit's voice bawling. What the fuck was he doing? That was my cue, the distraction I needed. I had to take out the man on the other side of the well before he made his way back. The nearest man shouted again. I sprang to my feet, but he had already started to return the building. I ran at him, but he turned around, confused and startled. I didn't stop my charge and, just as I got alongside him, I stuck my right arm out across his chest, knocking him clean onto his back.

It had taken the wind out of him. Taking a step back, I put my hand across his mouth and then punched him as hard as I could on his cheekbone. He shook his head and tried to release my hand, trying to scream under the pressure of it. I hit him again, but he didn't stop. Jesus. He tried to bite my hand, so I hit him another two times. His eyes flickered and then his body went limp. His friend was screaming at Rabbit. Surprisingly, Rabbit was still shouting back. What the hell was he playing at? Had the sun really fried Rabbit's brain?

I made a quiet quick run to the corner of the building. The armed man indeed had his AK47 pointed at Rabbit, who stood swaying a few strides in front of him with his hands up. The fighting male was raising his voice and gesticulating with his weapon, but Rabbit still refused to stop shouting back. The situation was at a critical point. I knew I only had seconds to react before he was slotted. The enemy's finger moved onto the trigger. I sprinted over to him and grabbed his black turban and weapon, pulling these backwards and down. In his panic, he fired his weapon, letting off three rounds. The noise deafened my right ear as I followed him to the ground. As he hit the deck I quickly rolled him onto his front and landed my fist in the back of his neck. Pulling it back, I hit him in his rib cage. I kept the pressure on his turban, forcing his face into the dust. After a few strikes, his body went limp; I was knackered. I leant over and grabbed his weapon and threw it aside. I rolled him over and raised my fist, but there was no reaction. However, I didn't trust any of these fuckers not to play dead.

'Rabbit, grab his weapon and watch over him.'

With no reply, I looked up at Rabbit who was lying on his side. I went cold.

'Roy. Oh fuck, no.'

Had he taken a fatal round? I picked up the AK47 and, pointing at the lifeless enemy on the ground, backed up towards Rabbit, still motionless. Kneeling, I frantically felt for a pulse whilst keeping an eye on both assailants. I couldn't feel a beat as he was in an awkward position. Dreading rolling him over, expecting to find half his face gone like with Planet, my guts churned. Eventually, I did.

'About fucking time you'd taken him out,' Rabbit blurted. 'You're slacking, mate.'

'You're OK?' I said, shocked.

'Yep, shit shot like you, mate.' He smiled.

'You were fucking playing. Unbelievable,' I shouted.

Quickly standing up, I kicked dirt over him. I was angry, but elated.

'I should kick your arse all the way home. I can't believe you, Roy.'

Through his laughter, he said, 'So my distraction worked then? Great plan, hey?'

Still incensed, I replied, 'You've been in the sun too fucking long. What would have happened if I'd not got to the first bloke in time?'

'I knew you would have beaten both. You're Special Forces, SBS. That's why I'm a great forward planner.'

'Idiot,' I muttered.

Letting him wobbled to his feet on his own, I checked the weapons magazine—empty.

'You're lucky he only had three rounds left,' I said angrily.

'Why's that?'

'Because I could fucking shoot you myself.'

'What's eating...'

'Right, we'll fucking talk about this later,' I interrupted. 'For now, let's dispose of these two and get back on track before we have any other unwanted guests.'

With my adrenalin still surging, I dragged the nearest body up to the well and threw him in over the edge. As I turned, Rabbit was searching the first man on the floor.

'Typical, no fags,' he said.

'Roy, give me a hand to drag him over.'

We dragged the man to the same fate of his comrade and threw the weapon in. I returned the wooden slats on the well. Looking back in the direction of the motorbike, I spotted a tiny flash high up in the mountains. I stared through the sweat running into my eyes until I had to wipe it away. There it was again, and then there was another glint further along. The sun was causing a reflection off something moving. This was roughly where we had made our LUP on the overhanging ledge. I knew then the hunters had found it, my heartbeat increased with my alerted state.

'Right, we gotta get moving, *now*.'

Rabbit walked back from the motorbike and said, 'Guess who forgot to check the rag-heads for the keys?' He nodded at me, smugly.

'Push the motorbike in the building and lock the door.'

I stared back at the flashes, and Rabbit looked in the same direction.

'What is it? What have you seen?'

'Now, Roy. We've got to go now.'

Whilst he locked the motorbike away, I tried to clear any signs that we had been here. I also checked the area in both directions of the track in case we had alerted anyone with the gun shots. There was nothing of any use in the building, so he snapped the lock shut. I told him to follow me as I made a quick dash across the track.

We picked up speed as we ventured back into the scattered trees and bushes, Rabbit a few metres behind. I headed towards the direction of the village, trying to stay as silent as possible and not disturb too may bushes and trees, but I had to keep the good pace going; the net was closing in on us.

I stumbled across a shallow ditch, surrounded by a clump of spiky-branched trees. Rabbit joined me about thirty seconds later, getting snagged on the spikes. He started cursing under his breath and tried to swallow what saliva he had, like me. Our breathing was rasping and we were wet through with sweat again. Our eyes met, but we were too knackered to say anything. The fight back there really had taken it out of me and I started to shake. As we took a little rest and shade in a clump of trees, goats bleated in the distance. We had to be close to the village.

'I'm not sure if that was a bloody daft or lunatic thing to do back there,' I said, still panting.

'Sorry about that, Johnny. I was playing dead in case he shot you when you grabbed him. I was going to attack him when he came over to check me.'

'You could have got yourself killed, or both of us, Roy. I strictly said stay put, didn't I.'

Looking frustrated with himself, he replied, 'I watched both men head towards the building and thought I'd try to help you. I must admit I didn't see one of them was armed. It shit the life out of me when he turned around and pointed his gun at me.'

'Well, listen next time. I had it under control. But thanks anyway,' I said, and smacked him on his shoulder.

'Holy cow, was that some thanks?'

'Yeah, and your last one. And just be thankful you are still around for me to say it after your stupid stunt.'

He nodded.

I stood up, feeling like a ninety year old, and said, 'Right, let's get to that village and find what we need. It won't be long before our friendly Elkhaba find our tracks.'

'But I really need more rest, mate,' came his sorrowful reply.

'If we don't get moving now, you'll be getting all the rest you fucking need. You'll be dead. They've found our last LUP, so no buts. Get up and get your arse in gear.'

He looked worried as he checked the direction of the reflective flashes.

# CHAPTER FIFTEEN

An urgency had replaced my fatigue to find the village and hide until the hunter force went by. Hopefully, we would find food and water, maybe some medical supplies; even some natural old wives' remedies would do. We could stop the deadly growing effects of dehydration. Feeling more positive, I decided to take a direct route to the trees, and the goats bleating in the distance. Time was desperate. As I staggered into another ditch, I looked back to check on Rabbit, but there was no sign of him. I waited, and waited, until intolerance got the better of me.

'Shit, where are you, Roy?' I said, under my breath.

Concerned, I started to climb out, but I caught the sight of Rabbit sitting with his back against a small wall some thirty metres away. His face was contorted with fear and he was hugging into the wall. He looked over at me and waved to me to get down into the ditch. As I sank back I tried to make eyes on what he could see that I couldn't, but my line of sight was obscured by an old wall to my left. He raised two fingers to his eyes and then pointed to where the wall ended. He held up three fingers, turning two over and making a walking sign. With my view just above the cusp of the ditch, it was then that three men walked past the end of the wall. My heart flew into my mouth. They were all carrying AK47s, but at least had them relaxed over their shoulders, and they were chatting and smoking. Rabbit's anxiety levels must have been sky-high. My only movement were the trickles of sweat running down my torso. I had to ignore my stomach cramps, which had worsened.

Eventually, after what seemed ages, the three men continued along the track and out of sight and sound. I felt as if I'd taken my Bergen off after a long run. I was soaked in sweat and my heart was thumping, but my tight shoulders began to relax, whilst my breathing became heavy. Making sure they were well out of sight, Rabbit came quietly scuttling across, stopping alongside me.

'Jesus. That was close,' he whispered.

'I was just about to come and look for you. Good heads-up, Roy,' I said, relieved.

'Too bloody right, mate. I was lagging and just spotted of their cigarette smoke in time as I ran across the field. I sprinted back sharpish. I can't get caught again…' He paused, searching for the right words. 'I can't go through all that shit again, mate.'

I patted him on the back. 'I won't let it come to that, Roy. Come on, let's move out.'

It was a brave statement to say the least, but without proper weapons or a getaway vehicle, there was not a lot I could do. It's not like in the movies, where you can throw your knife over ten metres and kill one of them, jump up, run, and pull the knife out and kill another, and then karate kick two more. That sort of shit happens in Hollywood.

As we crept forward together, I was hyper-alert. Out of the corner of my eye, Rabbit was scanning all areas, his face full of concentration. I could clearly hear goats and chickens. We made it to the bottom of a large mud wall. At one end it stopped where the track continued past to whatever was on the other side. Nearing the other end was a small wooden gate set in the wall. I scurried along to the gate with Rabbit following closely. The wall was too high to see over, so I opened the gate gradually, just enough to peek through. Directly in front, about three metres away, was the rear of a building and an old vehicle, faded blue in colour and which had seen better days. In the rear window it had a sticker: 'SAFI PETROL'.

I opened the gate enough for me to squeeze through. Rabbit kept tight to me. I whispered to him to close it quietly, and then we both crept to the building. Peering around the wall, a large area of crops covered most of the courtyard. Beyond these were smaller individual buildings with wooden and metal doors. The wall we had come through via the wooden gate continued around the whole of the village. I needed to see what was on the other side of the yard. I turned to Rabbit and, in a low whisper close to his ear, I told him to stay put.

I silently moved around to the other corner of the building, praying that I would not bump into Elkhaba. Slowly, I leant one eye around the edge. The landscape was as much the same as the other side, except in one corner were neatly erected wooden posts which had all been bolted together. At the base of each post, small plants grew up, encouraged by wire. Opposite the track was a poppy field with the easily recognisable tall stems and bulbous heads. This was obviously an illicit opium farm, most probably under the control of the Elkhaba; maybe in the past the Taliban had controlled it.

Goats were milling around the edges. A door opened from one of the buildings and out of the shadows came a boy, a teenager at most. He threw the goats feed and gently stroked them. An unarmed man came out of the same doorway and patted the boy on the head, before walking over to a lean-to covered by corrugated sheets. The man was fatter and of bigger build than most Afghans I had seen. He didn't have the typical beard, but instead sported a thick, bushy moustache; the sort Saddam Hussein had.

A vehicle started, and then out of the lean-to, Saddam, as I now called him, drove a beaten-up rusty tractor. The goats fled, bleating, jumping, and kicking. One of the larger goats started to wander in my direction, I quickly pulled my head back in. I hoped it hadn't spotted me and was curiously venturing over. I wondered for a second if terrorists were training goats to hunt out Special Forces.

I crouched swiftly backwards to Rabbit and quietly told him what I'd seen, then I continued towards the blue vehicle. Even though this Nissan Bluebird looked like a pile of junk, it had signs it had been used recently. I watched the tractor ploughing the field and waited for the driver to turn at the bottom and make his way back up and out of sight. Stealthily moving up to the driver's door, I checked inside. First, the keys were in the ignition. Second, a pair of sunglasses rested on the dash. The last sign that this car had been used recently was a scattering of food crumbs over the driver's seat, most probably bread. I also noticed all the windows on the car were dirty, except the front screen.

'We've got company,' Rabbit hushed behind me.

I turned around sharply, expecting to see armed men coming through the gate, but next to him was the large goat. He was stroking and patting the animal on the head. I pulled my knife out, to the horror of Rabbit.

'What are you doing? He's OK, he's not doing any harm,' he whispered.

'If it follows us, or makes the slightest sound, I'm gonna slit its throat,' I whispered. 'Right, this is our escape vehicle, but first we need to find water and food; also, some weapons would be ideal. Now put your new lover down and let's get to work.'

Around the front corner of the building, a large group of chickens were busy doing what they do best. Saddam had nearly come to the end of the field before he would turn around again.

'Quick on me, stay tight,' I said.

I shuffled low to the front of the building, opened the door, and hurried inside. As soon as Rabbit was in, I closed the door. I pulled my knife out as I searched the gloom, then put my mouth right up to his ear.

'Stay here and watch outside through this crack in the door.'

As I stood away, he motioned me to turn my head and whispered, 'What do I do if someone comes over?'

'Come find me. Nothing heroic or any daft ideas this time. OK?'

He put his thumb up. 'Roger, mate.'

The interior was made up of wooden shelves with straw on each level, and was laden with chicken shit everywhere; the stench was awful. On the floor under the shelves was a mass of feathers and broken eggshell. There were no lanterns or candles, the only natural light came from the cracks in the main door and from the adjacent room. At least it was cooler in here, even if it reeked. I warily moved into a doorway at the back of the room, looking at where I placed my feet. I gripped my knife down by the side of me, being relaxed but ready to strike. In the doorway a stone staircase met me.

The tractor, chickens, and goats still went about their business. I took a quick glance at Rabbit, who was still watching outside. Sensing someone was upstairs, I held my knife slightly forward and, without any noise, took each step painstakingly slowly. Nearing the top, a gentle snoring sounded; I stopped. My breathing and body were relaxed, but my heartrate picked up pace. I edged to the top of the stairs until my eyes came level with the wooden planked floor. On the wall hung maroon textiles, like draped palace curtains. Along one wall were large, flat, oblong cushions. At the end of these, religious artefacts and candles were laid out. The inside of the roof had woven, patterned panels. The stench from downstairs had gone, replaced by a perfumed aroma. This didn't look like your normal Afghan farmer's home.

I listened in to the left part of the room where the snoring was coming from. My legs began to shake where I was holding my stance so I carried on stepping up. The room was shady as the window shutters had been closed, except the window behind me. To my left, a body was curled up with the back facing me. To the right was another bed. Past these were table and chairs and an old kitchen Welsh-style dresser. I crept up the remaining stairs, not taking my eyes off the person, unsure if it was male or female, and more crucially, if the person was armed. Tiptoeing stealthily closer, I searched for signs of weapons from the stocky-framed man. Adrenalin was driving my killer instincts to turn the person over and, if not friendly, thrust my knife into him. I took a side glance at the solid-looking dresser. Along the shelves were baskets filled with neatly placed eggs. On the next shelf up were open baskets of succulent dates, wholesome seeds, and colourful fruit. Above this shelf were jars of what looked like delicious chutney or jam. On the rustic table next to this feast, irresistible small rolls were on top of each other; all were placed on a white cloth.

Imagining the taste of each item, I began salivating, licking my lips. Maybe I should just steal some and clear off in the vehicle with Rabbit. Creeping backwards towards the table, not taking my eyes off the man on the bed, the table touched my legs. I put my knife back and turned around, feeling like a kid in a sweet shop; I didn't know what to grab first. Snatching bread rolls, I shoved them down my shirt, quickly glancing back as the snoring had stopped, being changed to a heavy breathing. Next, I quietly moved backwards towards the dresser, but the back of my foot caught a wooden chair, scraping it along the floor.

As I froze, the person on the bed looked over their shoulder. It was a woman of about fifty years old. Her hair was as black as the night, all squashed where she had lain on it. Her skin looked as tough as an elephant's arse. Her eyes went wide and her mouth opened as she locked eyes on me. In this two-second state of shock, I felt like a naughty boy again, caught stealing from a local shop in Newquay. This sense was shattered by her screams. At first, she shrieked in terror, but then as she stood up. Still hollering, her expression turned to anger and her scream to one of vicious intent.

The woman came at me, clenching her fists, raising them above her head. She had no front teeth, and when she yelled, spit lashed around her tongue and gums. Instead of drawing my knife on an unarmed woman, I stepped towards her, restraining her arms. I put my hand across her mouth to shut her up, but she tried to bite me; thank fuck she had no teeth. She thrashed about and kicked me in the shins as I tried to calm her. She certainly was strong; it didn't help that I was very weak.

The crazy bitch managed to pull her other arm away and slap me a few times around my face, all the while verbally abusing me. Her fingers dug into my face, trying to gouge at my eyes. I pulled my head away, but then she brought her knee up in my bollocks—they had certainly taken a battering lately. This wasn't going how I had imagined it. An image flashed into my mind of the other SBS lads laughing at this pathetic show, jeering the woman on. She managed to break free and, running to the dresser, pulled out a large kitchen knife from a drawer. Without even a pause, she charged at me, blaring a high-pitched shriek, and then took a lunge at my face. I side-stepped her knife, swerving my upper body. I quickly grabbed the wrist of her hand holding the knife and pulled it across me. With the momentum, I turned her arm around her back. In the same move, I gripped her shoulder, pushing it down, and lifted her arm up. With a cry she released the knife and it clanged on the floor. I kicked her hard in the face. Her head jerked up and her body wilted, dropping to the ground with a thud. At last, she had gone quiet.

'Jesus,' I said, shaking my head.

Whilst she was momentarily knocked out, I clutched the basket of eggs and placed handfuls of other food inside. Lastly, I picked up a wooden water jug. As I stepped over the woman, making a quick exit, she started to stir with a moan. I didn't want another round with her, so I sped down the stairs to Rabbit. He turned; eyes wide on my loot.

'The bloke on the tractor has stopped and he's gone back in the building with the boy,' Rabbit said. 'The goat keeps nudging the door with its foot.'

'I told you I should have slit the goat.'

'What the hell was going on up there?'

'To get this food I had to take on some mean blokes.'

Roy had a worried expression.

'Best we get to the Nissan before they wake. You lead the way,' I ordered.

Rabbit was transfixed on the food and water, and didn't move.

'Oi,' I hissed.

He looked up at me.

'Like the fuck now,' I said.

He checked through the door once more before opening it and then darted through it. The psychopath woman upstairs started wailing. Clutching my treasure, I made a hasty exit and opened the Nissan door.

'Take these,' I said, almost panicking.

Passing the basket and water, I then turned the ignition keys, but the only response was a click from the starter motor.

'Bollocks. Come on girl.'

I tried again. This time the engine turned over, but didn't start. Again, I turned the key.

'Start you bitch.'

'Watch out, mate,' Rabbit shrieked.

I turned to look out my window, just catching a glimpse of a knife as it lunged through it. I crooked my head, but the blade sliced across my cheek. The engine revved into life and I let the clutch out, flooring the accelerator. It didn't respond like the Toyota, but it was enough to send the crazy, knife-wielding woman bouncing down the side, ending up in a heap.

I checked the mirrors, hoping she had fallen onto her knife. However, she got up and started chasing. We bumped and bounced over the newly-ploughed field and headed for the compound's exit. The Nissan struggled in second gear, and we fought to stay in our seats, holding on for dear life. We were grunting and cursing simultaneously. It felt as if the psycho woman was breathing down my neck. I couldn't see her through all the shit being thrown up. Saddam and the boy came running outside to see what the commotion was about as we neared their building. Saddam darted back in, and as the Nissan tyres took to the smoother track, he came out brandishing an AK47. I floored the pedal, but it was like waiting for an elevator.

'Jesus. Might as well have stolen a fucking pushbike,' I fumed.

As we passed Saddam aiming his weapon, he let out a burst of fire. We both reacted simultaneously by ducking. The rounds impacted all the way down the side of the bodywork. Lifting my head slightly, the rear seat's stuffing floated around us. The AK47 stopped, but then further rounds ripped into the rear as we fled down the track. I overshot the bend and ploughed straight through the poppy field. The Nissan slowed, struggling through the dense crop. Slamming her into second, I veered sharply back towards the track. Still jostling around in my seat, I changed gear.

'Who the fuck was that woman?' Rabbit asked.

'Some crazy bitch, hey?'

'Did she catch you in bed with her man or something?'

'Ha, very funny.'

'Was *that* the group of men then?' He roared laughter.

'Dish the grub out. I'm starving through to my bones,' I said.

# CHAPTER SIXTEEN

Watching the village disappear in my door mirror, Rabbit passed me some dates. They tasted amazingly sweet; I spat the stones out onto the dash. Next, we scoffed the bread rolls like savages. The yellow plums were as I had imagined, sweet and juicy; these were heaven. I didn't go much on the seeds and nuts as they played havoc with my sore gums, but they were a vital source of protein. Speeding through the desert, I tried to pick the food remnants off my lap and shirt and put them quickly back in my mouth. I didn't even take the peel off the orange, just ripping into it like eating an apple, sucking at the juices, trying not to waste any running down my beard. With one hand on the wheel and one eye on the road, I cracked the eggs raw into my mouth. After the fourth one I turned to Rabbit, who was staring at me with a look of disgust.

'Oh my God, have you seen yourself, mate?' he said.

'What do you mean?' Food spat out.

'You're fucking gross. That's what I mean.'

I looked at myself in the rear-view mirror. Apart from the growth of mud and dust, I now had bits of raw eggs and juice around my mouth and nuts matted in my beard.

'Not been the best all-inclusive holiday I've had,' I said, and burped.

He pretended to gag. 'You've put me off my food now. Don't know if I can finish it, mate.'

'Good. Give it here then.'

'Bollocks, I'll suffer.'

'Yeah, like I had to suffer watching you eat with your humungous lips,' I joked.

We both laughed.

'Do you think that's it now from the Elkhaba?' he said seriously.

'I reckon they've stopped at the farm. Shame as I wanted them to give chase to test this high-performance vehicle out.' I scoffed—Roy didn't.

Most of the dashboard instruments didn't work, including the speedometer and the clock. The fuel gauge wasn't reading at all, but at least the jet-washers and wipers worked. Rabbit took lots of small sips from the jug and, passing it to me, I gulped the water. I let out a big burp, which displeased Rabbit. The track disappeared into a desert plain with small rocks scattered about. The suspension, or what was left of it, took a hammering; we felt every jolt. I tried to steer round the obvious sharp rocks as the last thing we wanted was a puncture. I set my bearings on a small mountain ahead. This would be my point of direction as the laws of physics would send me around in a right arc, back on myself without a visual point.

Rabbit chuckled almost under his breath.

Dreading asking, I said, 'Come on then, share the joke.'

'I reckon the crazy woman could have taken on that black mountain bear, mate.'

He had tears running down his face, obviously finding his joke hilarious, or maybe he was on a high from the pleasure of our feast, or the simple fact that we had got away from the hunters.

'Maybe we should've had her on this operation from the insertion,' I jested.

'She was fucking nuts.'

Mentioning the crazy woman reminded me of my cheek wound. I ran my fingers through the congealed blood in my beard. As I probed deeper, I touched the cut and it began to sting. Close shave, I thought, and sneered at my own joke. Wanting a closer look, I lifted my face to the mirror, but my beard was too overgrown. Bringing my eyes back down, I noticed behind in the far distance a large cloud of dust rising in the air.

'Rabbit, look out the rear window. Can you see that cloud of dust?'

He turned around and said, 'I can't be certain. The glass is covered in shit and dust.'

Stopping the Nissan, I got out quickly and took a long hard look back. The dust cloud was a way in the distance, but still it looked ominously large. Then out of the haze and cloud the sun glinted off two vehicles; very much like white Toyotas. Getting back in, slamming the door, I thrust the Nissan into gear and floored it, but again the response was pathetic. I warned Rabbit what was behind and his face drained white.

I didn't have any plan other than to keep as much distance between us and whoever was in the vehicles. I was pretty sure who they were. I had to make for the mountains. A big worry was they had better and faster vehicles. Maybe if both vehicles had rear-mounted Dushkas and were loaded with men, then this would stop them closing on us. But on the other hand, that would mean they had devastating firepower. I had tried to remain positive since my first run from the forest, which now seemed a very long time ago, but our vehicle was an uncontrollable heap of junk, and I had no idea how much fuel it had. We had no weapons except my knife, no map, and at best half a jug of water and three eggs, let alone being chased by the Elkhaba, looking for blood. We were both physically burnt out and Rabbit's arm had become a major concern. My bouts of griping pains had become more frequent. To top it all I was now battling with my negativity.

'What's the situation on the vehicles behind us?' I asked.

'I can't see much, mate, it's too...'

'Well, stick your fucking head out the window,' I snapped. 'And they let you fly a Chinook?'

He didn't answer as he wound down his window.

I shouldn't have bitten his head off, but the pressure was building. I was normally the calm squad member, but no training could have prepared me for this survival trip.

'They're without doubt nearer, Johnny. I've just seen muzzle flashes.'

A solid stream of rounds smashed into the earth in front and to my side of our Nissan. Every so often a tracer round would zing over the top of us. The impact of one of those Dushka rounds would tear big holes in our vehicle and could easily take our limbs off.

'Shit. How close are they?' I yelled.

'I reckon about a thousand yards plus.'

'Come on you piece of shit, go faster.'

Thumping the steering wheel, my mind was working at speed, trying to figure out a plan. The only answer was to head for the mountains and find a path on foot. I hoped we had enough energy to climb and outrun them when we ditched the Nissan. It seemed too much to dream of a nice, smooth road through the mountains. It also seemed our last chance.

The terrain took a gradual steep incline, our vehicle struggled, the clutch slipped and fumes entered through the vents. The rounds came in more concentrated and were extremely close. As we veered to the top there was an almighty bang like a grenade explosion. The wind rushed in through the roof along with a burning smell. Rabbit began smacking the interior roof-liner as it had caught fire, hitting me in the face as he did so. The smoke filled the rear, but was sucked out of our open windows. We both started to cough, my eyes began to stream. As we came over the cusp of the incline, another round took off our passenger door mirror, sending shards of plastic into Rabbit's swollen arm. He let out an agonising scream and, gripping his arm, he vomited over himself.

As we levelled out, the engine got a new lease of life and gained speed. I slammed the Nissan into third gear, waited till the engine was screaming its nuts off, and crunched her back into fourth. The air rushed through the gash in the roof, I got the whiff of Rabbit's vomit. We were out of sight from the Elkhaba. To my left, in the very far distance between trees and a compound wall, tracer rounds zipped across the desert. Veering slightly to the right, almost running parallel to the battle, I couldn't tell if it was friendly fire or the enemy. Even though Rabbit was in extreme pain, he pointed to my far right.

'More rounds coming inbound from the opposite treeline, Johnny.'

He then dropped his hand and cradled his bloodied broken arm.

It was like watching a mirror image: the opposite barrage was approximately a thousand yards away from the left treeline. The mountains we were heading towards took us nearly dead-centre through the battle. That would be a suicide run. I still had no idea which were the friendly side.

Rabbit looked to our rear out of his window, gasping, grimacing as he did.

'They have now come over the crest, but at last we have made some distance,' he managed.

'Which way forward though, left or right?' I bellowed.

'Head right, Johnny, that's our force, but the only problem is they don't know we are.'

'How do you know for sure, Roy? You have to be a hundred per cent sure.'

'Well the enemy have stopped following us and pulled up. I reckon they don't want to follow us to the right. Also, this area to the right is approximately the route I flew in to extract you guys. I remember the mountains and the lie of the land. Trust me, mate, I'm ninety-nine per cent sure.'

Just as I veered slightly further to the concentrated fire, a projectile smashed into the ground about fifteen metres in front of our route. The earth exploded, sending sand and dirt over our Nissan. I swerved to miss the crater and switched the wipers on, trying to clear the debris off. The passenger wiper blade ripped clean off. The projectile had no smoke trail, so it had to be a mortar.

'Fuck; now we're being mortared,' I raged.

Another thud of an explosion went off behind us. The Nissan sucked up the shockwave, its bodywork vibrated. Further large Dushka rounds followed up the incoming mortar rounds and smashed up the area around us. I decided to weave, turning left to right, as more mortar rounds landed perilously close.

My intermittent stomach cramps had now turned into one painful ache. I desperately needed a shit. I tried to hold it, but as hard as I tried, the weaving and jolting made it impossible and I let it go. Things couldn't have got worse. I was deeply embarrassed. In a few seconds the smell inside the Nissan was terrible.

'What the hell is that smell? Oh my God, it's vile,' Rabbit said.

I made out I didn't hear him due to the noise of incoming bombardment and the Nissan screaming its nuts off.

'Can't you smell it?' he persisted.

The thought-to-be friendly force was set out in an arrow formation and had started to move forward. The outer flank of this formation nearest to me started to engage us with machinegun fire. We were now taking flak from the hunter force behind, and both left and right positions.

'What the hell? We're on your side, you morons,' I fumed.

Swerving left, I started to flash my headlights in the international SOS code: six long flashes followed by a six-second pause, and then another six flashes. The large calibre incoming rounds ceased, and for a moment my hands slightly relaxed. However, I didn't relax for long as a barrage of rounds erupted behind us. The Nissan took direct hits. In my mirror, fragments of our lights and the bumper exploded into the air. One more of those could ignite our petrol tank, that's if we weren't driving on fumes. Incoming rounds from the front arced over the top towards the stationary Elkhaba hunter force. It was chaos.

Suddenly, the Nissan's boot-lid flew up after an almighty bang, shattering the rear window and sending sparks, glass, and metal fragments inside. The noise was ear-shattering. The distinctive smell of burning rubber flared my nostrils. Without giving them another chance to get a further direct hit, I swung the Nissan right.

'Fucking good choice you had chosen the friendly side. If we get out of this I'll buy you fags *and* beer for the rest of your life,' I said.

He didn't answer, which was unlike him.

Trying to miss the incoming fire, I glanced over at him: his head was down and had a hand to his neck. My glare froze as the blood trickle through his fingers. Further splats ran down the B-pillar to the side of his head. Another loud bang from the rear sent us into an uncontrollable swerve. I heaved the wheel left and right, trying to sustain a straight line of direction. One of the rear tyres had blown. It then disintegrated and the rim sunk into the desert floor.

I opened my door and crawled out. Rounds whizzed in all directions. Unclipping my smoke grenade, I pulled its safety pin and threw it as far to the rear of us as I could. As it bounced along the ground, it gushed with smoke, totally obscuring our position from behind. Deathly rounds still came from the enemy, but were aimed indiscriminately, but that's all it took, one lucky round. I moved around the front on my hands and knees and wrenched open Rabbit's blood-stained door. Dragging him out, he was alive, but unconscious. As his hand fell, he had a large golf ball-sized chunk ripped out from his neck, with his arteries and muscles still pulsating. Putting firm pressure on the wound, I leant into the passenger foot-well and whipped the cloth from the egg basket. Releasing my hand, the blood flowed at an alarming rate. Quickly, I made a ball shape with the cloth and shoved it in the wound. Smaller calibre rounds whizzed all around us. With my knife, I cut the seatbelt and wrapped that around his neck, tying it at the rear.

Our Nissan Bluebird sucked up these smaller rounds at a horrendous rate. I half-stood up and heaved him far away, keeping us low, staying in the screen of the blue smoke. All the remaining glass, including our front seats, was now being peppered by rounds. The noise was horrendous. I checked his pulse—very weak. With tears in my eyes, I shook him.

'Don't you die now, you bastard. Stay with me, Roy, stay with me. We're supposed to roll up with laughter after every crisis. Come on, Roy, wake up and laugh.'

I pressed my hand harder on his neck as the cloth had become saturated. Looking around for further cover, I realised how extreme the battle was. Three vehicles, still firing at the enemy, made their way across the desert to our position. Further mortars thudded near to us, sending shockwaves through the ground. The vehicles became recognisable: a WMIK Land Rover, a Foxhound, and the last, a Mastiff. The Foxhound raced ahead under the cover of the other two. The WMIK fired an awesome display of firepower with an array of weapons before stopping just right of our beaten vehicle. The grenade had almost stopped smoking; we were now in full view of the enemy.

The WMIK fired its Gimpy, a 50 cal heavy-machinegun and its 40mm grenade launcher. The back blast of an Interim Light-armour Weapon filled the void behind the vehicle as the rocket blasted across the desert out of my view. A couple of seconds later, a huge explosion boomed; it had found its target. Smoke grenades popped out to the side.

I turned my attention to the Foxhound, which had pulled up five metres in front of me. I put one hand on my head, but kept the other hand on Rabbit's neck. A soldier came from the rear and knelt on one knee with his weapon aimed at me. The passenger door opened and a soldier with his weapon raised gingerly moved towards to me.

'Johnny Vince, UK Special Forces,' I shouted, above the battle. I looked at Rabbit cradled in my lap and said, 'Roy Franklin, 7 Squadron RAF pilot. Am I fucking glad to see you guys.'

Looking like he had found the Holy Grail, he lowered his weapon and through his walkie-talkie shouted orders for the Mastiff to immediately advance to his position to extract a T1 and T3 casualty. He then proceeded to radio the JTAC to advance to his position immediately. One he had finished, he knelt beside me and passed me a water bottle. I gulped the water.

'Lieutenant Simon Kellett. Where are the others? Are there any more of you?' he yelled.

'Negative. We're the only survivors. Roy and I were on the Chinook extraction from Operation Blue Halo. Are you aware of that?'

'Yes, we're the search party. My brother was on that operation.' He looked pitifully at Rabbit. 'I know Roy. Are you sure my brother is dead? His name was Ashley Kellett.'

'Affirmative. He is.'

His expression and head dropped.

I knew I had to tell him the truth, but I thought how awful and regimental it sounded so I squeezed his arm.

'I'm sorry. If it's any consolation, he died instantly, according to Roy. He didn't die in vain either; he tried to save the lives of us all.'

Simon looked up with a distant expression and said, 'Thanks. Are these the bastards we're fighting now?'

'Yep, sure are. Well, what's left of them. Me and Roy took care of quite a few. You've got to mallet the rest. Don't let any of them escape or they will destroy an entire village further west. Some of these villagers have helped me and Roy evade capture. You owe this to your brother.'

His whole demeanour changed in an instant. 'Oh, don't you fucking worry,' he said, 'the fucking rag-heads are going to have it big style.'

He turned to the JTAC who had come alongside him and ordered the en route Apaches to take out all enemy positions.

'Make sure all of them don't have another breath, you understand me, not one of them,' he finished off.

A medic piled out of the Mastiff and began treating Rabbit, who now appeared barely alive. I shouted his symptoms to the medic, who then wrote notes on the back of his latex glove. Grabbing his arm and fixing him a steely glare, I told him it was imperative Roy didn't die. Whilst a drip was inserted, two other guys prepared a stretcher. Noticing the Pathfinder's badge on the arm of the JTAC, I listened to his commands on his TACSAC handset with the 'donkey dick' aerial poking out of his rucksack.

'Ugly Five Zero, Havoc Three Zero, copy?... Ugly Six Zero, Havoc Three Zero, copy?... You are now in my ROZ, and I alone command this, confirm?... Friendly grids are 98055618, friendly grids are 98055618, repeat?... We are on the ground engaging multiple enemy, grid reference 97055620, enemy grid reference 97055620, repeat?... You are to engage all multiple enemy targets, confirm visual... Clear to engage... from the top... Affirmative, from the top... I want a full BDA.'

A stretcher was laid out for me, but I refused it as I wanted to see the enemy get a pasting, even though I didn't have a visual on the Apaches yet. The medic held my arm.

'We can't make two trips. You have to come now,' he sternly ordered. 'Your friend is in a bad way.'

Reluctantly, I made my way around to the rear of the Mastiff, watched by a few soldiers in disbelief. Was it because we looked so wasted and unrecognisable? Or was it because we had survived against all the odds?

Lieutenant Kellett radioed ahead, shouting above the noise for an immediate CasEvac as he leant over his map, giving the grid reference. He then ran back over to me, showing me his satellite-imaged map.

'Do you remember where the village was?' he asked.

'Sure.' I studied the map, then pointed to a position between the bases of the two valleys.

'This is the village here, and this is the point where the Chinook crashed. When you get to the village, please find the doctor, Haleema, and her mother, whose name is Anoosheh. Please tell them that we have both made it and I will return one day.'

'Will do.'

I moved up to about two inches away from his face and glared into his eyes. 'Make sure you do this. If it wasn't for them, we both would have died. You got that?'

'I understand,' he answered.

'One last thing,' I said, showing the satellite-image. 'It's not marked on your map, but about here I believe to be an IED-making facility. There are three small buildings just outside a farmed village, which, by the way, is being run by the Elkhaba for opium. You'll know when you find it as it has a brick-built well. However, you won't find water in it.' I threw him a wry smile.

'Thanks, appreciate the heads-up.'

'Thanks for not blowing the shit out of my Bluebird with us in it.' He scoffed.

I took one last look at the wreck, now sunk into the sand, and said, 'Take care out there, Simon. Make sure you mallet those motherfuckers.'

Simon spoke on his radio for half of the platoon to move to a grid reference, and the other half to head to a different grid reference on his orders. He then informed the JTAC he wanted a BDA once both Ugly call signs had engaged the enemy. He reminded them again that no runners were to survive. He then instructed the JTAC to inform the Apaches to oversee the advance of both platoons, splitting to the two grid references of the village and the crash site. A surge of pride and relief flooded me, but at the same time a part of me was envious I wouldn't be taking merciless revenge on the Elkhaba.

A soldier held the rear door open and put his hand out, so I shook it. I achingly climbed in and he patted me on the back. The door swung shut and the beast slowly began to roar forward; rounds ricocheted off its armour. The medic in the back was still leaning over Rabbit, checking vital signs. He looked a bloody mess and pale as ice. The air was very stuffy in the back. It was then I started to smell the shit I sat in. Looking around, some of the other soldiers could too. I wanted to tell them it wasn't because I was afraid out there, but I couldn't be bothered; I was exhausted.

As we rocked and jolted, I began to tremble and ached from head to toe. I was handed a fresh bottle of water, but could hardly lift it to my mouth, my arms were too heavy. As I sipped, the Apache's mastery weapons erupted, but I was too shattered to even smile.

'Yes. Now they're 'aving it. Go boys, take them all out,' the driver joyfully shouted.

The battle was drowned out by the sound of the Mastiff's engine. I could barely keep my eyes open and my thoughts drifted into a dream of the family and friends of my dead squad, my mates.

★

Their emotions upset me as I told them individually of their loved ones' deaths. Pain, loss, confusion, and anger all hit me in a barrage of verbal abuse. I was stuck to the spot. As I looked down at the sticky stuff holding my feet, I realised it was a pool of blood. Panicking, I looked at the faces of the family who were melting into the forest where we had landed. The sticky pool started to swallow me. I grappled with the forest floor, being sucked in further. Desperate, I gazed up. Planet was sitting in the Chinook seat.

'Ye should have dragged me out of *your* seat,' he yelled. 'Why did ye leave me here, mate, why?'

I tried to answer, but the blood had entered my mouth, and then my lungs.

I sat upright, lashing out my fists, landing on objects in front of me. Opening my eyes, two soldiers pushed me down.

'Easy, buddy… easy. It's OK, you're safe now,' one of them reassured me.

'Where the fuck am I?' I said, above a familiar sound.

'You're en route to Camp Bastion, in the back of a Chinook.'

Fear ran through me. Images flashed through my mind of the SAM hitting us again. I half-sat up and watched as a group had gathered around a man on a stretcher administrating CPR. As I was assisted to lie down again, I recognised the soldier: Roy.

'No, no, he cannot die,' I yelled.

'Clam down.'

I began to wrestle the two soldiers holding me, the cannula dug into my bone as tubes lashed around my arms.

'You bastards should be helping him, not restraining me. Get the fuck off. I want to talk to him.'

A third medic came over and I felt a sharp scratch on my arm. I found it hard to resist; I became feeble, almost drunk.

'Roy… Roy, I'm sorry… stay alive,' I mumbled.

# CHAPTER SEVENTEEN

Meticulously, I pulled apart the two halves of my medication capsule and out poured tiny white micro balls onto my dining table. I had moved the table and one chair from the dining room into the lounge because of the amount of mess in there. As the little balls landed, I tried to keep them contained, but they fell between the letters I'd carved out many times, venting my inner demons. The vandalism had become a ritual after finding comfort in drinking Jack Daniels. In fact, it hadn't stopped there. My house had been repeatedly despoiled with my own graffiti and I'd smashed it up. I didn't have much left in the way of furniture and items anyway as Ella had moved out ages ago. The day she had left, I didn't give a shit who owned what, and in a rage threw most of our items into her rented van. It was Lee Brown who was driving the van. He didn't intervene in our ranted arguments; he just sat in the van reading a newspaper.

My outbursts of anger and depression were one thing, but in our last row I'd grabbed Ella and thrown her up against the wall, coming very close to hitting her; the woman I'd cherished, the woman who'd stuck by me. At the time I couldn't see my behaviour changing from rash to uncontrollable. I'd always have an excuse, blaming something or someone else. That morning I had received a letter from her parents, expressing their disgust after Ella had told them everything about the last eight months, and that our relationship was over. The letter mentioned that I would be hearing from her solicitors about the sale of our house and a rapid divorce.

On the table in front, I set out, slightly apart, an empty bottle of Jack Daniels, a box of anti-depressants, and a P226 Sig Sauer pistol. It had an engraved anchor sign on the left side of the slide.

★

I had won the pistol in a bet with a US Navy Seal who had come over for training with our unit. After a heavy drinking session in our local pub, I was pretty much wasted; a habit that was growing. I couldn't remember how the conversation came about, but it ended up with me saying I bet I could climb to the top of the Twin Sail Bridge and recite the American national anthem whilst naked. Joe, the Navy Seal, thought for a while until he named his prize if I forfeited the bet. The forfeit being that I had to give him my full-dress uniform and beret. A few of the lads at the table tried to talk me out of it; however, a few encouraged me by calling me a chicken shit, one of them being Lee. Once we had shaken hands, I named my prize if I completed the bet: his personal P226 Sig Sauer pistol. More banter added to the pressure until Joe agreed, even though I guessed they all thought I wouldn't.

Bundling out of the pub and jeered on, we reached the Twin Sail Bridge. I stripped off naked, took a deep breath, and started to climb the side of the huge structure. I had not really taken into consideration how drunk I was and how cold it was. Strangely, I felt spurred on by the thought of winning, not so much for the challenge, but the thought of claiming the prize. My hands soon went numb on the icy steel. A few times I'd slipped, much to the delight of the drunken group below. The alcohol rushed around my body. My warm breath vaporised into the clear, starlit evening.

Once at the top rung, I leant my upper-half above the top of the sail and stood up naked, proud, and then sang the American national anthem. The world around me was a blur. I had to squeeze my eyes shut and open them to try to focus. Objects in the distance seem to merge as one, as if the Twin Sails were moving, like on a big pirate ship at sea. I estimated I was about fifty metres up, my vice-like grip not letting off as I continued to sing—more like a drunken holler. When I looked down, one of the lads was filming me on his phone and a few of them were jostling Joe. Once I'd finished the anthem, I moved down a rung and clung on for dear life. I was numb and started to shiver. A wave of fluid came into my mouth and I was forced to spit it out. Fermented alcohol burnt my nose and throat, tasting rancid. The jeers below turned into abuse. Some of my vomit must have landed on them. The climb down was harder than climbing up. A part of me just wanted to stay and go to sleep, and I really had to dig deep to continue. Feeling heroic once I swayed on the ground, Joe and the lads had made a run for it with my clothes. Fortunately, help came in the way of an old friend, Meryl, who put her coat around me. I don't remember the journey home. It wasn't till the morning that I felt deeply embarrassed for her as I discovered her note, explaining the night's shenanigans.

Meryl was the widow of my best mate Planet. Even though she was out of the military circle, she had tried to stay in contact. I'd done many brave and fearless things in my time, but couldn't find the balls to look her in the eyes and talk to her about the events eight months ago. I had found the funerals of Rob, Tony, and Gary incredibly difficult. The weight of guilt and loss bearing down on me was too much. I was paranoid about what friends and family, including our unit, were saying. I felt the finger of blame was on me. The joint funerals were a blur. The only part I can properly remember was handing over Fish's watch to his parents. I didn't say much; I just apologised and walked off. Ella had supported me on the day, but I didn't go back to the wake with her. Instead, I stole a bottle of whiskey from the mess and sat between the headstones in the pouring rain, drinking myself into oblivion.

The next day at work, after the Twin Sails Bridge bet, I confronted Joe. He tried to back out, explaining the trouble we would be in if he handed over his personal weapon. An argument followed, which escalated to a fight; fortunately for him, he was also trained in martial arts. Once we were broken apart by several lads, we both felt the wrath of my CO, Dick Brown. The truth never came out; we said it was banter that went too far. I was asked to stay, whilst Joe was dismissed.

Dick informed me these meetings were becoming too frequent. Even understanding my recent stresses and continuing therapy, the ice was wearing very thin. I was warned this would be my last chance. Dick had been very patient with me; I wasn't too sure why. I had not been put on any further operations and he always encouraged me to take time off.

"Let your hair down to get it out of your system. Go out drinking with some of the new lads," he had prompted.

His son, Lee, was in the SBS, but a different unit. Lee was happy to tag along, and Ella liked him being around. Something didn't seem right, but I couldn't put my finger on it. Eventually, I was only sent on further training, which frustrated me. I wanted to get back in the thick of it. It was Dick who made the appointment for me to see the military doctor. I was very hostile and uncooperative with the doctor, who repeatedly told me I was in denial and suffering from PTSD. I was given the chance to see a therapist, but instead I went to the pub and got very drunk.

Two days before Joe was due to return to the Navy Seals, and after continuing pressure from me, not to mention some of the other lads, he kept his side of the bet, handing over his pistol. The very same day, Dick summoned me to his office. On the way, two new lads walked passed me and one, Scott, muttered something. I didn't catch what he said so I turned back.

'Speak up, or shut the fuck up,' I said.

Without stopping, he replied, 'Not healthy for your credentials, all this trouble, Johnny. Have you seen your film?'

They continued on their way, still joking.

Before I entered the room, more than one voice spoke. The voices were slightly raised, so I tried to listen through the door.

'I want this meeting on record, but gentlemen, this is my office. You play by my rules,' Dick said.

I didn't knock, I just entered. The sight of two military police stopped me in my tracks. It seemed incredible to them that I hadn't knocked or wasn't stood to attention. I had the utmost respect for the military police, but that day I hated them, and I gave them both a steely glare.

'What do these muppets want?' I asked.

'Johnny, you will stand to attention and address them professionally,' Dick barked.

'Johnny Vince, we have reason to believe you were involved in an incident, being in a drunk and disorderly state in public last night. Is this correct?' one of them said, glaring.

'Are you charging me with this incident or asking me?' I replied.

Dick cut in, 'Just answer the bloody question, Johnny. Don't go down the road of being a smart arse.'

'We have gained evidence through an internet video clip,' the MP said. 'Furthermore, colleagues have named you, that you gained unauthorised access to private property. You proceeded to strip naked and then climb the structure. Finally, you indecently exposed yourself to passers below.'

'Well, if you have enough evidence in the video clip, why ask others? Are you sure you're not just jealous the man in the film had a bigger knob than you?'

'Johnny Vince,' Dick intervened. 'You...'

'I deny all knowledge of this incident and have an alibi,' I over spoke. 'So, you either fucking arrest me or you go back to your desk job.'

Dick put his head in his hands and I could sense he was about to read me the riot act, when the shorter, young, spotty-faced muppet, who was now very red in the face and fit to burst, stepped forward.

'We have the power to arrest you here and now. We understand you have been through a lot lately. We are…'

'Understand?' I interrupted. 'What the fuck do you know? You're barely out of nappies. How the fuck can you say you understand? You know jack shit what I've been through. You either arrest me here and now or fuck off. And by the way, I won't make it easy for you.'

'OK, Johnny, that's enough,' Dick ordered. Turning back towards the stern-faced men, he said, 'It's blatantly obvious you have the wrong man for the incident. If I can assist any further in finding the culprit, please don't hesitate to contact me. However, chaps, this meeting is over. I'm sure, as you have stated, you understand the pressure Johnny Vince has been under. He and I do not want any further tit-for-tat, unjustified accusations to unbalance and stain this regiment, or his outstanding character. Please submit a full report to me in writing. Do I make myself clear, gentlemen?'

'Please head for our finest canteen and make yourselves known to the lads,' I butted in. 'I'm sure they'll make you very welcome.'

They started to leave.

'And please put your bill on the slate of the *colleagues* who dobbed on me,' I said.

The younger of them glanced back and gave me a filthy look before slamming the door shut behind him. I faced Dick, feeling smug, but was brought back down by his cold, angry stare.

'Who the fuck do you think you are?' he barked. 'You were treading on thin ice with me, but now you've gone through it. You will now take immediate leave from when you exit this office. I will sort the paperwork and cancel any dates for training and operations.'

'But…'

'For once, shut your mouth and listen. I've stood by you, putting my neck on the block. I've tried to get you help, but you have turned it down, therefore I've cancelled your therapist. You can do this on your own now.'

'But…'

'Listen,' he interrupted again, 'you have a court case in the next three to four months, therefore I want you to take leave and get your shit together. I would advise not contacting any of the lads; keep yourself to yourself. Its best you go home and drink alone, and get it out of your system. My son can take your position here until you're ready to come back.'

'I'm fine, I just need…'

'Dismissed,' he said sharply.

With mixed emotions, I left his office, this time shutting the door more respectfully.

With the pile of micro balls gathered, I labelled the empty Jack Daniels bottle as friends and loved ones I'd lost due to my recent behaviour. The anti-depressant box I labelled as friends and loved ones I'd gained, and reasons to continue to take the medication. I hadn't taken my medication for two weeks since I was told to go on leave to get my shit together, as Dick had instructed me. I believed the tablets were making me angry and clouding my judgment. The Sig, which now felt darkened with evil, I labelled as reasons to live. I wanted a drink to make me feel more at ease.

Going into the kitchen to fetch a bottle of JD, I passed the mirror on the wall. Through the marker-pen graffiti, I stopped to judge myself. I looked aged, not just because I'd not shaven and washed. Staring back was a pale, gaunt, haggard man. I looked deep into the eyes of the almost-stranger.

'What the fuck has happened to you dude?' I questioned the mirror.

My mind scrambled for an answer, but was taken over by a weird, deep, slow voice.

*You've fucked up. You oversaw the operation. You should have checked the area before extraction, called in for air support. It's your fault your mates and others died. Now, nobody wants to know you; they are vindictive behind your back. You wonder why you have lost your wife.*

I shook my head, quickly walking to the kitchen. I found the bottle of JD. Trembling, I ripped off the seal, unscrewed the top and took a long swig.

'Awwwww,' I said.

Wiping my mouth, I passed the mirror on the way back and raised the bottle in a 'cheers'. I sat down on the solitary chair at the table. After taking a large gulp, I looked around the room at the mess. I started to read the graffiti spread around the walls:

'I'M SORRY. YOU FAILED. FUCK OFF OPERATION BLUE HALO. SBS WANKERS. ELLA IS A BITCH.'

Reading the next graffitied wall, I caught sight of a cracked glass photo frame in the corner of the room. I went over and picked it up, brushing the glass off with my fingers, cutting them, watching the blood trickle.

'Hmm,' I smirked.

I brought my eyes back to the frame, staring at the photo. In the picture, I was stood with my now ex-wife, Planet, Fish, and Shrek. The photo had been taken at a barbecue just prior to Operation Blue Halo. All were dead except Ella, but she might as well have been. Her parents' letter this morning just added to my loss. A sadness swelled in me and tears began to form in my eyes. I poured a little of the JD onto the photo.

'Cheers, lads. I'm sorry you can't be here to see my prosperous life. Ella, your parents were right from the beginning: being with me was trouble.'

My sadness turned to irritation in a blink of an eye and I threw the frame against the wall, taking another swig from the bottle.

'Fuck you, Ella. Right, let's get down to business.'

Lifting the cushion on the stained sofa showed the remnants of too many alcohol-fuelled nights. I picked up my knife, the same knife I'd brought back from Operation Blue Halo. I marvelled at the marks on it.

'We've been through quite a bit together. Now I want you to help me choose what is right and what is wrong.'

I sat back at the table and glared at the pile of micro balls. The room was gloomy, not just because the curtains were shut, but from the feeling radiating through me. Carefully, I moved one tiny ball between the carved letters with the tip of my knife.

'Right, Ella, you can go over to the bottle of JD,' I slurred. 'Now, my CO and all the Head Sheds can go with Ella.'

I carried on the laborious move of many individual micro balls over to the bottle. Not taking notice of the time, I managed to build up quite a pile of friends and loved ones I had lost. Staring at the box of tablets, I racked my brain for friends and loved ones I had gained.

*See, you've gained jack shit, dude. You're on your own, you're a loser,* said the voice.

'Hold on, what about Joe?' I said.

*I don't think Joe is happy with you. Probably court-martialled because of your stupid bet.*

I moved another micro ball over to the bottle pile and took a large swig of JD. Again, I searched my mind.

'Well, there are my workmates who are my best drinking friends,' I said triumphantly.

*You wanker. Can't you see they're just using you to buy them drink? They're planning to get you into trouble. They all want to see you gone. They mock you behind your back.*

With the voice squashing my triumphal statement, I became frustrated. I fastidiously moved six further micro balls towards the bottle. In despair, I looked at the objects on the table and a name popped into my head: Meryl. With a broad grin, I proudly moved one ball towards the box of medication. Looking at the one and only micro ball at the base of the packet, I couldn't think of any more people. My grin soon changed into a frown. I started carving a new hole in the table with the tip of my knife. Images of my brother and parents came into my mind. They had all tried to contact me a couple of weeks ago, but I had told them never to contact me again and ripped out the house phone. I'd woken up after my first night's leave and found my mobile sitting at the bottom of the toilet with a post-it note on the lid which read: 'Peace and quiet!!!' I had been so drunk that in the morning I couldn't remember doing this.

I started to push three balls over to the packet of medication, but I buckled under the pressure and moved them to the bottle. I stared at the last object: the Sig, labelled reasons for living. I felt a cold, empty feeling inside; one of guilt and unease. I had to face the last object; I couldn't fail now. My thoughts turned to Operation Blue Halo. I hated it, again.

'Well, you know you've lost your best mate, Planet,' I slurred, 'so let's start by moving a micro ball for him.'

Gulping down the rest of the JD, I then I shuddered at the taste. Once I'd finished screwing my face up and my chest had stopped burning, I stared closely at the empty bottle. Enraged, I threw it at the wall, but it didn't smash, just bouncing off. It hit my display cabinet, smashing the glass-panelled door. Through the damage, splinters of glass laid on my prized collection of signed military books. I asked myself why I had become angry and thrown the bottle.

*Stop shirking and move the rest of the micro balls for each one of your mates you have lost. It was your fault after all.*

Depressed even more, I kept my hand still, trying to fight off the urge to do what it has said.

'It wasn't my fault. I tried my best. I managed to save Roy and myself. I killed quite a few of the enemy, and…' I'd run out of reasons. 'Just go away,' I shouted. 'Leave me alone.'

*But Roy has ended up in a nut-job ward and is paralysed. So, you've not really saved him, have you?*

Feeling even lower, I put my hands over my ears and screwed my eyes tight shut, but I knew there was more to come, and it did.

*Don't be so fucking soft. You can't escape from the facts. It's your fault, all of it. When you go to the court hearing they are going to throw the book at you, and you will be court-martialled and thrown in prison.*

'Shut up,' I yelled. 'Shut the fuck up.'

*Just think of all the families in the room, all jeering as you go down.*

'Arghhhhhhh,' I raged.

I grabbed my Sig, stood up, and kicked the table from underneath, sending it crashing over with the objects and micro balls.

'Shut up. I mean it,' I said, snarling. 'I'll fucking sort you out in a minute.'

I didn't stop there. My rage worsened and I kicked the chair behind me, sending it across the room. Walking over to my cabinet, I swung the doors open and started pulling out the books, letting them drop to the floor.

'It's entirely your fault, Dad. Why did you have to start collecting fucking military books? In fact, I blame all of you, the authors, for writing them.' I was grasping at straws.

Not satisfied, I picked out one of his books and threw it across the room. As it landed, the dust jacket was damaged. The inside of the book lay with its inside photos showing. I crooked my neck at a group shot of SBS men, all in their battle gear and their faces blacked out. Intrigued, I went over to it.

*Why don't you just end it here and now, then it will all be over.*

The voice stopped me in my tracks, my heart raced and I was trembling. I sank to the floor on my knees, head bowed, and started to sob like a child. Opening my eyes, the tears dropped onto my Sig in my hand. I wiped my face, took a big sniff, and then lifted my head, taking a last look around.

'God, is this what I've become?' I said, and sighed.

I raised the Sig to my temple, pressing it hard, feeling the cold barrel. My finger tightened on the trigger, but I pulled it away. I slowed my breathing.

'Do it,' I ordered.

This time I believed I could squeeze the trigger. Holding my breath, I put the pistol back against my temple, trying to block out emotions and any thoughts. Then I gently started to squeeze the trigger.

**Bang, bang, bang!**

I jumped, opened my eyes, and released my trigger finger. Confused, I looked down the end of the barrel. I dropped the Sig and felt my head, expecting to find it shattered with my brains out.

**Bang, bang, bang, bang!**

'Johnny, are you in there? Answer the fucking door or I'll kick it in.'

Startled, I grabbed the Sig and moved to the front door.

*It's the Elkhaba. Best shoot through the door.*

I took aim, approximately at chest height to the Elkhaba.

'Johnny, it's Oliver. Open the door. I know you're in there. I'm gonna count to ten and if you don't open it, I'll kick it in.'

Imagining evil terrorists on the other side, I took a firmer grip of my pistol.

'One... two... three...'

*Shoot, Johnny, it's a trick.*

'Four... five...'

I re-gripped my Sig. My breathing became frantic, my eyes wider than ever before.

'Six... seven...'

*What are you waiting for, Johnny? Do it, do it.*

'Eight...'

Then something deep inside, a different voice, female, said, 'It's all fine, Vinnie. Put the gun down.' I'd heard it before, but couldn't remember where.

'Ten.'

I swung open the door and, just as the person standing there kicked, I grabbed his shoe. Pulling his leg in hard towards me, I sent the butt of my Sig into his face, but his arm blocked it, sending it up past his forehead. I felt sharp pain to the side of my head. I recognised the move as an outside knife hand strike, but my reactions were too slow. I stumbled back and, falling over the chair, landed on my arse. I raised the pistol, but my vision was blurred. Rapidly blinking, I focused hard on the intruder, his hands defensively out.

'Johnny, what the fuck are you doing? It's me, your brother,' the intruder said.

As his face came more recognisable, it dawned on me he was indeed telling the truth. I felt ashamed, not just because I had come close to slotting him, but also because of the state I was in; I lowered the Sig. Gingerly, I clambered up, but the walls moved and the floor tilted; I fell over.

'Jesus, dude, what the hell has happened to you?' Oliver asked.

Trying to hide my shame, I slurred, 'Ah, just had a little too much of the good times. Welcome to my five-star accommodation.'

Another person came through the door and she said, 'He needs help, serious help. Take him home, Oliver.'

Once the person had stopped spinning along with the room, I recognised Meryl. I bowed my head.

'I'm truly sorry for his death,' I garbled. 'Please forgive me.'

'Like I said at the funeral, when we found you outside in the rain, none of us think you are to blame,' Meryl said. 'We love you now as much as we did before Operation Blue Halo. We're all proud of you, so stop this moping and get yourself back on track. What do you think Rob would be saying if he could see you now? Don't waste the life that has been given to you.'

They were the best words I'd heard for a very long time, and it was a poignant slap around the face.

'Thanks,' I managed to mutter.

As I was helped to the front door, Dick grabbed the Sig from me, making it safe. I hadn't seen him enter.

'Where did you get this?' he asked.

I stayed silent.

'I'm going to have to report this, Johnny,' he said.

'I don't think you should, sir. It's not going to help, is it,' Oliver said.

'This can't be swept under the carpet, young man.'

'Yes it can. You're his boss. What would you do if it was your son?'

Dick turned and squared up close to Oliver, who was still holding me up. 'My son wouldn't have got into the mess your brother is in now. Ella should have had a decent man like my Lee, not this pathetic waste of space. He wouldn't have let the needless deaths of so many good men happen.'

Oliver dropped me and pushed Dick back. 'We're brothers, so if you slate him, then you start on me. I'll kick your fat arse in here, right now.'

'Guys, stop it,' Meryl bawled.

'I'm sorry, Meryl,' Dick said. 'I suggest we call the military police and get him taken somewhere safe.'

'No, Dick,' Meryl said. 'I don't want the police involved. Johnny needs support. How could you think of a thing like that?'

Dick turned back to Oliver. 'No doubt we will meet again, Oliver. Hopefully we can start where we left off.'

'No doubt, but we won't be discussing anything. I'll be pasting your face up the walls.'

Dick defiantly laughed.

They both lifted my sorry arse to Oliver's vehicle. Just before I was helped in, I chundered across the bonnet.

'Oh fucking great, Johnny,' Oliver said.

Bundled in, the seat belt was fastened to keep me from falling forward. I lifted my wobbly head.

'Thanks everyone, it means a lot, I love...'

Oliver slammed the door, cutting my speech short. I drifted off with the sounds of the three of them talking.

# CHAPTER EIGHTEEN

The morning after, I'd felt like a camel's bollocks in a sandstorm: rough and battered. However, two months had gone by and it felt great to be back in Newquay. I was staying in Oliver's swanky apartment overlooking the sea. I felt better than I had for a long time and I started getting my head sorted. From time to time I got the severe headache which had begun after receiving the injury to my forehead in the Chinook. I apologised to my parents for the hurt I'd caused them, but they dismissed this, saying there were no apologies to make. I hadn't touched any alcohol or medication. I had made no contact with Ella; I'd accepted it was over between us. I felt a free young man, and sexually potent, getting into the swing of chatting to other girls; I'd been let off a lead.

The beaches and rock-climbing seemed to be the therapy I needed. I revisited my *dojo* and started training to get fit and sharp. *Sensei* Trevor was still at the club. After the karate lesson when everyone had gone home, we sparred together. This always ended up with me letting off steam, venting my past problems and feelings; he was a great listener. But something was still bothering me, missing, like being incomplete. I just couldn't put my finger on it. Even though back on track, I was still getting nightmares and flashbacks, but at least the voice had gone.

Oliver invited me to a RAF charity event in St Mawgan. A part of me didn't want to go, feeling raw to be around military personnel, but another part of me wanted to go. I put my concerns to Oliver.

'What's the worst that could happen?' he replied.

The charity event was going well and I was enjoying it. Thump, thump, thump: a distant Chinook flew into view. The noise seized my attention, my insides started to panic. The children and parents cheered, but then, weirdly, these turned into the cries of men dying in battle, women screaming at the hands of the Elkhaba, children shrieking after being forced to watch atrocities. The idyllic Cornish scene turned into the battle grounds of Afghanistan. My nostrils flared at the desert heat, like walking into a sauna. Sweat dripped from my forehead and hands. Panic-stricken, my stomach churned and my fists clenched. I had the urge to run as I spotted terrorists amongst the crowd. Instinctively, I checked for my weapon, but couldn't understand where it had gone. Looking down, I was now dressed in the shredded and blood-soaked uniform again. The pain in my leg returned, along with the rotten reek, and I started to get the familiar headache.

As the Chinook came closer I caught the side view of Planet in the porthole and I began waving my arms.

'Planet, over here,' I yelled. 'The Elkhaba are here, help me escape.'

As Planet turned to me, the other half of his face was missing. My breathing became erratic and I started going dizzy. I knew this wasn't right, but couldn't figure out why. I couldn't get enough oxygen in. I decided to make my escape and I ran through the onlookers who had gathered. Sprinting at full speed, knocking villagers who didn't move out of the way, the valley was up ahead with the boulder I'd hidden behind when making my escape from the forest. As I neared the slopes, a thought entered my head: where were all the small rocks on the floor to dodge? My mind was gyrating on its common-sense axis. I knew something wasn't true, I had to get a grip.

Almost reaching the large boulder, stalls and marquees replaced the images of Afghanistan. I ran inside a marquee and clattered into a table, tumbling over the other side, landing on my front. Laying there catching my breath and thoughts, laughter came from the other side. A few moments later I was helped up by Oliver.

'What the fuck happened, Johnny?' Oliver asked.

I couldn't speak.

'Look, let's get out of here.'

As he helped me up, I looked up to the crowd drinking at a bar. Unexpectedly in the crowd I saw Ella. I don't know who was more shocked, me or her. A bloke had his arm around her. Seeing me stare at Ella, he moved in front of her, displeased.

'Oh fuck, here we go,' Oliver muttered.

'Think you've had enough, pal,' he threatened. 'Best you trot along and gate-crash another bar.' His mates laughed along with him.

'Ella, it's good to see you. We need to talk,' I said—Oliver tried to pull me away.

'Do you know this drunk then?' the boyfriend asked Ella. 'Run along, pal, with your hippy boyfriend,' he said to me.

'Come on, dude, they're not worth the hassle,' Oliver said.

'I just want to talk to Ella. I know it's over, but I just want to clear the air, tell her what a moron I've been,' I whispered to Oliver.

'Yeah, pal, civvies don't belong 'ere, especially a pair of drunken tossers like you two,' the boyfriend said.

Ripping my arm from Oliver's grasp, I started making my way to him. Oliver grabbed me and held me firm. The boyfriend took a step closer and his mates did the same in unison.

'Paul, stop. Leave him,' Ella ordered. 'Johnny, go home. I don't want to talk to you ever again. It's over. I've got a new life now, something I should have done years ago. I wish I'd never got married to you or the army life.'

That hurt. 'Lee was in the army. Did that stop you sleeping with him. Maybe you've been around the whole base,' I sneered.

'What? she said, perplexed.

I knew what I'd said was untrue. It was a golden rule you didn't sleep with your mate's partner. 'You heard.'

'Why do you say that?' she blurted. 'I've been faithful. Honest.'

Now it sounded guilt to me. 'Oh, now you want to talk, huh? Going out with an ugly Northern twat from the RAF is any better than the army?' I said, and turned my back to walk away.

'*This* is Johnny? Oh my God, I expected so much more,' Paul chipped in.

'Leave it, Paul,' Ella said.

I stopped in my tracks but didn't turn around. Oliver tightened his grip on my arm again.

'Keep going, Johnny, they're not worth it.'

'*We're* not worth it? You taking the piss, pal? This is the loser that got his team mates killed in Afghanistan. In fact, he got some of our boys killed,' Paul fumed—the crowd muttered.

Oliver's grip loosened and he charged past me. I didn't need an invite. I followed him and, as he launched himself at this mouthy twat, I waded in on those who came forward. A mass fight erupted, the marquee getting wrecked. As I took some hits, I found I wanted more, so I started yelling for more. Additional blokes piled in, but rather than joining in, they started separating us. Some of the RAF lads were in a bad way with cuts and bloody faces; one lay motionless on the floor. Tables and chairs were damaged and lying on their sides, glasses strewn amongst them.

Oliver was being held down by four burly blokes. Through the arms holding him, he managed to wink at me from his puffy eye. More onlookers gathered on the fringes of the marquee, adding to the tension. I was also being restrained, but I stopped struggling and started to laugh. I looked around for Ella, but she had obviously made her exit. The twat boyfriend's face had started to swell, blood was pouring from his nose. He looked dazed and beaten. Fantastic, I thought.

'What the hell is going on in here?' someone bellowed. 'This is a charity event with kids. Who started this fight?'

As everyone went quiet, a cold shiver went down my spine and my eyes grew wide. I turned my head sharply and was stunned at the last person on earth I expected to see in full uniform: Roy.

'Johnny... What the...? What are you doing here? How did you...? Did they let you out?' he said, looking whiter than the strew table cloths.

I looked him up and down in disbelief. 'I could say the same to you. I was informed you were paralysed from the neck down, with no speech. They told me you had ended up in a nutty ward.'

I took a glance at his neck where a large scar had healed his wound, and he put his hand to his neck.

'Are these the same people who told me you had ended up in a psychiatric hospital, never to be released or even have visitors?' he asked.

'Reckon he should have been locked up in one,' Paul muttered.

Rabbit sharply turned his head. 'Flying Officer Berry, I suggest you keep absolutely quiet. Take your sorry arse home now. Make sure you report to my office first thing Monday morning. The rest of you, clean this disgraceful mess up, right now. I want all of you to donate one hundred pounds to this charity event. I'll be checking. Any questions?'

'No, sir,' a few mumbled.

Whilst the tables and chairs were being picked up, Berry left, still holding his nose. Oliver got to his feet, looking at his torn clothes. I was still being held tight. I looked at one of these blokes, fixing him with a mean stare. He must have read my mind; he released his hold and took a step back, looking uneasy. The other blokes holding me did the same.

'Make yourself useful and go mingle. Now,' Rabbit barked.

'Yes, sir,' they all replied, shifting out of the marquee.

I made myself more respectable, tucking in my shirt and retrieving one of my shoes that had come off. Nobody said a word or made eye contact. I wiped the blood from my lip.

'Should have known,' Rabbit said, picking up a table.

'I didn't start it. Berry did,' I retorted.

'I didn't mean that, Johnny. I meant I should have known better than believe you had ended up in a psychiatric ward. You've always been mad. I had a feeling it was bullshit, but your CO made it very convincing. But why the lies?'

'My CO? You mean Dick Brown told you that?' I said, confused.

'Yeah, every time I phoned.'

The penny dropped. 'Well it was the same Dick Brown that told me you were paralysed and in a nutty ward. He said I couldn't make contact.'

Rabbit looked at me puzzled.

'We've been kept apart, Roy, because of the enquiry and the court case. I reckon we're going to get the blame. They're plotting to hang us out to dry.'

'Sorry, mate, but I've been informed I don't have to appear at court,' he said. 'Once discharged from hospital, I found it strange I wasn't asked for an accurate statement, so I started contacting my senior officers. I was eventually given the chance to make a statement and I revealed the whole truth. Very soon after, I was decorated, promoted, and posted to RAF Odiham, all in quick succession. Missions for flying UK Special Forces have been passed by me, which I thought strange. I was obviously being kept out of the circle.'

'I knew something wasn't right, I could sense it. I've been too off my face to see it,' I said. 'So, are you going to court now?'

'I've been tasked for a mission around the same time: to drop some unsavoury American Marines into Afghanistan. I can't go into details here. We need to talk further. I think you've been stitched up for the fall, mate. Rest assured, I will go to court with the truth if I can.'

I held out my hand and as he stepped forward, but he put his arms around me. I patted him on the back.

'I never got to say thanks for saving my life, twice, mate,' he said, choked.

'You're really gonna have to stop hugging me. Anyway, I think that makes us even.'

He continued to hold.

'Rabbit, you can let go now.'

'I still want my fags and beers as promised though, mate,' he said.

Stepping back, Oliver quickly came over and gave Rabbit a firm handshake and then passed him a business card.

'It's bloody good to meet you, Roy,' Oliver said. 'Here's my address and contact details. Pop around this weekend. I'll leave you two alone to chat, but please, no alcohol. He needs to get better. Do you understand me, Roy?'

'Yeah, I understand. We both must be going through the same shit.' He looked over my shoulder. 'Oh hell, my boss is coming this way. Now clear off both of you, before you're arrested. I'll handle it from here.'

'Oh, that reminds me. I never got to tell you about that big black bear,' I said, and winked at him.

It was amazing to have seen him again. On the journey home, I didn't say a word and neither did Oliver. My mind was catching up with questions from our conversation in the marquee. At that moment, I made the decision to get my body and mind back to the Elite soldier, the person I was before. I would get through the court case untarnished and then leave the British Army. I also decided to banish Ella from my thoughts, move on, and accept a quick offer on the house. Thinking on, I now recognised the calming voice I'd heard just before almost shooting my brother through my front door: Haleema. Remembering my promise to return and visit her and Anoosheh, come hell or high water, I would get back to Afghanistan to find them.

# CHAPTER NINETEEN

Elated, I walked out of the court room. I hadn't realised how much I'd been sweating. Taking of my suit jacket, I unleashed my tie, as if pulling a python from around my neck, and threw it over my shoulder. As I reached the old wood-smelling main corridor, Dick Brown stood with his back to me, talking to his boss, Richard Reddin.

'Unlucky, boss,' I said. 'Your stitch-up didn't quite work.'

I could see the hairs on the back of his neck stand up, or so I imagined. He didn't turn around and, through fumbling words, he tried to continue to talk to his superior. Reddin looked over his shoulder and then raised an eyebrow as he stared down his nose at me.

'Nice to meet again, Rich, sorry, Richard,' I said. 'Oh, sorry, excuse my etiquette, sir.' We never used the word 'sir' when addressing an officer, so I'd said it with as much sarcasm as possible.

'Think you have some unfinished business to attend to, Dick,' Reddin said. 'You know where to get hold of me if you need me.'

'Playing croquet with the other Ruperts, sir?' I butted in.

Dick swung around fast, his face redder than ever, like his head was going to explode. 'You'll never know as you won't make it to officer, or in fact, even your next rank,' he raged.

Nonchalantly, I wiped his spit from my shirt and took a step back from him. 'You wanna take it easy, dude. Watch that old heart of yours.'

His fists tighten and his shoulders tensed, appearing he was going launch at me. I was having the desired effect.

'You little fucking waste of space. I'll kick your…'

'Dick,' Richard said, stopping him just as he was getting into full stride. 'I suggest you deal with this in your office, not in public. Then you can visit me for a long chat.'

Dick reluctantly turned around; I could only wonder what his face looked like. Behind Richard, looking on, were the families of the deceased soldiers and RAF crew. As Dick turned back to me, I grinned. Striding past him, I forcefully bumped his shoulder with mine.

'See you Monday morning, Dick,' I said.

'Oh yes, I'll be there. Be ready for what I have in store for you. Oh, by the way, it's a shame Ella left. She was getting along fine with Lee.'

As I walked to the watching crowd I wondered what he had meant. I hustled my way through everybody. They must have thought I was being very rude, especially after the support they had given me leading up to the court case, but I had my own agenda, my own plan, and nothing else mattered.

Outside, I waded through a small group of reporters, all wanting to stick their microphones in my face. A barrage of questions came from all directions. My lawyer came bounding down the steps, trying to stop the questions and filming.

'Stop, stop. This is not to be broadcast. This is of the highest confidentiality. This man is an Elite soldier,' the short, fat lawyer bleated.

'Now the whole world knows. Thanks, fat man.'

A couple of the reporters found this highly amusing.

'Tell you what, chaps, if you pixel my face out, I'll give you the best lead on the outcome,' I said. 'Deal?'

It was like hanging a piece of raw meat in front of a pack of wolves. The short, fat lawyer tried to intervene, advising me not to speak.

'You ready?' I said calmly to the reporters.

'Ready when you are,' the nearest one said.

A microphone nearly went up my nose, this action prompted the others to bombard me with foam-ended microphones. I wrenched my arm from the lawyer's hand.

'Thanks for turning up today, fat man,' I said, 'but to be honest, I didn't need you. I stuck to the truth, and I have come away with my morals and integrity intact. I didn't want to enter a plea bargain with the prosecutor as you suggested. Whilst you hide behind your little desk doing what you do best, there are men and woman out there fighting for the rights of your country. So, run along and pick up your handsome pay cheque.'

The colours drained from the lawyer's face and he walked off, smaller in stature than he already was.

'If you want the complete story of Operation Blue Halo,' I continued, 'including today's verdict, coming down the steps in the next minute or so is my boss. He's dressed in a grey suit, which, by the way, is too small and dates to the seventies, and has an awful choice of tie.'

Right on cue, Dick came out of the main doors; perfect.

'That's him there,' I said. 'He would love to answer all your questions.'

Without me having to say another word, the marauding reporters made a charge for Dick, shouting questions. See you Monday, Dick, I thought.

It was a beautiful summer's day. A massive load had been lifted and I now walked with a purpose to my stride. I threw my jacket in a waste bin. Time check: 13.45 hrs. I was now three minutes late for my lift. I had begun to hate being late. In fact, I had found I'd become more agitated about petty things since discharged from hospital just over a year ago. My stride now turned into a fast walk. Johnny, slow down, I told myself. Again, I looked at my watch: four minutes late. I bounded into a sprint as if being chased. As I rounded the corner into St James Street, I searched in vain for my lift.

'For fuck's sake…' I started, but then I saw vehicle over the road, flashing its headlights.

I strolled over to it and, sure enough, Oliver was waving with both hands, like a crazed kid. I opened the door.

'You've changed your motor,' I said moodily.

'So?'

'So? It's the little details that can fuck your day up. You should have told me.'

I settled into my seat and slammed the door shut. I had got to the stage of yanking my seatbelt repeatedly as the inertia reel had locked out. I slung it behind me. There was an awkward pause.

'Bad day at the office, Johnny?' He burst out laughing.

I started laughing with him. My mind flashed back to when Rabbit and I had fits of laughter after almost being vaporised by the missile. My amusement fizzled out and my mind wandered off.

'Johnny, are you all right? Johnny, Earth calling Johnny…'

I shook my head and looked at Oliver's worried expression. My eyes welled up. 'This court case has stirred some old ghosts. Just take me back home please, back to my house in Poole.'

'What? I've driven up from Newquay, and now you want me to take you all way to Poole?'

'Got a problem with that, Oliver?' I snapped.

'I thought we were going to stay in a hotel here in London, you know, have a few beers with me. That's why I brought your luggage you'd packed after you caught the train.'

'Well, you thought wrong. That's not part of my plans. Now you either drive me home or I'll catch the train.'

Oliver, pissed off, started the car and, thrusting it into gear, wheel spun away.

'So, you brought my bags, the ones I'd asked you to, right?' I asked.

'Of course, I did, I'm not a total idiot,' he snapped.

I grinned at him whilst getting out my mobile, and I phoned Roy.

'Vinnie, tell me it was good news,' he answered.

'Sorry, Roy, it's not good. I've been court-martialled. They've blamed it all on us two. I heard you're next to give evidence; you're in the firing line. I'm on the way to prison.' I waited for his response, biting my lip.

'No fucking way, you deserve a fucking medal not a court martial. No fucking way. I'll give evidence all right; I'll blow the lid on... hold on, on the way to prison on a mobile? You wanker. Ha ha, very funny.'

Hearing his relief, I laughed with him. 'It's all good, dude,' I said. 'I'm in the clear.'

Oliver happily silently punched the air; he must have been itching to know what happened.

'Brilliant news, mate,' Roy said.

'Should have seen Dick's and the prosecutor's face, especially when I gave them your signed written statement,' I said gleefully.

'I'm really sorry I couldn't go. They kept postponing the start date. You know I would have, but...'

'I understand,' I butted in. 'As I said before, we both owe each other nothing now but friendship. We've been to hell and back and saved each other's arse a few times.'

He paused and let out a sigh. 'You still owe me fags. I had to go through a lot of therapy after you destroyed my fags in that cave.'

'Rabbit, I won't be able to afford fuck all if I spend much more on the phone to you. Are you still flying off to Afghan on Wednesday?'

'Yep, still at 4.30 a.m. Why?'

'I'm gonna be on that flight. I want you to go along with it in whatever form. Got it?'

'What...? Why...? How? You're not booked on,' he said, confused.

'That's on a need-to-know basis. Just go along with it. Don't let your pilot take off without me. See ya Wednesday.' I ended the call.

'What are you up to, Johnny?' Oliver asked.

Taking no notice of his question, I checked the battery life on my phone: one bar left. This agitated me. Bad planning, Johnny, I thought. I delved deep into my trouser pocket and pulled out a scrap bit of paper. I texted to the mobile number scribbled on it:

'Meeting still on time. Don't be late. Post code BH15 1QG. No. 3. You can stay the night. Have a few beers. I've so much info to give you.'

I found myself looking at my phone every minute. Where the hell was the reply? I decided to shut my eyes and get some sleep.

'Oh great, I'll bloody drive in silence,' Oliver moaned.

I drifted off and my thoughts turned back to the court case. It had been hard going, very emotional, but I had felt the strangest thing. Next to me in the courtroom were Planet, Shrek, and Fish, all watching me. I couldn't see them physically but could feel their presence. I don't believe in ghosts or shit like that, but I drew strength from this. Dick's lies and accusations were outrageous; he had orchestrated a web of deceit. He also informed the courtroom of all my bad conduct since returning to base, including the conversation in his office between me and the military police. Just as the prosecution thought they were going to turn the wheels on the rack, we presented Rabbit's full statement. This was the bombshell I'd dropped in Dick's lap. This court case had made me resolute. I'd spent the last eight weeks making a lot of phone calls and calling in a lot of favours.

Bzzzzzzz!

My phone went off in my hand. Opening my eyes, I opened the text.

'Can't wait Soldier X. Yes to the beers & overnight stay. As you know I have an important flight the next day, so must be up early. Lol. Hope your intel is juicy. Neal.'

Smirking, I said, 'Twat.'

'Who's that then?' Oliver said, still sulking. 'Oh don't tell me, you can't say or you will have to kill me.'

'I cannot answer that question, sir.'

'Ha bloody ha, you're not being interrogated now,' he retorted.

'Loosen your knickers, dude. It was just some knobhead I befriended when Rabbit told me he was doing an interview.'

'You, friend someone?'

I noticed we weren't on the motorway but pulling off on a slip road into the Fleet Services on the M3.

'What are you doing? This wasn't in the plan?' I said angrily.

'What plan? Whose plan? I don't know anything, but what I do know is I want a piss and I'm bloody starving.'

I began getting anxious. 'Bloody starving? You don't know the fucking meaning of starving. You wanna try surviving days without food and water in the searing heat and cold of the desert.'

Looking perplexed, he replied, 'You wanna find your little brother with a gun at his head and about to end it all without a care about his family, the family who has always been there for him. Now, if you want to carry on, Johnny, then start fucking walking. I'm off for a piss and some scoff.' He got out and slammed his door.

'Bollocks to ya,' I shouted back.

Sitting in silence, it hit me hard what he had just said. His words went over and over in my mind. He was right: what a dickhead I'd been.

Out of the car, I slammed my door and slumped on it. The anger was still growing. Turning around, I pounded the roof a few times. At the same time, a BMW pulled up two spaces alongside me with music blaring and windows open. The blokes in the back started mimicking my actions and laughing at me. All four of them were now taking the piss. Something made me go over. I swung open the passenger door. The young man looked shocked; however he didn't have time to react. Pulling him forward, I wrapped the seatbelt around his neck, leant in and punched the driver straight on his nose. A sharp cracking noise preceded a trickle of blood. I pulled back and hit him again. Whilst the driver sat there moaning and holding both hands to his face, I turned my stare to the blokes in the back who had now stopped taking the piss and were holding their hands up.

'Sorry, mate, but it was only a bit of fun. We don't want any more trouble,' the young lad on the right said.

I lowered my fist and leant back out of the car. The passenger let out a gasp for air and started coughing and spluttering.

'Bad day at the office,' I said.

Slamming the door shut and, without looking back, I strutted the way Oliver had walked.

I found him sitting at a table, about to tuck into his food, so I sat next to him.

'Sorry, Oliver. Once I've finished my objective, I'll tell you everything, maybe even write a book about it one day. Now, you gonna share that pasty or what?'

Through a mouthful of food, he replied, 'Tastes like shit, not like a traditional Cornish one. And no, buy your fucking own.'

After he had finished, we made our way back to the car park. Parked next to the BMW was a police vehicle with its blues flashing. This didn't bode well.

'Meet me at the exit slip lane,' I said. 'If the police ask you any questions, you know nothing. You travelled alone. Got it?'

Oliver, watching the policemen inspecting his vehicle, started to ask what I'd done, but I'd already left. I didn't run, so as not to raise suspicion, but causally strolled around the rear of the petrol station. When it was clear, I walked across the slip road and tucked myself in a bush just on the fringe. Whilst I crouched, I cursed myself for attracting attention with the BMW lads. To mess up my plans at this stage was damn stupid.

Ten cars went by and I started to fear the worst. Had Oliver been arrested? Then I caught sight of him heading slowly up the slip lane and he pulled over with hazard lights going. Checking the police weren't behind him, I came out from hiding and made my way quickly to him. I lowered the back of the seat into a lying-down position as he drove off.

'Fill me in then,' I said.

'No big deal. I just told them you were some loony on the run who went around pissing everybody off, which is the truth.'

With a smirk, I closed my eyes and went over the details of my plan.

# CHAPTER TWENTY

Fun times filled my thoughts, remembering when Fish and Shrek had played a prank on me and Planet. We were taking a well-earned rest on a training exercise. The next stages of the mission were to head out after sunset on a rigid inflatable boat and navigate the jungle waters to a set destination. From there we were to set out on foot and recce a small village to gain information. Suddenly, I was woken up with Fish putting his hand over my mouth.

'Quick, boss, we have to move. We're being tracked and the enemy are preparing a raid,' he whispered in my ear. 'No time to dismantle the camp, let's go.'

Shrek had said the same to Planet. I picked up my weapon and sack and moved quickly to the RIB which was tied on the water's edge. Behind me was the hulking frame of Planet. We dived into the boat and, sliding across the bottom, almost out over the opposite side. To stop going all the way over, I grabbed the hand rope.

A second later, Planet crashed into me, knocking all but the top half of me over the side. I tried to hang onto the rope, but my hands were covered in something slippery. Dragging myself out of the water, I had a terrible taste in my mouth. In front of me were Shrek and Fish rolling around on the ground in fits of laughter; I was fuming. They weren't trying to help us avoid capture. Up popped Planet, covered in a slimy blue substance with white foam covering most of his face.

'What the actual fuck?' I burst out laughing.

'Ye two better start running. I'll beat ye stupid until you beg for mercy,' Planet ranted at Fish and Shrek, who were now hysterical with laughter.

As Planet went to get out, he slipped back in and reappeared in a worst state.

'Look, it's Papa Smurf,' Fish said.

I looked down at myself: I was the same, which now didn't seem as funny. Slipping and sliding, Planet clambered out. He looked at me and started to laugh. He then strode over to Fish and picked him up by the scruff, dragging him back to the RIB. Fish was tossed in like a rag doll. Next, he turned to Shrek, but Shrek had already taken a run, and he jumped in behind Fish. After a bit more piss-taking we calmed down and cleaned up. It transpired they had filled the boat with shampoo, shaving foam, and used the dye from inside a blue smoke canister.

As most pranks go, it was hilarious, but as most pranks go, it has its downside. We couldn't get rid of all the slimy soap, which made the next part of the mission's journey hell. We reckoned our host enemies could smell us from miles away. Our hands and faces were stilled dyed blue at sunrise, a question we couldn't answer when asked by our CO. Fortunately, the exercise was a complete success, which let us off the hook.

My eyes opened gently with the sound of the radio softly playing through the noise of the traffic. Shadows and lights flickered through the side window. I had an empty feeling in the pit of my stomach, a sense of loss and sadness. My dream about the good times was now just a nostalgic memory, one I could never share with my lost mates. Shaking my head to clear the grogginess, I sat upright and moved the back of the seat up. I looked down at my watch, shocked to see I'd been asleep for just over an hour.

'Afternoon,' Oliver said. 'Blimey, you were flitting all over the place. Chasing chickens in your sleep, were you?'

'Something like that, dude.'

I had to start being kinder to him, not only because he was my brother who really had saved me from the grip of desperation, but also as I had a few more favours to ask of him.

'Thanks for driving me home. Maybe have a few beers tonight, yeah?'

'No big deal,' he said. 'Yeah, I could do with a few tinnies.'

A mix of emotions and thoughts flooded through me as I focused on the street sign, the place where I lived. I thought of Ella, the promise of our own family, my last kiss and embrace before Operation Blue Halo, our barbecues and parties with mates and family, the mess I had got into before I was found. In that short journey down my street I'd packed so many past emotions in. Oliver drew up outside my house.

'Are you all right?'

I didn't answer; in fact, I couldn't. The lump in my had throat stopped me. Studying the property in detail, it didn't seem a happy house anymore. The garden that we both took pride in was overgrown with weeds and littered with rubbish. Hanging baskets were dead, pots choked by weeds. All the curtains were shut. It was as if a recluse was living there, someone with something to hide. I felt sick. Oliver put his hand on my arm and gave it a squeeze.

'Come on then. I'm dying for a cuppa,' he said briskly.

I took a deep breath and let it out slowly. I knew there would be more demons inside, waiting to stir my conscience.

Pushing the gate open, I looked at the lounge curtains, imagining Ella pulling them back and waving with tears in her eyes, like she used to when I returned from an exercise. However, this time she wasn't going to swing open the front door and greet me with hugs and kisses. I thought I had banished thoughts of her; how naïve I was. I took the front door key from inside the little compartment in my wallet. Lifting the key to the door, my hand was slightly shaking. I tried to shield this from Oliver.

'I'll give you a minute, dude. I'll go and get your bags,' he said.

Again, I lifted the key to the door. Turning it, I slightly opened the door and was rewarded with my house's familiar scent. Everyone's home has its own smell. I then got a whiff of the destruction and evil I had wreaked on the place. Memories came flooding back of the months of trouble I was in, including my last night of desperation. Quickly, I pulled the door shut. Follow the plan, Johnny. Get yourself sorted and get inside, you big girl. It's not exactly a bloody war zone, I told myself sternly.

For some reason, I looked both ways up the street, like I was checking the coast was clear before breaking in. How stupid; this was my house. Taking a deep breath, I turned the key again and pushed the door, but there was something on the other side. I pushed harder until I could just squeeze in. Mail and local papers were piled on the mat. The lounge was dingy, cold, and musty, with an eerie quiet about it. I was half expecting someone to jump out, like in a horror movie.

Oliver came inside and said, 'Jesus. You've got some reading to do.'
I scoffed.

'Oh, by the way, lucky Mum and Dad have been paying money into your account, otherwise you wouldn't still have electricity, let alone a house,' he remined me.

I knew this of course. Maybe Oliver knew I hadn't thanked them.

He stepped over the mound behind the door. Squeezing past, he turned the light on. Looking around, I was horrified to see the destruction and the sickening words scrawled over the walls. I didn't want to read anymore but found myself compelled to. Coming back was harder than I'd thought; this wasn't detailed in my plan.

'Nothing a lick of paint won't sort out,' Oliver said. 'I've seen worse places finished on *60 Minute Makeover*. Now, I'll find the kettle, you clear the doorway and bring your bags in. It's about time you helped on your mission.'

I dropped the luggage and walked to the dining room. I caught a glimpse of myself in the mirror, still with the graffiti on it; a shudder went down my spine. I turned away sharply and moved into the kitchen. The smell was putrid. Remains of food and empty Jack Daniels bottles were strewn across the worktops and floor. Dead insects lay among these; some had fallen foul of the remaining dregs of alcohol at the bottom of the bottles. A wash of guilt came over me and I hung my head.

'I'll get some milk and food from the local corner shop,' Oliver said. 'You can clean some cups while I'm gone. Won't be long.'

I was shocked at how much destruction and mess I'd caused, not just to my house, the person I'd become back then. Right, Johnny, this is part of the healing process, I thought, reminding myself of my plan. A tidy camp is a happy camp.

I started by opening the blinds and windows in the kitchen, which spurred me onto the dining room. I felt a lot of the demons blow out with the stench. The sun coming through lifted my spirits. Wading through the bottles and rubbish on the kitchen floor, I found a roll of garden refuse sacks in the larder. With every piece of waste I picked up, I slung it in the bag with a purpose, making me feel better. I couldn't clear quickly enough, like a man possessed. Really, I was trying to hide my past, my embarrassment.

With each full bag now holding a wretched past, I threw them out the back door. On my fifth sack I looked up to see Oliver standing there with a bag of groceries, and a big smile. Nothing was said; I felt what he felt. He came past and started to make a brew. With the rubbish cleared in the kitchen and dining room, I moved into the lounge. I opened the curtains and windows, where yet more insects lay dead. Dealing with the mess in the sunlit room was more challenging. My prized collection of books was jumbled in the broken glassed cabinet; others lay in a heap at the base. This fuelled my guilt further.

I started to pick them up and brush the shards of glass off. A tiny white object on the floor caught my eye, nothing normally of any significance, except this tiny object had played a massive part. A white micro ball had stopped me in my tracks, derailing my healing process. I visualised myself kneeling, slumped on the floor, letting my pistol do the talking. I couldn't turn my stare away, like time had frozen.

'Tea up, dude,' a soft voice came from behind me. 'Come sit in the garden. I've got some Jaffa cakes.'

Oliver put his hand on my shoulder and turned me towards the open patio doors. Outside, the sun warmed the tears in my eyes. I pulled up an overturned chair and sat at the patio table, which was covered in a blanket of green mould. Oliver brought me a brew and the Jaffa cakes out on a Tupperware lid.

'I couldn't find your plates,' he said, and threw me a big smile. 'Must have had one hell of a party before you left.'

The sun glinted off his brilliant white teeth. I'd faced the demon in the lounge, the one I had feared the most. No more upsets now. I'm back, this is my house and the demons can all fuck off, I thought. With that, I dunked my Jaffa and sipped my brew. Looking around the back garden, it was worse than the front. Oliver had shut his eyes, looking directly into the sun.

'Oliver, when have you got to go back?'

'Tomorrow. I've got work Monday.'

'I need a favour, bro,' I said meekly.

'Oh God, you called me bro. Must be a big favour.' He smirked.

'It is, bro, I mean, Oliver. I need help to get the place cleaned and the graffiti gone. I need some new, basic furniture, and shopping. Also, the gardens need sorting. All by Tuesday morning.'

'Shit. You've been watching too much *60 Minute Makeover*. Anything else?'

'Yes, I need you to put it on the market by the end of the week and take care of the sale.'

He stopped sunning himself and looked me in the eyes. 'Are you being serious? I've got to get back to work. I've got a big contract to sort.'

'I wouldn't ask if it wasn't important,' I said, emotionally blackmailing. 'Anyway, you've never had a big contract, and you're your own boss. I'm sure the waves will be there to catch when you get back. Just one week, bro, then you can deal with the house sale from Newquay. Please?'

Oliver rubbed his stubble, contemplating.

'I've already signed the sale of the house over to you through the solicitors: Bennett & Webster in the High Street. All you need to do is go in there Monday, show them your ID and sign some forms,' I added, trying to make it sound easier.

'But how did you know if I would agree? And what about Ella's half?'

'All covered. My solicitors are in contact with her solicitor. They will transfer her percentage over to her; simple. She has signed and sent her letter back agreeing to this. Tell you what: I'll give you two thousand pounds from the sale. Think what that would do for you: new surfboard, more surfing, more girls, more beer, and more pasties.'

'Why have it all done by Tuesday? Where are you going? I mean, you must be off somewhere or you could sort the house sale yourself.'

'I'm busy, going away to tie up loose ends,' I said.

'You're going back to Afghan aren't you, bro. Is it to find that female doctor?' He knew he had hit the nail on the head.

'Sorry, I cannot answer that question, sir,' I replied.

'You're a dumb arse, but I suppose we all have different dreams. Three thousand quid and you got yourself a deal. In fact, I'll even wear a pinny when I'm cleaning.'

'Fuck off. Now you're taking the piss. I don't want a long-haired, scruffy bloke in a pinny in my house. I have standards. Done deal, Oliver, three it is,' I said, and slapped him on the back. 'Right, let's get clearing up. We'll start upstairs. You take the bedrooms and I'll take the bathroom, and then downstairs you take the kitchen and dining room. Leave the lounge to me. If we have time, we'll start on the gardens. I want it spotless. OK?'

'Bloody hell, dude, have you always been this bossy? Not related to Adolf, were you?' he asked.

Rabbit had asked me something similar in Afghanistan, but this time I smirked and headed upstairs.

By Sunday evening we had totally cleared the house. Even throwing out photos of Ella seemed to have a real purpose to a new beginning. Between trips to the local dump, charity shops, and DIY stores, we had slapped some paint on the lounge, kitchen, and dining room walls. Admittedly, it was a bit slapdash, but we had put in many hours, going to bed very late and getting up extra early. Whilst putting the last of my signed books back, I found one which I had received from Planet on my birthday. It was a signed copy of *Touching the Void* by Joe Simpson. Planet had added his own signing next to the author's: 'When it gets tough out there, remember this book. A faint heart never fucked a pig. Your best mate, Planet.'

God, I miss him, and the rest, I thought.

'Got something for you, dude,' he said, exhausted.

Delving into his rucksack, he pulled out a bottle of Rattler Cornish Cider. He levered the bottle-top off with a key-ring bottle opener and handed it to me. I hesitated, as I'd not touched alcohol since the last night in my house.

'Just the one. If you want, that is. Celebrate your new, clean house,' he said.

Oh what the hell, I thought, and took it. I waited for him to open his and clunked mine with his. I took a long swig and it tasted good.

'I'm not here tomorrow. Got to go in and see the boss.'

'That wanker,' Oliver said.

'Can you finish here? Also, can you make yourself scarce all-day Tuesday and Wednesday?'

'Why? Where the hell am I gonna stay?'

Not wanting to give too much away, I replied, 'I've got a friend coming over Tuesday, staying the night, if you get my drift. Been a while, dude. I've booked you into a Premier Inn just up the road. It's all paid for. You can come back Wednesday evening.'

Putting his cider down and sitting on the second-hand sofa, he said, 'Booked? You hadn't even had my answer.'

Sitting next to him, I said, 'If you had gone as long without it, I would do the same for you.'

'Not a five-star hotel then?' he replied. 'OK, I get the message, I'll do it.'

'Cheers.'

'When are you going to Afghan then?' he said, changing the subject.

'Wednesday, but do me a favour: don't tell a soul. If anyone asks where I am, I've moved to Edinburgh. Tell Mum and Dad once I've settled that I am going to invite you all up to stay. It's very important you don't mention Afghan to anyone. OK?' Before he could question me further, I said, 'Goodnight,' and went to bed.

# CHAPTER TWENTY-ONE

After a crap night's sleep, thinking of the meeting with Dick, I decided to get up early and have a brew. It was just after 05.15 hrs. Opening the back door, I took a deep sniff of the beautiful, fresh morning air and watched the vapour of my breath as I exhaled. I looked up at the stars and moon. Funny to think that fourteen months ago I was looking up at the same stars and moon, but in quite a different way. It's mad how dramatically your life can change, I thought. Not wanting to dwell on this, I walked to the shed at the bottom of the garden. The door was padlocked, and I didn't have a clue where the key was.

'Bollocks,' I loudly whispered.

Returning from the kitchen, armed with a screwdriver, I started to prise at the padlock. After some swearing and brute force, I managed to pull the slide bolt completely off. I threw the screwdriver, trying to land the blade in the grass, like throwing a knife. I caught movement from the neighbour's curtains. I looked up and gave a wave. The curtain gap shut again, and I could only imagine what he or she was calling me. I flicked the switch in the shed, but the light didn't come on. Flicking the switch repeatedly didn't help. Between the moonlight and streetlights, I could make out my bike handlebars at the back. The only problem was it was blocked with other crap. Rather than trying to get everything out first, I tried to lift the bike up and over. As I leant forward and pulled the frame up, it seemed to be coming, but then it got snagged. The weight of the bike pulled me off-balance and I toppled forward.

I felt a sharp pain above my left eye as I fell among the clutter. A little dazed, I put my hand to my eye and felt a stinging sensation and then the moisture of blood. It was dark and damp at the bottom of the shed. I started to panic; I had to get out. Thrashing about and breathing heavily, I managed to kick some of the items off me and get up. Once outside the shed, the fear dispersed, but my headache had come back.

Sitting down, I touched the lump on my head. My hand was covered in blood. I went back to the kitchen and looked in the new mirror in the lounge. I had a nasty two-inch cut above my eyebrow which was still seeping blood. In the kitchen I found a white tea towel and wrapped it round my head, pulling it tight at the rear.

I needed my bike, so, not to be beaten, I returned to the shed. Pulling some of the items out and throwing them on the lawn behind me, I saw what had caused the wound: the edge of the barbecue. I yanked the contraption out and threw it aside. Once it had toppled over, I gave it a good karate kick, and then decided it needed another one. Triumphant, I rolled my bike out. Both tyres were flat. Great fucking start to a day, I thought.

With the dawn breaking, I leant further into the shed to find my foot pump. As I was leaning over, I felt a presence behind me and suddenly a kick sent me crashing head first back to the bottom of the shed. Quickly I got up, spun round, and lunged forward at the attacker, but was pushed aside onto the lawn. I swung around and leg-swiped the attacker's ankle. He fell to the ground and let out a yell. I immediately jumped up and leant over him, fist in chamber to strike.

'Whoaaaa, Johnny, it's me,' Oliver said.

'You fucking idiot, I could have killed you. What the hell are you playing at?'

He looked at the blood-stained tea towel around my head. 'You look like Kato from the *Pink Panther*.'

I let go and sat next to him, sharing his amusement. The neighbour's window opened.

'Will you two keep the bloody noise down please. You've bloody woke my new-born baby up, and the bloody wife now.'

'Sure, sorry,' I hushed.

'Jesus. Best you get cleaned up,' Oliver whispered.

Getting up off the damp grass, I helped Oliver up and asked him to get my bike ready. After sorting my head with steri-strips and washing the blood off my face, I got ready for my meeting with Dick, remembering his words to me: "be ready for what I have in store for you." They continued to play on my mind. What else could he do that he hadn't tried already? I had to stick to my plan, I thought.

Riding to work brought back memories of how it felt really wanting to go to work, relishing the new challenges, meeting my mates, the camaraderie, the thrill of being in the Elite, the best in the world. This time, though, I knew it would be different. Most of the old gang were dead or had taken a dislike to me on my return from hospital, maybe poisoned against me by Dick; or was I just being paranoid? I did have a few loyal friends left and had called on them to help me in my plan to get back to Afghan, the true friends that tried to support me when I hit the ground at a hundred miles an hour, the ripples ruining everything around me.

I arrived at the main gate and was met by two lads I'd never seen before. I handed them my identification.

'God damn, what happened to the other handsome two?' I joked. 'When did they let you two out of the chemical testing lab?'

Checking my details, one of them said, 'Maybe you are handsome. I just want to tell you somethin'; there are more of us ugly motherfuckers than there are of you. Hey, so watch out.'

The lad next to him found this funny.

'Keep talking, dude, one day you will say something intelligent,' I said.

Then this lad other started, 'Maybe we shouldn't let this handsome guy in. Doesn't look like the sort to be in with our lot. Never heard of this lady before. You sure you got the right place, mate? Are you sure you don't want the hairdressers down the road?'

'I'm shocked you even know what a hairdresser is,' I retaliated. 'I've seen a better hairstyle in a shower plughole. Now, if you want to give my CO, Dick, a quick call and let him know you've cancelled his meeting, then be my guest. I'll just pop down to the hairdressers and book you in.'

'Best you get on your bike and fuck off then,' he retorted, but gave me a flash of his broad smile.

I kept my head down whilst riding up to the office block. Lads were milling about and didn't take much notice. I wanted to get this finished and get home. Too many bad memories spoiled the good ones. I tried not to focus on the gym and canteen where I'd had some good laughs with Planet, Fish, and Shrek, plus a few others. I took off my rucksack, pulled the lock out and secured the bike to a post. You couldn't trust anyone in here; everyone seemed to borrow what wasn't theirs. After taking a swig from the water bottle, I retrieved letter I had written before the court case. I took a deep breath, not that I was nervous, but I didn't want to come across with a weak voice.

I walked up the stairs and, just as I reached the top, I bumped into Richard Reddin.

'Ah, Johnny Vince,' he said drolly. 'Glad you could grace us with your presence. It's been a while hasn't it. I hope we will have you to stay for a bit longer.'

'Cut the niceties, sirrr.' I left him standing there.

Going through each door in the corridor, my resistance grew to whatever Dick had in store for me. Don't get angry in here, Johnny, play it cool, I thought. I knocked on the door and waited. It was like being at school again after being sent to the head for beating up the school bully. No reply, so I knocked again. Whilst waiting, I looked at the sign on the door which had his name on it. It was then I thought of crossing out his second name and writing 'HEAD' in its place. If only I'd brought a marker pen. Still no answer, so this time I banged with my fist and let myself in.

'You can go back outside and wait to be called in,' Dick barked, raising his eyeline.

Slamming the door behind me, I said, 'Sorry Dick, I haven't the time or patience to play your fucking games.' Not playing it cool, Johnny, I thought.

I threw the letter at him and he looked at the front of the envelope. 'What's this?' he asked.

'I think you know what that is. If not, you're dumber than I thought. It's my resignation. I quit, capeesh?'

'Well, that cuts our meeting short. But I wonder, especially with a good word from me, if your old regiment would have you back. You may even be demoted and become the ridicule of the barracks,' he said, amusing himself.

'I wouldn't expect a *good* recommendation from you. I'm not planning to go back, you fucking moron. I quit the army,' I said, seething. 'And furthermore, it's useless officers like you and Reddin who tarnish the reputation of this Elite establishment.'

Dick stayed silent, whilst I clenched my fists, the adrenalin gushing through me. The familiar headache returned. Dick picked up his gold-plated pen and studied it. Slowly, he leaned back in his leather swivel chair and smiled.

'Well?' I burst.

'You think you can just walk out on this regiment and the army without a stain on your character? What about the blame for the loss? I think not, Johnny Vince.'

'There is no blame. I was acquitted. If there's any blame, it's down to you for not getting us out sooner, for not sending air support, for not making sure a quick response team was ready to go. Need I go on?'

'Lee bought this fountain pen for me,' he said. 'Talking of Lee, how's Ella?' His tone had changed.

'What's that supposed to mean?' I had taken the bait.

'Someone had to keep Ella happy whilst you were missing in action. They seem to hit it off, don't you think?' He ran the end of the pen over his lips.

'I've spoken to Ella about that; he never made her happy. Apparently, he has a tiny cock, like you.'

'She needed a shoulder to cry on you whilst you were boozing your life away.' He smiled.

I was at boiling point. Calm it, Johnny, don't let him get to you. Think of a cool answer. 'Goodbye, good riddance,' I said—pathetic.

As I turned to walk out, he said, 'Aren't you forgetting something?'

I heard him opening a drawer. I turned around but wished I hadn't. I stared at the pistol in his hand. He was looking over it, gloating as if to say, 'Oh, look what I've got, naughty boy'. I stayed silent and tried not to look concerned. Now I knew what he'd meant by "something in store for me."

'Nothing to say, Johnny? Makes a change. Or is your complex character thinking of what to do next?'

'You're still pissed off I led the operation instead of your son, Lee, aren't you? In fact, no one else recommended him except Daddy.'

'It was the right action for Lee to inform the military police of your reckless behaviour.'

'Well, that's in the past. Adios,' I said, and went to leave.

'Oh, you're going to be dragged back to jail, then through the courts, and then through the media.' His voice had changed from smug to menacing. 'And I'm going to be the one who comes down on you like a ton of bricks. I hope when they find out you won this in a bet that they throw the book at you. And the poor bastard who gave it to you, I hope you can live with his punishment.'

He slammed the pistol down on his desk and the thud made me jump. I launched across the room, sliding my knees across the table, knocking his papers, pen pot, and desk name badge in his direction. Grabbing him by his tie, I thrust it up under his chin. He tried to land a fist to the side of my head, but I blocked it on his inner arm joint. I gripped that arm and pulled it in close, and then pushed my forehead hard against his.

'Listen, you fuck-head, I'm quitting the army, and if you mention this pistol matter to anyone, if I do time, I swear I will not only blow the lid on Operation Blue Halo, I will blow the lid on all yours and Lee's lousy plans to set me up.' I squeezed him harder. 'One last thing: I will make your life so miserable, you'll beg me to finish you off.'

I loosened my grip, and with the release he headbutted me on the bridge of the nose, sending me back. He managed to push my arms off and throw me back off the desk. I landed on my back, winded. Before I could get my breath, he had come around and landed a boot to my side. The pain rippled through my ribcage as I sucked in air. I let out a groan. Seizing his opportunity, he pulled his leg back for another kick. Reactions took over and I lifted my foot up, catching him right, square in his bollocks. Doubled over in pain, holding his groin, he sank to his knees, drawing in air.

I stood up, wobbling from my painful ribs. My head was a daze and the blood ran down my face.

'Get out, get out,' he shouted through his pain.

Doors began bashing in the corridors with the sound of feet. I moved behind the desk and stood ready for anyone that came in wanting trouble. The door swung open and two lads stood there, looking in disbelief.

'What the fuck is going on?' Mike said.

Mike was one of the good guys. The lad who stood next to him, Scott, was one of my recent drinking friends, one of the culprits who joined in at the pub. He was also best mates with Lee.

'Just showing our CO some combat moves,' I said. 'Do you want me to show you? I'm happy to oblige, maybe both at once,' I threatened.

'Listen, mate, best you just clear off before you have the entire base breathing down your neck,' Mike said.

As he pushed Scott out of the way of the door, I quickly bent down and searched. Picking up my rucksack from among the items on the floor, I then fastened the drawstrings. I moved past Dick, his face red. He went to speak, so I hit him hard once more, and he fell to the floor. I threw my letter on him.

'Consider this the end, Dick. Remember what I said.'

Mike took a step to the side and, as I went past, Scott went to help Dick.

'Good to see you back to yourself, Vinnie,' Mike said. 'I hope you will look back and realise there are quite a few blokes who looked up to you, and still do, me being one of them. Need anything else, just ask, got it?'

I shook Mike's hand and then left without saying a word. I didn't have to; I knew Mike had meant it.

A crowd had gathered outside to see what the commotion was about. The blood from my swollen nose had run on to my white shirt; also, the cut had opened above my eye. All was silent as I unlocked my bike and cautiously got on.

'Didn't get your promotion then?' a voice said from the crowd.

Everybody laughed. Not wanting to show I didn't find the comment funny, I laughed with them.

'Listen, lads, all it takes for evil to triumph is for a few good men to do nothing. When that time comes, don't be that man. Be lucky,' I said, quite choked up.

I rode back the way I had come. As much as I was glad the meeting with Dick was over, and as much as it didn't go as calmly as I wanted it to, I was very sad to leave the SBS, very sad. Riding up to the gate, the young lad stood in my way.

'Fuck me. Now you're uglier than me.' He laughed.

'Piss off. Your face is like one of those chewed-up dog toys,' I retorted.

His mate came out and said, 'Pork chop; great fucking nickname.'

I set off and left them to their banter.

Once home, I threw the bike back in the shed and slammed the door. Oliver came out of the kitchen. He shook his head as I grinned at him.

'Bad day at the office again?' he said. 'Why is it everywhere you go trouble follows you?'

'Get us a brew on. I'll tell you all about it.'

I followed him inside, but made a quick move to my bedroom. I took off my rucksack and pulled out the pistol I had shoved in it. I sat down and marvelled at it for a second, a worthy prize. Then I thought of Dick's face once he realised it was missing, which made me even happier. I wrapped it up in an old T-shirt and shoved it in the top of my Bergen. Except for a few bumps and bruises, my plan was working. However, I knew the next part was audacious. I also had to get Joe's pistol back to him and invent a cover story as to why we had it.

Over a brew, I filled Oliver in with most of the details of my morning's meeting, leaving out the pistol.

'You all packed for tomorrow then?' I slipped in casually.

Dunking another biscuit in his mug, he then stuffed the whole thing in his mouth and nodded.

'Good. I don't want to be disturbed,' I ordered. 'Got one tiny, tiny favour to ask,' I added.

'You take the piss. Now what?'

'Thursday night, I need you to go to the Baker's Arms pub at 20.30 hrs and meet an old friend of mine there: Mike. You will find a box under my bed. I need you to give this to him.'

He frowned. 'But how do I know who Mike is? And what's in the box?'

'You won't have to look for Mike. He will know you. Mike will come up to you and ask you for a fag. I know you don't smoke, but go outside the front with him. He will then say, 'The moon is high tonight, don't you think?' Then if the coast is clear, discreetly hand him the goods. The box will contain some medals of mine, but these medals were never accounted for in the public domain. You must only give the box to him. Find some inconspicuous way to carry it in. If the person who asks you outside for a fag doesn't say 'The moon is high tonight', do not hand it over. You clear on this?'

Oliver narrowed his eyes. 'Bit cloak and dagger for a set of medals. Why can't you hand them over?'

'Are you going to do this for me or not?' I said, raising my voice.

'Sure, dude, but that's the last favour. OK?'

'Of course.'

Oliver leant over and picked a book from the cabinet, then said, 'Don't mind if I have a read, do you?'

'No, go ahead, but please take care. They mean a lot to me.'

He flicked through the pages of the book, looking at the photos, and said, 'By the way, what am I supposed to do with all your stuff when the house is sold?'

'The only items I want to keep are my books and a few other personal items. I'll get you some boxes and you can take them back to Mum and Dad's house.'

'Oh for God's sake, anything else?' he said.

'I don't think so,' I said flippantly.

'Have you phoned Mum or Dad yet? They were worried sick about the court case.'

'Shit. I forgot. Right, I'll go get some boxes from the local supermarket, grab some scoff, and then I'll have an early night. I'll make the phone call then. Thanks for reminding me.'

Jumping up, I grabbed Oliver's car keys and bolted through the front door, not hearing exactly what he was shouting, but it didn't sound good.

By the end of the evening, after a good meal, a few beers, and a good old chat about growing up in Newquay, I'd made the phone call to my parents. It was great to chat to them. After, I phoned Mike and told him of the situation with the pistol, and how I had to get it back to Joe, but without raising any suspicions, especially Dick Brown's. I also told him to be very wary of Lee and Scott; he got the message. Mike suggested asking his best mate, who worked in the armoury, to phone Joe's boss and express his deep embarrassment by saying he had accidently stocked the pistol, and that he would get it dispatched immediately. In the meantime, he would contact Joe and let him know the real situation. I asked Mike to give my sincere apologies to Joe, and to say that if we met up again, I would buy him countless beers. Last of all, I told Mike to meet my brother with the coded message at the designated place and time.

# CHAPTER TWENTY-TWO

Getting up early, I woke Oliver in bed with breakfast.

'Blimey, Johnny. I could have done with this service every morning.'

'Bollocks. I just want you to hurry up. I need some time alone before my date arrives.'

'Oh charming.'

I left him to eat and get ready whilst I packed my books and personal items in the boxes. I put the pistol on the top shelf of the kitchen larder, along with some paracord and gaffer tape. Oliver came down about an hour later, all showered and carrying an overnight bag.

'OK, Johnny, I'm ready to go,' he said.

He looked sheepish and I knew how he felt; it was the white elephant in the room. I broke the awkward silence.

'Listen, bro, I can't thank you enough for everything you have done. Not only for saving my life, but for being my bro from the day I was born. You've also restored some dignity in me. I'm not sure when I'll be back, but I will be back. I'll try to keep in contact with you, and Mum and Dad. Remember, I've gone to Scotland. I love you, bro.'

I passed him the spare set of house keys. Oliver bit his lip and sighed; he began to speak but I guess he couldn't find the words as he closed his mouth. He came over and gave me a big bear hug, patting me on the back.

'Make sure you do return,' he said, and he turned and walked out the front door, shutting it behind him.

I had to remind myself what this was about, why I was doing this. The doubts came flooding in. Oliver's vehicle headed off into the distance, and I felt alone, almost vulnerable. I went into the kitchen and made myself a brew, and the biscuit tin was empty. Greedy git, I thought. Returning to the lounge, I picked up the signed book and read the inscription. Once again, I drew strength from this. I sat down and started to read as I had some time to kill.

A vehicle pulled up outside. I checked the time, and I'd been reading for just over three hours. I sat still as a person walked up to the door and knocked; dead on time. I went to the door, but before I answered I thought I would play along a bit.

'Who is it?'

'It's Neal, Neal Caselton.'

'Pass me your press ID badge through the letterbox.'

I was enjoying this pretence that this was a secret meeting. With the jangling of the letterbox the badge came though.

'Right, hold on there. I'm going to make some checks,' I said.

I returned about three minutes later. 'OK, you check out. I'm going to pass the key through. Bring all your bags in and don't hang around. Make sure no one follows you in. Do you understand?' Visualising him looking around, trying to be covert, I sniggered.

Through the letterbox, he whispered, 'Roger that... the coast is clear. Pass the key through.'

I handed the key through and took a few steps back. As soon as the door was open, I said, 'Quick, inside, now.'

Neal rushed in, nearly falling over his luggage. He stuck his hand out and said, 'Neal Caselton.'

'Soldier X.'

Instantly, I moved in and turned him around, aggressively pushing him against the wall, pulling his hand up tight behind his back.

'Arghhhhh, that hurts. Take it easy,' he whined.

Talking close to his ear, in a gruff voice, I said, 'Just want to make sure you're not carrying a piece, or that you're wired.'

I searched him from head to toe, having trouble holding back the laughter. I let go of him and spun him around. Letting out some of my laughter, I tried to disguise it as joy.

'Phew, you're one of the good guys,' I said. 'You can't be too careful these days. How's your arm?'

Rubbing his shoulder, he seemed a little relieved. 'Yeah... OK, I suppose.'

'Good. Well, make yourself at home. I'll put a brew on. Milk, sugar?'

'Just milk, thanks.'

When I returned from the kitchen, Neal had sat down and was holding a notepad and pen. He had a recorder on the table.

'You don't hang around,' I said. 'Listen, I want us to get to know each other first. How about we do the interview after some dinner, in about two hours?'

Looking slightly disappointed, he agreed.

After about an hour, Neal had run out of things about his life to talk about; thank fuck. He was itching to ask some questions about me, so I'd thought I'd get in first.

'Fancy something a bit stronger than tea? I mean, you've had three already. I've got some beer in the fridge.'

'Sure, Soldier X, might make you loosen your tongue.' He laughed at his own joke.

I tried to laugh along with him, whilst thinking what a twat he was; hopefully it didn't come across as too false. I grabbed some beer from the fridge.

'So, you said you were flying out to Afghan tomorrow,' I shouted back. 'Where you off to? What part?'

'I'm flying out to Camp Bastion. But I suppose you've been out there quite a few times. I mean that's what we're here to talk about, Operation Blue Halo, right?'

I handed him the beer and said, 'Yep, I've got loads to tell you. Did you say on the phone that you were doing a cover story?'

'Yeah, I'm flying out with a group of American Marines. They've come over here to train with our Marines. You know, learn from each other. My colleague broke his leg training alongside them. Fell off a high pole or something; idiot. My editor has picked me to take his place.'

'Poor bastard; I mean your mate. Have you met these Yanks yet, got all acquainted in the showers?' I said, making a joke but really probing for further answers.

Laughing, he replied, 'No, not met them yet. Had a good chat with a Captain Leon. They call him the lion. He has arranged with the pilots for me to have a tour of the cockpit. How cool, hey? Can I have another beer, bud?'

'Yeah, sure.' I went back into the kitchen. 'Did you say his name was Lion? Wow, he sounds ferocious.' I had to bite my hand, trying not to laugh.

He shouted back, 'Yeah, I reckon he is. He sounds hard as nails. Best fighting force in the world he tells me, and I agree. No offence, bud.'

'No offence taken,' I replied, shaking his beer as hard as I could. 'Who are the pilots? I might know them.' I handed him the beer.

'There is a Franklin, erm... Roy, that's it, Roy Franklin, and...'

He paused to think and opened his beer; it fizzed, shooting over his trousers. He tried in vain to stop it and catch the mountain of froth spewing out.

'That's weird. Mine didn't do that. I'll get you a cloth,' I said.

As I handed him the cloth, he said, 'I've remembered the other pilot's name: Steve Snape. Sorry about the mess. Can we get down to our interview now?'

Body-swerving his question, I said, 'Not heard of those pilots; must be new. What's Captain's Leon's first name? It rings a bell.'

'He said it was classified. I was to call him Captain Leon, or Lion, throughout the whole tour. Any notes and recordings must be authorised first by him. So, how about we get started on Operation Blue Halo.'

'Do you not fancy something to eat first? I'm starving. I couldn't possibly tell you everything on an empty stomach. Here's a good piece of Special Forces advice: always eat when you can as you don't know when your next meal will be. If you're offered food, take it,' I said, trying to keep a straight face.

'Great advice. Yes, let's eat first. Can I use that in my recording?'

'Sure, Neal. Fancy another beer?'

'Top man, Soldier X.'

'I've only got microwave meals as I'm used to eating it rough. Eating a microwave meal is SAS jargon for 'hard routine',' I said, seeing if he would notice what a load of shit I was talking.

'Yeah, sure, I'll eat anything. I'll use that hard-routine detail in my notes as well. We're getting along like buddies now.'

As I heated up his meal, I couldn't believe this bloke. What a total moron. I reckoned this was his first time around the likes of me, let alone any military service personnel. Whilst I waited for the dinners to cook, I put the pistol and paracord on my person.

I had to endure sitting next to him in the lounge as we ate. At the same time, he opened his notebook and got his recorder set on the table.

'What gear have they given you for Afghan?' I asked. 'I could advise if it's any good.'

With his mouth full, he spluttered, 'I've been told to buy khaki or beige trousers, tan shirts, and lightweight walking boots. Those also must be tan. I've got all the gear packed. Most of it I purchased cheap off the internet. I put in a larger expense bill. They sent my office a helmet and flak-jacket. The flak-jacket colour has changed from blue as the press were being easily recognised, so now we blend in. I get a pistol once we've reached Afghanistan. How awesome is that.'

Choking on my dinner, I replied, 'Yeah, really awesome. Reckon you will definitely blend in. Have you ever fired a gun?'

'I used to have an air pistol when I was younger, so that might help.'

I found Neal irritating now. Enough of the silly talk, I thought. 'After the interview, I'm off to Scotland for a few months for a break. I want to learn to track and snare wild animals, live off the land and learn how to survive alone. Place just outside Dornoch. Have you heard of it?'

Neal sat back, drinking the last of his beer. 'Burrrrp. No, not heard of it.'

'Have you ever seen how a snare works?' I asked.

'No.'

'I'll show you. Stand up and put your hands together in one big fist.'

As he did, I stood up and pulled out the paracord. I then started tying it around his wrists. All done, I told him to lie in the foetal position, which amazingly he did. I tied the remaining cord around his ankles, and he looked a bit uncomfortable with the situation. Helping him up, I pushed him on the sofa.

'I don't get why you are showing me this,' he said.

'Well, I thought it would be good for you to know how the animal felt, like a rabbit or a fox. Now hold still. Last bit now.'

I pulled another piece of paracord from my pocket and put a noose round his neck, tying it off to the display cabinet and then took up the slack.

'Now you see, if you move you will asphyxiate. That's dying by strangulation for the lame, the likes of you.'

'How would the animal get its feet tied together before getting in the noose?'

Raising my voice, I said, 'It fucking wouldn't as it's not as fucking dumb as you. You know what I do when I've caught a weasel?' Before answered, I went up close. 'I put it out of its fucking misery.'

'Is this sick joke? Untie me now,' Neal said sternly.

'Do you really think I would sell out my regiment and those that have died doing their job for the likes of you to have freedom, so you can portray them across your headlines in a sleazy bag of lies?' I opened his case and rucksack.

'Hey, that's my stuff. Look, joke's over, Soldier X. Untie me and we can forget about the whole thing.'

I ignored him and found the items I was searching for: his flak-jacket, helmet, clothes, and boots. In the side pocket I found his passport.

'Ah, these should come in handy in Scotland,' I said.

'You can't take those. I need them tomorrow. Listen, bud, you'll be in serious trouble if you don't untie me. Why did you invite me if not to inform me?' he said, growing more anxious.

I disregarded the question and went upstairs. I pulled my Bergen up onto the bed. I didn't have to check it as I'd double-checked everything before. Not forgetting what I'd said to Oliver, I placed the pistol in the box and hid it under the bed. I had planned to threaten Neal with it as a last resort, but the snare trick had worked well. By now, he was shouting that he needed a piss. He really was irritating me. I grabbed a sock, my Bergen, including Neal's items, and then went back downstairs. I walked into the kitchen and dumped my gear, and then went up behind him.

'Open wide please,' I said.

'What? What are you doing?'

I poked my finger in the back of his head. 'Open your fucking mouth or you'll see your brains come past your eyes.'

He opened his mouth and I stuffed the sock in and then wrapped the gaffer tape around his mouth.

'Ah, peace and quiet. It's amazing what a finger can do,' I said, showing him my finger.

He started to struggle but the paracord tightened round his neck. I told him it wasn't wise to skirmish, and I loosened it off. I got a pillow and laid him on his side to make him more comfortable.

'There you go, Neal. No hard feelings. I'm leaving for Scotland tonight, but don't worry someone will be coming in tomorrow.'

He started to mumble under the gaffer tape, his eyes fiercely straining at me.

'Make sure you don't piss on my sofa now.'

'Mmmm… mmmm.'

Ignoring him, I picked up his notebook and recorder and then started to write a note for Oliver:

'Bro, I know this is going to look strange you finding this reporter tied up, but sorry forgot to mention this part. Please make sure he has a nice brew. Maybe you could give him a lift to the station as I've borrowed his vehicle to get to Scotland. When I get to where I'm going, I will give you a call. Good luck on the house sale. Don't forget to go to the pub and have a few beers on me. Johnny.'

I folded a fifty-pound note inside the written note and put it on the table in front of Neal. I turned around and searched his pockets. He was frozen with fear. I took his ID card, wallet, and car keys.

'Cheers, Neal,' I said, and walked off, listening to his muffled objections.

In the kitchen, I changed into his clothes and footwear. The boots were slightly too large, but they would have to do. I locked the back door behind me and, on the way to Neal's car, I posted the back-door key through the letterbox. I pressed the remote car fob and the Vauxhall Astra's lights flickered.

Once I'd loaded up, I sat and took a long last look at my house. So many good times, I thought, feeling the emptiness in me. I then thought of Lee coming around. This made my blood boil. I hope one day I will meet up with him to have a little *chat*. I turned the ignition over and set his satnav to RAF Lyneham. Driving away, I chuckled at the vision of Oliver finding Neal tied up. Further into my journey, I got into Neal's character, thinking and acting like him. I practised talking aloud the kind of phrases I would say. Hopefully, I would stay the grey man, keeping myself to myself and blending into my surroundings, but if asked any questions, I had to sound convincing, especially to the gate guards and Captain Leon.

After nearly two hours of driving, I pulled into a superstore car park. Inside the store, after having a piss, I stocked up on sweets for the journey, and sandwiches to eat beforehand. I pulled out Neal's wallet and paid with his cash. Nice of you, Neal, I thought. Back in the Astra I sat and ate my sandwiches, running different scenarios through my mind of being questioned by the guards. I took Neal's ID badge and studied the photo, not the best resemblance. Maybe my beaten face, beard, and the night would help. I really needed a miracle to get in, and then it came to me: Rabbit. I pulled out my mobile and texted: 'Hi. Remember you owe me a favour. I need to call it in.' I pressed send.

Thirty seconds later my phone vibrated. The text read: 'I'm sure it was the other way around, LOL. Busy now with work, little aeroplane to sort. What's up?'

No use beating around the bush. 'Going to be late for take-off. Meet me at 4 a.m. My new name is Neal Caselton. I'm driving a silver Astra. Just get me on that plane!!!'

Two minutes elapsed and I was getting agitated. 'Come on, Rabbit, bloody reply,' I murmured.

I was about to forward it to him when my phoned beeped. It read:

'Are you fucking mad, or drunk!!?? Where's the real reporter? What the hell are you up to?'

I imagined him sweating as he typed, which made me smile. I texted back: 'He's fine. Just meet me at four. Fill me in later. Buy you some duty-free fags.'

Within twenty seconds Rabbit came back. 'You're mad. I can't do this. If I get caught, end of.'

I didn't reply on purpose, not wanting him to put up any more excuses. I just hoped he had it in him.

It was just after eleven o'clock. I punched the postcode into the satnav again and it informed me I was eight minutes away. I put the flak-jacket on and hung the ID badge's chain around my neck, and finally, threw Neal's wallet on the dash. I then set my watch alarm for 03.50 hrs, put my head back and shut my eyes.

# CHAPTER TWENTY-THREE

My dream turned back to Operation Blue Halo, right from the beginning at the successful insertion. It felt good to be with all the lads in action, and to be with Planet, Fish, and Shrek again. I went through the whole mission once more. My feelings changed when the vision arose of the Elkhaba prisoner smiling at me in the Chinook. I went through the frightening crash in detail, this time playing out Rabbit's version as he had told me. I had to undergo the horror of finding my dead mates. I tried to wake myself but couldn't. I burst into the room where Rabbit was being held, only this time I riddled him with bullets by accident. I woke up shouting.

Beads of sweat had collected on my shirt collar and I had large patches under my arms. My face was blotchy with perspiration and I was breathing erratically. I thought back to what I'd just dreamt, but was interrupted by the tiny chime of my watch. I put my helmet on; time to go. I followed the satnav's directions until ahead I noticed the large blue steel main gates to RAF Lyneham. I sped up and, nearing the gates, I braked suddenly and then put the window down. An armed guard came out through the side door and shone his torch in the window.

'Are you being chased or late for war?' He laughed.

'Sorry, officer, I'm late for a flight,' I said, trying to look flustered. 'Neal Caselton is my name. I'm supposed to be on the Globemaster flight with the American Marines. I'm press.'

'Derek, come and look at this guy,' he yelled to the other guard in the small room by the gates. Turning back to me, he said, 'Identification please, sir.'

Derek shone his torch through my window. 'Bloody hell, mate, you've been cooking up a sweat. Why are you wearing your flak-jacket and helmet? You don't have to wear all that now.'

In my best pleading voice, I said, 'I've never been on a military plane before, officer. I've never been to Afghanistan. Captain Leon told me to dress ready for action. My flight leaves at four-thirty. I'm very late. My boss will kill me if I don't make that plane.'

He started to search down the paperwork on his clipboard, which I presumed was the load manifest.

'I can't afford to loose my job,' I said.

'He's listed here, Mark,' Derek said.

'You've changed a bit from your ID card, Neal, and why the beard?' Mark said.

Shit, where was Rabbit? 'So would you if you'd been beaten up in town.' I tilted my helmet to show him my forehead and nose. 'I've been at the hospital, that's why I'm late. I was told to grow a beard as I would blend in out in Afghanistan. The locals wouldn't find me so strange, apparently.'

They both took a harder look at my face. 'Nasty, Neal, and the beard,' Derek said, and grinned.

'Got any other ID?' Mark asked.

'Yes, officer, but I'm really running late.'

Passing him my wallet and passport, he looked through them, and then both went off into the little guard room.

'Rabbit, where the fuck are you?' I whispered under my breath.

A set of headlights drove up to the guard room and, to my relief, Rabbit got out. He ran inside, and I could see him gesticulating with his hands, looking as if they were getting a bollocking. The heavy gates opened and the spiked ramp sank into the ground. I didn't need a second invite. I pulled up alongside the doorway to the guard room.

'Mr Caselton, you're bloody late,' Rabbit shouted, throwing me my credentials. 'Follow my car.'

Not looking sideward at the guardsmen, I quickly followed Rabbit's vehicle to the outskirts of the runway. There sat the enormous Globemaster C-17. The grey beast had its four turbofan engines running and its tail ramp down. I got out and took my Bergan out of the boot. The noise emanating from the engines was deafening. Rabbit grabbed me forcefully by the arm and marched me over to the ramp, where we were met by another man in a boiler suit and ear defenders. He snatched my gear, not before giving me a filthy stare. I lowered my eyes as if in shame. Rabbit pulled me up the ramp, past the giant mass of tied-down Marines' personal equipment.

'Sit there, Mr Caselton, and strap yourself in.'

After shouting his orders in my ear, he moved back towards the front of the plane. I parked my arse quickly next to my dumped kit as the tail ramp began to close. Before it was fully shut, the Globemaster began to taxi to the runway. I buckled up my lap belt and pulled the two straps tight. The fluorescent strip lights dimmed. I was sitting in the last row opposite the luggage, all by myself. Opposite, to my left, was a row of seats where some Marines sat. I could almost smell their anger. Quite a few irritated faces were staring at me. I put my hand up and mouthed my apologies. One of the guys gave me the wanker sign before turning back to his mates. The enormous power of the beast gained in speed. It was amazing this bulking plane could even get off the ground; it is known that it can carry a tank.

The fuselage vibrated. Looking down the rows of blue seats, I saw some of the men had yellow earplugs in and some had iPads and Kindles. Further seats in rows of five sat facing the front. The flooring had grip stickers on and the ceiling was a mass of pipes and cables that ran the length of the fuselage. Crewmen were pressing buttons and checking equipment right at the far end. As we took off, the roar and vibrations were taken over by the sound of mechanical components clunking and the hum of the engines. I'd been in one of these beasts before. It was quicker, larger than, and far superior to the Hercules. My first time in one had reminded me of a futuristic aircraft from a sci-fi movie, where the military were heading to do battle with an unknown alien enemy.

I put my fingers in my ears and swallowed. Quickly unclipping my helmet, I started to retch over it, faking motion sickness due to the turbulence, much to the amusement of the Marines. One of them was saying something to me, but I couldn't really hear him. Good, my cover was working; the more I played a non-military person, the better. I pretended I was amazed at the inside of the fuselage. I wrote down details as a journalist would. After I'd written a page and become bored, I shut my eyes and relived the part with the gate patrol. I couldn't believe I'd made it. I felt euphoric.

'Fucking outrageous. Not by strength, by guile,' I muttered.

I'd been dozing for about an hour when I felt something move my foot. I wearily opened my eyes to see a very tall Marine standing over me, and he had my notebook in his hand.

'You gonna staannd up when speaking tooo an officer?' he said, in a loud, drawling American twang.

Normally, I wouldn't even bother to answer, but I had to play it different, not cause any problems or raise suspicions. I went to stand up immediately, but I couldn't due to the lap belt. In the process, I dropped my pen. I struggled to unclip the buckle. Captains Leon's face changed with frustration. Eventually, I unclipped it and bent down, making a big deal trying to find the pen. I thought my impersonation of Mr Bean, was good. Once I found it, I stood up.

'Sorry, Captain Leon. It's good to meet you. My name is Neal Caselton.' I thrust my hand out.

'Nooo shiit. You loook a bag of neeerves, sonny boooy. Hope you ain't gonna be chicken shiit out there,' he drawled.

'No, sir. I'm here to capture the full story of you and your tough men. And, as you told me, I will check with you before print.'

'You'rre damn right, sonny boooy.' He spat a mouthful of chewing tobacco at my feet.

'Wow, what a big plane,' I said, looking around.

'Thaat's aircraft, boooy.'

I still had my hand out and he looked down, smirked, and marched off. Now more than one Marine was giving me the finger sign. I smiled politely, then sat down and pretended to make notes. I felt like writing 'Just met the biggest cock of the entire universe'. But I decided not to.

Captain Cock, as I now named him, was your typical Yankee Marine in the movies; in fact, you couldn't imagine a bigger stereotype: tall, muscular, athletic, with a short blond flat-top haircut. To add to this, he had piercing blue eyes, a chiselled jawline, and a butt chin you could abseil on. He had long legs and a muscular triangle-shaped torso. No doubt he'd served his country and been through the mill, but to act so big, so untouchable, would be his or one of his men's undoing one day. Imagine him on a close quarters recce, or undercover, trying to blend in, or worse, trying to sort a problem out with the Afghan locals. I couldn't see him letting anyone else speak freely in a Chinese parliament session, where British SAS involved were in an open operation briefing session and could speak freely to give their input, regardless of rank.

I made notes on the recorder as I knew I was being watched. Opening my small rucksack, I pulled out a pack of Starburst sweets. I waved at the Marine lad who had enjoyed his hand signal to me. As he looked, I threw him the bag of sweets. He caught them, checked the front and then proceeded to open them. Once he had opened the tiny wrapper with his sausage-sized fingers, he popped it in his mouth. He gave me the thumbs-up and continued to chew. His friend next to him tried to grab one out of the packet, but he was denied. They started to jostle and argue. I reached in and pulled out a packet of sour jellies and threw them to him, landing on his lap. He gave me the OK sign and ripped open the packet. This time I didn't catch his reaction, instead I started writing notes about the two of them. I had to win over their trust; a hearts and minds strategy. I didn't have an exact plan for how to get off the RAF base when we landed and I might need their help.

Between the boredom of note-writing, recording, and sleeping, the three-hour flight so far started to do my head in. I stood up and stretched, then decided to take a small walk around my own space. Most of the Marines were asleep. Captain Cock was making his way down towards me. Oh hell, here he comes, I thought.

'Ah, Captain Leon. Do you mind if I call you Lion?' I asked enthusiastically.

'Thaat's what I said, boooy.'

'When can I visit the cockpit to meet the pilots? You did say, right?'

'You reeead my mind, boooy. I was just comin' tooo get ya, boooy. Follow me.' He turned and made his way through the sleeping Marines.

If he called me "boooy" once more, I would deck him.

As I knocked on the door, I turned and thanked Captain Cock, keeping my arm across the doorway to show I wanted him to go no further. He got the message and went back the way he'd come. The cockpit was lit up with illuminated green dials, handles, and switches; too many to think what they were. I closed the door behind me.

'So, now what's your fucking plan then?' Rabbit blurted.

I gave him a glare to say shut up, as Steve was listening. 'I cannot answer that question, sir,' I replied.

'Oh, you're worried about talking in front of Steve. Well don't be, he knows everything. I had to tell him, otherwise he wouldn't delay the take-off.'

The pilot turned his head and said, 'Steve Snape. Nice to meet you, Johnny, or shall I carry on calling you Neal?' Before I could answer, he put his hand up to stop me. 'I've heard you don't let anyone get a word in, so please let me finish. I would like to say a big thank you for saving Roy's life. Not only is he an outstanding RAF asset, he's godparent to my children. Anyone else I would have reported for their outrageous attempt to board my aircraft.'

'Thanks, Steve. I'm curious to know who said I don't let anyone get a word in.' I glared at Rabbit.

'This is bloody mad, Johnny,' Rabbit blurted. 'How the hell are you going to get out of Camp Bastion?'

'I'm not going to Camp Bastion. Steve, how long will you be stationary at RAF Akotiri?'

'After we disembark, refuel, and embark, not less than two hours.'

'I need some help to leave the airport. Any ideas?' I said to Steve.

'You can't get us involved any further, Johnny,' Rabbit said. 'Steve, you could get in serious shit for this.'

'Oh loosen your knickers, Roy, he's a grown man,' I said.

'Same old Johnny, with his bossy ways and stupid plans,' Rabbit replied.

'Oh piss off, you knob-jockey,' I barked.

'OK guys, that's enough,' Steve broke in. 'Johnny, I've got to hand over pilot duties to another pilot, regulation. So I will take you to the airport gates, about a mile away. I'll get one of the crewmen to sort a ground car. What are your plans after?'

'I need a taxi. Rabbit can book me one,' I said, and smiled at Rabbit.

'Sure. Anything else?' Rabbit said flippantly.

'Yeah, there is,' I said. 'I need you to tell Captain Cock, sorry, Captain Leon, why I couldn't make the second leg of the journey. Tell him my wife has been involved in a serious accident and I'm making my way to Larnaca Airport for a return flight.'

'Fuck me, who put you in charge?' Rabbit said.

'I did,' I said, and gave him the wanker sign.

He looked me hard in the eyes.

'What's your fucking problem, Roy?' I asked.

'I can't get my head around why you're risking your life to go back. I mean, just for some pretty doctor?'

'It's...'

'Shut it and listen for a change,' he interrupted. 'We went through some shit together, yes, and barely came out the other side. I'm concerned you'll be coming back in a body bag this time, Johnny.' He rubbed his neck scar, upset.

'I'm not going back just for Haleema. I've got other issues to deal with.' It was the first time I had admitted it to myself.

'Why then?' he asked.

'Well it's not because I favour the inside of a body bag.' I decided to change the subject. 'Steve, do you mind if I stay in here for the landing?' I knew Rabbit would be squirming.

# Chapter Twenty-three

'If you don't bore us with your boring SAS stories, mate,' Rabbit replied.

I knew he was waiting for me to bite, but instead I answered calmly, 'But I'm not in the SAS, I'm the press.'

Chatting with Steve kept the last part of the flight entertaining; Rabbit hardly spoke. Buckling myself in the spare seat, I watched and listened to these two pros bring the hulking beast towards the runway lights. As we touched down, the wheels made a screech. Again, I was impressed by how soft the landing was. I'd had harder landings falling off the sofa, drunk. Once the checks were sorted, I checked my watch: 08.40 hrs. I set my watch two hours forward in line with Cyprus and stayed in the cockpit whilst Captain Cock and the Marines disembarked. Once out of sight, I grabbed my gear, but decided to leave the helmet. All three of us went in another direction towards a building which had a sign over the door: 'RAF Personnel Only - Restricted Area'.

'Wait here, Neal, I'm going to sort a car,' Steve said. 'Roy, book a taxi for eleven outside the main gate, please.'

The plane was being refuelled and the ground staff made their vital checks. Even though I was in the shade, I was starting to sweat profusely. I could smell the hazed tarmac as it baked in the sun. There was only a small breeze for comfort and I felt sorry for the blokes who weren't in any shade, and those working around the hot engines on the Globemaster. I guessed it was about thirty degrees. A few of the staff walked out of the office and gave me funny looks, as if to say, 'what the hell does he want? He's not one of us, he shouldn't be here.'

I'd checked my watch. I'd been stood there for nearly ten minutes when a black Mercedes pulled up. The young driver got out and made his way over to me.

'Sorry to hear about your wife. Hope she is all right. Have you heard any further news?' he said, putting my gear in the boot.

'No, I'm waiting to hear from the hospital if there are any changes.'

'Well, I hope she gets better soon,' he said, and went into the restricted building.

Steve came out soon after and said, 'OK, Neal, get in. Roy has booked you a taxi for eleven.'

'Cheers, sir,' I said.

It was lovely and cool inside, the vents blasting out the air-con. Steve drove us out of the main area to the airport's outskirts. So far, so good, I thought.

'Only the main gate to go,' he said. 'I'll deal with the SBA security. Shouldn't be any problems.'

'SBA?'

'Sovereign Base Area. I'll tell them you've been cleared, but have you got your, or should I say, Neal's passport, just in case?'

'I have indeed, and his wallet and press ID.'

'Don't forget to look upset. Your wife is in a critical way in hospital,' he said, and took my ID.

Steve parked in a small lay-by opposite a large building. He got out and went inside. I stared out the window, using the thousand-yard stare I'd seen many blokes have after their first battle in theatre. A guard looked out his window as Steve was talking to him. I rubbed my eyes on my sleeve, pretending to wipe away tears. To mislead him further, I anxiously looked at my watch. Steve came out and got in. The barrier went up and he shot off, pulling over on the road further up, opposite a roundabout.

'Obviously went well then,' I said cheerfully.

'The gods above must be shining on you; the security guy lost his wife six months ago in a car accident. He said he knows how you're feeling. I told him we have passport checked and cleared you.'

'Maybe the gods are going to make it smooth from here on in. Really appreciate your help, Steve. I hope you won't get in any trouble.'

'Why should I? Just helping Neal Caselton get back to his dying wife after he asked me,' he said, making clear the point.

I got out, took my Bergen out of the boot, and went up to his window, which he put down. Putting my hand through the window aperture, I shook his hand.

'Thanks again, I owe you one,' I said.

'When we met up at Christmas with Roy and his family, I sat there and imagined if you hadn't rescued Roy, how our family and his wife and kids would be feeling. And for the record, make sure you come back. Roy would be devastated. Here comes your taxi. Take care, Johnny.'

# CHAPTER TWENTY-FOUR

A silver Mercedes Viano came hurtling towards where I was standing. I liked the look of it, but wondered if this would be reflected in the fare. It seemed a bit excessive for one person. The driver put his window down.

'Taxi for Jonathan?'

'It's Johnny, actually,' I replied. Bastard, Roy, I thought, and chuckled.

The driver didn't bother getting out, so I lifted the tailgate up and put my luggage in. He wouldn't be getting a tip from me. Inside, the aroma of new leather instantly hit me. It was very stuffy as I shut the door. I handed him the name and full address. Then he typed it into his satnav. Once it gave him the route, he flew off at such a rate, it was like he was being chased. His fare meter already read: 20.2.

'Couldn't have some air-con back here, could I?' I asked as the windows were locked.

He didn't reply, but just glanced back at me in his rear-view mirror.

The driver was a short, chubby, bald man and was sweating like a pig. He had quite serious black bags under his eyes, which looked as if they were keeping up his oversized, thick black glasses. He reminded me of Danny De Vito. He also needed a shower, as his odour started to filter back to where I was sitting.

'Excuse me, could you put the air-con on back here, dude,' I asked again politely.

Again, he just stared at me, but at least he gave a grunt this time. However, again he did nothing.

I squinted at him, showing my displeasure. 'Bollocks to ya then, Danny,' I said.

Mr De Vito was still driving at a stupid speed, so I rashly opened my door. The sandy dust clouds started swirling inside. I smiled back at him in his mirror. He raised his hands and said something which I guessed wasn't polite. I sat waiting for him to put the air-con on, but he didn't.

'Please shut,' Danny shouted.

'Not until you put the air-con on.'

The traffic sounded their horns.

'OK, sir. I will do for you.'

'Thank you. Wasn't hard was it?' I said.

This made him drive more erratically, reckoning he was trying to scare me. I shut the door and sat back, smiling at him, and then casually looked out the window, showing his driving didn't bother me. In fact, I was enjoying it, especially after the flight. I could do with a bit of action.

At last the cool air began to chill the rear. Cyprus was a beautiful place. I'd been there a few times. I checked my watch. At this rate I was going to be too early.

'Hey, Danny, can you speed up a bit? I'm going to be late.'

I couldn't see his face, but his eyes gave away his sadistic smile and, right on cue, he slowed the Mercedes down to what felt about thirty miles per hour. I shook my head in disgust, but little did he know I was smiling inside. I didn't want to be too early, knowing David would be late.

David 'Will' Charles had left the SBS nearly two years after I passed selection. I had met him in the Paras and I remember him leaving for selection. He looked very similar to Will Smith; in fact, he started copying his hair and beard style. Of course, the ladies in Catterick and Poole fell for his looks and charm. He originated from Grenada, but moved to London just before his sixteenth birthday. On leave, he always returned to his family in his homeland, as he called it. He was discharged on medical grounds after a vehicle crash. On this operation, the pinkie he was sat in, him being the main gunner, overturned and rolled down a bank. The weight of the vehicle landed on his legs, crushing them both. It was fortunate, though, the 50.cal took some of the impact and weight. However, after many months of surgery and rehabilitation, the regiment couldn't keep him, the Paras didn't want him back. He loved Cyprus, so he decided to start his own business in Nicosia. This was where I was heading.

Woken suddenly by the Mercedes erratically braking to a stop, I lurched forward, but managed to put my hands out to stop myself hitting the seat in front. I got the feeling he enjoyed slamming the brakes on for no reason. It was very stuffy again, the illuminated air-con button was switched off.

'Here, sir,' Danny said, and grinned his yellow teeth.

'How much, you smug bastard?'

'Eh?'

'How much?' I said again.

Danny frowned, so I rubbed my thumb and index finger together. Danny then pressed a few buttons on the meter, which doubled the fare amount to 160.9 euros.

'Listen, bellend, I might look stupid, but there's no way I'm paying that much.'

He leant forward into the foot-well and produced a baseball bat. 'You pay, or I smash your brains.'

'Really, Danny?' I sighed.

His expression became more aggressive. He turned around, leaning on his seat and gripped the bat in both hands.

'You pay now.'

His hairy, fat fingers grip and re-grip the bat's handle. He looked nervous and out of his comfort zone. I didn't believe he would do it. I sat back, feeling cool and relaxed.

'Put the bat down, Danny, there's a good chap.'

'I want money, now,' he yelled, trying to intimidate me.

A second later, his door was flung open and a pair of hands grabbed and dragged him out. The bat was ripped from his hands and he was hit across his legs as he lay on the ground.

'Man, dat's no way of treatin' me friend,' Will said in his calm, easy twang. 'He comes all de way from Blighty.'

I jumped out of the Mercedes and stepped over Danny to give him a big bear hug. 'Will, good to see ya, dude. It's been ages. You've put on weight.' I let him go.

'So, man, what's up with dis taxi driver? Ya not payin' up or someting? And what's with all de hugs? Are ya going soft?'

I looked down at Danny, who was trembling and looking up at Will's six-foot muscular frame, still tapping the bat in his hand like a gangland thug.

'Apparently, the fair goes up if you put the air-con on.'

Laughing, Will said, 'Is dat right, man? Maybe we should kill him and bury him out in dis desert.'

Will leant over Danny and his broad white teeth with a gold gap smiled at him. Danny scrambled to his feet and headed for the safety of the Viano.

'I go now,' Danny said, flustered.

'Hold on, Danny,' I said. 'Bring me my luggage and I'll pay you half, agreed?'

As he went to the Merc's rear, I pulled out a roll of notes from my pocket. Sheepishly bringing me my Bergen, I handed him half of his outrageous fare, which was more like it.

'Always de nice man, Johnny,' Will said.

We walked off together, joking about what had just happened. Will still walked strangely. Over a rum-filled coffee and lunch, he told me how he had started his dream business with the money he raised, buying the airport outright. He had certainly done well. Half a dozen small aircraft with covers on were parked neatly in a row at one end of the runway. He had contract pilots teaching those that wanted to learn to fly. Apart from the flying lessons, he chartered private clients anywhere around the world, but for a high fee. He told me he laid on special female entertainment on certain flights. Over the last year he had taken on an ex-SF skydiver who used his airport to give lessons on skydiving. Some of the students were ex-SAS from Australia and Britain. He was also contracting out these old friends for whoever wanted special work carried out. I'd always wondered what I would do if I left the army; the Private Military Contractor seemed appealing. In the past, the letter 'M' was deemed to be a Mercenary, but I prefer Military, even though there probably wasn't much difference.

Across the way, inside a small hangar, was parked a larger plane with a few crew busily working around it.

'Dat's me baby, a Beechcraft B60, man. She's better dan any woman. I should know, I've ridden a few,' Will remarked.

'Is that what we are flying in?'

'Sure ting, man, she's a beauty,' Will said proudly. 'You got de money?'

'What do you think, David?' I snapped.

'Easy, man. Tell me again, why are ya going back?'

Over a few more rums, I told him the whole story of Operation Blue Halo and how I had ended up here. I'd been avoiding telling him of the deaths of my squad when we were previously setting up my plans. He looked solemn, understanding why I'd given him a bear hug. We laughed and joked about some of the old times and bragged about our different operations, some of it exaggerated for bravado. It was a warm, beautiful day. I could understand why he had fallen in love with Cyprus and the job. It was very different from the bodyguard 'circuit', which most of us went into after leaving. Will went off to make some phone calls. I sat slouched in my chair, took a last swig of rum, and shut my eyes. I now had time to dwell on recent events. Things had worked out way better than expected.

Will broke the tranquillity by kicking my feet. Yawning, I checked the time: 13.28 hrs. Will sat down in the chair next to me.

'So, what you got for me then?' I asked. 'A nice assault rifle, I hope. Maybe some grenades, flash bangs, NVGs, rocket launcher, light armoured vehicle, etcetera?'

'Yeah, man, sure I would have. But your money only buys me baby, and she is beautiful. And it doesn't cover any flight entertainment, man. Why ya need all dat stuff? You startin' a war?'

'Doesn't look like it now. You got nothing for me, not even a weapon?'

'I got a cam net. Anyway, I had to buy a chute. Dat ain't cheap out here.'

'A cam net, without a pinkie? What am I supposed to do with that?'

'I'm sure ya'll find yourself a nice Datsun again, man. Ya want it, or not?' he said, and grinned.

'It was a bloody Nissan, *man*, mighty fine as well,' I said, proving a point. 'Yeah, I'll take it, not,' I added, sarcastically.

I delved into my bag and pulled out a fat envelope filled with euro notes, three thousand in total. I tossed it at him and asked him to check it as it was time to go. He didn't count it, but just stuffed it in his shirt, telling me he trusted me, same as I trusted the parachute was not stuffed with his washing. Again, he threw me his gold-toothed smile.

We walked over to the hangar where the crew were doing their last pre-flight checks. The single front nose propeller plane had three porthole windows down the side. It was gleaming white with red decals down its bodywork. Will opened the little door just behind the wing and went in. I climbed up the small steps to the rear door and chucked in my gear. The interior had been finished in cream leather. Two of the seats were missing, a walnut table and units replaced these. It was swanky. I made my way to the cockpit.

The dashboard was a mass of dials and switches set in a walnut finish. Protruding were two cream leather U-shaped steering wheels. They reminded me of some accessory for the Wii console. In the foot-well, two large pedals sat on each side. Both seats had sheep's wool seat covers on them.

'Bit swanky this, Will. You must be earning too much. I see you have two steering wheels. Does that mean I can fly?'

'No,' Will replied bluntly. 'And dey're not called steerin' wheels.'

'Oh. Am I allowed to even sit up front then?'

'Sure, man, just don't touch anyting. Can ya imagine Planet tryin' to squeeze in de cockpit?' He grimaced with embarrassment. 'Sorry, man.'

'Ah, no worries. He would've had trouble fitting in a Hercules.'

Looking straight into my eyes, he said, 'Are ya sure ya've got your head screwed on de right way around, Johnny? Ya sure ya want to do dis? It's bonkers.'

Nodding my head towards the cockpit, I said, 'Let's go.'

I squeezed into the front seat after Will and watched him with awe as he ran through all his flight checks and started the engine. He flicked and pushed more controls and we started gaining speed up the runway.

'Tree hundred and eighty horses fly dis baby, man. Top speed of two hundred and forty knots,' he bragged.

I looked out the window. 'I can't see any horses.'

'Still have no sense of humour den,' he retorted. 'I've got ya loads of food in, all of it fresh. Ya know de drill: eat as much fresh as ya can before a mission.'

Rather disappointed, I replied, 'I would have rather had some scantily-dressed Russian girls.'

'Ahh, now de single man, hey? Just de thought of slim Russian girls must have ya a boner.'

'Let's not get into a measuring competition. You know I'm far superior to you.' I held out my hands about a foot apart.

Will burst out laughing. 'Sure, man, ya keep tinkin dat, ya're bound to get a nice, little Afghan doctor. Do ya want me to meet her first?'

'No, fuck off.'

I undid my belt and climbed through to the back. In the fridge I found a stash of fruit, nuts, salad, bread, olives, and halloumi. At the back was something wrapped up in a plastic bag; I pulled it out. On the front a label read 'Pastourma-loukaniko'. Unwrapping it, a strong smell wafted out even before I got into whatever it was. Finally, with my mouth watering, I undid the package. Inside, six stumpy, rich-looking sausages perfumed their essence. I took a sniff and they knocked my block off. I thought of the moment when I was hiding under Anoosheh's bed and imagined the outcome if I'd eaten these. The entire Elkhaba would have smelt the garlic and herbs oozing from my pores. I decided not to eat the sausages and instead swapped them for a four-pack of KEO beer. Setting it all out in front of me, I tucked in like I hadn't eaten for weeks.

The food was delicious. Relaxing back in the reclining leather seats, I gulped the beer. I closed my eyes and thought of the next part of my mission. A part of me was a little apprehensive. I had to expect the unexpected, always keeping on my toes. These thoughts fell aside, and I dreamt of Will's lovely girls making a fuss of me here in his plane.

# CHAPTER TWENTY-FIVE

A small bump and a screech from the plane's tyres on touchdown woke me. I looked out the porthole window and could see only a single light on the outside of a building. I moved towards the cockpit for a better view, kicking the empty cans on the floor.

'Where are we, Will?' I asked.

'I have to refuel. My baby needs a drink, a bit like you have. Hope ya're gonna clean up.'

I looked at my watch, it was just over four hours since take-off. 'So, where are we?'

'We're at an old friend of mine. He owns dis little airport. Just outside Tabriz. It's off de radar, man, if ya get me drift. We can't stay long. I want ya to stay inside, ya get me?'

'I need a piss though,' I said.

'Use one of de beer cans. Now stay here.'

Will opened the cabin door and jumped out. I moved over to the porthole and watched him walk over to the building with one light. After he knocked, the door opened a couple of inches. I couldn't make out who was opening it. Will went inside and closed the door behind him. I decided to get my gear ready. I fastened all the toggles and zips on my Bergen as I didn't want anything snagging or flying out. I pulled the parachute out from under the table and checked all the straps and fasteners.

In the distance, headlights turned on and started to make their way over to our plane. As it neared, the truck turned broadside on. It was the refuelling truck and Will was driving it. He worked the pipes and levers and then started to refuel. Whilst I was waiting, he turned and stuck both his thumbs up. I wanted to help as sitting here didn't feel right, but decided to listen for once. When the plane was refuelled, he drove the tanker away. Out of the building came the silhouette of a man.

I still couldn't see who it was; maybe he was ex-military, and maybe I knew him. I was itching to find out. They shook hands and the stranger went back inside. Will did his familiar walk back and climbed aboard, locking the door.

'OK, man, let's fly dis baby. Buckle up,' he said.

I followed him into the cockpit and buckled up. Again, I marvelled at the dials, leavers and switches he used before turning around. Then a long row of lights came on, illuminating the runway. We roared off. It was a lot bumpier than his runway back in Nicosia.

'Bloody hell, Will, is this a runway or gravel pit?' I asked.

Will didn't answer; he was in his zone. The rumbling stopped as soon as we were airborne. I looked back out of the window and the runway lights were instantly switched off.

'So, who was your friend back there? Would I know him?' I asked.

'No. He's kinda shy.'

'Ex-military, is he?'

'No. After a sex change, he became a nun; hates open spaces, and lots of questions, man. Any more questions and ya know de kind of answers ya'll get.'

'Fair enough. Not that bothered about him,' I said, lying.

I reset my watch forward to 19.12 hrs in line with the GPS monitor on the dash. Will poured himself and me a hot drink from his flask. As he handed it to me, I got a whiff of very strong coffee.

'Hope there's no rum in this,' I said, and took a sip.

'I don't drink and fly, man. It's double espresso. Ya won't be able to shut your eyes for a few hours.'

'Jesus. That's fucking strong,' I exclaimed.

'Here, present from me old friend,' Will said, and chucked me something.

'Well, I know what it isn't, an assault rifle. Unless it's one of those kits you put together, as in the films. So, what is it?'

'It's an inflatable tank,' he said, mocking.

I ripped open the Jiffy bag and inside was a mobile phone. But it looked like it was from the Ark. I tipped out the rest of the contents. Only an AA battery, a piece of paper and a SIM card fell.

'Has Cyprus not got into the twenty-first century?' I asked, studying the phone.

'I tought ya *special* guys would know about dis type of ting, man. Dat's an emergency phone, runs on one AA battery and can last for fifteen years. SIM card is untraceable and de piece of paper has me untraceable mobile number on it, and de one dat belongs to de phone. Log em and get rid of de paper. Don't go callin' your mum and dad; ya never know who is listenin'. Don't want a load of extremists descendin' on Newquay, man.'

'Ah yeah, I know about this kind of technology,' I replied, lying through my teeth.

Will smiled. 'Next landin' point is tree and half hours away. Ashcabat, Turkmenistan. Be on your guard; not a trustworthy bunch.'

'Don't suppose you're carrying any weapons, M-60, Minigun, by any chance?' I joked, hoping he was.

'Nah, man, I've got me charm.'

'Don't suppose you've got an Xbox back there? Three more hours with you is gonna kill me. I might have to jump now.' I slumped forward, pretending to die.

'I have, man,' he said smugly. 'Turn de rear seat around and pull down de panel.'

'Good, I could do with some action. This trip is getting boring now.'

'Hey, man, be careful what ya wish for, especial on me aircraft,' he snapped.

I jumped over and found the Xbox One, with *Battlefield 4,* plus a few other games. Ah well, missed the Russian fuck, but this will do, I thought.

Three hours soon went, only feeling I had only played an hour. I'd been holding off going for a piss for a while and, as we touched down, it jolted my bladder. My eyes were as wide as saucers. I wasn't sure if it was playing the Xbox that long or the double espresso. I turned the console off. Time check: 01.15 hrs. Will, on his headset, was talking to someone. I sensed something wasn't quite right. Now at bursting point, I knelt, found an empty beer can and proceeded to piss in it.

'Bastards,' Will said, unbuckling.

'What's up?' I asked, still concentrating my aim.

'I'm off to refuel. Do me a favour. Go over to de small office and make sure de fat controller is kept occupied.'

'Problems, Will?'

'When ya hear me sound de horn, be ready to board. OK?'

'Sure, but...'

Before I could finish, Will had leapt from the plane. As I followed, he sprinted awkwardly to one of the small hangars. I made a hurried walk to the small office. The building was a Portakabin with large, tinted windows. I wasn't sure how many staff were inside. I knocked on the door and waited.

'*Garashmak*,' a voice shouted from inside.

Assuming this meant come in, I entered. A shifty-looking man looked up from his desk, frowned and began ranting and waving his arms. I held out my hand to greet him. His feet pushed his swivel chair back, the wheels sliding on the nylon floor tiles, and he put one hand on a desk drawer handle. His eyes had a menacing look about them. He had a white, pointed beard that hung down to his neckline. The rest of his tanned, wrinkled face was clean-shaven, which gave the impression it was a false beard, like the ones you put on Santa at a Christmas panto, but without the moustache. He looked like a tanned gnome for sale in a garden centre. I thought of the character name from the *Gnomeo and Juliet* movie: Tybalt.

'Good morning, Tybalt. What seems to be the problem?'

He replied sternly, '*Gum Bol*,' and pointed towards the door I'd come in.

Sitting relaxed on the desk next to him, trying to block the view of our plane, I said, 'I'm not here to cause any trouble. Got any coffee?'

'I telephone *howpsuzlyk*.'

Tybalt picked up the phone receiver and pressed a button. He started to talk quickly, sounding concerned. I pressed the end call button.

'No need to call anyone,' I said. 'We'll be off in a few minutes.'

Tybalt replaced the handset and made a quick reach for the same drawer. Rapidly sliding it open, the office equipment shot over the edge and onto the floor. He pulled out a pistol, kicked his chair back further on its wheels and pointed the weapon at me. He took the safety catch of the pistol. This wasn't what I expected. Will did say they were an untrustworthy lot; I should have known better.

'Don't move, I *zelel* you. *Owrum, owrum*,' he said, circling his pistol for me to turn around.

'I don't understand.'

'Err... hands up, turn around.'

Reluctantly, I got to my feet and turned around, but didn't raise my hands. I heard him get out of his chair. I stayed still, keeping my hands out in front of me, out of sight from the gunman. He shouted at me in broken English to move again and to go outside. I walked forward, sliding my feet slowly. He impatiently shouted more words I couldn't understand. He stuck the pistol in my back, pushing me forward. Bingo; he was now too close. I didn't have to think of the next move, it came instinctively. I'd trained many times in this situation with a variety of weapons and set-ups.

I turned sharply. At the same time, I swiftly swung my left hand, the one he couldn't see in front of me, and pushed his wrist to the side. The pistol fired as I grasped his wrist, sending the round into a metal filing cabinet. My other arm pushed his shoulder in the direction his weapon had just fired. He tried to resist, but the momentum carried him into the cabinet. I had to keep the pistol pointing away from me. He fired off more shots in a panic, three in total. The air was filled with whatever the rounds were impacting on, including the cordite. His foot contacted my shin as he tried to kick his way out; adrenalin blocked any pain. Keeping his wrist away from me, I moved my hand up to his shirt collar, put my knee in the soft back of his knee and yanked him back, keeping his arm upright.

He fired three more rounds as he fell back, glass shattered between the violent shots. As he hit the deck, I knelt on his arm and punched him hard, square in the face. He wrestled his arm, trying to loosen the pressure from my hand and knee to bring the pistol's death sentence on me. With his other hand, he punched me in the chest. I felt the pain this time and I tried to get my breath. In that second, he managed to raise the pistol slightly and fired one round after another. I wasn't counting this time. In the mayhem of rounds destroying where they hit, I thumped him again, and again, and again.

The weapon fell silent; he went still. I was breathing fast. The air was tinged with smoke. His white beard collected the blood from his face. I still had a tense grip on him, the end of my fingers pushed into his relaxed forearm muscle. Loosening my grip, I took the pistol from his hand and moved off his body, keeping the weapon aimed at his head. I backed up towards the desk. The area was littered with paper, glass, and splinters of the prefabricated walls. Between the ringing in my ears, other sounds started to filter in.

Glancing out the broken window, in the distance Will was still refuelling the plane. I gave Tybalt a good kick to see if he was faking his unconsciousness—silent. Putting the safety catch on, I tucked the pistol in my trousers behind, and then dragged the swivel chair over. Tybalt was heavier than I'd thought when I picked his inert body up, slumping him in the chair. I ransacked the drawers and found some Sellotape, then wrapped the tape over and over around his arms and legs, securing him to the chair. The rest of the reel, I wound around his face and head, leaving only a small gap for him to breathe. I wiped his blood off my hands onto a tea towel which lay next to the coffee machine. I poured myself half a paper cup of coffee. As I lifted it to drink, my hands were trembling and I noticed my shirt cuffs were covered with blood splats.

Before sitting down and facing the door, in case there were any unwanted visitors seeing what had gone on, I pulled the pistol out. It was a Kanuni 16, Turkish military. I unclipped the magazine, annoyed I'd not kept a tally of the number of rounds fired, even though I knew it held sixteen when full. Fortunately, it still held rounds. I kept Will and the plane in view. In the silence the phone rang, its little orange button flashing away. After ten seconds it stopped.

Beep, beep, beeeeeep!

That was Will's signal. 'Happy Christmas, Santa. Well-wrapped.' I laughed at my own cheesy joke.

Leaving the Portakabin, I scanned the area for threats. Will was frantically waving his arms, beckoning me over. He then pointed to the distance. A pair of vehicle headlights in the far distance were coming down the hill, flickering between the rocks and trees. Running over to Will, I made the pistol ready.

'You took your fucking time,' I said.

He pulled me inside. 'Why is trouble always followin' ya around, Johnny? A simple job of takin' care of de fat controller and den all hell breaks out.'

'Thanks would be nice. Who are our visitors?'

Will started the plane, rushing at everything he did. 'Dey're not here to wave us off,' he said, slightly flustered.

'They've entered the far gates,' I said, looking out the side door. 'How long before we're airborne?'

'Tirty seconds.'

A black SUV, like an American federal agent would drive, headed towards our direction under the airport lights.

'Haven't got that sort of time. Their windows are down, armed men in back,' I relayed. 'I've got an idea. Start moving towards the runway.'

Jumping out of the plane, Will moved the Beechcraft towards the runway. I opened the valve on the tanker. Aviation fuel gushed out, some of it spraying upon me as the propeller picked up speed. Running alongside the doorway of the plane, I hitched myself up. We steadily picked up speed. Muzzle flashes came from the rear of the moving SUV, whizzing very close.

'Incoming,' I yelled. 'Get us the fuck airborne.'

The plane's engine revved its nuts off. We were only about thirty metres from the tanker truck, crazy to hit it now. I aimed to the side at the closing SUV, not that I could hit anyone; that would be an unmistakable fluke, but it might keep their heads down a bit. I fired, then another, in slow succession. The SUV's driver's response was to veer away slightly. Five shots in total, then the Kanuni 16 was out of ammo. More rounds came our way as the gunmen intensified their fire; their rounds ricocheted off the tanker's cab as it came between us and them.

Whoosh... **BOOOM!**

The tanker's contents had ignited, sending a massive fireball into the air, the cab and shell blowing outwards. A vortex of intense yellow and orange colours made me shield my eyes. Thankfully, we were now a good eighty metres away; however, I still felt the shockwave. The air was rushing by as we reached the pinnacle of speed. I tossed the pistol out and then struggled to shut the door. As I slammed and locked it, all the commotion stopped, like pausing a film on a DVD player. I moved to the porthole, trying to get a look behind us, but Will had banked the plane on its side. The only reminder was the strong smell of aviation fuel on the bottom of my trousers and boots.

Moving into the cockpit, there was an edgy atmosphere. As we got to cruising height, I broke the silence by cracking a joke about what we had just been through. This led us each to tell our own side of the events. After, we sat quiet for a while.

'I'm not goin' to be able to return to refuel now, so I'm goin' to land at Kabul. I'll work out a plan later,' Will said.

'How are you going to get clearance, though? They won't just let you land.'

'I'll make out I have a malfunction, put a mayday out. It's either dat or I crash in de desert, talkin' of which, P Hour minus twenty, so get your chute ready.'

Fitting into the flak-jacket, I made sure my knife was at the front in case I had to cut away any tangled guide ropes and pull my reserve chute. Whilst I harnessed the parachute on, we went over the new rendezvous details, including our special contact codes when using mobile phones. With the skydiving goggles on my forehead, I tied a long length of rope to my Bergen. I squatted down, clipping it on my front as it was easier to stabilise yourself whilst freefalling. Staying in this position, I went over the exit, skydive, and landing in my mind. I set my watch to the Afghan time zone: 06.26 hrs.

'P-minus four,' Will said, watching his GPS monitor. 'Wind speed eight knots at IP.'

I had successfully made a lot of jumps in my time, both in the Paras and SBS. However, my heart was still pounding. I tapped the altimeter strapped to my wrist and tightened all the straps and buckles for the second time. Falling at terminal velocity, around one hundred and twenty-five miles per hour, things can get ripped off. The last thing you want to see is your chute and Bergen come loose and freefall away. Also, when the chute is deployed, it slows you up dramatically, putting a lot of strain on those straps and buckles.

I put a thin pair of leather gloves on as I wanted to make sure my hands would operate the pull lever, and not be numb. Making my way to the exit door, I pulled the goggles over my eyes. I opened the door, the sound and force of the wind rushing in. Facing my back towards the aperture. I hung onto the edge, the awaiting world trying to suck me out. I watched the sign for me to jump. From the corner of my eye, the empty beer cans blew around the cabin's floor.

'P-minus twenty seconds,' Will shouted. 'Thirteen thousand feet. Good luck. See ya in a few days. If not, see ya in hell, man.'

My arms and legs were aching, holding on with the pressure.

'Go, go, go,' he yelled.

My body was sucked into the slipstream, sending me over into a turn. Once I was out of it, I stabilised my dive and looked up to see the black silhouette disappear into the distance. With the exhilarating air rushing past me, I looked down towards earth, trying to fix a point. I had one eye on the altimeter out in front of me. Forty seconds had elapsed. At the five thousand feet mark, with my right hand, I pulled the release handle. In the back of my mind I was already going through the dreadful drill option of cutting loose and pulling my reserve chute if necessary.

A small parachute deployed, dragging the larger chute out. As it did, the slipstream roar almost stopped and the flap of the chute opened. My body endured the G-force as my plummet to earth was almost halted. I checked the canopy above after counting the familiar one thousand, two thousand, three thousand, in my mind. All was going well. This felt amazing. I seized the steering toggles and pulled them up and down simultaneously to drive more air into the chute. Apart from the swish of air and the odd ruffle from the chute, all was tranquil. Gliding down, I made small adjustments with the toggles. I went through the drill of touchdown at the IP. Normally, as a group, we would form an all-round defence and tune into our surroundings, weapons ready. Only this time, I had no rifle, and I was alone.

I checked my altimeter again: one thousand five hundred feet to go. I unclipped the system holding my Bergen and let it drop. The pulleys managed its fall. The line became taut; it was now dangling eighty feet below me. I could make out a dark matter to my left. If Will had got his GPS coordinates spot on, this should be the forest. I slowed my descent slightly, and then felt my Bergen hit the ground. Staring into the abyss, I focused on the distance where I thought the ground was; also looking for any obstructions. Then, it came rushing up and my heart gave a little flutter. I yanked both toggles to slow my descent and lifted my feet up. As the ground came up, I put my legs down and tried to run along, letting the parachute fall behind me.

My feet contacted the sand. I wasn't prepared for how much they sank and, as I tried to run, my feet became too heavy to lift. Inevitably, I went arse over tit, the parachute continuing over me. Fighting off the guide ropes, I got up on one knee and started to drag the chute in. I wasn't hurt, just a bit of bruised pride. It would have been a great piss-take for the lads. I made my way over to my Bergen and untied the rope, and then lifted it onto my back. In the distance was the black outline of the forest. I took a quick scan around me, but even with the full moon, I couldn't see anything of significance. I dragged my chute over to the forest, appearing denser than I remembered it. I scrambled through the bushes and trees, where I threw my kit off and sat on it. Tuning into my environment, I let my eyes adjust to the blackness. If only Will had given me a pair of NVGs. At least he had kept his side of the deal and hadn't filled the chute with his designer boxer shorts.

# CHAPTER TWENTY-SIX

After five minutes, all was calm and quiet. Apart from the little stumble, that was a textbook skydive, and I felt alive. I decided to find the part of the forest where Planet and I had crash-landed. With dawn breaking, I buried my chute and skydiving equipment underground at the base of a bush, trying not to make the area look obvious by covering the soil with dried leaves. I pondered burying Neal's ID. It was necessary on a mission to be sterile of identification. However, this time I might be able to bluff my way out of a situation. It had got me this far; I decided to keep it.

This wooded area was thick. Roots tried to trap my feet. Ahead was a clearing in the gloom. Reaching it, I stopped and let my eyes adjust. My sixth sense started to nudge me, telling me someone was following or watching me. I sank low and waited for the slightest movement or sound, but it was silent, except for my breathing. Two broken trees caught my attention as I searched the dimness. Both had been snapped halfway up; half-lying on these was another larger tree. It then dawned on me: this was where part of the fuselage had crashed with me and Planet still strapped in. It felt as if I'd found the lost City of Ubar.

I waited for the sun to rise a little more whilst I went over what had happened on that dreadful morning. Only this time, I wasn't feeling morose. I unpacked my Bergen to find the box hidden at the bottom. Taking the lid off the box, I took out the small plaque which I'd had specially made. It was only two inches in diameter, but made of solid silver. I dug further down and pulled out a tack hammer and nail. Feeling proud, I nailed the plaque high to the tree which had held his body and mine. The inscription read: 'Evil may have taken away a courageous friend, but your legacy lives on in my soul. I will not forget you, Planet. SBS 2013'

Taking a step back, I stared at the inscription, reading it again. I smiled as an image of Planet popped into my head. Good memories from now on; I had closure. Wiping the tears, I picked up my gear and roughly followed the same path towards the crashed Chinook. The sun's beams were filtering through the forest, like before. It didn't feel at all eerie though. I found the route the Chinook had made through the trees and followed this to the edge. Only small fragments of the wreckage poked out of the sand; the rest had been cleared away. A few years from now all evidence would be lost. Maybe someone in a hundred years would find the plaque and research it, which was kind of comforting.

I returned to the forest and roughly established the spot where I'd found Fish. Opening the box again, I pulled out the second silver plaque. Standing on my Bergen at full stretch, I nailed it to the closest tree and took a step back to read the inscription: 'Fish, Shrek, & RAF Crew. All true heroes. Operation Blue Halo 2013'

I took a deep breath. Now I had full closure. The niggling part of me that had felt emptiness was now full. It was almost as if I relaxed properly for the first time. This was the real reason for my return. Only the good memories would live on. Taking hold of my pack straps, I dragged it away a short distance, but left the tree in sight. I emptied it and sorted the items I wanted to take on my last part of the journey. The webbing I had packed would carry my Pelican micro E&E case, and a cannula, drip and two saline bags, two water bottles, GPS, compass, map, standard battlefield medic kit, ration packs, energy and glucose bars, Hexi-stove, spare mug, poncho, beanie hat, and fleece jumper. I had not forgotten some powder for my feet and bollocks, as on the previous adventure I'd got a nasty sweat rash. I didn't want it again, or my bollocks to drop off. I put the water-filled Camelbak on my back, pulling the tube forward.

I needed a brew, so I dug a small, square hole in the ground, lit the Hexi-stove and placed it in the hole. With my mug on top, I filled it with water and put a teabag in. I set up the poncho sheet with some sticks and paracord, shielding any light given off. At night it was essential to move away from the light and not look over the stove, as a well-trained shooter could pick off your silhouette. My sixth sense began screaming at me. Was this training? I couldn't take the chance. I took a dogleg route the way I had come in to ambush any pursuers. Only this time, with only a knife, this was more of a recce.

Sitting between a group of three tree trunks gave me good concealment and great eyes on the path I had entered earlier. The thick-bushed area behind me covered me from the outside view. I pulled out my green netted veil and placed it over my head, camouflaging my face. Feeling relaxed, I went through scenarios of what might be following: expect the unexpected. Whilst I waited and watched, I thought of my brew. It wouldn't be long before it boiled the teabag to dust, or it would be too hot to drink. This made me think of the hot, sticky bread in Anoosheh's home, burning my mouth. I wondered if they had both made it out alive. I pictured Haleema's beautiful face and elegant body. I now knew what the strange feeling standing in front of her naked was. Hopefully, I would get the chance again, but not for medical reasons.

The thoughts of Haleema were sharply interrupted by voices. I slid back further into the bush, trying to break up the shape of a human form. Ahead of me, coming from the right, were three figures. I caught a better glimpse of them when they went through the sun's beams. As they drew nearer, I established they were all male and all dressed in *dishdashas*. The leading male was dressed in brown attire. Over his shoulders he wore a belt of ammunition. He wasn't wearing a turban, but a beige *swati pakol*. He was checking the way ahead like a tracker, armed with the typical AK47. The man walking directly behind him was also wearing a brown *dishdasha*, but he had a blue jerkin on. His headwear was a maroon and beige chequered *shemagh* and he only had his eyes showing. He was carrying an RPG with a crude back-sack attempt at carrying further warheads. The third man at the rear was telling the other two in front of him where to head. He had a black eye-patch with a turban to match, and the typical white *dishdasha* and black jerkin. Through his long, black, bushy beard, he spoke in Arabic. Occasionally, he looked down the sights of his weapon. He wasn't carrying an AK47, but what looked like an American M16A2 assault rifle.

So, my sixth sense had proved right yet again. My heart was beating faster, but not through my chest as before. They were heading to where I had made the brew. I had been very careful to hide any tracks along my dogleg ambush. I went through the options of my next move. The answer was to stay where I was.

After about ten minutes, my elbows and shoulders began to ache where I was lying on them. I had to get into another position. I managed to get both arms out, leaving my chin on the top of my hands. A branch cracked directly to my left side. I froze; I held my breath. A pair of black boot trainers walked past within two metres of my face. I waited for the nudge from his weapon, or worse, a shot. Something crawled on my leg, coming up towards my back. The sensation stopped, and then I felt it again on my shoulder. It stopped once it got to my neck and just sat there. It felt like a crab, or a large spider. My impulse was to jump up and brush it off. I stared at the trainer boots. The end of his AK47 pointed towards the ground. Why was the armed man just standing there?

A match fell to the ground, its little trail of smoke wafting into the air. I didn't even dare twitch my nostrils. It became more difficult to hold my breath. When the fuck would this guy go? I heard a loud Arabic voice from the distance, and then the trainer boots made off in that direction, along with the smell of his cigarette. Slowly, I released my breath, taking slow and shallow breaths after. Whatever it was on my neck now started to crawl up onto my head, as if it, too, had been waiting for the enemy to leave. The legs had moved down to my ear as little sharp points probed it. This was starting to freak me out, but I had to remain perfectly still. I heard the leaves move to the side of my head as the creature jumped off. My eyes moved left to the direction of the creature now in front of me, my ears tuned into the voices of the three men. I studied the spider's body form. It had an ugly, dark main body with a reddish-coloured head and eight yellow legs, sprouting tiny hairs.

It scurried around the leaves, using its large front legs to feel. I could now make out the two pincer jaws. It wasn't venomous, but this six-inch camel spider could give me a nasty bite. I was torn between staying perfectly still, hoping I wouldn't be its next victim and giving my position away. Or, reaching for my knife and stabbing it, also giving my position away. My eyes behind the veil were wide as I watched it creep closer. The spider put its front two legs on the netting. It was so close I could hardly focus on it. The hairs on my beard move. It just sat there. Was it sizing me up?

I moved my eyes in the direction of where the three men were standing. I couldn't see or hear them. I eased my hand under my flak-jacket for my knife. The spider's front legs raised up as I did, showing its pincer jaws. Fuck; it was ugly, and now agitated. I touched the handle of my knife and pulled it out ever so slowly. As I moved my arm to the side to extend it, my shoulder joint cracked, the noise like a whip being cracked. Suddenly, the camel spider shot off into the undergrowth. I laid my arm to rest on the cool earth, feeling relieved. I didn't know who was luckier, me or it.

Letting time go by as I lay there, I hoped the three of them, including the camel spider, had disappeared forever. Gradually, I lifted my head and scoured the surrounding area. Once I felt it was safe, I pulled my stiff body up into a kneeling on one leg position. I was still concealed behind the group of trees. Hugging the tree formation, I listened intently. The surrounding area was devoid of life; however, my intuition told me that someone was close by. I moved forward, squatting at a deliberate deathly slow pace, watching where I put my feet, making sure I didn't brush any bushes or branches. Every ten paces, I remained completely still and listened: nothing but a gentle breeze and the sound of my pulse thumping.

Twenty metres of painfully-slow, measured movement went past. I was in view of the point where I'd made the brew. Slowly, I took off the veil. The poncho had been taken down. Sitting in the shadow of a tree was the third enemy figure. He was drinking my brew. Wanker. His M16 was lying across his lap and he seemed very chilled, too relaxed. I searched the whole area for the other two. After watching for another ten minutes, I concluded that they had gone, most probably to alert further Elkhaba, or maybe the Taliban had claimed the land back. I couldn't stay hidden forever; I was left in the same sinking position as before. Lightening surely didn't strike twice. Maybe Will was right for saying be careful what you wish for.

Drinking the last out of *my* mug, the fighter got up and threw it into the bushes. He stretched his arms out and took a big yawn. He seemed to spot something in front of him. Putting his weapon against a tree, he walked over to the tree where I had nailed the memorial for my friends that had fallen. He studied it and then made a jump to get it, but it was just out of his reach. He tried again. As he did, I moved stealthily closer. Not to be beaten for a third time, he jumped higher. I moved a few more metres, keeping the tree with the weapon against it between us. This time he managed to touch the plaque, but he couldn't prise it off. He stood there with his hands on his hips. Go on, have another go, don't give up, I mentally screamed. I was within metres of the tree, now in no-man's land. He then grabbed the trunk and his lanky physique started to shimmy up. Bingo.

I made a dash for the M16, seized it, and aimed it at him as he grappled with the tree. He hadn't realised I was there. The weapon didn't have its foregrip and optics attachment. I slipped the safety catch to three-round burst.

'Hey, best you leave that the fuck alone,' I said.

Peering over his shoulder, looking shocked, he jumped down and faced me. The first thing he looked at was his M16, and then he gave me a stare of loathing.

'*Ahlan wa sahlan. Mā ismak/ik?*' he said.

He had welcomed me and asked me my name in a casual way, far too casual. 'Do you speak English?' I asked.

'I speak many languages, my friend. Please put the gun down.' He took a step towards me.

'I wouldn't take any further steps, *my friend*, or I'll slot you. Turn around, get on your knees, and put your hands on your head. Now.'

'*A'id min fadlak*,' he said, smiled and took another slow step forwards.

Asking me to say it again was classic stalling technique. I moved my finger onto the trigger and leant forward in my stance, showing I would squeeze the trigger.

'You move another step, you streaky piece of piss, and I'll send you to your promised land. Now fucking turn around and put your hands on your head.'

He appeared arrogant. 'You infidel pig. You won't shoot me. Do you know who I am?'

'I'm not playing a game of *Who the fuck am I*. Last chance or I will slot you. That's *qutal*, kill, if you don't understand slot.'

He loudly laughed, tipping his head back, and when he brought it forward he spat at me. 'Then slot me, as you say. I hope you have enough bullets for the rest who will come.'

He had moved his right hand slowly inside his *dishdasha*. However, I had him tracked. He made a slight move forward.

**Bang, bang, bang**!

I'd fired off a short burst at his forehead. The impact threw him back to the floor. The burst echoed around the trees. '*Threat neutralised*.'

'You had your chance.'

Lifting his clothing revealed his hand holding a small grenade with the safety pin still in; thank fuck. I wrenched it from his grip. Examining it through the years of grime, I established it was a Russian F-1 grenade, most probably seized when the Russians invaded Afghanistan in a nine-year battle. No point in trying to hide his dead body. In fact, I had an idea, but speed was of the essence. It wouldn't be long before the other two, if not more, would swoop on this position.

I rifled through my webbing to find a length of 12-lb transparent fishing wire and a small reel of clear tape in my Pelican case. I taped the grenade to the tree at shin height, thinking that the next enemy to arrive would be looking at his body or at eye-level. I tied off the trip wire at the same height at another tree three metres away and made my way back to the grenade. Very carefully, I tied off the end through the safety pin, leaving the wire a little slack; too taut and the victim may feel the wire and halt.

Picking up the Hexi-stove and tucking it away, I left my mug. I didn't want to catch any nastiness from it. I'd rather take my chances kissing a slobbering camel. I took one more glance at the silver plaque and then made my way to the fringes of the forest where the Chinook had burnt out. I checked the area both sides of the valley—all clear. But which way was best? My original plan had been to head the same way at night, like before, but now it was Plan B. I decided I would head straight across the open and over the mound, the same route the truck had made. Again, I couldn't see the other side of the mound. I readied my rifle.

'Who dares wins,' I muttered.

I sprinted out of the woodland and headed for the mound. This time I wasn't holding my breath. The only noise was my webbing and the items in it. Reaching the mound, I continued to run up it, weapon tucked in my shoulder, aiming down its sights. I don't know if I was more surprised or thankful, but I was met with nothing but a slope of sand. I continued to sprint to the edge of the track where it went between the two sloped sides.

I had been running for about one hundred and twenty metres, my lungs were hurting from the lack of oxygen in this dry heat. Slowing to a fast-paced jog, the track wound its way through the valley. A large boulder lay to one side of the track and, sheltering behind it, I faced my weapon back the way I'd come. I was lying on the floor, my chest moving at the same time as I was sucking in the air. Sweat poured out of every orifice. Jesus; it was hot. I searched for the Camelbak's tube and sucked it between my teeth, taking long, hard sips. The water was warm, but it did the job.

Once I had got my breath back, I followed the track further away from the forest. Approximately a kilometre of a fast-paced tabbing later, the valley's sides became lower and opened out. Sixty metres or so in front of me was the village. Getting down on one knee, I took another long, hard swig from the tube; salty sweat ran into my mouth. Wiping the sweat that was dripping into my eyes, I scanned the area behind, then to the front. All quiet, I travelled up the slope to within a couple of metres from the top ridgeline, moving forward all the time. As I got to the last point of the ridgeline before it became a sheer drop, I lowered myself down into the prone position and studied the village, feeling weird to be back.

Most of the buildings had either collapsed entirely or were part-standing. The larger ones that still stood had battle scars from various types of ammunition. Different sized craters pock-marked the ground. Haleema's home was part-standing. The roof had half-collapsed in at an angle across the doorway. There must have been quite a standoff when Lieutenant Kellett brought his firepower in. I hoped that none of the villagers had been caught up in the barrage, especially Haleema and her mother. A small explosion echoed down the valley. I hoped that was the end of any pursuers, but in reality I knew there would be more. Time to find Haleema, I thought.

# CHAPTER TWENTY-SEVEN

Jumping over the ridge, I slid down the slope, using my free hand to try to control my descent. As I reached the bottom, continuing my momentum, I ran over to the familiar wall behind the home of Anoosheh. I kept to the side of the building as before, only this time there was no hessian over the doorway. I managed to squeeze through the damage into half of the remaining ruin. It was murky inside. Objects were strewn across the floor, but thankfully no decayed bodies. I started to reminisce, but quickly slapped myself to remain focused.

The next building's door was securely locked with a steel bar across it and two padlocks, as were the windows when I checked the parameter. I checked behind the way I'd entered again. I didn't feel alone. My heartbeat had picked up dramatically. I wasn't sure if it was the thought of finding Haleema dead or alive, or that my sixth sense knew someone was coming.

I skipped the damaged buildings and made my way to an oblong-shaped building by the cropped fields, the same cropped fields I had dived into before, when thinking I had seen the enemy. This time there were no goats; a small mercy. Out of the front door came an old man. Instantly, I raised my weapon, finger poised on the trigger, aiming directly at his chest. He put his hands together in the greeting gesture, only, one of his hands was missing.

'*Pakheyr,*' the old man welcomed.

'*Salam,*' I replied.

He was probably in his late-sixties. His white, wispy beard hung misshapen. His rugged facial features displayed many wrinkles, like Waterloo Station's network of rail tracks. His left eye was missing, only scarred skin remained where it had healed. Underneath his tanned jacket and white robe, his frame was skinny and frail. His brown, dirty feet protruded past the end of his battered sandals and his discoloured brown toenails were in serious need of a pedicure. I wondered if he had been around since the first Afghan war in 1839. Through the only two teeth remaining, he tried to fix me a welcome smile. I cautiously lowered my weapon.

'You look for Haleema?' he said, in his local accent, but at least in English, which was better than my limited Pashto.

'How did you know?'

'I am Ghulam Rasool, village elder, former Mujahedeen fighter. I remember you from first time. I never forget foreign face.'

'Where is she? Where is everyone? Are you alone?'

'I am alone. The villagers will return one day, this for sure. We built village many times since I was boy. The...'

'Where is Haleema?' I interrupted, knowing it was rude, but I had to get a move on.

'She back at Kabul hospital. I warn you, she under guard. Her boss make sure this.'

'You mean Baha Udeen?'

He spat on the ground. 'Yes. Be wary. You need car now, yes?'

'You have one?' I said, looking around.

'Money?'

I pulled out a large roll of Afghan notes, took the band off and counted out ten one thousand Afghani bank notes. Ghulam gazed at the money, and then to my other hand that held the larger amount. I tutted and counted out another ten and thrust it to him. He smiled and took them. He then waved me to follow, his frail frame staggering past me into his house. As I trailed behind him, I heard an approaching vehicle. I peeked back around the doorframe. To the far end of the village was another Toyota pickup, red in colour. Standing on the rear was a lone fighter with a mounted machinegun.

'Fuck,' I said.

I slowly shut the battered wooden door behind me. Becoming impatient as the elder looked for his keys, I hurried him, telling of the approaching vehicle.

'Here are keys. Please tell Haleema to come home. I will go speak to enemy, *Insha Allah*.' He handed me the keys, but held onto my hand for a few seconds, and then he let it go.

'Where's your car?' I asked with urgency.

'Near old hospital.'

Before I could say no to him, he had pulled the front door wide open. The Toyota made its way over to our position. Shit; no time to make a dash. I took off the safety catch and switched it to semi-auto. With no rear exits, I noticed a small ladder leading up to another level. Above this point was a small window, letting in the sun's rays. Once I got to the top of the rickety ladder, I found a wooden slat bed strewn with dirty sheets. Positioning myself back from the window, I secretly looked out, calm and in command.

The elder made his way over to the waiting band of enemies in the Toyota. They all got out, three in total, the rear gunner staying put. I scrutinised their weapons. The better you know your enemy, the better you can kill them, rather than they kill you. Sometimes knowledge drives out fear. Still standing back from the window, I took aim. Once I had made the first kill, it would be harder for the others to judge my exact position from my muzzle flash. The further back I was, the better shield I had from the building and window framework. I preferred close contact, especially when low on ammo: less risk of missing or injuring the enemy so they can return fire.

First in my sights was the machine-gunner. I waited, still as a statue, rock solid in my stance. The driver, who had his AK47 slung over his shoulder, slapped the elderly man to the ground. I felt the distaste in my mouth and swallowed my spit like a bitter pill. The man behind him lifted his boot up and trod down on Ghulam's head. Ghulam grunted with pain, but he didn't squeal or beg for mercy. They shouted abuse at him. He just held his hand up to protect himself. The driver again slapped Ghulam's head; my finger squeezed the trigger a little further.

'Come this way. Go on, give me a reason,' I whispered under my breath.

The third menace, deciding he hadn't inflicted his prowess over Ghulam, moved between the others and put his hand up the old man's *dishdasha*. The sick bastard gritted his teeth and then Ghulam let out a sickening scream of twisted pain. Whilst the other three laughed, he continued to squeeze the old man's bollocks.

'*Aaeen how?*' he yelled.

In a way I now hoped he would answer their question of where I was, as it was cruel to watch. Ghulam began to scream louder as his testicles were twisted and yanked. Ghulam gave in after spewing up in the dirt, and he frantically pointed at the building I was in. The rear gunner pointed his machinegun over towards the front door. The twisted fuck let go of Ghulam and spat on him. They made their weapons ready and walked slowly towards me.

'Little bit further,' I whispered.

I let rip. A single shot hit the gunner just under his chin, like a water bomb balloon exploding, only red liquid. *'Threat neutralised.'* Immediately, I lowered my sights to the first man of the three, who had looked back to see his comrade's body fall backwards. I hit him in the chest, and then a second round hit his upper shoulder. He fell back into the man behind him, covering him in blood. Panic overtook the other two. The man at the rear fired erratically at the building, bits of debris flew up into my line of vision. But this didn't stop me aiming and letting rip at him. Three shots hit him in quick pace, throwing him around like a rag doll. His weapon began firing as he turned, and he shot the last man standing in front of him. He shuddered as each bullet impacted his back, sending his innards out.

I fired at their crumpled bodies, just to make sure. Shit; stoppage. I turned the M16 on its side and cocked it, facing the ejection opening downwards. No round came out. I quickly pulled the magazine out. Bollocks; out of ammo. Still pumped up, adrenalin running through me, I jumped through window. Landing on the hard-baked surface below, I rolled over to break some of the shock. I continued into a standing position and ran towards the victims' bloody bodies. I picked up the first AK47 and fired a shot into each of the three on the ground.

'Threats neutralised,' I hushed. Oh shit. I'd actually said it aloud. I put it down to over-excitement.

On the rear of the Toyota lay the dead gunner. Placing the weapon down, I helped the elder up. He was weak and he stayed bent over for a while. Once he'd stood up, stretching his limbs, and caressing his groin, his clothes showed the blood splats. With his eyes bloodshot, his long, aged, yellow teeth smiled at me.

'You fight strong. I have you fight next to me in Mujahedeen.'

'It's a shame you weren't taking the opium you were back then. You wouldn't have felt the pain,' I said, pointing at his hand rubbing.

He had started to enjoy the joke when we heard another vehicle. I didn't have time for pleasant goodbyes; instead, I made my way to the driver's side of the Toyota. However, I stopped as one of the front tyres was flat. I don't remember hitting that, I thought. I turned and ran down towards the makeshift hospital where Haleema had been forced to help. As I sprinted, I hoped Ghulam had hidden himself well in the village.

Then I thought of the RPG and the other AK47 lying on the ground. Why didn't I pick them up? I slapped my forehead for being so stupid, hoping this didn't come back to bite me.

In the distance, was the same small treeline which I hid in for a rest amongst the baked sewage. My eyes followed the trees to the left, towards the makeshift hospital building. I was shocked to see it all but gone. A huge mound of earth and debris was all that stood. Strands of metal and timber poked out of the rubble. A spine-tingling chill ran through me when I thought how close Rabbit and I had been. It only now dawned on me what the UAV was for. It was obviously taking live feed or photos of this building. Keeping close to the buildings, I darted round the rear of one and got down on one knee. I couldn't hear the approaching vehicle. Where was Ghulam's vehicle? With each cautious step through the scarred village, I checked all around.

There it stood, a faded orange long chassis Pak Suzuki Jeep, most probably from the eighties. It was covered in rubble. Parts of the tanned convertible roof had lengths of timber sticking through. Lying awkwardly against the rear was a large side of what seemed like a section off a wooden boat. I opened my webbing pouch and pulled out the keys. A single gunshot resounded around the village. I looked back in the direction it had come from, the area where I had killed four of the enemy.

As I reached the rubble around the jeep, I started quickly clearing it. A sharp stinging pain to my left hand stopped me. I held it up and, between the dust and grime, blood started to seep through, but I didn't have time to dress the long slit. The boat-shaped panel on the rear was part of the gate from the compound. The driver's door handle was missing, so I rushed over the rubble around to the passenger's side. Another gunshot in the distance made me yank at the door handle. The door opened with a loud creak. I threw all the mangled debris out and climbed across. The leather seats were blistering hot, my hand wound stung. Leaning across, I slammed the door shut, catching sight of blood down my dirty arm. As soon as the key was in the slot, I turned the ignition. The engine slowly turned over.

'Don't you die on me,' I pleaded. 'Come on, bitch.'

Rather than waste the battery, I turned the key back to the beginning stage. Maybe I should be like Will and talk nicely to it.

'Right, baby, please start this time.'

I tried again. This time it started, but it sounded as if it had no oil in it. Ten seconds after I had revved the engine, a plume of exhaust smoke filled the area behind me. The knocking engine quietened as if oil had been put in. The exhaust pipe rumbled below my seat. I looked for the window button; instead, I found the manual winder. I started to cough as the fumes and smoke hampered my view. The window had only opened a couple of inches when the winder handle came off in my hand.

'Oh for fuck's sake,' I said, livid. And I paid two hundred pounds for this privilege, I thought.

Selecting first, the gearbox crunched and I let the clutch out, pushing down the accelerator more.

Bang!

The exhaust had backfired. All four wheels moved as the brakes unbound. The car rocked forward over the small pile of rubble. Exhaust smoke filtered out the holes in the cloth roof lining. Suddenly, a round hit the rear. I took a quick look to my right as I floored the Suzuki, but couldn't see who had fired it. The jeep jolted and jumped around as all four wheels tried to find traction. The bodywork was taking a battering. I hoped this wasn't from further incoming rounds. Hunched down, I selected another gear and I lurched backwards. As we hit the track, the seat-back behind me collapsed. I held onto the steering wheel to keep upright and rammed it into third gear. The blood dripped down my arm, my heartbeat keeping up with rev counter.

As I sped down the track past the ruins of the hospital, a lone gunman opened up to my left just as I wrenched the jeep into fourth gear. Rounds slammed into the bodywork and the front screen smashed as it took most of the incoming. Hot shards hit my face and I squinted to protect my eyes. Leaning forward whilst trying to steer, I punched at the window, swerving all over the place. The screen became loose. I dipped the clutch, braked hard and the screen flapped forward. I selected second, let off the clutch and sped off.

I hadn't seen the small roadside ditch in front, and as the Suzuki landed the other side after becoming airborne, my face contacted the steering wheel. The horn sounded, my neck and head were pulled back as the car continued to snake off-road. I thought of Rabbit making a joke about how at least the horn worked. Blood poured into my beard and I poked my tongue out to taste it. We were now moving along at top speed, my adrenalin keeping up with it. The noisy flapping roof-liner eventually gave in and was ripped away. This gave me a better all-round view, but I felt more vulnerable.

Frantically searching for the pursuing vehicle, I spotted it coming from the left; another fucking white Toyota. Only this time, the gunner was missing from the rear, the mounted weapon jerking up and down. The terrain ahead was featureless, endless miles of baked sand. A little orange dash light flickering in the middle of this mayhem caught my eye: the dreaded fuel light.

'Give me a fucking break,' I bellowed.

Rounds hit the side of the Suzuki. I could have kicked myself for not picking up the RPG or AK47. I glanced over at the gaining Toyota; windows down, it was filled with crazed faces.

**BOOOM**!

A huge orange fireball, with rolls of black, erupted into the air. I kept looking back in astonishment. Small, unrecognisable black metal pieces rose out of the fireball. The vibrant flashes of colours were replaced with clouds of earth and dust. A large, odd-shaped object rolled over in mid-air, then disappeared as the smoke and dust engulfed it, obscuring my view as the mass hit the ground.

I slowed the Suzuki to a standstill and pulled the handbrake up. Leaving the engine running, I tried to open the driver's door, but it was stuck. I gave it a shoulder barge, but that didn't work either. I had to climb across again. The exhaust still bellowed fumes from the now rolling-away jeep. Bits of fragments from the devastation hit me from above. Dust clouds rolled at my feet. I could smell burning, not wood, but like hot metal and paint. My Suzuki had continued forward another five metres. Worrying that it may have been a jet strike, I looked to the skies. Nothing but the sun, not even a bird or cloud.

'Bloody great big mine,' I said, realising.

I laughed at the irony. Then thought how it could have been me. I stared back at my tracks, which went off in the direction of the damaged wreckage.

A tiny tap on my boot broke my gaze on the mangled, burning Toyota. I looked down to see red-stained blotches around it. I touched the bridge of my throbbing nose and pulled my hand away, covered in blood. Holding up my other hand, it too, was bleeding. I pulled out and ripped open a surgical wipe and cleaned the areas. Once the bleeding had eased, I dressed the serrated wound on my palm. There wasn't a lot I could do with my nose, so I just placed a pad over it. I swallowed two painkillers with a good suck from the tube.

Walking back to the car, smoke coming from out underneath, I bent down and looked, making my nose ache. The exhaust was broken in two and made a deep rumbling sound. The bodywork had soaked up many rounds. I cleared the glass from the seats and climbed back over, pulling the back of the driver's seat upright. I checked my GPS and worked out where I was on the map. Someone would have heard the explosion. Time to get the hell out of here. I set the trip meter and let off the handbrake. Time check: 09.11 hrs. I looked out in the direction to head and wondered how many other mines there were.

# CHAPTER TWENTY-EIGHT

Even with the cool air blowers on max, and the screen gone, the heat was relentless. My clothes soaked up the pools of sweat on the warm leather seat. My face felt taut from the burning sun. Continuing to wipe away the sweat from my eyes, I began to miss the roof. Sometimes a gust of wind would throw up the dust from the desert, my eyes bulging with grit. Shouldn't have ditch the skydiving goggles, I thought.

On every bump, the fuel light had flickered on. The route hadn't been straight forward, following tracks carved through beautiful mountains. I had made three stops just to reset my direction; without my GPS and map I could end up anywhere. Ahead was a clump of trees, all alone in the open. I veered towards them, thinking of the shade. Nosing the Suzuki up to the tree, using it as a handbrake, I cut the engine.

Clambering across, out of my sweat bath, I found a small, shady spot at the base of an old tree. In front of me was a massive wadi. Only small, dark-stained sand running down the middle altered the featureless ground. At least there had been a water supply at some stage, maybe before my arrival there had been rain. My stomach gurgled and I looked at my watch: 12.13 hrs. I took a hard suck on my water tube, but only got a small amount out. The hot engine ticked as it cooled down. I made a mental note to check the water level later. The midday sun was at is hottest, 40 degrees, if not higher. It was getting seriously heated, even under the little shade. I crawled forward and took a quick peek over the edge of the wadi bank. The concave bank showed the dried tree roots, but at least it gave better shade and concealment.

Taking off my webbing, I slid down with it and climbed under the bank between the roots. I wasn't alone; a small lizard the size of my palm had poked its head out of a small burrow. It had a metallic-blue flash on the underside of its head and further around its body, where its legs started. The lizard's eyes flitted about. I made a move to touch it, but it shot down the bank to the base of the wadi. There it sat, still as a rock. I was fascinated. My stomach growled louder. My Hexi-stove was slightly bent, so I had to straighten it before I set it up. Once alight, I got the familiar smell, which always brought on a bit of nostalgia. I used my spare metal cup to boil some water and put a sealed ration pack in. As it heated, I thought back on Haleema's trips from Kabul to her village and back. How did she get through the mines, IEDs, militants, and checkpoints? Was she paying her way through, or had she known a secure route?

Once the water had boiled, I carefully took the packet out and put a tea bag back in. I ripped it open. The aroma was better than it tasted. However, meat, potato and beans were a luxury compared to no food at all. When I had finished my gourmet dinner, I tucked into some glucose bars and boiled sweets, finishing off with dunking oatmeal biscuits in my tea.

The breeze had picked up, which was refreshing. I had found a brilliant LUP by accident and was chuffed. I had lost sight of my only companion out here, the lizard. I threw some bits of oatmeal on the sand below and waited. I could do with some company or a distraction, I thought, and then wished I hadn't as 'Be careful what you wish for' seemed to be getting me into trouble. The wind had radically increased, little pockets of sand whirled around the wadi floor. Crawling out of my little hotel, I raised my head above the bank's ridge. I had to squint my eyes almost shut as a large sandstorm obscured my view. I scuttled back in and put my beanie hat on, pulling it over my face, my nose reminding me of its injury.

The driving storm and creaking of the trees played tricks on my mind. I questioned my reason for carrying on. Was Rabbit right: would I end up in a body bag? Or rot in the desert, or, even worse, my head on a pole outside a village? Why was I risking it going to find her? More to the point, was she alive still? Even Will, with his experience, had questioned me. I didn't feel negative, just a bit more realistic. I tucked myself further into a ball as the wind and sand tried to find its way in. I closed my eyes and tried to answer all the questions in my mind.

Woken by the pure silence, I pulled up my hat, sand falling down the back of my neck. I was covered head to toe in it. I felt stiff when I stretched and climbed out. Brushing myself down, I checked the time. I must have been tired as I'd been asleep for nearly three hours. Looking back to where I'd been asleep, I watched the lizard scurry out of its burrow. I threw the used teabag and an oatmeal biscuit back in as I climbed to the ridge. I scanned the surrounding area for any signs of unwanted life. It was as bleak and barren as before. After messing about, trying to get the Suzuki bonnet up, another thing that was broken, I checked the oil and water. Both were on the minimum levels. After going through the ritual of getting in, I decided to text Will with coded a message via the emergency phone.

'Wilfred. Newquay. Running late. Had Barney Rubble this morning. Gooseberry puddin' at her hospital. Jam jar on route now.'

I knew Will had used Cockney rhyming slang many years ago. I hoped he hadn't forgotten it, otherwise he might think I've gone mad. I pressed send, and then I rechecked my position and the best route. I'd had enough of the off-road and planned to pick up a better road. The engine knocked its head for a few seconds before the oil smoothed it, but at least it had started.

I had been driving for about forty-five minutes and was amazed how the landscape had changed. The drab colours of the desert were broken up with greenery of trees and bushes dotted around. The other thing that had changed was the Suzuki's temperature gauge. It was creeping up to the red. I pulled off into an eight-foot-wide ditch. I was about eye-level with the track. To my left were fields. Some were plain earth-coloured, some mixtures of green. Looking around further, I could see randomly positioned buildings. I checked the GPS and map. I was close to Qala-e Ilyas Khan, only eighty kilometres to Kabul. I weighed up the risks in taking the main route, the Kabul Gardez Highway, against a more off-road one. Either way had its pros and cons, plus I had to take into consideration the piece of shit I was driving.

Sitting there for nearly an hour made me feel very vulnerable, even though the only sound was a barking mutt. At least I had water and snacks to occupy myself with. I thought of Oliver finding Neal tied up, and the kind of reaction and their conversation. This kept me amused. Had the police put out a search in Scotland for his car or me? I knew Steve and Roy would cover each other's backs. I would love to have been there when Captain Cock found out who I really was. I turned on the ignition and the temperature gauge had dropped. Time check: 17.59 hrs. Another hour and the sun would be setting. Maybe this would be an advantage. I decided to wait it out.

It didn't take long for dusk to settle. I had kept myself amused by thinking of past times with the lads. I didn't think about the disaster of

Operation Blue Halo; hopefully, the pain was now laid to rest. Before setting off, I decided to take a piss. At head height, with a part of the ditch lower down in front of my position, I started to go. To my right, it was a stark difference to the fields and buildings on the other side. The sun was in its last stages and the moon wasn't fully up. All was peaceful.

A cacophony of sounds and lights erupted high in the air in the distance. It was like a scene from *Star Wars*. Tracers streaked towards the earth, spitting fire out from their source. The sound echoed towards me for a short time after the display had finished, but then the spewing fire would start in a different position. I couldn't see it, but I knew of only one machine with that type of powerful calibre: the Apache. Another Apache let hell break loose from another position, adding to the awesome display. I could hear different types of explosions. I scrambled out of the ditch and lay down, taking it all in. I guessed that what they were mulching was about two kilometres away. My energy levels were up and I wanted to join in. However, I could easily be mistaken as the intended victim.

Two small glows, one after the other, lit up the night's horizon, followed by large booms. The helicopters were drowned out for a second, but they continued to move and fire. Then all went silent, except for barking mutts. All the lights in the distant buildings were out. I took a sip of bottled water as my mouth had dried. I tuned into the silence, expecting it all to start again. Now wasn't the best time to set off, so I decided to stay put for another hour. Anyway, in the past we [British Army] always let the Taliban collect their dead.

Cupping my hands around my watch, I illuminated the time: 20.11 hrs. It had been just over an hour since the final two explosions. The night was still quite warm, but a chilly breeze had picked up, bringing me goose bumps. Or were the goose bumps rising as I thought other militants might be in the area? This time I didn't have my Diemaco C8 to pull into my shoulder for reassurance. Time to head out on the main highway, but the draw of going to look at the battle scene was too much. I could hear Will and Oliver saying trouble always followed me around. Maybe this was why, and maybe I craved it. I climbed back in the Suzuki and started her up. I was getting used to the noise and smells. This time I wasn't concerned about driving on black light; in fact, I wanted to be seen just as a local, less conspicuous. After making a meal of getting out of the ditch, I drove off the main track towards the area where the

Apaches were striking. On the rough terrain, the hanging back part of the exhaust fell away.

This had to be the area. I pulled up to an edge of a small wadi, killing the engine and lights. This time, before clambering out, I left it in gear. Peering into the blackness, I could see a good entry point. In the centre, water reflected off the moonlight. Across, on the far bank, a section had collapsed: that would be my exit. I drove the jeep on black light down into the wadi, parking it close to the side. I was well-hidden. Crossing to the other side, my boots soaked up the cool water, refreshing my feet. I clambered up the collapsed bank and I knelt on one knee, waiting for my eyes to adjust to the dark. It seemed I was on a plateau. Thirty-five metres below me, I could make out dark-shaped objects. I put my nose up slightly, like a dog, and tried to register a new smell that had drifted into my senses. I thought of a bonfire, like burning, dried leaves in a back garden in England.

I crept down low to the darkened objects. As I did, the smell became stronger. Focusing hard ahead, my foot trod on something what felt like a branch. I looked down to see the skin of an arm. I missed a beat and went to reach for my knife, but stopped when I noticed it didn't have its body attached. The soggy end was scorched, like a burnt, split sausage on a barbecue. The ground area around was peppered with holes; grass tufts had been upended. Approaching cautiously closer to the shadowy shape, it became more recognisable. It was a collapsed large building, imploding into a grave for anyone inside. I scanned the area as I moved towards it. An abundance of body parts was strewn around, reminding me of feeding time in the lions' den at Newquay Zoo. It was near impossible to work out each part and how many dead there were.

Moving through the ghastly remains, I found half an AK47. The earth around looked like it had been rotavated and the smell was putrid. The burnt-out shell of a large vehicle stood out in the distance. There was nothing left there, so I decided to head back to the Suzuki, but take a different path from the lions' den. As I crossed a small ditch, I heard something. I stopped in my stance, eyes wide, ears pricked up like a caracal cat. There it was again: a muffled moan from a human. I slid my knife out from my flak-jacket and gripped it firmly. I was still in the crouching stance, the strain taking a back seat whilst I concentrated on where the noise was situated. I fixed my stare to the point, swallowed, and crept towards it. I couldn't see who was making the sound in the shallow ditch in front. The moaning stopped. I stopped. I turned my head slightly, pointing my ear at it.

'Aghhhhhhhhh.'

A large hole was in the side of the bank, just under a metre in diameter. I moved out of the direct firing line of the void; in case the person was armed. I questioned what to do next. Did I need to find out who it was? What if it was a local, or even a kid? Was this person armed? Were there more than one armed in there? I looked at my knife. Not much help if there were. I decided to say hello.

'As-salam alaykum.'

The moaning stopped and there was a short pause before a faint voice said, 'Wa alaykum e-salam.'

At least I now knew it was a male, but why the vagueness of reply? Surely if this man was hurt and in bad need of help, he would be overjoyed to be found? He started moaning and speaking very quickly, but I found it too hard to decipher.

'La afham,' I said, telling him I didn't understand.

A standoff of silence proceeded. Then he broke it, speaking very good English, 'I'm injured, unarmed. Can you help?'

Slightly surprised, I asked, 'Are you alone in there?'

'Yes.'

'What's your name?' I moved position above the hole.

'My name is Tariq Sunny. Are you a military man? What is your name, please?'

'Why?'

'I am but an Afghan journalist. I wonder if you will kill me.'

'I am also a journalist, but I am armed. I will cause you no harm if you comply. Come out with your hands showing, very slowly. I can help you with your injuries.'

'Do I have your word?' he asked.

'Wallah.' This promise wasn't completely true. If he came out and even blinked wrong, I wouldn't hesitate to use my knife. 'Do I have your word, Tariq?'

'You do, you have my word, sir. I have lost part of my hand. Excuse, but I need to hold it to my chest to stop the bleeding.'

Tariq grunted and groan in pain as he shuffled forward. He poked his head out first; his black scruffy hair had a bald spot on top. I told him to keep coming out very slowly. He got to his waist and then literally fell into the ditch below. He let out an awful scream. His clothes were in tatters and blood-soaked. He managed to roll over and face me, but then his puffy eyes flickered, going to the back of his head. His eyes shut and he let out a breath. Studying his injured arm, I could tell he was telling the truth. He had removed his *shemagh* and wrapped it around the wound. This was blood-soaked and the blood had seeped through to his shirt.

I jumped down and faced the hole, gingerly checking inside. The tunnel went back further than I could see. I turned to Tariq and rapidly checked for a pulse—very weak. I doubted he had long to live. Should I just leave him there? He didn't have the characteristic and dress of an enemy fighter. He was dressed in a shirt, trousers, and shoes, but then so was I, almost. I thought of Fish and the others. Would they have wanted to be left? I was Tariq's only chance, even if very slim. I picked his unconscious body up. He certainly wasn't scrawny. After an arduous journey, I managed to get him back to the jeep. Laying him down, I checked his pulse again and waited. I thought I'd lost him, but a trace could be felt.

Pulling down the tailgate I went back and then placed him on the side bench seat. From my webbing I pulled out the torch and stuck it between my teeth. In the light beam I undid his soaked *shemagh* and revealed his wound. He had lost the whole of his hand. His skin was burnt black around the stump. Vessels and bone protruded; blood began to pour. I put the material back whilst I pulled out the two bags of saline, a large dressing, and tapes. I cut out the smell and apprehension, something I had got used to doing. I tied a tourniquet around his arm. Again, I pulled off his makeshift dressing and slit a bag of saline open, pouring it over the end of his wrist and arm. The solution washed the blood away. I then wrapped the new large dressing tightly around where he had lost his hand, taping it off around his forearm.

My hands and clothes were a mess. One thing I didn't have was latex gloves. I cleaned up with surgical wipes. The second bag I made ready with a line and cleaned his other arm up. He had a tattoo on the underside of his forearm. I had seen it before, but couldn't remember where. It would have to wait. Once I'd established a vein, I stuck a cannula in, plugged in the saline and taped it off to his arm. I rigged up the bottle to the soft-top's metal frame with paracord from my micro case. He had abrasions and burns to his body, but it was pointless cleaning them until he survived this. The drip was on max, but I gave the bag a gentle squeeze. His pulse became a little stronger. I was soaked in saline and blood; the back of the jeep looked like a scene from a surgical unit. That was about all I could do for him. I checked him for weapons, but he was sterile. After making him secure with cut seatbelts and the lap belts, I cut out the foam from the opposite seat and elevated his arm with it.

Driving through the wet bottom of the wadi and up the collapsed bank was very easy for this Suzuki. I drove past the lions' den and the tomb, keeping my speed down the best I could, taking as much care not to jolt Tariq. After a slow drive, almost a crawl at times, I found the main road. I checked the GPS: the Kabul Gardez highway. It wasn't like the M1 in the UK, but better than the tracks I'd become used to. Weirdly, there were no vehicles around. It had been half an hour since I'd seen to Tariq. Checking his pulse from the driving seat was too hard, so I pulled up. Before I got out, he had started to stir, then began to mumble.

# CHAPTER TWENTY-NINE

I took a large swig of water before holding it to his lips. Tariq sipped slowly. Each time he swallowed, he let out a sigh. He looked at his arm.

'You're a very good medic for a journalist,' he said. 'I owe you my life, *Shukran*. What is your name?'

'No need to thank me. My name is Neal Caselton. It's only basic first aid. All English journalists are taught.'

He had another sip of water, staring at my face, and then said, 'You've been through some recent trouble, yes?'

'Not as much as you've been through.'

'Do you all carry military webbing?' he probed, again.

'No, not all, but I do. I have been reporting on war zones for some years. I like to come prepared. Your English is outstanding. Where did you learn it?'

'I went to Durham University in England in 1994,' he said proudly.

'Really? It serves you well. So what newspaper do you work for and what brings you this far out?'

'Pajhwok Afghan News, but I also freelance for others.'

I gave him a glucose bar, which he devoured. Something didn't feel right about him though. I administered a morphine injection before telling him I'd better get him to a hospital. He asked what direction I would be taking, so I told him and asked why. He said he was friendly with the Afghan National Police at the checkpoint on our route, so it would make it easier to get through.

Driving further, I handed back a couple of unwrapped boiled sweets. Something was nagging me, so I questioned him.

'How do you feel?'

'Much better. Again, thank you. *Allah Yusallmak.*'

'God won't protect me, as I don't believe,' I said. 'So, what went on back there? Who were the others that died?' I waited for any waver or pause in his answers, tying to ascertain if he was lying.

'I was given a lead into the shooting of innocent villagers by US forces back in 2010. I and four other colleagues headed out to the meeting. I forgot my laptop from the vehicle, so I returned to get it. Then the helicopters attacked us. I managed to run into the nearest ditch. I found a hole, where I hid. The rounds poured into the ground above me. My hand was hit. I was terrified. I thought this was where I was going to die.'

He seemed to be telling the truth. 'Why were you carrying weapons?'

'I wasn't, but as you know, everyone carries a gun. You can't be too careful, especially with the Taliban snatching innocent people.'

I deflected my questioning from the Taliban. 'You know of the Elkhaba then?'

'I do. I need some rest, Neal. I'm feeling faint. Please wake me before the checkpoint,' he said, his voice weak.

Heading further towards Kabul, the traffic and area became more built-up. Time check: 23.19 hrs. I thought back to the tattoo. I had seen the symbol, but couldn't place where. The flickering low fuel light now stayed completely on. As I passed more drivers, no one batted an eye at the piece of junk I was driving, or the bag of shite driving it. I felt drained; I hadn't thought I would have to go through this much bullshit on my return visit. I fumbled through my webbing until I found my phone. I watched the screen as I turned it on and it then vibrated. Keeping one eye on the road ahead, I opened the message:

'Vinnie. London. Found old friends. Have 48 hrs before Baby and I must leave the main. Hopefully you can join us.'

I felt relieved he had landed safely and, reading between the lines, he had met up with some ex-military friends, most probably now working privately. Knowing Will, he was doing some dodgy deal with them, hopefully sorting a return flight refuel schedule, but not visiting Tybalt, the gnome at Tabriz.

I texted back: 'Men in black. Poole. Received. On route down Gardez Highway. Doctor in Karte Naw. Defo join you and baby. If late, stall.'

I hadn't noticed a vehicle had drawn alongside me. Once the message had sent, I looked across. A typical white Toyota crew cab, only this one had blacked-out windows, stayed dead level with me. My shoulders tensed, my hands grip, and it didn't feel good. I turned back, trying to look blasé; also keeping my speed the same; so did they. What did they want? I glanced back over. I wasn't sure if they were looking at me or even down their weapons. I had to know. I put my right hand over my heart and bowed my head.

'*Lhumdulilah*,' I said, thinking that saying praise to God might help them.

I increased my speed a little, just nudging ahead. They did the same. Out of the corner of my eye the passenger window lowered about an inch. I dropped into third gear and floored the Suzuki; at least this motor moved better than the Nissan Bluebird. I positioned us in the centre of the road. In my cracked door mirror, the Toyota was gaining on us. I thrust it into fourth as we came up to Muhmud Khan Square. The roads were clear at this time of night as we raced through it. I felt a nudge from behind; we were bumper to bumper. Suddenly, the Toyota rapidly slowed to a stop. I wasn't sure why it had.

'Unexpected visitors?' Tariq said from the rear.

Sarcastically I said, 'Didn't know carjacking had caught on out here. I mean, we are driving a top super sports car, Tariq.'

'Where are we?'

I looked at the nearest sign or landmark as I slowed down, leaving behind the Toyota making a U-turn. 'We're just coming up to the Hotel Araina.'

'We are approaching an ANP checkpoint very soon. Please let me do the talking. I may have some contacts on shift tonight.'

'Be my guest,' I said.

Tariq was right: ahead was a checkpoint. A hefty-sized, sandstone-coloured building stood to the right. It had HESCO barriers fortifying the front and the choke point of the checkpoint. Concrete blocks sat at angles in the road leading to the barriers. Razor-sharp barbed wire glinted off the high-positioned bright lights.

I slowed my speed as a single ANP dressed in his blue-grey uniform and hat put his hand up to halt us. He had his AK47 over his shoulder and a beige flak-jacket on. Behind him in the distance, another one looked on. Crawling across the passenger seat might spook him. I yanked at the inner door handle and, at the same time, gave the door a shoulder barge. It flew open easier than I thought. I wondered why now and not before as the large moustached, young ANP nervously swung his weapon in front of him. I raised my hands, clocking the other bloke going down on one knee, aiming his weapon; itchy trigger fingers came to mind.

He shouted for me to get out, which I had understood. Keeping my hands raised, his eyes stared me up and down. I knew I was covered in dirt, sweat, and blood. My own dressings were bloodied. He became nervous and confused.

'*Masa al-khayr*. Good evening. Do you speak English?' I said confidently.

Keeping his weapon raised at me, he shouted over his shoulder, turning sharply back towards me. Two further ANP ran out from behind the HESCO barriers and spread apart, both dropping on one knee, pointing their weapons. A tall man walked boldly out towards me. His uniform looked clean and crisp. He had red badges with silver motifs on his shirt collars. The silver badges on his shirt and hat glinted off the high-powered lights. As he strode over, he unclipped his holster strap. He came within two metres of me, stood with his legs slightly apart and put his hand on his pistol's grip. He was very good-looking, with a clean complexion. His beard had been trimmed to a neat design; only a thin vertical hair strip from his mouth to his chin was left. He reminded me of the French footballer Robert Pirès.

'Sir, do you speak English?' I knew he did, so I continued, 'I have a wounded Afghan reporter in the back of my vehicle. He urgently needs a hospital.'

'Please get down on your knees and put your hands on your head,' Robert Pirès replied.

I did as he said.

'Do you have your documents?' he asked.

'Yes, here in my right webbing pouch.'

As none of them had looked in the rear of the jeep yet, I told Pirès again about Tariq. One of the young policemen from the rear came sprinting over as he'd been ordered by a hand-wave of Pirès. I glanced at the eyes of the other man, still pointing his AK47 at me. His hand kept re-gripping the weapon, his finger twitching on the trigger. I was sure if a negligent discharge happened, I would be set up with another weapon and my vehicle planted with IED equipment of some sort. I didn't trust any of these guys. I quickly smiled at the young man, trying to ease him; a thought of my cheesy smile at Anoosheh entered my mind. His tentative grip and his rabbit-in-headlight eyes didn't move.

The young policeman moved curiously behind me and first took out my knife, throwing it aside. He unclipped my webbing and stepped backwards, not taking his eyes off me. He passed it to Pirès.

'What is your business here... Mr... Caselton?' he asked, fumbling through my passport.

I knew he had studied the press ID, but I played along. 'I am a journalist from England, writing about the withdrawal of our British troops.' What was annoying me was that he wasn't listening or taking me seriously about the injured Tariq. 'Listen, sir, in the back of my vehicle is a badly-injured man, he needs...'

'Who are you attached to?' he interrupted. 'Where do you stay?'

It was like talking to an automated machine on the phone. My knees had started to ache, and my patience had worn thin.

'Who are you attached...'

'For fuck's sake, sir, are you not listening?' I said, raising my voice. 'There's an Afghan man fucking bleeding to death in the rear..., sir.'

His eyes switched from me to the young policeman next to him and he mumbled something to him. The young man took his orders and went to the jeep. Pirès emptied the contents of the webbing on the floor. Just as he found the roll of Afghan bank notes, he was alerted by a frantic yell from the man checking. Calm and cool, he waved another armed policeman to take his spot. He then strode past me, fingers tapping on the grip of his pistol. Pirès shouted orders and then Tariq faintly spoke. Handcuffs ratcheted around both my wrists and I was forcibly stood up and marched off behind the HESCO barriers, where I was pushed down on my arse. A weapon's cold muzzle poked my neck. Orders were being shouted and walkie-talkies squelched with further talking. It was all a bit quick as I tried to translate it. A hood went over my head and all went dark.

My breath had caused droplets of moisture on the cloth and my beard as I had sat for approximately five minutes. No light came through the material. It smelt old and musty, or was that my own odour? I thought back of past training at the interrogation selection process. This was a walk in the park if this was all they'd got, I thought, then wished I hadn't thought it. A powerful vehicle roared past and then stopped. The doors opened, with the sound of feet running. My eyes instinctively turned to where the feet went. I tensed, waiting to be manhandled into it the car. I tuned into further chit-chat and movement of feet. The vehicle doors slammed and then it roared off in the direction it had arrived from, towards the city.

All went quiet. It was like they had all pissed off and left me here for a laugh, like I was the stag at the do. However, deep down I knew I was the target of many wannabe heroes. I was lifted to my feet and marched off, and then the handcuffs were removed. The hood was whipped off.

In front was Pirès, with no facial expression to reveal what his mood was or what was coming next.

'You can go now,' he said.

Is that it, I thought? I bent down and started to stuff the kicked-about items back in the webbing.

'I would take this opportunity to go, return to your homeland,' he said, cocky.

'Hey, Robert, what about my money? Can I have that back. Oh, and my knife.'

He strode off, but then turned around. 'Robert?' He paused, waiting for an answer—I didn't reply. 'Enjoy your evening,' he said.

I mentally cursed him as I knew I wouldn't see the money again. 'Where have you taken Tariq?' I yelled.

'Tariq?' A broad smile came across his face before he turned and strode off. Without turning around, he gestured at a young policeman, who walked over, also smiling.

'Hey, dickhead, can I have my knife back,' I said—it was a rhetorical question.

He didn't reply and walked past. I wanted to kick him in the back of his knees and when he dropped, rip it from him; satisfying, but stupid. He went to open the driver's door, but his fingers slipped where the handle should have been. I laughed at his expense and he turned sharply. He'd understood that part. I casually walked around the passenger's side.

'Hey, dickhead, you really should brush up on your vehicles. Didn't you know you have to climb across on this model to get in? Wanker.' I wondered how much he understood as his eyes scrutinised me.

I climbed across, looking to where Tariq had lain; only stained medical material was evident. I revved the engine once it had eventually started. I looked at the policeman through a haze of smoke. He was tapping my knife on his hand, all smug. I gave him the middle finger and then drove off past the other guards.

Fifty metres down the road, I stopped briefly and pulled out the GPS, along with my phone from under the seat. I set the route for Karte Naw; the directions wanted me to turn around the way I had come. The hassle wasn't worth it, I was so close now. I turned left and continued to drive until the route changed. Once it had, I quickly checked for messages, but none had come in. I texted:

'I Robot. Catterick. Clear-ish checkpoint. Fifteen mins from doctor's. Wait out.' I pressed send.

A white Toyota parked down a small side road caught my attention. It looked identical to the one that had nudged me from the rear. As I crooked my neck further, a man in a turban and *dishdasha* was talking to the driver of a vehicle parked behind. Maybe I was getting paranoid; perhaps I had been through too much shit lately. I dismissed the sighting, focusing on the hospital. I tried to imagine Haleema's reaction. Would she be pleased? Would she come back to Cyprus with me? Was she even there? I hoped so. I couldn't wait to say hello. I thought of embracing her, which lifted my spirits. Her image in my mind was of stunning beauty. A shit, shower, shave, and a new suit would be nice first though. My appearance hadn't changed since I had last left her. I also wondered if Tariq's health had been sustained. Maybe he knew Robert Pirès well and that was why it had been so easy for me to be let go. My niggling suspicion of him had vanished; maybe my sixth sense was in tatters.

# CHAPTER THIRTY

It was best to take the last short distance on foot, I decided. I switched the phone and GPS off as they were coded, so nobody could use them if found. I hid with the webbing the best I could, hoping the Suzuki would be there when I returned. That was if it had enough fuel left to get us to the airport. I had no cash for fuel or a taxi. Hopefully, if we needed it, Haleema would pay. Not the best start to a relationship. Looking back on the jeep parked in an unlit side street, it looked a pile of junk, and I doubted anyone would steal it. The streets were empty, only bags of litter lying around. Some had been ripped open and their contents scattered about. The clouds had settled in above me.

Turning the last dimly-lit corner, the hairs on my arms stood up. In front was the hospital, all lit up, showing off its vibrant colours; reds and oranges. The sign above the main door was written in Arabic and English and the car park was half-full. It was a stark difference from the other rundown buildings around it; some even had scars from previous encounters at war. As I strode towards this impressive structure, the recently raised hairs were joined by a feeling of dread, sensing I was being watched. I scanned around for the littlest sign of trouble.

Bounding up the stairs, I was so excited and nervous at the same time, like being on a first date. Entering the glass double doors, the lobby had marble floors, ornate ceilings, flamboyant plants, and flowers. Empty seats lined the corridor ahead. The air was cool and clean. One staff member looked at me with uncertainty. I walked up to the main curved reception desk where a carved wooden plaque hung above. The woman behind it was dressed in a white coat and black shawl. She looked up from her computer screen. I was not what she expected to see. Now, what was Arabic for, Hello, pleased to meet you?

'*As hlan wa sahalan, motasharefatun bemarefatek,*' I said, 'I have an urgent appointment with Haleema.'

'*Ahlan wa* sahlan,' she said, welcoming, then looked at her watch, frowning. 'What is your name?' she asked.

I paused and wondered whether to give my real name or Neal's. 'Johnny Vince,' I said.

'I cannot see you on the list, Mr Vince, and it is very late.'

'I know, and she'll be angry, but please tell her I am here. It has been one hell of a journey today.' I tried a begging face.

Maybe I had some charm after all as she punched in numbers on her phone. As soon as the line was answered, she picked it up and apologised for the rude awakening. She said I was here in the reception. There was a slight pause and then the receptionist repeated my name and listened. My heart was beating faster. I noticed my hands were rubbing together in anticipation. Get a grip, Johnny, I thought. The receptionist put the phone down. I was on tenterhooks.

'Please take a seat, Mr Vince. Doctor Gulza is on her way,' she informed me.

I walked over to the first seat opposite the reception. I took a glance of my reflection in the one-way glass doors. I couldn't believe the state I was in. I tried to adjust my clothes and hair, but nothing I did made any difference. I smelt under my arms. Jesus. I wondered if I had time to go to the washroom; maybe there was a shower. I turned around to look for any shower signs. Walking quickly down the main corridor was Haleema. Her slender figure strutted on every high-heeled step, her breasts bouncing under her blouse. Her eyes seemed wider and deeper than I remembered. Was it because her silky hair wasn't tied back? I was transfixed, and I was nervous. I prepared my greeting and opened my mouth—nothing came out.

'Johnny, what the hell you doing here?' Haleema said.

I was mesmerised by her voice, but it wasn't the kind of greeting I was expecting, or wanted. She grabbed my arm and pulled me over to a door on the left. She opened it and hurried me through, as she followed...

The deafening crashing sound was insignificant compared to the explosion's adverse power. The blast thrust me forward to the ground, my ears pierced a loud-pitch ring. My breath was sucked out as something landed on my back. My face crunched into the cold marble floor. Debris showered my neck and hands as I lay sprawled out. I tried to gasp for air, but I was suffocating. Dust engulfed the room. I shut my eyes, lying pinned in the grave amongst the confusion of sounds. My lungs opened, gasping in the rubble that fell from the ceiling. The ground shook as I tried to cover my face and mouth, but my left arm was restricted by something heavy. I turned my face; sharp, stinging sensations grated my cheek as I did. I brought up my weak trembling hand and cocooned it over my mouth.

I was breathing erratically, listening to distant muffled alarms. My head was banging with pain. As my senses returned to something a bit more normal in the chaos, my legs felt wet at the front. I shook my head vigorously, my mind frantically trying to catch up with events. Through the eerie silence over the alarms, the sounds of screams filtered in. I turned my face back towards my pinned arm, scraping the other cheek. Little shards of glass glistened in the darkened atmosphere. I focused on the object on my arm: it was the door that Haleema had opened. Oh fuck. Haleema? I pulled my arm out and it burned with pain. I let out a yell as I yanked it further. I knew it had been broken. I tried to press upwards to lift the object on my back off, but my arm gave way. I had a sense how Rabbit must have felt.

Instead, I rolled over pushing the object off. The ceiling plaster continued to drop in lumps as I sat up dazed, looking out at the carnage of tables, chairs, rubble, and flickering lights. A limp upper-body rested across my legs. Through the blown-off white blouse, shards of large glass poked into her delicate tanned skin. Her hair draped across the floor. Looking down the rest of her beautiful body, she now lay naked, blood seeping from her. I tried to stop the bleeding from the largest wound on her inner thigh, but it continued to pump through my fingers. In desperation, I searched in the murkiness for help. The reception area was demolished; the mirrored glass doors ripped away; only a gaping hole with twisted strands protruding was left.

Gently, I pulled my legs out, lowering her delicate body to the floor. I swept her hair from her neck and felt for a pulse—nothing. I held her slender wrist and searched for a sign of life—nothing. I didn't want to, but I knelt up, the glass crunching under my knees, and caressed her body. She still had one shoe on; I couldn't see the other. Brushing her silky brown hair away revealed her deep brown eyes. I gazed intently, wishing for them to blink. There wasn't a sound in the room. Her eyes were empty. My tears bounced off her perfect jawline. My gut knotted up. I rested her head and closed her eyelids.

The aftermath sounds returned, as did the pain of my injuries. Wobbling as I stood up, I took a step over the rubble. I fell forward, smashing my head on the twisted door frame. Hitting the ground, I sent up a cloud of dust. I lay there blinking it away. I didn't want to move.

*When it gets tough out there, remember this book. A faint heart never fucked a pig.*

Planet's voice played out in my mind. I managed to smile and the blood from my nose entered my mouth. It suddenly came to me: the tattoo on Tariq's arm was the same tattoo on Anoosheh's intended rapist. This wasn't the only time I had seen it, that I was sure of. Hearing Planet's voice again, I staggered back up and made my way to the hole in the wall, my feet crunching over the glass. Just in front of the scarred steps, a large crater smoked. Vehicles in the car park were brutally damaged. I managed to navigate my way around the precarious pit of death. Trying to remember the direction I had entered, my vision became blurred. Lights came towards me; my legs gave way and I slumped to the tarmac.

I woke with my head bowed forward and my hands tied behind my back. I listened to the voices around me: none were speaking English. The pain flooded back to my body. For a moment I thought I was back in the ripped part of the fuselage, hanging in the trees. I coughed a bit of the blood out of my mouth; the coppery taste had now become very familiar. The voices went silent. I was jerked upright and a hood ripped off my head; I hadn't even realised I had one on. My eyes were swollen and they watered as I peered through my puffy eyelids. The single light was very bright, so I shook my head slightly. A lone figure in front of me sat behind a camera on a table, silhouetted against the light facing me. A red light was illuminated on the camera.

'Tariq? Is that you?' I croaked.

A sharp pain on the back from whoever was behind me made me coughed up some shit. Tariq waved him back. I looked behind me: two men either side of me were dressed all in black with only their eyes showing. They didn't take their gaze off Tariq. I twisted further, looking up at a white banner with an Arabic inscription which hung behind them. Below the inscription, 'L-khaba-a', the words had been written in English. Was this for me? At the end was a symbol, the same as Tariq's tattoo; the same symbol I had seen in the briefing room before Operation Blue Halo.

'You know why you are here, don't you,' Tariq said. 'Do you know who I am?'

'I doubt your name is Tariq or you're a journalist. So, it only leaves you are going to throw a surprise party for me for saving your life,' I said cockily.

With a tiny movement of his finger, one of the guys behind hit my broken arm. The pain was unreal. I screwed my face up and gritted the agony away. I didn't want to yell.

'You are right, I am not Tariq. Do you know who I am?'

'I've never been into the game, *who the fuck am I*, and to be honest I don't give a shit.'

He stood up with his only hand on the table. The expected hit on my arm came as he waved his finger again. It was as painful as the first time. I wanted to make a joke about it: if only he had lost both hands, then he would have nothing to wave. Instead, I thought I'd keep my mouth shut. I blinked through the tears of aching and looked squarely back at him.

'Let me tell you then,' he said proudly. 'My name is Baha Udeen. I am the leader of the L-khaba-a.'

The penny dropped. 'So you're the sick cunt who terrorised Haleema and Anoosheh. But why kill her and blow up your own hospital?' I waited for his finger to wave.

'I didn't blow up my building,' he said angrily. 'The Taliban have claimed responsibility. They must have followed you. A suicide bomber let off a huge car bomb.'

'Fuck,' I muttered.

'How did you know Haleema?'

I smugly smiled. I knew what the result of this meeting would be. I had been trained not to answer questions and play their mind games in interrogation. This time I thought, sod it, and stared straight at the camera.

'Let me tell you who I am,' I said. 'I am the survivor of the helicopter crash, the crash your pathetic men found by Haleema's village. Haleema and Anoosheh helped me escape with more of my men. Who do you think killed your pitiful soldiers in the village, and those that hunted us? I enjoyed killing every one of them. Who do you think orchestrated the revenge mission to kill your men with the Apaches? Me, you bellend. So, you're not as good as you reckon. It's a shame you weren't killed by the Taliban bomb at the hospital. My only mistake was to save your fucking deplorable little life.'

I tensed up before his finger waved, but this time he threw his whole hand into the air in anger. The back of my head took the first of their orders; my face hit the table with the impact. I stayed down as more weapon butts rained in on my body. I sucked in air and held my breath. My chair was toppled over and I let out my breath as I hit the floor. I caught a boot directly in the face. I could taste my own blood as a tooth dislodged, falling to the back of my throat. I spluttered it out. I had now become their punch bag, but it was better than the weapon butts. One large hit on the side of my head and I blacked out.

*You fucking loser, I knew you would fail. Now you are going to die. Deserved for the loss of your own men. Dick was right, you are a fucking little waste of space.*

I thought the voice in my mind had been banished forever. The anger raged through me.

I was sat upright again with my hands still tied. My whole body was swollen, hot and aching. I had no idea how long I had been unconscious. With my best eye, I focused on the object in front of me. My heart punched through my chest when I saw the large machete. I had no shirt on. I looked up to see Baha sitting in front of me, arrogantly superior.

'This is the end for you, and you know that. So tell me your real name,' he said softly.

'I'm sorry, I cannot answer that.' I half-smiled. 'Are you going to break your word and kill me? I thought that went against your religious beliefs.'

I waited for the whacks, but this time Baha gave a quick small shake of his head at the men behind me.

'My word was to Neal. I'm sure if I gave you gun now, you would turn it on me as I am not who you made your promise to, right?'

'Wrong,' I ranted, spit and blood flying. 'I'd kill you and all the fucking cronies behind me.'

'Exactly. Any last words?'

He pressed the camera and the red light came on. He nodded at the guards behind me. They seized me by the shoulders and bowed me forward.

*You gonna let these pussies do this? You wanker, you're SAS.*

'That's fucking SBS,' I shouted.

With all my will and remaining strength, I stood up and twisted the hands off my shoulders. I turned sharply, the chair legs hitting one of the men behind me. I butted the balaclava-hidden face in front of me as hard as I could. His eyes went wide, sending him backwards. I was floored by a kick to the side of my knee. Punches and kicks followed. I lashed out with my legs and spat vicious words at them. I wanted them to shoot me, better than having my head hacked off alive. I fought on, but eventually I was overpowered; I had given it my all. I gasped for breath as I was replaced at the table. My head and shoulders were forced down with firm pressure, pressure I couldn't release, even though I struggled. I heard the scrape of the metal blade on the table, most probably exaggerated for effect. I tried to relax, not giving them the satisfaction of knowing I was scared shitless.

I thought about joining Planet, Fish, and Shrek, but because I didn't believe in the afterlife I found this hard. Maybe I should have believed. I tried to picture Haleema's beauty, but I could only see her death. Fingers gripped my head and shoulders. I knew it was coming. I shut my eyes.

A white flash lit up my eyelids. I hadn't felt a thing. Then another flash almost instantly.

**Bang, bang**!

More sounds, exactly the same, echoed around my head. Something warm sprayed across my back and a metallic sound hit the floor. I lost count of the deafening bangs. Strange thumps and scuffles happened as I had my eyes screwed tight.

'Clear... Clear.'

I was gently pulled back by a pair of hands on my shoulders. Trembling uncontrollably, I searched the eyes of the person in front. He started saying something, but it was too muffled to understand. Then, halfway through his sentence, the sounds of his voice and all around came rushing back, like warp speed coming to a stop.

'...to stand. Come with us, Johnny,' he said.

The straps were cut away and I was helped to my feet, but I couldn't stand. Another person came and put his arm around me and they both quickly dragged me out the door. In the corridor, another person in black had his weapon raised and was crouched low, walking towards the end of the corridor. The two men holding me were breathing fast. The door in front was kicked open. The daylight was too bright. I turned my head away. My feet had totally given up. I was dragged down the steps and bundled in the awaiting vehicle. I blacked out as I tried to make sense of what was happening.

A familiar sound hummed. I felt warm and cosy—no pain. Opening my eyes, I recognised the cream leather interior. I tried to sit up but had been restrained. I was covered in bandages.

'Will?' I mumbled.

'Welcome back, man,' he replied.

'What the fuck happened? Where are we?'

'Ya is flyin' in de best baby in de world. We owe some good old friends of mine a lot of money, man.'

'Old friends?'

'Ya don't tink I would let ya alone in Afghan, do ya? Not with your mad plan. I had a friend stake out de hospital when I got your text. He called me once de car bomb went off. He saw ya bundled into a car and followed. De rest, my friend, is history, or your hosts are.' He laughed at his own joke.

'I take it these *old friends* of yours trained in the killing house?'

'Well, ya're still around to tell de tale.' His tone changed, 'What happened to de doctor?'

I didn't answer; I just let the silence tell him.

'So, ya want to come and work for me now, a private military contractor? Get some rest. Tink of de adventures ahead we could have.'

Lightning Source UK Ltd.
Milton Keynes UK
UKHW020630160821
388939UK00011B/925

9 780993 575013